Praise

"Jannine Gallant gives you a satisfying read."—Kat Martin, *New York Times* bestselling author

"Jannine Gallant is an exciting new voice in romantic suspense."—Mary Burton, *New York Times* bestselling author

"*Every Step She Takes* delivers enough twists and turns to keep the reader guessing until the end."—Nancy Bush, *New York Times* bestselling author

"*Every Move She Makes* will have you looking over your shoulder long after the lights go out."—Nancy Bush, *New York Times* bestselling author

"Jannine Gallant is a talented author who knows how to grab your attention and keeps the suspense in high gear until the end."—*RT Book Reviews* on *Buried Truth*

"Gallant's well-wrought second Siren Cove contemporary…will keep the reader enthralled until the explosive conclusion."—*Publishers Weekly* on *Lost Innocence*

"The novel's best quality is the relationship between Nina and Teague…A pleasing romantic story."—*Kirkus Reviews* on *Lost Innocence*

"In Gallant's gripping third Siren Cove romantic thriller…mystery adds intensity to this fast-paced story."—*Publishers Weekly* on *Hidden Secrets*

Books by Jannine Gallant

Leave No Trace
Midnight Reckoning
Relentless Dawn
Twilight Deception
Chilling Moonrise

Counterstrike
Fatal Encounter
Lethal Memory
Imminent Danger
Ominous Legacy

Siren Cove
Buried Truth
Lost Innocence
Hidden Secrets

Born To Be Wilde
Wilde One
Wilde Side
Wilde Thing
Wilde Horses

Who's Watching Now
Every Move She Makes
Every Step She Takes
Every Vow She Breaks

Secrets Of Ravenswood
We'll Never Tell
She'll Never Rest
He'll Never Know

A Deadly Love
A Deadly Game
Christmas Snow and Mistletoe
Double The Trouble
Road To Serendipity
An Uncertain Destiny
Bittersweet

Desperate Alliance

Truth and Lies

JANNINE GALLANT

Desperate Alliance

Copyright © 2023 by Jannine Gallant

This book is a work of fiction and all characters exist solely in the author's imagination. Any resemblance to persons, living or dead, is purely coincidental. Any references to places, events or locales are used in a fictitious manner.

ALL RIGHTS RESERVED. With the exception of quotes used in reviews, this book may not be reproduced or used in whole or in part by any means existing without written permission from Jannine Gallant.

Cover Art by *Creative Author Services*

Published by Jannine Gallant
United States of America

Publishing History

First Electronic Edition: August 2023

First Print Edition: August 2023
ISBN-13: 9798852886323

Dedication

To Margo and Alison, the women who help make my writing journey possible. You're the best!

Chapter One

Something about the Pissarro made her heartbeat falter and her breath seize in her throat as she stopped and stared at the painting.

Stepping closer to the masterpiece hanging in a place of honor on the focal wall of the Impressionist room, Annalise Quintrell blinked. Surely, her imagination was working overtime. She'd walked by the landscape hundreds of times since the Chestnut Street Museum had acquired the piece three years before, and never once had she noticed anything odd. After all, she'd authenticated *Sheep in the Meadow* herself.

A chill shivered through her, despite the temperature-controlled room. There was nothing specific she could put her finger on. The picture of four wooly sheep in a meadow with apple trees in the background and a fence in the foreground was perfect in every way. The color and texture were exceptional. But the depth of feeling, the quiver of excitement she got in her middle when looking at Camille Pissarro's work, was inexplicably missing.

"You okay, Annalise?"

"Huh?" Jerked out of her contemplation of the painting, she turned to face the museum's tour guide.

Lydia Mendoza's brows drew together over curious brown eyes as she regarded Annalise. The tall brunette was one of her best friends, and the two had worked at the museum in the heart of Philadelphia's historic district since graduating together from UPenn. Still, Annalise resisted the urge to blurt out her concern about the Pissarro. No need to worry anyone else until she'd thoroughly examined the landscape.

"You look a little pale. Did you see one of our resident ghosts?" A wide grin lit her pretty face. "Six years in this place, and I've never caught even a glimpse of a lingering spirit. I keep hoping."

Annalise's lips twitched in an answering smile. "Nothing so exciting. I'm just tired. And hungry. I think I forgot to eat lunch."

It had been a long, frustrating day, beginning with a breakneck rush to work after spending ten minutes searching for her damn phone, then an argument with Marcus Poole when the museum curator seemed less than enthusiastic about her ideas for a late fall exhibit, followed by a call from her mother, who was upset because Nash was incommunicado somewhere in Ukraine. As if Annalise could magically make her oldest brother phone home.

Now, she was freaking out about a painting that wasn't giving her butterflies. Lydia would probably tell her if she wanted all the feels, she needed to find a guy who would make her stomach flutter. Which wouldn't be wrong.

Lydia broke into her musings. "We closed a half

hour ago. Why don't you go home? That's where I'm headed."

"As you should. You have a terrific guy waiting to hear all about your day. I have a cat with attitude." Annalise rubbed the back of her neck beneath her messy blond ponytail. "Anyway, I planned to put in a couple of hours on those paintings Marcus acquired at last weekend's auction. If I can get a little more of the grime off, we might be able to identify the artist."

"You mean *you* might be able to identify him. Or her. You're the wiz at restoration and authentication." Lydia checked her phone and frowned. "I need to take off. Don't work too late. You really do look frazzled."

"Gee, thanks."

Her friend rolled her eyes. "We all aspire to look as good as you do at your worst. I'll see you tomorrow."

"Now you're just being nice. Have a lovely evening."

"You, too." With a wave, Lydia hurried toward the central staircase leading down to the main floor of the nearly three centuries old building.

Most days, Annalise loved her job, loved being surrounded by beauty and history, and loved working just down the street from Independence Hall. Today, however, wasn't most days. She was irritated with her boss, which seemed to be the case more often than not lately, but with the added worry about her brother and general exhaustion from too many long hours spent in the museum's basement, the last thing she needed was this niggling sense of unease over *Sheep in the Meadow*.

When her phone buzzed, she pulled it from the hip pocket of her tweed pants and read the text from her dad. Nash had sustained minor injuries from Russian shelling in the small Ukrainian town where he was taking photos, but he would be fine.

She texted back. *Thank God. Love you. I'll try to come home soon.*

Her phone dinged with a happy face emoji from her dad, and she pocketed her cell.

With one concern appeased, she squared her shoulders and faced the painting. If she didn't take a closer look at the Pissarro, she'd never get any rest tonight. After another ten minutes of intense scrutiny, her stomach was fluttering with all the feels—none of them good.

When Oscar Jessop, the museum's nighttime head of security, strolled into the room on the beginning of his rounds, Annalise made a decision. "Evening, Oscar. How's your wife feeling?"

"Better." Relief brightened brown eyes in his dark, craggy face. "The chemo is working, and her prognosis is good."

Annalise gave the older man a high-five. "That's terrific news. Give her my best."

"I definitely will." He crossed his arms over the front of his uniform shirt above the belt containing his holstered sidearm and walkie-talkie. "You working late again?"

"I'm afraid so, and actually, I need a favor." She nodded toward the painting. "Can you turn off the alarms on the Pissarro and carry it down to my work area? I'll only need it for a few hours."

Both of his bushy gray brows shot up in surprise. "I didn't see a work order for *Sheep in the Meadow*. Did Mr. Poole sign off on the removal?"

"No, he didn't. He left early today and will be gone all weekend, and I just noticed a hairline fracture in the gilding on the frame. I want to get a sealant on that before it gets any worse. The frame is contemporary to the artwork, and you can't be too careful."

Oscar stepped up close to the painting and frowned. "Your eyesight must be better than mine because I don't see a crack."

"Right here." She pointed at a tiny inconsistency in the elaborate gold scrollwork.

He scratched his head and then adjusted his cap. "I suppose it won't be a problem if we have it back on the wall before we open tomorrow."

Annalise let out a relieved breath. "Thank you, Oscar. I would have lost sleep over it."

"A pretty, young girl like you should have better things to think about on a Friday night."

"I know, I know." She threw up her hands. "I need to get a life, find some hot, intelligent, entertaining guy to date, and quit obsessing over my work."

He patted her shoulder before walking away. "At least you realize you have a problem."

Annalise smiled. "You're a funny man, Oscar."

"I try. I'll turn off the alarms and ask JR to carry the painting for you. That frame you're so worried about weighs a ton."

"I appreciate it."

The minute Oscar disappeared down the hall, all her humor dissolved. She hadn't lied. There was a tiny crack in the gilding, which she intended to fix while she had the Pissarro in her workroom. Right after she ran some tests on the painting itself.

Heavy footsteps alerted her to JR Hendricks' arrival before he strode into view. A couple years younger than Annalise, JR was built like the linebacker he'd been in college. With his wild ginger hair, blue eyes, and scruffy beard, he reminded her of Ed Sheeran on steroids.

"Oscar wants me to carry a painting for you." His tone was blunt, and he failed to make eye-contact. "He'll notify me as soon as he turns off the alarm system."

Annalise sighed. "Thanks, JR."

Shortly after the disastrous end to her engagement two years earlier, JR had asked her out. She'd declined in the kindest way possible, but he'd gone out of his way to avoid her ever since. When his walkie-talkie squawked with an all clear a few moments after the subtle green light below Pissarro's masterpiece blinked off, the junior security guard set to work disconnecting the trigger wires from the back of the frame. Once he'd lifted the painting off the wall, Annalise led the way down the hall past the colorful Pop Art exhibit to the back staircase that had originally been used by the servants.

Descending two stories, she waved at Oscar when he emerged from the old butler's pantry off the kitchen that was now the security center for the museum. After unlocking the door at the top of a final, squeaky set of steps, she headed into the basement where she worked.

"You can put the painting on the table. Thanks, JR. I'll let you know when it's ready to return."

He carefully laid his burden on the sturdy, wooden surface and backed away. After a quick glance in her direction, he merely nodded before pounding up the stairs like a rogue bison fleeing a predator.

She forced down a twinge of guilt. JR's issues weren't her problem.

Flipping on the light over the table, she donned a pair of surgical gloves and then simply hovered, studying the brushstrokes beneath the bright light. They were nearly perfect. Too perfect. Precise but lacking the feeling Camille Pissarro imparted with each touch of his brush on the canvas. Still, a gut feeling wasn't the proof she needed, even though she felt like she might throw up at any moment.

Swallowing back a surge of nausea, she deftly removed the canvas from the frame, then chose a sharp, thin blade from her rack of tools. Taking a scraping of the verdigris pigment used for the meadow from the edge of the canvas covered by the frame, she put the sample on a glass slide. She'd soon know the truth beyond a shadow of a doubt.

Twenty minutes later, she sat on a straight-back chair in the far corner of her work space, as far from the forgery as she could get, and forced herself to breathe. The green paint sample was a synthetic verdigris, not the toxic copper acetate used by Pissarro. The painting was a stunning replica. If she hadn't been in a lousy mood and stopped to gaze at the masterpiece, hoping to lift her spirits, there was no telling how long the fake would have gone undetected.

Had she possibly made a mistake in authenticating the painting when they'd acquired it from the collector whose family had owned the piece for over a century? The provenance documentation had been destroyed in a fire, and only rumors that *Sheep in the Meadow* even existed had substantiated their claim. But she'd been absolutely certain the painting was Pissarro's work.

Marcus would crucify her if she'd been wrong, and her career would be over. She squeezed back tears and pressed a hand to her churning stomach. Except she hadn't made a mistake. She'd put the painting through every test possible, and it had passed with . . . maybe not flying colors, but certainly authentic pigment.

Which meant someone had swapped the original for an outstanding copy. She had no idea when the theft had taken place. It could have happened any time after the painting was first hung on the gallery wall three years before.

Rory might have stolen it.

Pushing up from the chair, she ran to the tiny bathroom and threw up everything she'd eaten that day. Which wasn't much. When the dry heaving finally stopped, she staggered to the sink to rinse out her mouth and wash the cold sweat from her face. Raising her chin, she stared at herself in the mirror.

Haunted eyes looked back at her. Quintrell blue. The same cobalt shade her sister and two brothers had also inherited from their father. Her dark lashes were wet and spikey with tears, and her normal peaches and cream complexion was ashen. She resembled one of the damn ghosts Lydia had been hoping to see.

What in God's name was she going to do now? Call Marcus at the beginning of the three-day weekend he planned to spend in Atlantic City to deliver the catastrophic news? Her boss would go ballistic and definitely blame the messenger. If she reported the painting stolen to the police, they would immediately contact the curator, who would be even more angry that she hadn't informed him before going to the authorities. Then there was the whole insurance angle to consider.

The place would be crawling with both law enforcement and insurance investigators for who knew how long, forcing them to close the entire museum.

She pressed trembling fingers to her lips as a whimper escaped.

What she really wanted to do was turn back the clock a couple of hours and hurry past the Pissarro without giving it a second glance. Ignorance would definitely be bliss. Another option crept through her brain like a rat scurrying into a hole for self-protection. She could simply repair the frame, rehang the picture, and not mention what she'd discovered to anyone. The forgery was so exceptional, no one would know the truth—except her. Could she live with the lie, or would it eat her alive?

Probably. Undoubtedly. Closing her eyes, she gripped the sink and held on.

The best-case scenario would be to recover the original painting before reporting the forgery. Proof positive that she hadn't authenticated a fake. Marcus wouldn't be able to throw her under the bus, and her life wouldn't be ruined. *Again.* Two years ago, she'd barely survived devastating heartbreak, clinging to her work to stay sane. This time, she'd have nothing at all to hold onto.

Except the only person who could possibly help her find the Pissarro was the same man who'd destroyed her entire world. Her ex-fiancé, Rory Cavanaugh.

When her phone rang, she jumped and smacked her hip against the cold porcelain sink. Backing out of the bathroom, she pulled the cell from her pocket and checked the screen. Brielle. Her calm, logical, younger sister. The baby of the family whom everyone turned to for advice.

She swiped to connect. "How did you know I needed to talk to you?"

"I didn't." Brielle's tone was slightly distracted. "I called to tell you I found an antique brass sundial for Mom's birthday present. It's a beauty but expensive. Want to go in halves with me?"

"Sure, except I might not have a job after tonight." Her voice rose. "If Marcus fires me, I won't even be able to pay my rent. I'm in trouble, Bri."

"What's wrong?" Her sister's voice was immediately all business. "What can I do to help?"

"Nothing. No one can help, except—" She broke off and bit her lip.

After a moment, Brielle spoke softly, "Tell me what happened."

The whole story came tumbling out in a rush of words. Finally, she stammered to a halt. "I don't know what to do. I'm pretty sure I'm screwed, no matter what."

"Let me see if I have this straight." Her sister was clearly organizing the chaotic sequence of events in her mind. "You had a feeling something was wrong with the Pissarro so you asked security to bring it to your workshop, where you verified it's a forgery?"

"Yes."

"And you're afraid your boss won't believe the museum was robbed and will instead blame you for authenticating a fake and fire you?"

"Exactly. If the police can't find the thieves who made the switch, how can I prove the original was stolen?"

"Did anyone stay with you and the painting while you ran the test on the pigment?"

"No." Annalise frowned. "Of course not. The security guard set the painting on my work table and left."

"So, if you come forward now and report the painting was stolen, wouldn't the police consider you a prime suspect? You could have made the switch tonight and reported the theft to cover it up. It would take the cops about two seconds to figure out you were once engaged to a master criminal."

Spots floated before her eyes as she swayed on her feet and slowly crumpled to the cement floor. Her breath stalled in her throat, and she couldn't speak.

"Annalise? Are you still there? You're scaring me."

"I . . . I . . ."

"Take a breath. Are you okay?"

She gulped in air. "No, no I'm not. I never thought . . . Oh, my God. What have I done?"

"You haven't done anything wrong. We can fix this."

"How?" Her voice broke on a sob. "The only way is to ask security to hang the damn forgery back on the wall. I intend to keep my mouth shut and pretend this evening never happened. This will stay between you and me. Period."

"Except, if at any point another authenticator determines the painting is a fake, you'll definitely be arrested. The security guard will have logged tonight's activity, and you can't make that go away."

"Then what are my options? Go to the cops, pray they believe me, and never mind that my career will be in the toilet? Or, do I live with the threat of certain imprisonment hanging over my head and keep this to myself?" She leaned against the wall and tried not to cry. "I don't know which is worse."

"Let me think." Brielle paused for a moment. "Back at the beginning of this conversation, you said no one could help but . . ., and then you stopped. What were you going to say? What are you holding back?"

An image of Rory flashed through her mind. Dark brown hair above sparkling green eyes. A smile that never failed to charm her out of a bad mood . . . or her clothes. The man she'd loved more than anyone or anything. Except the truth. Learning that he was living a lie, that he was nothing but a con and a thief, had broken her heart into a million little pieces. She was still trying to put them all back together, but some big chunks had been lost forever.

"Annalise?" Brielle's tone was hesitant.

"Rory. I stopped because I couldn't bring myself to say his name."

Her sister sucked in a harsh breath before letting it out in a whoosh. "How can that rat bastard help you?"

"He might know who has the painting. It's his business, after all. Or was." She swallowed hard. "Maybe he's the one who stole it in the first place. I wouldn't put any level of betrayal past him."

"Do you think he'd tell you if he was guilty?"

"I have no idea. Probably not."

"Do you know how to get ahold of him?" The anger in Brielle's voice came through loud and clear. "If you do, Nash and Lincoln will beat the crap out of him to get answers."

Annalise didn't doubt for a minute that both her

older brothers would love to use her ex-fiancé as a punching bag. "I haven't a clue where he is, but he gave me a phone number once. Said it was only for emergencies. I'm not sure if he'll answer, but I still remember it."

"Call him." Her sister's tone was fierce. "Tell Rory he owes you. Tell him that for once in his pathetic life, he needs to do the right thing."

"I don't know if I can."

"What do you mean? If there's even a chance that jerk can help—"

"I haven't spoken to him in two years." She pressed a hand against her aching chest, wondering how it was possible to hurt this much all over again. "Wow, today is September first. Two years exactly. No wonder I've been feeling like crap all day."

"Why would you stay in touch with him? He's a low-life, bold-faced liar, but—"

"Not one single conversation since the day he was arrested."

Several seconds ticked by in silence before Brielle finally spoke. "After he cut a deal with the feds and was released from prison, surely—"

"He called me dozens of times, but I wouldn't answer. Finally, he stopped." She gripped her phone so hard, the case dug into her palm. "When I broke down and called him back a few months later, determined to speak my mind, the number had been disconnected."

"I can't believe—" Brielle broke off. "You know, maybe this whole forgery debacle is actually a good thing."

She closed her eyes. "Are you crazy?"

"You need to talk to him. You need closure. Maybe then, you'll finally be able to open your heart to a man who's actually worthy of you. Because we both know Rory Cavanaugh damn sure wasn't."

Chapter Two

Rory clutched a short glass of Glenlivet in one hand and the remote in the other as he swore at the Yankees' pitcher when the idiot gave up two more runs. "I told you to walk him and go after the next guy. Unbelievable."

He was tempted to turn off the game rather than watch his team go down in flames to the Red Sox. When the next batter also got a hit, and the manager headed out to the mound, he muted the game, swallowed the last of his neat, single malt scotch, and pushed to his feet. Standing in front of the plate glass window overlooking Central Park, even the spectacular view from his Upper East Side apartment didn't improve his mood.

Maybe if he'd gone out with friends instead of brooding at home, he wouldn't be taking the Yankees imminent loss so hard. Then again, if he was being honest with himself, his crappy frame of mind had little to do with his team's equally shitty pitching. Tonight was the two-year anniversary of the biggest regret of his life. He'd decided to spend it alone with a bottle of scotch and a baseball game, the same as he had the year before.

When a muted ringing sounded from somewhere in his apartment, he frowned and checked his pocket. His cell was right where he'd stuck it after calling for takeout Thai food an hour ago. Before the game had gone to hell.

Following the sound, he approached the antique rolltop desk in the corner. The cumbersome piece didn't blend with his modern furnishings, but he kept it because it reminded him of his childhood in the days before his entire family had fallen apart. Flipping up the oak front, a final ring shrilled before going silent.

Comprehension dawned. Shifting the stack of electrical schematics for his most recent client's security system, he uncovered the cell he'd stuck in one of the cubbyholes when he'd first moved the desk into his new apartment. A cord led from the phone through a slot in the back to the outlet on the wall. His emergency burner phone, the final tie to his past, hadn't rang once since he'd ratted out the entire art forgery operation to the FBI. Only one of his accomplices had managed to escape when the sting went down, and he couldn't imagine any reason why Archie would call him now. Last he'd heard, the man had fled to someplace in South America.

Probably a wrong number.

Pulling the cell out of the cubby, he disconnected the charger and checked the screen. One missed call. The phone number on the display nearly stopped his heart.

"Annalise." Her name was a mere whisper on his

lips. With a shaking finger, he tapped the screen to return her call. It rang once, twice, while he held his breath.

She picked up before the third ring. "Rory?"

"Annalise." He cleared some of the gruffness from his throat. "How are you, love?"

"Don't you *love* me. This isn't a social call."

A grin stretched his cheeks so wide they hurt. That was the Annalise he knew and loved—never afraid to speak her mind. The woman he'd missed more than he'd imagined possible for two long years.

"Okay, but can I at least tell you how sorry I am? I tried to call you over and over, but you wouldn't pick up." His eyes burned, and he blinked back tears. "Not that I blame you or expect forgiveness. It's just so damn great to hear your voice."

She didn't answer. If not for her ragged breathing, he wouldn't have known she was still there.

"Annalise?"

"I need to know if you stole the Pissarro from my museum. I want you to tell me where it is. You owe me that much."

On unsteady legs, he crossed the room and collapsed onto his recliner, then blinked at the TV screen. The Yankees had come back to win. This must indeed be his lucky day.

"I didn't steal anything from your museum, love. Ever." He winced as the term of endearment slipped out. "I would never have done that to you. Anyway, since I cut the deal with the feds, I've gone completely legit. Hell, I even work for the FBI when they get a security breach their guys can't handle. Irony at its finest." When she didn't respond, he continued,

"What's this about?" His tone was soft and coaxing.

"A painting I authenticated is a forgery. For some strange reason, I thought you might help me." Her voice rose, and her harsh laugh held a note of hysteria. "I should have known better. Good-bye, Rory."

"Don't hang up!" He sprang to his feet and paced to the window to stare out across the lights of Manhattan. "I'll help. I swear. I'll figure out who took it and get your painting back. What do the police have to say?"

"I haven't reported it yet. If word leaks out that we're sitting on a fake Pissarro, my career will be destroyed. It's not like I can prove *Sheep in the Meadow* was stolen and not simply an authentication mistake on my part. God knows how long the forgery has been hanging on that wall." A sob escaped. "Are you sure you didn't *liberate* it? I believe that's the term you used during the one press conference I saw."

"Positive. I swear on your life, which I value a whole lot more than my own." He turned his back on the view. "Are you at the museum now?"

"No, I'm at home. I fixed a tiny crack in the frame and had the security guard rehang the picture without saying a word to anyone except Brielle. She's the one who convinced me I should call you, even though she knows you're a lying bastard. Then I left. I didn't want to have this conversation at work."

"In that case, just hang tight. I'll be there in two hours. Maybe less since the traffic won't be bad at this time of night."

"No!" The word cracked like a shot in his ear. "I'm not going to see you or talk to you ever again. You *say* you didn't steal the painting, so I don't see how you can possibly help me. I'm sorry I called."

The phone went dead.

Rory dropped the cell and swore. Annalise wouldn't have contacted him if she wasn't completely desperate. There was no way in hell he was going to leave her to handle this alone, even if facing him was the last thing she wanted.

Fifteen minutes later, he'd thrown a few clothes, toiletries, and his laptop into a bag and was on the way down to the garage where he kept his car. The attendant had his Porsche waiting for him when the elevator doors opened.

"Thanks, Stuie." He handed the teen a twenty and slid onto the driver's seat. Shifting into gear, he accelerated up the ramp and turned onto the street.

He would finally get to look into Annalise's beautiful blue eyes, maybe touch her, a casual brush of his hand. He was under no illusions she'd let him do more. The fact that she hated him for what he'd done and the lies he'd told wasn't important. All that mattered was somehow finding a way to make up for the pain he'd caused. He certainly didn't deserve her forgiveness, no matter how much he wanted it.

The drive from Manhattan to Philadelphia gave him far too much time to think with zero distractions as he weaved between slow-moving semis on the expressway. He tried to keep his speed to a reasonable level since he didn't want to get pulled over, but the need to reach Annalise without delay was fierce. At least he knew where she lived. She'd moved out of the house they'd shared on the outskirts of Philly and into an apartment not far from the museum where she worked. Apparently, being surrounded by memories of their time together had been more than she could stand.

He hadn't persisted when she refused to answer his calls, hadn't intruded on her privacy, but he couldn't sleep without at least knowing where she was. He'd driven by her new place, stopped on the street and watched her walk back and forth in front of the window before she lowered the blind, regretting every stupid decision he'd ever made. Afterward, he'd stayed away, respecting her wish to have nothing to do with him. Besides, spying on her made him feel like a psycho stalker.

But this situation was different. Someone was threatening her livelihood, and he wasn't going to stand idly by while some asshole torched her career. Art forgery was his world, or at least the one he'd left behind, and he was confident he could use his old connections to discover who had stolen the Pissarro.

It was shortly after ten when he cruised past a small park and turned onto the side street where Annalise's apartment was located in an eighteenth century rowhouse in Philadelphia's Old City neighborhood. Finding a parking spot two blocks away in front of a coffee shop, he maneuvered his Porsche up to the curb and debated taking his overnight bag with him. Maybe she'd offer him her couch for the night, but that was wishful thinking and would definitely be pushing his luck. Better to make it clear from the beginning he had no expectations, and pray she'd at least agree to talk to him.

He stepped outside into the cool evening air, locked his car, and strode down the cobblestone alley until he reached the black-painted front door of the building where she lived on the second floor. Taking out his phone, he texted her. *It's Rory. I'm outside. Please let me in.*

Above his head, a blind rose and a window creaked open. Stepping back, he craned his neck to meet her gaze. Illuminated by a streetlight, eyes flashing with anger and pain stared back at him, and his breath caught in his throat.

"I told you I don't want anything to do with you. If you don't get the hell out of here, I'll call the police."

"You wouldn't have contacted me in the first place if you weren't desperate. I may not have stolen that painting, but I have the means to find out who did. Hear me out, and then I'll leave. I promise."

Her lips tightened, but she finally nodded and shut the window. A couple of minutes later, the door opened. He didn't say a word as she stepped to the side. Instead, he clenched his hands into fists to keep from touching her.

"Come in." Her voice was abrupt.

He brushed by her, catching a whiff of the vanilla-scented lotion she liked, and waited in the entry beneath an antique chandelier while she relocked the door. "It's good to see you, love—uh, Annalise. You look beautiful as always."

"Right now, I look like hell." Turning, she led the way up the curving staircase to the second floor and pushed open the door on the right.

He followed her into her apartment. Hardwood floors and crown molding, along with a padded window seat and an ancient, cast-iron radiator, gave the main room charm. He recognized the small, wooden dining table against the wall near the kitchen, but she'd replaced their oversized couches with a loveseat and matching chair upholstered in off-white. As he stood on the braided area rug, a calico cat tore out of what he assumed was her bedroom to launch itself at his ankles.

"Maizie!" He scooped up the furball and snuggled her close.

Purring like a well-tuned engine, the cat rubbed her head against his neck and chin, green eyes slitted in sheer bliss.

"I've missed you, too, you silly cat."

Annalise crossed her arms over the front of her fuzzy, purple robe and bit down on her full bottom lip. Her face was pale, and she wore no makeup. Her silky-smooth hair hung down her back, the color of the early morning sun steaking through their bedroom window on a warm summer day. His fingers itched to slide into the soft mass, but he settled for petting the cat.

"Say what you came to say. I want to go to bed."

He swallowed hard and refrained from commenting that going to bed would be his first choice. "Why don't we sit down? You're a bundle of nerves. Relax. I won't come near you without your permission."

She released a long, slow breath. "Fine. We'll have a civilized conversation, despite the fact that just looking at you makes my blood pressure skyrocket. There definitely won't be any touching unless I completely lose my temper and punch you."

When she sat on the edge of the chair, he settled into one corner of the couch with Maizie draped across his chest. "I deserve it, so hit me if it'll make you feel any better."

She gritted her teeth. "It won't. Start talking."

"The offer stands. Sorry doesn't begin to cover

how badly I feel, but I was in too deep with those people to get out, and I knew if I told you the truth, I'd lose you."

"You're right. Sorry isn't close to enough for the lies you told, and I guess we'll never know if I could have lived with the truth. Why are you here, Rory?"

"Only to help. I swear."

"How?"

He finally tore his gaze away from the misery in her eyes and forced himself to focus on the current situation. "If the forgery is high quality—"

"It's definitely first rate."

"In that case, there are only a handful of artists in the business who could have done the job. The key is to determine which artist painted the fake and who commissioned the work. From there, I can follow the money trail to discover which collector bought the original." His voice hardened. "If that fails, I'll beat the answer out of the thief who stole it. I won't pretend this is going to be easy, but I *will* track down your missing Pissarro."

"Fine. So, you make a few calls, and we go from there?"

"First, I need to see the actual painting. Since I've handled pieces by a couple of master forgers, I may recognize one of their signature tells. How did you discover the painting was a fake?"

She stared at some spot over his head and frowned. "I was having a bad day. No one in the family had heard from Nash in a while—"

Rory's hand stilled on the cat's back. "Is your brother okay?"

"Yeah. Minor injuries sustained in Ukraine while

he was taking photos in some small village. Anyway, I stopped in front of the Pissarro to take a deep breath and try to chill. Just looking at *Sheep in the Meadow* always calms me, but today, it didn't. There wasn't any magic, and I'll admit I freaked out. I had one of the security guards carry it down to my work station in the basement, and I ran a test on the verdigris paint. It was synthetic, not the old, toxic pigment." She shuddered.

"You didn't report the theft after you confirmed the painting wasn't the original?"

"No. I started thinking about how there was no proof other than my detailed report that the piece we acquired was actually a Pissarro since it didn't come with a provenance. Marcus Poole—he's the new curator who replaced Josephine when she retired—would have gone ballistic. I was worried he'd accuse me of making a mistake when I authenticated it."

"The guy sounds like an asshole."

"He kind of is." She grimaced. "I was in a panic, trying to decide what to do, when Bri called. I told her the whole story."

"And your sister suggested you contact me?" His brows shot up. "I figured Brielle would be the last person to give me the benefit of the doubt."

"Oh, she hates your guts, but she said you owe me, and we were grasping at straws. She also pointed out that if I reported the painting as stolen after taking it down without prior approval, the police might think I was the one who made the switch. Guilt by association." Her knuckles turned white as she clutched handfuls of her robe. "My ex-fiancé was an art thief."

Rory's gut clenched. "Shit."

"Exactly."

"But you haven't had any contact with me since—"

"I have now."

When his hold on Maizie tightened, the cat dug her claws into his chest and leaped to the floor.

"Ouch. Dammit!" He stared at Annalise, ignoring the sting of pain, only now realizing he'd made the situation for her even worse. Unless he found the original painting.

"I'll locate the Pissarro and get it back." His tone was controlled, despite how angry he was with himself. "I promise."

"Even if you have to steal it?"

"Damn right. I'll make this problem go away." He rose to his feet. "But we can't accomplish anything tonight, and you look exhausted. Tomorrow, I'll stop by the museum and check out the forgery. Then I'll be in touch."

She also stood. "Where're you staying?"

"I'm not sure. I'll find a hotel with vacancies and check in. You have my new cell number, the one I texted you from, not that old burner phone. I had to ditch my previous number shortly after I cut a deal with the feds. The press got ahold of it and kept hounding me." He took a step closer but resisted the urge to brush his fingers along the soft skin of her neck. "Call anytime. If you're worried or want an update or just need to vent. Day or night."

Her eyes darkened to the color of a stormy sea. "I do my venting to my sister, and I assume you'll keep me in the loop. My major concern is that there'll be a record of your presence here in Philly on the night I removed the Pissarro from the museum wall. If this plan of yours fails, and the forgery is discovered before you can recover the original, who do you think the police will blame first?"

He clenched his teeth to keep from swearing. "Good point. I'll choose a fleabag motel that doesn't ask for ID and pay cash."

She ran one hand through her hair and closed her eyes. "I can't believe I'm saying this, but your face was all over the news two years ago. Someone is bound to recognize you, so it's probably best if you sleep here." Her eyes popped open. "On the living room floor. Don't get any ideas."

Maybe not the words he'd dreamed of hearing, but damn close. "I know better than to assume you meant in your bed, Annalise."

Her cheeks colored. "Just so we're clear. If one of the neighbors saw you come in, we're already screwed, but I want you to stay out of sight until the museum opens. Tomorrow, you can wear a hat and sunglasses and my Sonny Bono wig and mustache—"

His jaw sagged. "Are you kidding me?"

A frown furrowed her brow. "Nothing about this situation is a joke. Lydia and I went to a 70s party as Sonny and Cher a few months ago. We even won a prize. No one will recognize you dressed like—"

"I'm not wearing a damn wig. Maybe the mustache."

"Fine." She stared at him for a moment. "The key is to avoid looking at security cameras while you examine the painting. Maybe hook up with a group of tourists so you don't stand out. Saturdays are always busy."

"I know how to avoid security cameras. I'll go grab my bag. I'm parked a couple of blocks away."

"I'll get it."

Before he could respond, she disappeared into her bedroom. The door shut with a thump.

"Alrighty then." He sat back down on the loveseat, which was far too short for him to sleep on, and Maizie jumped onto his lap. The cat circled a couple of times, purring wildly, before settling down and closing her eyes.

A minute later, Annalise emerged, dressed in a pair of navy-blue sweatpants with UPenn stenciled down the side of one leg and a white T-shirt. When she stopped in front of him and held out her hand, he shifted the cat to pull his keys from the front pocket of his jeans and dropped them onto her palm.

"I have a new car. It's the black Porsche parked in front of Cuppa Joe. Thanks for doing this, Annalise."

"I should send you straight home and then have my head examined for even considering such a wild idea. I feel like I'm making a deal with the devil just by having you in my apartment." Her brows lowered in a scowl. "By the way, how did you know where I live?"

"It isn't exactly a state secret." He scratched Maizie's ears, and the volume of her purring increased. "I drove by once, after you wouldn't take my calls, but I left without stopping. I figured you didn't want to see me, even if my only intention was to apologize."

"You were right, but Bri told me I need to face you in order to get closure. So, this is me, getting closure. Nothing else."

"Got it. Closure. For both of us. Just as soon as we solve your problem."

"Once the original Pissarro is back on the museum wall, we go our separate ways. That's all I want, Rory."

He cradled the purring cat and met her gaze. "If that's how you feel, I'll walk away and never bother you again, because my only goal is for you to find the happiness and peace of mind I destroyed two years ago."

And if his heart got crushed all over again, it was no more than he deserved.

Chapter Three

Dressed for work in a simple, coral-colored sheath dress, with her hair twisted up in a knot, Annalise snuck out of her bedroom and tiptoed to the kitchen. She needed coffee and would have to risk waking Rory to get it. He'd always slept like the dead, and she wasn't surprised to see him sprawled across the thin mattress she'd dragged out from under her bed the previous night, sound asleep on the living room floor, bare chested, with a blanket tangled around his legs. Maizie, the traitor, was curled up at his side.

Damn the man for being so undeniably sexy. His thick, hickory brown hair was cut shorter than when they'd been together, controlling the hint of wave, and black lashes were fanned out against tanned cheeks. He'd always loved spending time on the water, sailing his small Hobie Cat and getting toasted by the sun. She'd nagged him to use sunscreen and couldn't help wondering who was currently rubbing SPF 50 onto those broad shoulders and across his toned chest sprinkled with dark hair. Rory was too handsome not to attract plenty of female attention.

When he groaned and stretched, sending the blanket sliding completely off the blue boxers he'd slept in, she jerked her gaze away and grabbed the coffee pot to fill with water.

"Morning."

She risked a quick glance over her shoulder. "Morning. I'm making coffee. You can shower if you want."

"I want." His voice was gruff. "A cold one. I'll be out in a few minutes to cook breakfast."

"I usually just drink a smoothie on my way to work."

He stood up and efficiently folded the blanket, seemingly unconcerned about his lack of clothing, despite his tented boxers. "You'd turn down my world-class French toast?"

She let out a frustrated sigh and looked away, feeling like she was being sucked into the vortex of Rory's charm. "Fine, make French toast. I was too upset to eat dinner last night, so I'm starving."

"Have a cup of coffee and relax. You'll be eating like a queen in no time." He flashed a grin before disappearing into the bathroom and shutting the door.

Lips pressed tight, Annalise scooped coffee into the filter and pushed the start button. She should have risked Rory being recognized at a hotel rather than put herself through this torture. Believing her anger and disappointment in him would make her immune to his charisma had been a mistake. As much as she hated what he'd done to her, she couldn't simply turn off the attraction between them. Not that she intended to act on it. Not now. Not ever.

Five minutes later, she'd recovered most of her equilibrium and was pouring herself a cup of coffee when he emerged from the bathroom wearing a pair of tan pants and a green polo shirt the same shade as his eyes. Taking a second mug from the cupboard, she filled it with the fragrant brew, added a splash of cream, and handed it to him.

"Thanks." He took a sip. "I've been thinking."

"About what." Bending, she pulled a bag of cat food from under the sink and filled Maizie's bowl while the cat twined around her ankles.

"For a thief to trade out the picture in the actual frame . . ." He paused. "Or did he switch the frame, too?"

Straightening, she frowned. "I didn't consider that possibility. There was a tiny crack, which I fixed while I had it off the wall. I hadn't noticed the imperfection before, but maybe that's because the frame wasn't the original. If so, the elaborate detail fooled me."

"Possibly the original was slightly damaged when the thief made the switch. However, he would have needed a fair amount of time to get the job done. How often does security pass through the gallery where the painting was displayed?"

"I think it takes about twenty minutes to complete a round of the premises. There are always two guards on duty at night while the museum is closed. One is in the office watching the monitors while the other is on patrol."

"If the thief froze the feed for the monitors near the Pissarro, he'd have roughly fifteen minutes to make the switch and get out before he got caught."

"Wouldn't he also have to disable the alarms? The

controls for those are in the security office, and all the electrical is down in the basement near where I work. The only way in is through a door right next to the monitor room."

"Maybe he planned a distraction to get both guards out of the security office while he tampered with the alarms and monitors." Rory set his coffee cup on the counter and walked over to the refrigerator to pull out eggs and milk. "I'll need bread, sugar, cinnamon, and vanilla." He glanced over his shoulder. "Do you have syrup?"

"In the pantry. I'll get everything."

He frowned as he took the shallow bowl she handed him. "Of course, the thief would have to reset the alarm after he switched the paintings, or the guards would realize there was a problem. I feel like he needed help to do that. Someone on the inside who could come and go freely without being questioned."

Annalise dropped the bag of French bread beside the stove. "Someone like me?" She gripped the edge of the counter. "This just keeps getting worse and worse."

"Maybe one of the security guards was in on it. Hell, it could have been any employee who worked late that day. The problem is, we don't know when the switch was made to narrow down the list of suspects."

Standing well out of his way while he mixed the French toast batter and soaked the bread, she sipped her coffee and considered his points. "If we figure out who the inside man—or woman—was, do you think we could somehow make that person tell us who took the painting?"

"All I would need is access to their phone and banking app. Any unusual deposits will lead us to whoever organized the heist. Of course, I'll have to sift through the shell corporations used to disguise the transaction, but since I've been on the receiving end of a few of those deposits, I have an advantage." He dropped the dripping bread onto the griddle before glancing her way, his lips curving in a smile. "No torture involved."

"Not funny." She frowned. "I guess that means we have two potential leads to explore, identifying either the artist or the inside helper—if there was one."

"I'll see what I can learn by studying the forgery." He expertly flipped the slices. "If that doesn't give me any insight, we'll plan our next move."

"Which is?"

He forked French toast onto two plates and poured syrup with a liberal hand before carrying their breakfast to the table. "I'm not sure, but I'll think of something. Let's not talk about grand larceny while we eat. It'll ruin your appetite."

"I'm pretty sure this whole situation is guaranteed to give me an ulcer." She dropped onto the chair across from him and picked up her fork. "Or maybe not. My stomach lining survived your betrayal. My heart, not so much."

"I hated lying to you, love, but I was afraid to tell the truth. Either way, I knew I'd lose you."

"Why did you do it?" She stabbed a bite of French toast and waved it. "You have an EECS degree from MIT, for God's sake. You could make six figures or more in a legitimate job as an electrical engineer or a computer programmer. You didn't need to steal to have a good life."

Tears threatened. She shoved the bite in her mouth

and chewed furiously, determined not to cry. Still, she deserved some answers.

"I won't make excuses for my bad choices. I own every one of them, despite my regrets." His hand shook slightly as he lifted his fork to his mouth.

"You had a reason, Rory. Tell me why."

"It's complicated."

She ate another bite. "All that means is you don't want to talk. Whatever. It seems like an explanation is the least you owe me, but you do you." She picked up her mostly full plate and took it to the sink. "This was a horrible idea. Closure isn't worth tying myself up in knots again."

As she stared at the cheerful picture of sunflowers hanging on the wall and blinked back tears, strong hands closed over her shoulders. When a tremor shook her, he pulled her against his chest and held on tight.

"You knew I grew up with old money. What I didn't mention was that the family fortunes had been in decline for a few generations, actually since the Great Depression, but my snobby forebearers were too proud to change their life style—or actually work. My parents were in debt up to their eyeballs when everything came crashing down. My tuition check to MIT bounced like a rubber ball the summer before my senior year."

Annalise jerked away from him. "You could have taken out loans or gotten a job like a normal student."

"Yeah, I could have. But my dad hanged himself when the bank notified him they were foreclosing on the mansion in the Hamptons. The Manhattan house was sold at auction soon afterward. My mom had a complete breakdown and needed inpatient care for a couple of years."

Slowly, she turned to face him. "Oh, my God. I'm so sorry."

"Yeah, I am, too. It was a mess. They'd let our health insurance lapse, and none of our relatives had the cash to get her into a decent facility. When I got drunk one night and confessed to a college buddy that I was in trouble and needed to make a lot of money fast, he told me he knew someone who could help."

"That's when you started stealing artwork?"

"Yep. I didn't feel like I had any other choice."

"You always have a choice, Rory."

"You're right, and I made a bad one. However, I got my mom the treatment she needed, and she's adjusted reasonably well. We aren't exactly close, but she's able to live comfortably and do the charity work she enjoys."

"Because you support her." Her tone was flat. "You always made excuses when I wanted to meet her. You told me your dad had died, but not how."

"I never talk about my father's death, and I don't see my mom often, once every couple of years. I'm a reminder of the life she lost, and she'd rather not face those memories."

"I'm sorry. I can't even imagine."

"That's because you're tight with your parents and siblings. Your family is great, and I enjoyed being a part of it. I've missed them."

Her throat ached with unshed tears. After a few moments, she managed to speak. "Our personal relationship wasn't the only casualty of your choices. Maybe you should have considered that."

"I honestly never expected my past to become an issue. I left that world behind a few years after I graduated from MIT. By then, I had a good job, and my mom had been released from the care facility and was living on her own. Once I met you, life was pretty damn perfect."

She crossed her arms over her chest. "You would have married me without ever telling me the truth?"

"I was afraid I'd lose you if I did. Why hurt you when there was no need? My past was just that, in the past."

"Until it wasn't." She gritted her teeth, doing her best to control her anger. "What happened?"

"The guy I'd worked for back in college contacted me. He needed my skills for a specific job."

"Why didn't you say no?"

"Believe me, I tried. Felix made it clear turning him down wasn't an option. If I wouldn't help him, he'd tell you exactly what kind of man I was."

"I thought I knew who you were. If you'd been honest from the start, none of this would have happened. You should have gone straight to the police."

"At that point, I didn't have any leverage to cut a deal. They would have charged me with a dozen counts of grand larceny, and I would have been old and gray before I got out of prison. You would have found a man who actually deserved you, and the thought of that nearly killed me. Completing one final job for Felix Lemmon seemed like the only way to keep you in my life."

"And how did that work out?" Her eyes narrowed. "Lying to the person you love is never the answer."

"You're right. I lost you anyway. I was an idiot, and I'm sorry."

Annalise gave an abrupt nod and glanced at the

digital clock on the stove. "If I don't want to be late for work, I need to head to the museum. When do you plan to show up?"

"Noonish. Best if there are plenty of visitors roaming around so I don't stand out."

"Do you have a hat and sunglasses?"

"Sure. My Yankees ballcap goes everywhere with me."

"Wear my Phillies cap instead. You'll attract less attention." Turning, she headed to her room and dug through the chest where she'd stashed the Sonny Bono costume. Her smile was grim as she took the mustache out of a plastic bag but left the wig. After grabbing her ballcap, she returned to the kitchen where Rory was standing at the counter, finishing his French toast. "The moustache is lighter than your hair, but since you'll have on a hat, no one will notice."

"I'm going to feel like an idiot wearing that thing."

"Too bad. It'll disguise your good looks, and we don't need half the women in the gallery checking you out."

"Only half?" he teased.

She didn't want to find him amusing, but her lips twitched, despite her irritation. "Okay, all the women. While you're at it, maybe you should stick a pillow under your shirt so it looks like you have a beer belly."

"Good idea. No one will give me a second glance."

"There's a spare key hanging on the rack by the door. Can you lock up when you leave?"

"Sure. I'll also make certain none of your neighbors see me." He reached out to squeeze her arm. "Are you okay, love? You look like you're ready to snap."

"No, I'm not okay. Nothing about this is okay, but

I'm doing what I can to hold myself together. Don't make it harder by being sympathetic and charming." She took a deep breath. "And stop calling me love!"

"Got it. I'll try harder to be an inconsiderate jerk."

"I'd appreciate it." She grabbed her purse off the end of the counter. "Give me a call after you take a look at the painting."

"I will."

Annalise walked out of her apartment, shut the door, and leaned against it. She wasn't sure she could handle spending any more time with Rory. Derailing her career and possibly getting arrested might be a better option.

Looking into his gorgeous green eyes made her stomach flutter and her heart ache with regret. She hated that she was still susceptible to his good looks and flirty attitude, had been from the first moment she'd laid eyes on him, standing in front of one of Andrew Wyeth's lesser-known Christina paintings. Which made her think she should check that portrait for authenticity, as well.

Pushing away from the door, she hurried down the central stairs to the entry. Once out on the sidewalk, she let the fresh morning breeze blowing off the Delaware River and the charm of the red brick buildings and quaint shops in her Old City neighborhood restore her perspective. Rory was a regrettable part of her past, but her career was front and center in the present. She'd do whatever was necessary to ensure she didn't torpedo her future, even if it meant working with her ex-fiancé.

Reaching Chestnut Street a short time later, she dodged visitors and ran up the shallow steps to the museum, shoved open the heavy, oak door, and crossed the parquet floor, her low heels clicking. When Lydia waved from the balcony one floor up, Annalise climbed the stairs to meet her.

"You marched in here, fired up about something. What's your schedule like today?" Her friend practically radiated well-rested cheerfulness.

Annalise wished she could say the same. "I'm determined to finish cleaning those new paintings Marcus acquired. I didn't get much done last night, and I'm off Sunday and Monday, like usual. Our boss won't be pleased if he gets back from his Labor Day trip to Atlantic City, and I haven't authenticated them yet."

"Well, you still have to eat. Want to try that new Indian place for lunch? I have a break between tours at twelve."

Rory would be here at noon.

She grimaced. "I'd better not. I plan to eat a sandwich in my dungeon."

"Wow, you really know how to have fun." Lydia rolled her eyes. "Please tell me you aren't going to show up tomorrow to work."

"Not if I finish my project today." She hesitated. "I might go visit my parents. I haven't decided for sure."

"You should go. Let your mom pamper you for a change." She glanced at her watch. "Almost opening time. I have a big group arriving at nine sharp, so I'd better head down to meet them."

"A bus from a retirement home was stopped in the middle of the street, clogging up traffic and disgorging senior citizens when I came inside."

"That would be my tour. Catch you later."

As Lydia descended the stairs, Annalise climbed to the third floor and paused in front of the forged Pissarro. JR had rehung the picture after she'd repaired the crack in the frame, and the little green light beneath it indicated the alarm was activated. Clenching her teeth until her jaw ached, she spun on her heel and headed into the portrait gallery.

Andrew Wyeth's painting hung on the north wall. Her steps faltered as images of her first encounter with Rory played like a movie through her mind. He'd turned and met her gaze, his mesmerizing green eyes and megawatt smile bringing her to a standstill. Before she'd gathered her wits enough to keep moving, he'd struck up a conversation, and fifteen minutes later she'd found herself having coffee with a complete stranger.

Biggest mistake ever.

Shrugging off the memory, she studied the painting of Wyeth's neighbor, Christina Olson. Unlike his more famous painting, *Christina's World*, this was a small, close-up portrait of the young woman who'd been crippled by polio. A shiver ran through her as the pain and stoicism in the girl's eyes gripped her emotions. Definitely the original. Maybe Rory hadn't lied about not stealing from her museum. At least not this particular painting.

Leaving the gallery, she used the back stairs to descend to her work area. As she pulled her keys from her pocket to unlock the basement door, Francine Childers hurried into the kitchen.

"Oh, good. You're here." The older woman's brows drew together. "I seem to have misplaced my key, and I need to restock the postcards in the gift shop."

"Security has a master." Annalise opened the door and flipped on the light. "Come on down and show me what you need. I can carry the boxes up."

"Thank you, Annalise. You're sweet to help. I left the new boy alone in the gift shop and don't want him to be overwhelmed, so I'm in a bit of a rush."

Annalise grinned as she led the way into the bowels of the building. Callen, the new *boy*, had to be at least her age, maybe older. He'd seemed perfectly competent the few of times she'd spoken to him, but Francine liked to believe she was the only one capable of overseeing her gift shop domain.

Reaching the foot of the stairs, she glanced over her shoulder at the petite woman. With her bobbed gray hair and glasses dangling from a chain around her neck, Francine was all business all the time.

"I can't imagine what happened to my key." She hovered while Annalise opened the supply closet door. "I don't lose things, and I was down here last week."

"I'm sure it'll show up. How many boxes of cards do you need?"

"Just one. They're heavy. I'll take up more of the Declaration of Independence scrolls. Those sell like hot cakes."

Hefting a box of postcards, Annalise headed back up the stairs to the kitchen, followed by Francine with the much lighter container of poster tubes. Turning down a corridor that led past an elaborately decorated dining room straight out of Ben Franklin's era where Lydia was holding court with her elderly tour group, she turned into the gift shop near the main entrance.

"I'll take that." Francine's new assistant set down the giant cup of soda he was drinking and rushed out from behind the counter to relieve her of her burden. Callen Ives was boy-next-door attractive, with clean-cut features, neat brown hair, and blue eyes. His hesitant smile revealed one slightly crooked front tooth that gave his face some character.

"Thanks. Do you need anything else, Francine?"

"No, that was it." She set down the tube container. "Thank you, Annalise."

"Anytime."

Callen followed her to the door and cleared his throat. "I don't suppose you'd like to go to lunch with me later?"

She'd been expecting this since the first time they'd met and he'd regarded her with puppy dog adoration. What she should say was yes. Callen was polite, good-looking, clearly interested in her, and just a little bit on the boring side. Which was exactly the type of man she should date instead of one who turned her insides into a fluttering swarm of bumblebees.

"I'm sorry, Callen, but I have so much work to finish today, I don't intend to take a . . . a break." She stuttered to a stop.

Over the clerk's shoulder, she met Rory's interested gaze beneath the brim of her Phillies hat as he sauntered toward the stairs, following behind two families with young children. He glanced between her and Callen, and the fake mustache twitched as he rolled his eyes.

She clenched her fists at her sides. "Maybe some other time."

"Yeah?" His tone brightened. "I'll check with you next week."

What the hell is Rory doing here already?

With an effort, she focused on the man facing her. "That would be great, but right now, I need to get back to work."

Turning, she walked swiftly toward the kitchen. Rory was up to something or he would have stuck with their original timeline. What, she had no idea, but she damn well intended to find out.

Chapter Four

Rory couldn't believe the starched and pressed dweeb had the guts to ask Annalise out. Okay, maybe he'd sucked up his courage to make a move, but why hadn't she shut him down hard? Hearing her tell the guy *maybe* had pierced his heart like the arrows in the Lenape tribe exhibit to his left.

Wandering the museum's second floor while he brooded over the fact that Annalise was apparently open to dating, he ditched the families he'd been trailing and followed a group of college students headed to the third floor. To anyone watching the monitors, he was just a guy enjoying a Saturday morning cultural outing. Curbing his impatience, he rubbed his upper lip. The damn mustache itched like crazy.

Right now, he needed to focus on the job at hand and forget about the way his ex-fiancée had smiled at another man. If he'd arrived later in the day, as he'd intended, he wouldn't have witnessed the dweeb asking her out, but waiting even an extra couple of hours had been more than he could handle. A little digging on the dark web after she'd left the apartment had turned up a name he hadn't expected to see. Maybe the rumor was a lie, but he'd know soon enough.

Finally reaching the Impressionist gallery, he waited impatiently while the college kids earnestly discussed the Pissarro, without any clue they were looking at a fake. When they eventually moved on, he stepped away from an early Berthe Morisot painting of a woman in a garden to study the forgery. The quality was excellent, each brush stroke precise, but if Archie Weber really was back in business—

There it was. Woven into the blades of grass beneath one of the sheep, discernable only to someone who was searching for a tiny AW. Archie had never been able to resist signing his work, even though Rory had warned him he was taking a huge risk.

Releasing a long breath, he turned away from the painting and strolled out of the room. He'd spend another half hour casually making the rounds from one exhibit to another, before getting the hell out of the museum. Making a hasty exit and attracting the attention of anyone studying the security tapes was the last thing he wanted. His heart thumped wildly, just thinking about it. Even though he hadn't stolen the Pissarro, there wasn't a cop on the planet who wouldn't consider him a prime suspect. And Annalise would be nailed as his accomplice.

Time crawled like a three-legged spider as he checked out the Pop Art gallery before descending to the second floor. There he mingled with a group of elderly patrons, until he realized they were part of a tour. Catching a glimpse of Lydia Mendoza, herding her charges toward the maritime display, he turned in the opposite direction. A cheesy mustache wouldn't fool Annalise's best friend if she got a look at his face. And if she recognized him, she'd probably murder him on the spot.

After spending five long minutes pretending to study Early American artifacts, he headed down the central staircase, smelling freedom. When his phone vibrated in his pocket, he pulled it out and glanced at the screen.

Well?

A smile curled his lips at Annalise's succinct inquiry, and he typed rapidly. *We need to talk.*

His phone buzzed again. *I don't want to risk being seen with you.*

He didn't blame her. Reaching the bottom of the stairs, he stepped out of the way as a pair of middle-aged ladies brushed by him on their way to the gift shop, avoided meeting the gaze of the pretty young woman taking entrance fees near the door, and finally made his escape. Once outside, he turned his face into the sharpening breeze and breathed deeply before checking his latest texts.

Rory? What's going on?

He clutched his phone tightly as he dodged pedestrians on the sidewalk. Head down, he tapped the screen. *Just left the museum. See you at your apartment.*

Seconds ticked by before she responded. *Can't you just call me?*

He could, but he didn't want to. Pausing beneath the awning of a neighborhood pub, he carefully phrased his reply. *Lots to discuss. Afterward, I'll leave.*

His phone buzzed again. *You definitely will.*

Clearly, Annalise wasn't in a charitable mood. Not

that he expected her to be. But if he could locate *Sheep in the Meadow* and return it to the museum, maybe she'd feel a bit more compassion. He certainly didn't expect forgiveness.

As much as he wanted to head straight into the pub for a stiff drink, despite the fact it was only ten in the morning, drowning his sorrows in public was definitely a bad idea. Instead, he hurried toward Annalise's street, waited at the corner while one of her neighbors left the building, then used the spare key to get inside. After climbing the stairs to the second floor, he entered her apartment and flopped down on the couch to consider his options. Unfortunately, he didn't have many.

When Maizie jumped up onto his lap, he rubbed the soft fur beneath her chin. "Don't get too used to having me around. Your mom isn't a fan." As his fingers stilled, her purring stopped, and the cat sank her teeth into his hand. A rueful laugh slipped out. "I probably deserved that, but let's see if I can fix this mess."

Pulling out his phone, he scrolled through his contacts until he found Theo DeWitt's name. A wave of emotion assaulted him—bitterness, anger, regret. When he'd needed help, his good buddy had set up a meeting with his Uncle Felix. However, he'd failed to warn him that once his uncle got his hooks into him, he'd own him for life. Maybe he should have figured that out for himself, but it was easier to blame Theo.

Scowling, he tapped the number. His old friend probably wouldn't be thrilled to hear from him, but Rory didn't give a crap. The call went straight to voicemail.

"It's Rory. Call me back. I need some information, and it wouldn't be in your best interests to ignore me."

Curiosity might not prompt Theo to return his call, but the implied threat should do the trick. Leaning into the corner of the couch, he stroked Maizie's back and waited. His phone rang two minutes later, and he swiped to connect.

"Hello, Theo."

"This is quite a surprise after you ghosted me for years."

"Blame your uncle for dragging me back into the family business, despite my vehement protests. He cost me the life I'd built and the woman I loved."

"But not your freedom. Uncle Felix and two of my cousins are rotting in jail thanks to the deal you cut with the feds. I heard you're living in a luxury apartment in Manhattan. Seems like you're the one who came out on top." He paused for a moment. "What do you want, Rory?"

"Information. Apparently, Archie Weber is back in the country. Tell me who he's working for."

"How the hell would I know? I didn't keep tabs on my uncle's associates before the feds busted his operation wide open, let alone afterward. I have a legitimate law practice with absolutely no ties to anything illegal."

Rory snorted. "You were always on the lookout to make an extra buck. Hell, Felix gave you a finder's fee for recruiting me."

"Maybe we've both changed. What's your interest in Archie, anyway? I thought you got out of the business when you ratted out my uncle."

"I did. Unfortunately, I discovered one of Archie's forgeries hanging on a museum wall. Anna . . . uh . . . a friend could get hurt if anyone figures out the painting is a fake, which is why I want to know who hired him and who stole the original. Archie's an artist, not a thief. He isn't working alone."

"I honestly don't know." Theo's tone was rough. "Even if I did, why should I do you any favors?"

"Because I didn't tell the feds you were an essential cog in your uncle's business. I kept your name out of it, so you owe me."

"I wasn't involved. I'm a corporate attorney, not a criminal, and Uncle Felix was just one of my clients. I didn't break any laws."

"Last time I checked, money laundering's a crime."

"There's no evidence I was anything other than an innocent dupe. How was I to know my uncle's auction house was a front for illicit activities?"

Rory rolled his eyes. "I know you, Theo. You like to stay informed. Rumors are floating around the dark web that Archie left South America and is working in the states. I'm positive you've heard something."

"Maybe." His voice was slightly muffled. "Tell Mr. Johnson I'll be with him in two minutes. Thanks, Patrice." A moment later, he spoke more clearly. "Look, I'm late for a meeting so let's wrap this up."

"Tell me what you—"

"Christ, you're persistent," he interrupted. "Fine. Back in July, whispers that Archie had been spotted in Miami were circulating. A couple of weeks ago, a second rumor surfaced that he's been working in Virginia, possibly near Richmond. That's all I know."

"If you learn anything else—"

"Don't hold your breath."

The phone went dead, and Rory dropped it on the cushion beside him. The lead was weak, but better than nothing. Frowning, he rhythmically stroked the cat as he debated how best to search for the artist. The chances of bumping into him on the streets of Richmond were slim, but he knew Archie's habits. All he had to do was figure out where he was likely to hang out and ask a few subtle questions.

If the man was still in Richmond.

On a positive note, he was familiar with the city since Annalise's parents lived thirty miles away in Wildwood, a small village on the James River where she and her brothers and sister had grown up. Maybe Annalise would want to drive south with him to hang out with her family while he did a little sleuthing in the city.

A road trip might lighten the mood and ease some of the tension between them. They'd always had great adventures together, exploring backroads to stop at yard sales and country auctions in search of lost treasures. On the other hand, Annalise didn't seem too keen on spending time with him. If she said no, he'd go alone.

He spent the rest of the day working remotely, repairing a security breach at a credit union, and had just finished the job when the door opened and Annalise walked in. He shut his laptop and smiled. "How was your day?"

"Better than expected, considering the way it started. A couple of landscapes my boss purchased at auction turned out to be paintings by Thomas Moran from his Luminism period." Her gorgeous eyes flashed with excitement as she hung her keys on the rack and swept her pale blond hair over her shoulder. "They were so filthy, I had no idea what a prize we had until I removed several layers of grime."

"That must have been exhilarating."

"It was." She bent to scoop up Maizie when the cat twined around her ankles. "You're still here."

"I told you I'd wait."

Holding the purring cat, she dropped onto the chair facing the couch where he'd been working. "Let's hear it. What did you learn?"

"I did a little digging on the dark web this morning and discovered Archie Weber had resurfaced."

A frown creased her brow. "Should that name mean something to me?"

"Archie painted the forgeries for Felix Lemmon's organization."

"Oh. The guy who got away when the feds raided Lemmon's estate. I remember Lincoln mentioning it. He followed the trial."

Apparently she hadn't.

Rory rose to pace across the room. "Yes, Archie escaped to South America. You said the fake Pissarro is excellent, and he was the absolute best when it came to Impressionist paintings. Once I knew he was active again . . ." He shrugged. "Anyway, I headed straight to the museum to see for myself."

"Patience not being your strong suit, waiting a few hours like we'd discussed was clearly out of the question."

He ignored her sarcasm. "Exactly. The sheep picture is definitely Archie's."

"Now what? Can you find out who he's currently working for?"

"I called Theo, hoping he could tell me."

When her hands stilled on Maizie's fur, the cat jumped to the floor and strolled into the kitchen. Strident meows echoed through the apartment.

"She wants her dinner." Annalise pushed up out of the chair and followed the cat. "Theo?" She turned with the bag of food in her hand. "Do you mean Theo DeWitt, your college buddy? Why would he know anything about an art forger?"

"Because Felix Lemmon is Theo's maternal uncle."

She stared at him for a moment. "Unbelievable. Theo is the guy who hooked you into a life of crime? The lawyer I introduced to *my sister* on a double date?"

"Yeah." He winced. "I guess it's a good thing he wasn't Brielle's type."

She closed her eyes and swore softly, only opening them when the cat meowed again. "Why didn't he get arrested with the rest of the crew?"

"No proof Theo did anything illegal."

She snorted. "Yeah, right." Bending, she poured food into the cat's bowl. Finally, she straightened and faced him. "Did he at least know where to find the forger?"

"Not exactly, but he'd heard a rumor that Archie is working in the Richmond area. I plan to drive down there, question some of the locals at the bougie bars Archie favors, and see if I can discover where he spends his free time. Once I find the bastard, he'll talk."

"Locating him might not be so easy. Would he use his real name? Isn't he still wanted by the police?"

"For a whole laundry list of crimes, and yeah, he'll definitely use an alias. My guess is he ran out of money wherever he was living in South America and came home to pad his bank account. I want to find him before he bolts again."

"Seems like your plan might have a few holes, but it's better than doing nothing. When are you leaving?"

He checked his watch. "It's almost six now. If I grab something to eat and start driving, I should be there before eleven. Not too late to hit a few bars and clubs this evening." He stuffed his hands into his back pockets. "Want to go with me? People might open up more to a couple asking about a friend, especially if you do the talking. Afterward, I can drop you off at your parents' house."

She considered him for several long seconds, her eyes narrowed. "Do you really think we'll learn more if I ask the questions, or is this just a ploy to spend time together so you can convince me you're a great guy worthy of forgiveness?"

He offered up his most convincing smile. "You already know I'm a great guy, even if I have a few faults." When her eyes turned a stormy blue, he continued, "However, I truly believe you'll get more out of male bartenders and bouncers than I will. I can handle the women."

"I bet." Her tone was curt. Finally, she nodded. "Fine. I'll go. I was thinking about driving down to visit my parents tomorrow, anyway."

"Great. Pack a bag, and let's take off."

"First, I need to ask my neighbor's daughter if she'll feed Maizie."

"That's right." He scooped up the cat and rubbed his chin against her head when she purred in feline pleasure. "How could I forget my favorite kitty?"

"If you want to save time, why don't you make a couple of sandwiches while I get organized? We can eat while we drive instead of stopping for dinner."

"Excellent idea." He set the cat on the floor. "I'm on it."

They left a short time later, taking his Porsche since, as Annalise pointed out, he'd need transportation more than she would. He wouldn't be staying with her parents, and she could borrow one of their cars if she wanted to go somewhere. Rory didn't press the issue, happy simply to have her company for the long drive.

They didn't say much while they ate their sandwiches and snacked on baby carrots and apple slices, completing the impromptu meal with a package of Thin Mints he'd found stashed in the freezer. But once they finished eating, the lack of conversation began to grate on his nerves.

"So, how's your family? Tell me what they're up to."

She crossed her arms over her chest and curled into the seat. "This isn't a date, Rory."

"If it was a date, I'd ask if you were seeing anyone. I'd ask if you missed Sunday mornings spent in bed together as much as I do."

"Dammit! I knew I should have refused—"

"Instead," he raised his voice, "I offered up an innocuous topic that's more interesting than the weather. Do you want to sit in complete silence for the next three and a half hours? Can't we be civil?"

"I suppose so, but this is . . . hard."

"I know." It took all his willpower not to reach over and squeeze her jean-clad thigh. Instead, he focused on the darkness shrouding the countryside beyond the expressway, and the steady stream of headlights traveling in both directions. "I don't want to make things difficult for you. I guess we don't have to talk."

Seconds ticked by, turning into minutes before she let out a shuddering sigh. "Mom and Dad are fine. Dad retired in June, but he still guest lectures a couple of times a month at the college."

"That's a big change for him. Dr. David Quintrell is practically synonymous with the history department at William & Mary."

"Yeah, but he doesn't seem bored with his new lifestyle. In addition to consulting, he spends plenty of time in his garden, and he and Mom have been traveling a lot. They bought an RV and have been touring the country in bits and pieces."

"Sounds like they're enjoying retirement. Is Ellen still volunteering at Colonial Williamsburg?"

"Of course. Mom adores dressing up in costume and showing tourists how to make lace. I can't imagine her ever giving that up completely." She clasped her hands together in her lap. "It was hard on them both when our relationship imploded. They loved you . . . right up until the minute they realized you were living a big, fat lie."

His stomach twisted. "I hate that your family got hurt in the fallout."

"I wasn't thrilled about it, either. You're lucky Nash is taking pictures in Ukraine right now. My very protective big brother would kick your ass into next week if he saw you."

"I don't doubt he'd try." Rory glanced over before focusing on the road. "Both your brothers are bigger than me, but I'm faster." He tightened his grip on the wheel. "Do you think Lincoln is on the warpath, too? Since he lives in Wildwood, I don't want to wind up with a black eye if we run into each other."

"Maybe not. He was the only one who defended you. He argued you must have a good reason for what you did." She hunched her shoulders. "I couldn't get past the betrayal."

The defeat in her voice hurt far worse than taking a few punches. He cleared the thickness from his throat.

"Linc and I are . . . were . . . good friends. I've wanted to call him, but I didn't think it would be fair to you. Anyway, he'd probably tell me to drop dead since I know his loyalty lies with you. Is he still doing historical restoration for that guy, Pete?"

"No, his mentor retired and sold Lincoln his business. Since half the homes along the James River are both falling apart *and* considered designated landmarks, business is booming for my brother."

"That's terrific."

"Yeah, it is."

Rory was quiet for a moment, wishing for the millionth time that he hadn't sabotaged his relationship with Annalise. God, he'd missed her.

"Brielle, on the other hand, isn't as forgiving as Lincoln. She mentioned more than once that prison was too good for you—until you walked. That really pissed her off." Annalise laughed softly. "She suggested cutting off your balls and feeding them to everyone involved in setting you free."

His scrotum tightened as her words painted a horrifying picture. "Remind me never to mess with your sister."

"You don't have to worry about crossing paths with Bri since she's still in Boston, doing genealogy research for people who swear their ancestors came over on the Mayflower. If they all had, that boat would have been bigger than an aircraft carrier."

"Good one. You still have your snarky sense of humor."

"I needed something to fall back on—afterward." She turned to face him in the dark. "Sorry. Those types of comments won't help, and I'm tired of feeling bitter. I appreciate your help solving my current problem. Let's keep things professional between us so we can move on with our lives once this is over."

"That's not going to happen, and you know it."

"Why not?" She sounded like a recalcitrant child who'd been told no.

He smiled. "Because, as much as you want to deny it, we still have feelings for each other."

"Maybe so, but none of them are warm and fuzzy."

He laughed out loud. "Maybe not now, but they will be." Reaching over, he patted her thigh. "Count on it."

Chapter Five

After three cocktails, Annalise was feeling a little unsteady as she and Rory entered the fourth bar just before midnight. Between the alcohol and the late hour, all she wanted to do was curl up and go to sleep. Instead, she teetered across the polished wood floor on three-inch heels and didn't jerk away when Rory gripped her bare arm to steady her. Reaching the long, mahogany bar, she avoided a hanging fern and plopped down on the only empty stool. The wall of mirrors behind dozens of booze bottles reflected the high color in her cheeks and plenty of cleavage exposed by the deep V-neck of her silk top.

When the man on the stool next to her edged closer, reeking of some woodsy cologne, Rory clamped his hands onto her shoulders and scowled. The guy backed off in a hurry.

The bartender finished filling the cocktail waitress's order and moved in their direction, giving them an inquiring look before his attention dropped to her plunging neckline.

Rory pressed up against her back and leaned in. "Can I get a glass of your best Chardonnay for the lady, and a neat scotch? Glenlivet, if you have it."

Warmth from his chest seeped through the silk, igniting a surge of feelings that heated her to her core, and he knew it. Damn the man. Their gazes locked in the mirror, and her cheeks turned even pinker.

"Coming right up." The man raised his voice to be heard over the lively chatter of dozens of patrons.

Finally, Rory shifted away, and she was able to breathe again. They'd followed the same routine at each bar and nightclub they'd gone to since arriving in Richmond, and Annalise had her part down pat, even if her head was beginning to spin. When the bartender returned with their drinks, she held out her phone with a picture of Rory and Archie Weber on the screen. Rory had cropped the two of them out of an old group picture he'd copied from one of Theo DeWitt's social media accounts. After blowing up the image, it was a bit blurry, but the best they had.

Taking the wine glass, she sipped her drink as she pushed the phone farther across the bar. "I don't suppose you've seen our friend? We heard he's living in Richmond now, and we're hoping to hook up with him while we're in town. Someone mentioned he might hang out here."

The bartender rubbed his bearded chin and frowned. "I don't think I know him. Sorry."

The woodsy-scented dude stretched out a finger to tap the screen. "I recognize that guy, although his hair is dark, not blond. His name's Elmer, right?" When Annalise nodded, he continued, "Definitely him. He has the same long nose and gray eyes, but he wears glasses now."

Annalise straightened and flashed a smile. "Do you know where he lives?"

"Afraid not, but I've seen him around the neighborhood."

"You're right." The bartender snapped his fingers. "The blond hair threw me off, but he does come in here every now and then. A couple of nights ago, he was talking to a sharp-dressed guy about getting tickets to the Governor's Labor Day Ball tomorrow."

"Yep, that sounds like my buddy, Elmer. He likes to hang with the movers and shakers." Rory took a swallow of his scotch. "We'll look for him there. Thanks for your help." He dropped a fifty on the shiny mahogany surface. "Put the gentleman's beer on our tab and keep the change."

"Sure thing." The bartender picked up the bill. "Thanks."

Woodsy-smelling guy raised his glass and smiled at Annalise. "Yeah, thanks."

Taking her arm, Rory helped her down from the stool and led her through the crowd to a table by the window. Still clutching her drink, she dropped onto the chair he pulled out. A frown puckered her brow as he sat opposite her.

"Now what?" She kept her voice low as she swirled the wine in her glass. "We know Archie hangs out here sometimes, but how does that help? What do we do next?"

"I take you home to bed. You look ready to fall over."

"Well, I'm tired, and maybe a little drunk." She propped one elbow on the table and rested her chin in her hand. "I didn't finish any of my drinks, but you know what a lightweight I am."

"I'm actually feeling the effects of that final scotch, but it would have looked strange if I'd ignored it. I probably shouldn't drive anywhere."

"Yeah, drinking all night wasn't the best idea." She blinked tiredly.

He pulled out his cell. "I'll order you an Uber, make sure the driver doesn't look like a serial killer, and then find a hotel room. Tomorrow, I need to somehow finagle a ticket to that ball."

"Dad and Mom always get an invitation. I'd forgotten all about it. The guest list is a mixture of state political figures, professors and administrators from local colleges, business owners in the surrounding communities, and sometimes a few entertainers. The event is a party, but also a major fundraiser."

Rory's brows shot up. "Seriously? Do you think your parents would give us their tickets?"

"I can ask, but not at this hour. I didn't call to let them know I was coming since I wasn't sure what time we'd finish barhopping. My mom would have wanted to know why I was arriving so late, and I didn't feel like explaining. Since I have a key, my intent was to sneak in and surprise them in the morning."

"Then why don't we both get hotel rooms tonight, and I can drive you to Wildwood early tomorrow. You can ask your parents about the tickets, and we'll make a plan once we know if we can use them."

She stared at him for a moment. "Honestly, that sounds better than taking a half-hour Uber ride. I'm exhausted."

"Great. I wasn't crazy about the idea of sending

you off with a stranger." He rose to his feet, picked up her wineglass, tipped her drink into a potted palm, and then pulled out her chair. "Let's go."

She rose, wobbled a little, and gripped the arm he offered. "Why'd you pour out my wine?"

"So the bartender wouldn't think we came in here just to ask about our supposed friend if the glass came back full. It's busy tonight, and I don't want to give him a reason to remember our conversation."

He pushed open the ornate glass and chrome door, and they stepped out onto the sidewalk. A cool breeze sent a shiver through her, and she hugged herself against the chill. Rory wrapped his arm around her waist, and she was too tired to protest as he guided her up the block to his Porsche. Once he'd unlocked the car, she settled onto the seat, leaned back, and closed her eyes. Her head spun, and she felt slightly nauseous.

He got in behind the wheel and shut the door. When he didn't start the engine right away, she cracked open an eye. "Now I remember why two drinks is my limit."

"You definitely don't have a head for booze." He tapped away on his phone.

"What're you doing?"

"Finding a hotel that isn't sold out. It's a holiday weekend, so rooms are scarce. I didn't think about that before."

Deciding accommodations were his problem, she shut her eyes again.

"I'd like to book two rooms for tonight." A pause. "You're sure? The availability on your website—" Another pause. "Okay, thanks."

"No luck?"

"Unfortunately not, but there's one more hotel that says they have space. Yes, hi. I'm wondering if I can get two rooms for tonight? Only one cancellation?" He waited a couple of beats. "Yeah, I know the Governor's Ball draws a crowd. "Fine, we'll take what you have."

Annalise's eyes popped open. "No way am I—" When he raised a hand and shushed her, she ground her teeth.

"The reservation is for Annalise Quintrell. She'll be arriving in a few minutes, if you can hold the room for that long. Okay, thanks." He dropped his phone on the center console.

"Rory—"

"I'll find a spot in one of the dive motels along the highway outside of town." He started the engine. "I can drive that far without falling asleep at the wheel. Your hotel is only a few blocks from here."

She didn't respond as he pulled away from the curb and turned right at the light. A minute later, he parked in front of the striped awning of a swanky-looking hotel. A valet attendant rose from the steps and approached.

Rory rolled down the window as the young blonde wearing a gray uniform jacket stopped beside his door. "Can I leave my car here for a minute while my friend checks in? I don't want to take off until I know there isn't a problem."

She frowned. "No longer than a minute. There isn't much traffic this time of night, but—"

"Are there two beds?" Annalise interrupted their conversation.

"Huh?" Rory turned to face her.

"The room." She released her seatbelt and wished

her stomach would settle down. "Does it have two beds?"

"Yeah, two doubles. The clerk said that was all they had left."

"Then you might as well stay with me. I don't want you driving any farther, even though you seem perfectly fine."

"Are you sure?"

"Not in the least." She took a couple of breaths, letting them out slowly. "But I'll survive. Just don't try anything."

"I won't."

Grinning broadly, the attendant stepped back as Rory opened the door and handed over the key fob. "Sounds like someone isn't getting lucky," she murmured.

Annalise got out and regarded the woman over the roof of the car. "Definitely not."

"Your loss. He's cute."

She rolled her eyes then gripped the side mirror as her world tipped and swayed. "Yeah, he is, but looks aren't everything."

Rory pulled their bags from the trunk and walked around to her side of the car as the attendant gave him a receipt. He took it and handed her a folded bill. "Thanks."

"You're welcome. Uh, try to enjoy your stay."

Carrying both bags, Rory followed Annalise up the steps and into the lobby. "That girl's a regular riot."

"A sense of humor earns better tips." Heading straight toward the front desk, she pulled her wallet out of her purse and removed her credit card.

The older man behind the counter smiled. "Can I

help you?"

"I'm Annalise Quintrell. My uh . . . friend called about a room."

"Yes, I have everything ready." He laid a form in front of her. "If you'll jot down your information, I'll make an imprint of your credit card."

She handed him her Visa and began filling in the blanks. Glancing up, she turned to find Rory hovering behind her. "Your license plate number?"

He rattled off the letters and numbers. Finishing the form, she pushed it across the counter.

The clerk took it and handed her a folder with the key cards. "You're in room 209. A complimentary breakfast is served starting at seven. You'll find the wi-fi password on an info sheet in your room. Enjoy your stay."

"Thanks." Annalise summoned a smile before following Rory toward the elevator.

He pushed the button, and the doors swished open. "Normally, I'd take the stairs, but I don't think you'd make it."

"Probably not." She stepped inside and sagged against the wall. "I can't wait to fall into bed. I never stay up this late."

He hit the button for the second floor. "I'm just happy you don't look as green as you did in the car. I was afraid you were going to puke all over my leather seats."

"I was worried about it, too, but I feel slightly better."

"Good." When the elevator bumped to a stop, and the doors opened, he wheeled the bags into the hall. "Looks like we're three doors down on the left."

Annalise pulled one of the key cards from the folder and pushed it into the slot. When the light turned green, she pushed the door open and walked in. "This is nice."

The room was decorated in shades of white and gray, with a few unique touches like roughhewn furniture and lattice shades instead of the usual heavy drapes. Crossing the room, she pulled the cord to shut them, blocking out the light from the street below.

"If you don't mind, I'll use the bathroom first. If I sit down, I'm not sure I'll ever get up again."

"I don't mind at all." Rory dropped onto the foot of one of the beds and stretched out a hand to grab the remote off the nightstand between the two beds. "Take your time. I'll find a news channel to watch."

With a nod, she trundled her small suitcase into the bathroom and shut the door. Then she collapsed onto the toilet seat and held her head in her hands. Spending the night in the same room with Rory was upsetting her stomach more than the alcohol, but making him search for a motel at one in the morning when he was only here to help her had seemed petty. She let out a long sigh. Nothing was going to happen because Rory would never violate her space without her permission. He might be a lying bastard, but he wasn't a creep.

Forcing herself to move, she stood, opened her bag, and pulled out a sleep shirt and robe. Finding the container with her toiletries, she brushed her teeth and washed her face. After stripping off her jeans, shirt, and bra, and putting on her nightclothes, she brushed her hair and stared at herself in the mirror. With no makeup, she looked a little pale, and her eyes were shadowed with worry. Her head was also starting to ache.

Whatever. Rory had seen her looking a lot worse during a bout with the flu, and she certainly wasn't trying to impress him. Because caring what he thought would be a huge mistake. Taking a pill bottle from her toiletry bag, she swallowed a couple of ibuprofens, then tightened the belt on her robe with a jerk.

Opening the door, she dragged her suitcase out of the bathroom. "It's all yours."

"That was fast." He pointed the remote at the TV, and the room fell silent. Rising to his feet, he stood beside her. "You okay?"

"Just tired. Good night, Rory."

"'Night, love."

He disappeared into the bathroom before she could complain about the endearment. With a resigned sigh, she pulled back the comforter, slid between the sheets, and closed her eyes . . .

The early morning sun was shining through the tiny cracks in the blinds, casting striped shadows across her bed. Annalise rolled over and blinked. The clock on the nightstand read seven fifteen. Beyond it, Rory lay sprawled across his bed, one foot hanging over the side, and the covers pulled down to reveal his bare chest, rising and falling with slow, even breaths.

She hoped to God he was wearing something on his lower half.

A smile curved his lips between rough-stubbled cheeks, and his eyelids twitched, as if he were dreaming. The sheet below his waist tented.

Cheeks burning, she crawled out of bed and headed to the bathroom, snagging her bag along the way. She didn't intend to wait around to discover what he had on—or what he was dreaming about.

After a shower, she felt ready to tackle the day. Dressed in denim shorts and a T-shirt, she pulled her hair back into a ponytail and slapped on a little mascara. The alluring woman in the lowcut shirt was gone, and in her place stood a girl who was much more comfortable walking through the woods or digging in the garden. She liked this version of herself better. After repacking her bag, she opened the bathroom door, hoping Rory was awake. And decent.

"Morning." His tone was cheerful as he turned away from the window. "How're you feeling after our night on the town?"

He was shirtless, but at least he'd pulled on jeans. His muscled chest was enough of a distraction.

"Fine. Surprisingly, no hangover."

"You look better." He approached slowly, his gaze locked on hers, and stopped a couple of feet away. "I'll take a quick shower and shave. Do you want to eat before we go?"

"Only if you're hungry." She backed up until her legs smacked the foot of the bed. "I can wait until you drop me at my parents' house."

"Okay. I'll grab something from the free breakfast bar on our way out. That'll tide me over. For now." He stepped around her, a twinkle in his eyes, and a knowing smile curling his lips. "I'll be ready to go in ten minutes."

When the bathroom door shut, she dropped onto the bed. Rory was fully aware of the effect his nearness had on her. Dammit. All this civility, not to mention his toned abs, made her forget all the unforgivable lies he'd told. He'd broken her heart, and if she wasn't careful, he'd do it all over again.

Her defenses were firmly in place when he emerged from the steamy bathroom, his hair still damp, and his face freshly shaved. He also wore shorts and a T-shirt, along with a determined expression.

"I've been thinking."

"On an empty stomach? This can't be good."

"Funny." He grabbed both their bags and pulled them to the door. "We need to call your parents about those tickets before we leave Richmond. That way we can strategize on our drive down. I want to get all our ducks in a row before I drop you off."

"Makes sense. It also occurred to me that I didn't come prepared to attend a formal event." As they left the room and headed toward the stairs, she frowned. "I still have a couple of prom dresses in my old bedroom. Maybe one of those would work."

"Hell. I'll have to rent a damn tux."

"Can't we just wait around outside the party venue and grab Archie when he shows up? Seems easier."

Reaching the lobby, he turned toward the dining room where a buffet was laid out. Taking a glazed donut, he wrapped it in a napkin and grabbed a banana. "Are you sure you don't want something?"

Annalise shuddered. "Just looking at all that sugar makes my teeth hurt. Maybe a banana."

He handed her one, then walked over to the coffee urns and filled two to-go cups.

"I definitely need coffee." She added cream to both and picked one up before heading toward the front desk. An older couple stood in line in front of them.

"I figure Archie has a reason for wanting to attend the ball." Rory kept his voice low. "Maybe he's meeting whoever ordered the last forgery to set up another deal. A fundraising event like the Governor's Ball attracts people with money, and he can mingle without anyone taking undue notice."

"Which means we'd need to be inside to see who he has a conversation with." The couple in front of them left, and she stepped up to the counter.

A middle-aged woman with lavender hair gave her a cheerful smile. "Checking out?"

"Yes." She laid the keycards on the counter and took a sip of coffee. "Room 209. You can put the total on my card and email me a receipt."

The lady tapped a few keys on her computer. "You're all set. Have a lovely day."

"You, too." Annalise turned to discover Rory had disappeared. Glancing around, she spotted him just outside the front door with their suitcases and joined him.

"I sent the attendant for my car." He eyed her steadily before crumpling his empty coffee cup and tossing it in a nearby trashcan. "I would have paid for the room."

"Why? We're here because of me, but you can rent your own tux."

"Whatever you say." He pointed. "Here comes the valet with my car."

After stashing the suitcases in the trunk, he tipped the man while she slid onto the passenger seat and dropped her purse at her feet. He got in a few moments later and pulled away from the curb. Steering with one hand and eating a donut with the other, he glanced her way.

"Go ahead and call your parents."

"What the heck am I going to say? That I have a mystery date and was hoping to take him to the ball? I'd originally planned to tell them I got a ride south with a friend, but now that scenario won't work."

"What about the truth? You're the one who made it clear lying only causes problems."

"True." She peeled her banana and took a bite, considering his suggestion. "The forged picture fiasco will cause Dad the greatest concern. Mom, on the other hand, will worry that seeing you will make me fall apart again."

His grip on the steering wheel tightened until his knuckles turned white. "I'm sorry, Annalise. Tell them whatever you think is best."

"You're right. I'll tell them the truth. The truth is always best."

Chapter Six

"No, Mom, I'm not getting back together with Rory. Yes, I do remember how angry and brokenhearted I was. He's helping me find the Pissarro that was stolen from the museum. That's it." Annalise was quiet for a moment, listening to whatever her mother had to say. Strain was evident in the tight lines bracketing her lips.

Rory focused on the road, feeling like he'd been kicked in the stomach by a bee-stung mule. He knew she wasn't deliberately trying to make him feel worse than he already did, but any hope that she'd be willing to start fresh disappeared with the sun as clouds bunched along the horizon. Clearly, her wounds were still deep and raw.

"We'll be there in about ten minutes. No, Rory isn't staying. He's just dropping me off and will pick me up again before that stupid ball." She drummed her fingers on her knee. "I know, but we have to go if we want to find the painting. Okay, I'll see you soon. Bye."

She laid her phone in her lap and sighed. "That was

painful. Mom fears the worst for my emotional stability, and Dad thinks I should simply go to the police with my story. He doesn't like the idea of me getting involved with criminals."

"If you want, I'll take you straight back to Philadelphia, and you can report the forgery to the cops."

"I don't. No matter how the situation plays out, I'm pretty sure I'd lose my job. Marcus will blame me for any upheaval at the museum, which we wouldn't be able to avoid, and after spending last night with you, I'd definitely be suspect number one." She grimaced. "Well, maybe suspect number two. You'd be number one."

"I agree, but I wanted to make sure you knew the stakes."

"Oh, I know. I'm probably a complete lunatic for agreeing to this, but I'm all in."

He was quiet for a moment as they turned onto a back road and drove along the James River. The trees were beginning to turn, bursts of yellow, orange, and red foliage dotting the verdant countryside. Under ordinary circumstances, he'd have enjoyed the hell out of the scenic drive. Today, however, was anything but normal.

"Your parents are willing to give us the tickets, despite their misgivings?"

"Yes. They weren't planning to go to the ball, anyway. Dad has a cold. They may worry, but they trust my judgement."

"I'm thankful for that. I'll rent a tux and pick you up around seven. I want to arrive during the middle of the influx so we don't stand out. I'd rather Archie didn't spot me the minute we walk through the door."

"I'm sure Dad wouldn't mind loaning you his tux since you're around the same size. Come a little early tonight, and you can change before we go."

He raised a brow. "You sure about that?"

She nodded. "Once I explain that you're only doing this to help me, he'll be on board."

"Great. I'd rather spend my morning hiking than driving back to Richmond to get measured for a monkey suit. Want to join me in the woods?"

A scowl drew her brows together. "Didn't I make it clear yesterday that we aren't on a date? Don't push me, Rory."

"Fine, but I bet you'd have fun."

Her only response was a grunt, and a couple of minutes later they entered Wildwood. The small town was situated along the southern bank of the river near the National Wildlife Refuge. With its broad main street, appropriately named Main Street, flanked by quaint shops, and a big park with a gazebo, Annalise's hometown reminded Rory of a Norman Rockwell painting. While it didn't have the historic feel of Williamsburg, the village was heavy on Americana charm. He smiled as they cruised down the main drag past antique stores and mom and pop eateries. On a holiday weekend, the sidewalks were bustling with tourists.

At the far end of town, he hung a right and drove down a narrow, dead-end lane past a couple of houses barely visible from the road, slowing as they reached the Quintrell home. The big, white farmhouse backed up to thick forest. A chubby yellow lab rose to her feet on the long, wraparound porch. Tail wagging, Buttercup ran down the steps and barked in excitement as he parked next to a red SUV and turned off the engine.

Annalise opened the car door and knelt on the gravel drive, rubbing the dog's ears as she danced around her. "Hi, sweetie. What a good girl. Are you happy to see me?"

Ellen Quintrell stepped onto the porch, letting the screen door swing shut behind her with a squeak and a slap. She waved and smiled hesitantly, her hazel gaze darting from her daughter to the driver's side of the car. Figuring he might as well bite the bullet now rather than later, Rory opened his door and stood to lean against it. A shield between him and the momma bear who knew only too well how badly he'd wounded her cub.

Annalise rose to her feet and regarded her mother with a wide grin. "Wow. You look terrific. Those gold highlights in your tawny hair are spectacular."

"They cover up the gray." Descending the steps, Ellen greeted her daughter with a tight hug before turning to face him. "Hello, Rory."

"Hi, Ellen. It's good to see you. Annalise is right. You look great."

"Flattery isn't going to work on me, not after what you put my daughter through."

Inwardly, he winced, but he kept his expression even. "Not flattery. Just the truth, and I don't expect forgiveness. As I told Annalise, I own my mistakes. All I can say is I'm sorry your family was hurt because of my poor choices."

"I appreciate that, and I don't want to make this awkward." Ellen spoke firmly. "Annalise said you're trying to help her, although I don't completely understand what's happened."

"I'll explain in more detail while you feed me breakfast." She laid a hand on her mother's arm. "If it makes you feel better, I talked to Brielle when I discovered the Pissarro was a fake. She agreed that I needed to do something pretty drastic. So, since your smart daughter thinks I'm right—"

"Don't fish for complements. You're both smart."

Annalise laughed. "True, but we both know she's the truly brilliant one." She turned as her father approached from around the side of the house. "Hi, Dad."

"Hi, honey. It's great to see you, even if the circumstances aren't ideal." David Quintrell hugged his daughter then faced Rory, his penetrating blue gaze assessing. "I appreciate you helping Annalise, Rory. It's good of you to drop everything when she found herself in a difficult situation."

"Of course. I intend to see that she isn't hurt in any way because of this." The comment was the best he could do to assure her parents he'd keep her safe from harm and not break her heart in the process. "I'll take off now." He met Annalise's gaze. "See you this evening."

"Wait." She glanced up at her dad. "Can Rory borrow your tux? We didn't come prepared for a formal affair."

"I suppose so." He glanced down at his lean frame. "The jacket might be a little tight through the shoulders, but the pants should fit well enough." He grinned. "Your mom keeps me too busy to lounge around eating all day."

"Thanks, David. I appreciate the loan." He attempted a note of levity when Buttercup strolled over to a patch of mud beside a rhododendron bush and rolled. "I promise not to romp in the dirt while I'm wearing it."

Staring at the dog in consternation, David pulled out a handkerchief to blow his nose. "Let's hope not, but I probably won't wear it again until one of the kids—" Breaking off, he grimaced.

Until one of his kids gets married. Rory guessed that's what Annalise's father had been about to say. He'd probably bought the tux when they'd set a date for their wedding.

Annalise's lips tightened into a grim line, and he decided it was time to make his escape. "I'll be here before seven to pick you up."

"Okay." Her tone was flat.

With a quick smile for her parents, he ducked into the car and shut the door, feeling like the biggest asshole in the world. A minute later, he'd backed out of the driveway and stomped the accelerator, only slowing when a squirrel ran across the road in front of him. Facing David and Ellen had been worse than confronting the line of cops with weapons drawn, just before they'd cuffed him and hauled him off to jail.

He hadn't expected anything else.

Reaching town, Rory parked on a side street and headed toward his favorite of the three cafés along Main Street. Wild Brew was crowded, but a familiar figure sat at the counter, reading a paper and drinking a cup of coffee. The stool next to him was empty. Deciding to risk a rebuff, he approached Annalise's brother.

"Morning, Linc. Is this seat taken?"

Lincoln turned slowly, his Quintrell blue eyes

narrowing slightly beneath shaggy, dark blond hair. He had strong features and a solid build and looked like the quarterback he'd been when he'd played in high school.

"It's been a while, Rory. What're you doing in Wildwood?"

He dropped onto the stool. "Helping Annalise out of a jam she's in through no fault of her own. She mentioned Pete retired and sold you his home restoration business. Congratulations. I bet you have more work than you can handle."

"I'm staying busy." Lincoln stared at him for a moment longer, not saying anything while the waitress, a fixture in the café, refilled his coffee cup and poured one for Rory without asking.

"Thanks, Marge. I'll have the strawberry waffles. Hold the whipped cream."

"Good choice." Your farmer's platter will be up in a minute, Linc."

"Great. I'm starving."

She laughed. "You're always starving."

After she walked away, the floor vibrating beneath her heavy steps, Lincoln scowled. "What sort of trouble is Annalise in, and why in the world would she turn to you for help?"

"It involves a stolen painting." He kept his voice low. "I'd rather not explain where a dozen people can overhear."

"Then you can tell me after we eat." He moved his newspaper out of the way as Marge returned with a plate full of scrambled eggs, bacon, sausage, hashbrowns, and pancakes. "Thanks. Looks delicious."

"More like an artery-clogging heart attack waiting to happen," Rory murmured.

"A guy's gotta keep up his strength." Picking up his fork, he dug in.

Rory poured a little cream into his coffee and stirred. "Look, I'm sorry for everything. There's nothing more I can say. I hate that I hurt Annalise. I hate that I blew up our friendship and worried your parents."

"Why'd you do it, Rory?" He pushed a bite of eggs into his mouth and chewed, the only sign of anger revealed by the slight tick beneath one eye.

"Because Felix Lemmon gave me no choice. If I didn't do the job, he planned to tell Annalise about our past association. I thought I could get in and out and not lose her. Basically, I made a stupid, stupid mistake."

"Maybe you should have told her the truth a long time ago. She's a pretty understanding woman, but she doesn't like being played."

"You're right. It's just . . ." He took a sip of coffee and stared at the counter. "I loved her so damn much, and she's so freaking amazing. Why would she have stuck with me once she knew I was a criminal?"

"Because she loved you, too, you idiot. I followed the trial and did a little digging into your past. Unlike my sister, who couldn't bring herself to watch. It hurt her too much."

"I saw you in the courtroom when I testified. I didn't blame her for not being there."

Lincoln ate steadily, talking between bites. "I found out about your dad's suicide, and I figured you put your mom into that care facility about the same time you started stealing art for Lemmon. I tried to tell Annalise you had your reasons, but she didn't want to hear about them from me."

Rory forced a smile when Marge delivered his plate and a small pitcher of syrup. "Thanks."

"You're welcome. Enjoy."

He'd lost his appetite, but he poured syrup over his waffles, anyway. "I told her my sad story after she called on Friday night. She was ready for some answers."

"And?" Lincoln raised a brow.

"She said I could have made different choices. She's right."

He washed down a final bite of pancakes with a swallow of coffee. "Did you mention why the cops busted you in the act at that art gallery?"

"No."

"Maybe you should."

"I wasn't trying to be a hero that night. If it wasn't for me agreeing to steal that painting, the security guard wouldn't have been shot in the first place."

"Maybe not, but he sure as hell would have bled out if you hadn't stayed behind to put pressure on his wound and call 9-1-1. The bullet nicked an artery."

"No guns. That was our rule. I didn't know Lemmon's sons were armed. I didn't know the rules had changed. That's why I cut a deal with the feds. Felix lied to me, so I didn't feel I owed him a damn thing."

Lincoln pushed his empty plate away and crossed his arms over his chest. "Being lied to doesn't feel great, does it?"

Rory didn't answer. Annalise's brother had made his point. Instead, he finished his breakfast and pulled out his wallet. When Marge strolled over to take their plates, he handed her his credit card.

"Put both our breakfasts on this."

"Sure thing. I'll be back in a minute."

"I'll let you buy me breakfast, but when lines are drawn, I'll always stand on my sister's side."

Rory turned to smile at his onetime friend. "You damn well better. Anyway, the breakfast bribe isn't about loyalty. If you have a spare room, I could use a place to crash tonight."

"Let's hear what you have to say about Annalise's problem before I make any decisions."

When Marge returned with his card, he added a hefty tip and scribbled his signature on the receipt. Sliding off his stool, he faced Lincoln. "That's fair. Why don't we take a walk?"

He nodded and rose to his feet. "Thanks, Marge. See you next Sunday."

A broad grin split her weathered face. "Since you're as regular as a prune lover, I'm sure I will."

Amused, Rory pocketed his wallet and followed the other man out of the café. They stopped on the sidewalk as a pair of young boys raced past.

"I was planning to take a hike through the refuge this morning. Do you have time to join me?"

"I suppose so." He checked his phone when it chimed. "Mom just texted to stop by the house this afternoon if I want to see Annalise while she's here."

"The trail isn't that long. We'll be back before noon."

"Fine." He pulled his keys from the pocket of his shorts and glanced down at his flipflop-clad feet. "I'll meet you there in twenty minutes. I need to put on some shoes first."

"Sounds good. See you, Linc." Turning, Rory jaywalked across the street and headed toward his car, happy that Annalise's brother was speaking to him. Clearly he had a few reservations, but Lincoln had been friendlier than he probably deserved.

With nothing better to do, he drove to the parking area at the wildlife refuge and sat on the low fence to wait. Lincoln's silver pickup pulled into the lot not long afterward, and he hopped down and walked over to meet him.

Lincoln eyed a family just getting out of their car, and an older couple heading into the woods. Otherwise, the lot was empty.

"I don't think anyone will overhear us. Start talking."

As they strolled down the trail, Rory explained about the forged painting, Annalise's panicked phone call, and his detective work that had led to the bar in Richmond. Birds chirped loudly in a thicket of maple, birch, and white oak while he waited for Lincoln to digest the news.

"You really think this idea of yours to find and return the original painting is the best course of action?"

"It would have been better if Annalise hadn't noticed a problem with the Pissarro and had never removed the landscape from the wall in the first place, but security will have a record."

"Which means, if at any point someone else verifies the painting is a fake, the police will investigate her as a suspect."

"Exactly, and since she was engaged to me . . ."

"Guilt by association."

"Yeah." Rory kicked a rock. "The whole situation

sucks since she didn't do a damn thing except be extremely good at her job."

They stopped at a bench overlooking a marshy area along Powell Creek. Reeds waved in the breeze, which carried the pungent sent of decaying vegetation. Across the water, a bald eagle perched at the top of a dead snag. A minute later, the bird spread its wings and took flight, soaring up into the hazy sky.

"What can I do to help?" Lincoln spoke abruptly.

"I'm not sure you can, at least not until we know more. The plan tonight is to keep an eye on Archie Weber at the Governor's Ball to see who he talks to. If he needed a ticket so badly, he may be using the event to communicate with whoever is ordering forgeries. I hope he'll expose a few viable suspects."

"Or you could just haul this Archie asshole outside and beat some answers out of him."

"That was my first inclination, and I might still have to do it, but what if he won't talk? If he warns his contact—"

"The stolen painting would disappear for good." Lincoln scowled. "Maybe the situation does call for finesse rather than hanging the creep up by his thumbs."

"After the ball, I hope to have a better idea of where to look next. I'll definitely ask if I think you can help."

Lincoln's lips curved in a grim smile. "Do you intend to steal the painting back?"

"Seems like the easiest solution."

"And God knows you have the skills to get the job done. Just make sure you don't put Annalise in any danger."

"Not going to happen. If I need backup, I'll call

you."

"That works." They started walking again, taking the looping trail back toward the entrance. "If you want a bed to sleep in tonight, I have a spare."

"Thanks. I imagine the local B&Bs are all booked for the holiday weekend. I could drive back to Richmond after dropping off Annalise, but this will be easier."

"No trouble for me. If you get in late, I'll leave the door unlocked." He met Rory's gaze, his expression implacable. "Just don't mess with my sister's head. If you hurt her again, I'll kick your ass."

"You'd probably have to get in line for that honor. Truthfully, I'm more afraid of Brielle."

Lincoln grinned, and after a few repressed snorts, they both laughed out loud.

Finally, Rory sobered. "Don't worry. The last thing I want is for Annalise to get hurt. She's far more likely to shred what's left of my heart, but I deserve it."

"You won't get an argument from me."

They didn't talk much for the rest of the hike, passing a few other nature lovers, and getting a close-up look at a doe that bounded across the trail. When they reached the parking area, Rory leaned on the roof of his Porsche while Lincoln unlocked his truck and opened the door.

"Hey, thanks for listening back at the café, instead of telling me to get lost. Or punching me."

"I was tempted, but I guess I'm able to see the big picture with a little more perspective than my sister. Then again, I liked you, but I wasn't planning to marry you."

"Good thing. That would have been awkward."

They both smiled broadly.

"Damn, I've missed you, Rory." Lincoln released a long sigh. "Maybe when this is over, we can find a way to be friends again."

"I hope so because I always considered you my brother. I still do."

Chapter Seven

Annalise eyed the four prom dresses spread across her bed. Two were hers, and the others belonged to her sister. "Bri's red mini is definitely out, and my purple one is a little too sparkly for the Governor's Ball."

Her mother nodded. "I like your blue one, but the ruffles look a bit young. I think the long, black dress your sister wore her senior year is probably the best choice."

"I agree. Bri was going through her Goth period, which thankfully didn't last long, but the dress will work. It's simple and elegant."

"If I recall correctly, she wore it with a pair of low-heeled work boots and long, fingerless gloves."

"And makeup that gave her a Morticia Addams vibe."

Her mother shuddered. "I remember. However, if you pair the dress with those three-inch, strappy sandals you brought, the length should be about right."

"Perfect." Annalise scooped up the three rejected dresses and hung them back in the closet. "Good thing

Bri and I have always worn the same size, even if she is a couple of inches taller."

"I have a silver necklace and earrings that'll match your silver shoes, and a black clutch purse you can borrow."

"Great. One problem solved." She just hoped getting answers from Archie the forger would be as easy. Somehow, she doubted it.

Following her mom down the stairs, she headed out to the front porch where her dad and Lincoln were drinking beers, deep in conversation. When they both shut up the second she appeared, she figured they'd been talking about Rory.

"I'm not going to break down in tears or throw something if you mention Rory's name." She dropped onto the padded swing and gave it a push with her foot to set it swaying. "I have a little more self-control than that."

Her brother studied her for a moment. "He seems hellbent on helping you, even though there's a decent chance he'll get caught by either the criminals or the cops during the process."

"The thought occurred to me, but not until after I'd called him. I didn't expect him to jump in with both feet. Honestly, I was hoping he was the jerk who stole the painting so I could shame him into returning it."

"You're sure he didn't?" Her dad blew his nose before stuffing his handkerchief back in his pocket. "This damn cold is driving me crazy."

"I'm sure. Granted, he can lie like a politician on the campaign trail, but I believe he's telling the truth about this. I may not be ready to forgive and forget, but I certainly don't want him to get arrested because of me."

"Or shot by the thieves who stole the Pissarro in the first place." Lincoln's tone was blunt. "I made him promise he'd call me if things get dangerous. We agreed he won't put you at risk."

A shiver slid through her, and she gripped her bare knees beneath her shorts. "I don't want anyone to get hurt, but the two of you don't get to decide what I will and won't do. This is my problem to deal with as I see fit."

Her dad's brows lowered. "If going to the Governor's Ball will put you in harm's way—"

"It won't." She and Lincoln spoke in unison.

When she simply stared at him, he continued, "Rory was clear this will be a scouting mission to learn who the potential players are. Nothing more."

Her dad leaned back in his chair. "Then I feel a little better about letting you go."

Annalise gritted her teeth. Both her father and brother acted like she was a brainless child, incapable of making her own informed decisions. Time to change the subject.

"What's new with you, Linc? Dating anyone I know?"

"No one you know or don't know." He tipped back his beer. "I've been too busy with work to manage a social life. When you ask a woman out, she generally expects you to show up."

"Funny how that works."

He grimaced. "After having to cancel on the last two ladies, I'm taking a break." His eyes narrowed. "What about you?"

"Oh, you know me." She kept her tone light. "I

have to beat off men with a stick."

Her mother chose that moment to push open the screen door with her hip. Turning, she set down the charcuterie board she carried. "I made snacks. You'd better grab what you want before your brother digs in."

"Don't I know it. This looks great, Mom." Annalise piled crackers, cheese, nuts, and olives on a small plate. "Thanks."

"There's no telling if you'll have time to eat at the party tonight." Her mother leaned against the railing and smiled fondly as Lincoln attacked the spread, then returned her gaze to her daughter. "Why would you turn away potential suitors? I'm sure you meet perfectly lovely gentlemen at the museum."

"All the good ones are attached." Annalise savored a morsel of smoked gouda. "Lydia insists on setting me up with her boyfriend's single pals, but so far, I haven't been impressed. Maybe I'm just gun shy."

"Or not over Rory." Lincoln mumbled the words around a wedge of apple and brie he stuck in his mouth.

She tossed him a dark look.

"Don't tease your sister, Lincoln." Her father neatly stacked salami and pepperjack on a cracker. "Did I tell you Nash called? He's on his way home from Ukraine with some spectacular photos that will rip out people's hearts. At least that's what he's hoping."

"He'll probably win another Pulitzer Prize for his work." Annalise finished her snack. "I'm just glad he's returning safely."

"I am, too." Her mother let out a long sigh. "I can't stop worrying when he's taking photos in a war zone."

"Which is most of the time." Lincoln popped an olive in his mouth. "Will he and Bri both be coming home in October for your birthday, Mom?"

"I'm not sure. It would be lovely to have all of you here at the same time."

"I'll definitely try to make it." Annalise rose to her feet. "But right now, I want to go shower. I'm sweaty from working in the garden this afternoon."

"You were a big help picking beans." Her dad smiled broadly. "I may have gotten a little carried away and planted too many."

"You think?" She grinned back at him. "Don't get me started on how many zucchinis are out there."

"Your dad still thinks we're feeding an army." Her mom headed inside. "I'll lay out your dad's tux for Rory."

"Thanks, Mom."

Annalise had showered, dressed, finished her hair and makeup, and was ready to go ten minutes before Rory was due to arrive. She took one last look in the mirror and decided she was appropriately attired. The old prom dress had a simple, corset-style top with thin straps that fit like a second skin to the waist before flaring out in a skirt with a tiny train. She'd pulled her hair up into a classic twist with a few strands left to trail down her neck, softening the overall look.

"Good enough," she mumbled. Grabbing the clutch purse her mom had lent her off the dresser, she strolled into the hall and glanced through the open door of Lincoln's old bedroom where her mother had left her dad's tux, along with a white dress shirt and black bow tie.

Voices from the entry alerted her to Rory's presence before footsteps thumped up the stairs. He appeared wearing, shorts, a T-shirt, and black dress shoes and socks.

"Nice look."

He grinned, his gaze travelling from her head to her feet and back up again. "The shoes belong to your brother. We're both a twelve, and your dad wears a ten." He stopped in front of her. "You look absolutely gorgeous."

"Thanks." The admiration shining in his eyes, along with a banked glow of desire, sent warmth surging through her, and she ruthlessly tamped it down. She wasn't a naïve girl excited for a date with the hottest guy in school, for God's sake. Taking a breath, she let it out slowly as his attention zeroed in on her breasts. "Dad's tux is in Lincoln's room. You can dress in there."

"Okay." He jerked his gaze away. "I'll be ready in a few minutes."

With a nod, she walked past him and hurried down the stairs, holding up her skirt so she wouldn't trip. If she didn't get a grip on her emotions, this night had the potential to rip open the scar tissue over her heart, leaving a gaping wound. Stopping the bleeding wouldn't be any easier the second time around.

"My goodness, you look lovely." Her mother walked out of the living room and beamed. "That dress is perfect on you."

"Thank you. Hopefully, I won't attract too much attention. The goal is to blend with the other guests and watch Archie Weber's every move."

Her dad turned away from the baseball game on the big screen TV to glance her way. His brows shot up. "You're beautiful. There's no way you'll go unnoticed, even in a crowd."

"If that's the case, I'll ditch Rory so our target doesn't spot him."

"If you leave Rory on his own, he'll be surrounded by women." Her mom's gaze shot past her to the top of the stairs. "He looks very handsome in your dad's tux."

Rory descended to her side, his eyes sparkling with humor, having clearly overheard the comment. "Thank you, Ellen, but your daughter is out of my league. Always has been." He took her arm. "Shall we go?"

"Sure." She forced a smile as his fingers practically branded her skin. "I don't expect to be home late, but don't wait up."

"Enjoy yourselves," her dad called. "And please don't do anything risky."

"We won't. Thanks again for loaning me your tux."

Rory opened the front door, and they stepped out into the cool evening air. A sleepy-sounding bird chirped somewhere in the trees, and the breeze caressed her bare arms.

Her mother followed them onto the porch. "Take care of her, Rory."

"I definitely will. No one is going to hurt Annalise. I can promise you that."

"'Night, Mom." Holding up her skirt, Annalise ran lightly down the steps and headed straight to his car. He beat her there and opened the door.

She met his gaze as she slid onto the seat. "This isn't a date."

"Funny. It sure seems like one, right down to being admonished by your parents." He shut her door and walked around the car to get in.

She glanced over as he started the engine and

backed out of the driveway. "True. All day, I've felt like a sixteen-year-old going to my first prom while my mom and dad hovered and worried."

"If you were this smokin' hot in high school, they had a reason to worry."

"I wasn't, and we're not doing this. No sexual comments. Got it?"

"Fine. I won't say a word." He drove through town and headed toward the highway. "Let's talk strategy instead. Lincoln told me the ball is being held at the Wentworth Plantation, which the organizers rented for the occasion."

"That's right. You'll need to take the bridge across the James since it's on the other side, not much more than a fifteen-minute drive from here."

"I checked out the location this afternoon and did a little recon. They have a giant tent set up out on the lawn with tables and a dancefloor. In one of the wings off the main building, the items for the silent auction are on display. People will be milling around, going in and out, all evening long."

"Sounds like it'll be easy enough to keep an eye on your forger."

"In general, yes. They were stringing a ton of lights in and around the tent area, but there'll be plenty of shadowy corners for people to meet in private. Our goal is to track Archie's movements without being obvious. If I get too close to him, he'll recognize me."

"No problem." She stared out at the dark river as they drove onto the bridge. "If he goes somewhere you can't without being spotted, I'll follow him."

"As long as there're plenty of people around, I'm not too worried. He won't know you work at the museum since he wasn't the one who robbed it."

Annalise turned sharply in her seat to stare at him. "Do you think the thief will be meeting Weber at the party?"

"Doubtful. More likely, he plans to talk to either the person organizing the deal or the actual buyer."

"Or, he's just a guy who wants to party with the Richmond area elite. If so, we're wasting our time."

After exiting the bridge, Rory turned east. "Doubtful. Archie wouldn't show up at a high-profile event like this without a good reason. He's not going to risk being recognized, despite his changed appearance, unless he urgently needs to speak to someone and doesn't have a better way to communicate."

"I suppose not."

"Anyway, if he doesn't single anyone out, I can always haul his ass down to the river and threaten to drown him if he doesn't talk."

"I thought violence wasn't the answer."

"Maybe not the best answer, but I don't intend to leave the party tonight without a lead on that damn painting." He slowed to join the line of cars entering the checkpoint on the driveway leading to the huge, red brick, Georgian mansion. "Do you have the invitation?"

"Yep." She opened her purse, pulled out the square card with gilt trim, and handed it to him.

He glanced at it and smiled. "Do we look like Dr. and Mrs. David Quintrell?"

"I guarantee security isn't going to ask to see our IDs. Maybe in New York City, but not in rural Virginia."

"Probably not. Besides, if someone really wanted to sneak onto the estate, all they'd have to do is park nearby and hoof it across the fields surrounding the plantation house. That's how I got in for my recon earlier."

When they reached the security guard dressed in formal attire, Rory rolled down the window and handed the man the invitation. The guy barely glanced at it before giving it back.

"Enjoy your evening, sir."

"Thank you, we will." Rory raised the window again and smiled. "Lax. Very lax."

"Well, it's not like the president comes to this thing, or even the governor, for that matter. I guess our governor used to come, back in the day." She was chattering nervously and wasn't sure why. Maybe because she intended to spend the next few hours with Rory, pretending like they were a couple, and she feared it wouldn't be easy to convince herself it was all make-believe.

He parked in a cleared field where the attendant directed them. By the time he got out and walked around to her side, she was already picking her way across the stubbly grass. Not an easy feat in three-inch heels. When he took her arm, she gave in to the inevitable. Better to smell his aftershave and feel his warm fingers cupping her elbow than twist an ankle.

They reached the mansion and ordered drinks at the outdoor bar. After the previous night's adventure, Annalise had zero desire for alcohol and asked for club soda. Rory got a beer and sipped it as he scanned the crowd.

She eyed the other guests, recognizing a few friends of her parents. "Do you see Weber?"

He shook his head. "Maybe he's inside. Wait.

There he is, just walking in from the parking area." He kept his voice low as he edged behind a large man who was telling a story about a court case that had his companions laughing. "I wouldn't have recognized him with dark hair if I hadn't been looking. As long as I keep a few people between us to obstruct his view, we should be good."

Annalise searched the new arrivals. "Dark gray suit with a maroon tie?"

"That's him."

"Good. He'll be easy to keep track of in the sea of black formal wear."

"Maybe he plans to be in and out in a hurry and didn't want to bother renting a tux. You watch him while I keep my back turned."

"He's headed this way, probably to order a drink, so let's drift toward the buffet."

"Sounds good. I could eat." Rory took her arm and led her to the end of the line forming at the food tables. "Just get appetizers you can eat with your fingers. We don't want to sit at a table and have our view blocked."

"I'm too nervous to eat much, anyway." Glancing over her shoulder, she froze. "Your artist stopped and is talking to a couple. They have their backs to me."

"Get out your phone and take a picture as soon as they look this way." Rory frowned as he reached the buffet table and picked up two plates. "Seems strange he'd meet with someone right out in the open."

"How long does it take to inform his contact he finished a forgery or that he needs a meeting? Seems less conspicuous than huddling in the bushes." Annalise discreetly raised her phone and snapped pictures as the female half of the couple turned to greet an older woman. A few seconds later, the man with her stepped away from Weber. She took his picture before lowering her phone. "I got photos of them both."

"Excellent. I loaded a plate for you. Let's walk toward the house. There's a bench in the rose garden where we can sit but still see most of the yard. Archie won't be able to get a good look at me."

Balancing both plates on one arm like a seasoned waiter, and holding his beer in his free hand, Rory led the way while Annalise kept an eye on the forger. He'd gotten in line at the bar and was casually looking around while he waited. Reaching the rose garden, Rory gestured for her to sit down and then handed her one of the plates.

"Way too much food." She popped a mini spinach quiche in her mouth. "These are delicious."

"Did you recognize the people Archie was talking to?"

"No." She tapped her phone to bring up the pictures. "Middle-aged. Probably husband and wife. They don't look like criminals." Her tone held an edge. "But then, neither did you."

Ignoring her comment, he studied the photos and frowned. "I saw that woman this afternoon. She drove up to the mansion in a Bentley, of all things, and pulled straight into the garage like she owned the place. Then she marched over to the event coordinator and spoke to her before going inside."

Annalise took her phone back and did a quick search. "Ha, that's because she does. Or, rather, her family owns the plantation. I glanced through the local paper earlier and saw a story about how the Wentworth family had offered to hold the ball at their property this year." She laid her phone on her knee. "Here's a group picture of the whole Wentworth clan in front of the mansion, and our couple is there in the middle."

"Let's see, second row, third from the left. They're Howard Starmer and Georgette Wentworth Starmer." Rory's eyes narrowed. "Clearly, they have money, and maybe they also have a thing for priceless artwork that doesn't belong to them."

Annalise ate a stuffed mushroom while she searched for Archie Weber and found him still at the bar. "You think the Starmers might be the buyers, rather than the head of a forgery ring?"

"Makes more sense. I'll see what I can learn about them first thing tomorrow."

"He's on the move." She nudged Rory. "Your buddy Archie is strolling through the crowd with his drink."

"He doesn't look like he's leaving the party anytime soon. Wait, he just veered right toward those people standing near the band."

The jazz ensemble was warming up behind the dancefloor that had been laid out on the lawn. A tall man with silver hair stepped away from the group as Weber drew near. They spoke for less than a minute before Weber moved on to say something to one of the musicians. The two laughed, and he wandered off. When the older man glanced in their direction, Rory snapped a picture with his phone.

"I wonder who that guy is?"

"He's a professor at William & Mary, I believe in the English department, although I can't remember his name. He and my dad participated in a couple of Civil War reenactments when I was in high school. I'd say their relationship is more friendly associates than actual pals."

Rory set down his plate and tapped rapidly on his phone, scrolling through bios for the English department staff at the college. "Here he is. Dr. Thomas Ellison. He has an impressive list of publications. I wonder if he also collects art. Your dad might know."

"We can ask him."

When she glanced up, Rory cupped the side of her face in his palm and swooped in, kissing her like he never intended to stop.

Chapter Eight

Despite Annalise's initial resistance, Rory held her tight and kept right on kissing her. After a moment, she stopped pulling against him. When her mouth softened, he almost forgot about Archie, who was heading straight toward them. His tongue slipped between her lips, and he moaned in pleasure as she kissed him back.

It had been so long since he'd kissed her. Holding her close, feeling her breasts flatten against his chest, tasting her . . . this was what he wanted. To have the woman he loved in his arms again.

When he finally opened his eyes to see the forger's gray-suited back as he walked by on his way toward the mansion, Rory came up for air and rested his forehead against hers. They were both breathing hard.

"Why did you do that?" Her voice cracked as she jerked out of his grasp.

He angled his head toward the wing of the house where the silent auction was being held. "Archie is on his way inside. He would have seen my face if I hadn't hidden it."

Color burned in her cheeks. "Oh."

"Not that I'm complaining, but I didn't have a better idea, and I needed to act fast."

She drew in a breath, and her breasts pressed against the neckline of her dress. "I should probably follow him."

He forced his gaze up to meet hers. "Don't get too close, Annalise. Not that I think he'll do anything, but still."

With a nod, she rose and straightened her skirt. With her back held straight, she marched down the path toward the east wing of the mansion.

He slumped against the bench. She'd responded to his kisses, even though she hadn't wanted to. The chemistry between them was as combustible as ever. There was a fine line between love and hate. Indifference was the real killer, but if he was any judge, she was far from indifferent.

Still, now wasn't the time to think about winning Annalise back. Standing, he made his way through the roses, across a short stretch of lawn, and skirted the far end of the wing. Staying in the shadows, he peered through a window on the back side of the building, which gave him a clear view of tables covered with various items and bid sheets.

Annalise was at one end of the long room, and Archie was at the other. Between them were a dozen people. The artist looked like he was writing something on a bid sheet. Putting down the pen, he strolled through the rows of tables, pausing occasionally, before finally stopping near a woman standing at the edge of a small group. She turned and said something to him.

Rory drew in a sharp breath.

Annalise's brows drew together. "Do you know where she lives?"

"No, but I doubt it would be terribly difficult to find her address, or at least the location of her business. I assume she's still an interior designer, and this is just a side hustle, but maybe I'm wrong."

"Then why don't we go home and regroup? We learned far more than we thought we would tonight."

"That's true." When the band struck up a slow number with a smooth sax solo, he pulled her onto the dance floor. "Let's dance and think about this."

"Rory." Her tone held a warning.

"What?" He pulled her tight to his chest and rested his cheek against her soft, fragrant hair. "Kat and her friends are heading this way. Let's see what she does next. I'm using you as a shield to make sure the woman doesn't get a good look at me."

He could practically hear her teeth grinding, but she didn't argue and swayed in his arms to the music. They stayed where they were, on the outskirts of the dancers, until the song ended. Even after the music stopped, he didn't let her go.

"Kat and a guy who's probably her date broke away from the group and are talking to Howard and Georgette Starmer." He murmured the words just above her ear, breathing in her intoxicating vanilla scent. "She seems quite animated, and the Starmers are all smiles. Now she and her date are heading over to the bar."

Annalise pulled loose. "Do you want to stay here until she leaves?"

"I guess not. I'm pretty sure she won't ditch her date to meet up with either Archie or whoever's buying the stolen artwork."

Turning, she glanced toward the bar. "Is the tall man with the dark hair the guy Kat's with? They're talking to some people I recognize. Thomas Ellison and another woman who taught with my dad. The others in the group are probably spouses. I wonder if Kat's date is a colleague of theirs."

"I'm not sure it matters, but we can check him out." He slid an arm around her waist as the music started again. "Want to dance? Or we can get more food. One of the waitstaff just dumped the plates we left on the bench in the trash."

"No, I don't want to dance." She pushed away from him. "Or eat. Let's go."

"Fine. I'll raid your brother's refrigerator after I drop you off." Placing a hand at the small of her back, he steadied her over the rough terrain as they crossed the field.

"Are you staying with Lincoln?" At his nod, she continued, "He didn't mention it. I guess he thought it might upset me."

"Does it? Because I can get a hotel room if—"

"I don't care where you sleep tonight. I'm not going to burst into tears if someone mentions your name."

"That's good. I really don't want to make you cry." He pulled the key fob from his pocket and hit the remote to pop the locks.

"Lincoln thinks I'm not over you."

"Is he right?" Heart thumping, he opened her door and waited while she slid onto the seat and adjusted her skirt.

Finally, she answered. "We're finished, Rory. I won't let the fact that we're currently working together undo two years of emotional recovery. I've moved on with my life."

His grip tightened on the door handle. "I only want you to be happy, love. I hope you know that."

When she nodded, he shut the door and walked around to the other side of the car. He truly believed she'd be happiest if they got back together, but he kept his opinion to himself. Starting the engine, he shifted into gear, and they bumped through the field to the access road. He certainly didn't intend to push her—or his luck—right now. At the moment, he was relieved she was even talking to him.

Annalise slipped off her heels and curled up on the seat. "What do we do next?"

As they reached the highway, and the headlights sliced a path through the quiet countryside, he considered her question. "The end goal is to learn who has the original Pissarro. If Kat took over her father's business, she's the middleman . . . I mean middle woman. The buyer comes to her. She hires the forgery artist and the thief, and handles the money. Archie probably doesn't have a clue who the buyer is since he's not dealing with him or her directly. Same with the thief. After I quit, Felix's two sons were stealing all the artwork, but they're both in prison with their father."

"Why did Felix need you for that last job if his sons could have done it?"

Rory turned onto the bridge, the tires rumbling over the surface in the stillness of the night. "The situation was tricky and required more than one man to pull it off. Plus, I'm better than they are. The whole thing went to shit, anyway, when one of them shot the security guard. You know what happened after that."

She was quiet until they reached the other side of the river. "So, without her brothers, Kat would have to find a new thief."

"Yes. I really don't care who stole the painting. I care about who bought it and where it's currently located. Once I know that, I can go in and retrieve the painting and put it back on the museum wall where it belongs."

"And no one will ever know it was gone."

"Exactly. Neither your boss nor the police will have a reason to question your integrity, and you can move on with your life."

"And forget this whole nightmare happened." She slipped her shoes back onto her feet as he drove through town and turned down the road to her parents' house.

"I hope not everything. Maybe you can text me now and then. If seeing each other is off the table—"

"It definitely is."

He almost smiled at the growl in her voice. "You might change your mind. Can I still be friends with Lincoln?"

"I won't, and you and my brother can hang out as much as you like. I didn't force him to choose sides."

"Alrighty then." He pulled up in front of the house and turned off the engine. "What time do you want to leave tomorrow?"

"I don't know. What's on your agenda?"

The porch light didn't quite reach the car, but it softened the darkness around them. She'd unfastened her seatbelt and turned to face him, and he could just make out the tension in the set of her jaw and tight grip she had on her purse.

"I plan to do some digging into Kat's recent activities. How did this client find her? Maybe she decorated his house or talked to him at a party, and I use the pronoun expeditiously. The buyer could be a woman. I'll start with social media and move on to her business records."

"You mean break into either her home or her office to get information?"

He flashed a grin. "It's not like I'll actually break anything. I have a little more finesse than that. Anyway, I can probably get most of what I need online."

"Fine. Whatever. I probably shouldn't ask questions if I don't want to hear the answers. Is there something I can do to help?"

He reached over and squeezed her knee. "Why don't you just relax and enjoy spending time with your parents? I'll text you once I figure out a few things, and we can decide when we want to take off."

"Okay." She opened the door, and the interior light flashed on. "Thanks, Rory. I really do appreciate your help. You certainly shouldn't feel obligated."

"I'm not going anywhere." He noted the shadows in her eyes and wondered what bothered her more, the stolen painting or his presence in her life again. "We'll figure this out, one step at a time."

With a nod, she hiked up her skirt, swung her legs out of the car, and stood. "Good night."

"'Night, love. See you tomorrow."

The door shut with a solid thump, and he waited while she walked up the steps and disappeared into the house. After a moment, he turned on the engine and backed out of the driveway. Time to give Annalise a little space. After spending the last two nights together, maybe she'd miss him if he wasn't around.

He could dream.

* * * *

Late the next afternoon, Annalise sat on the porch with her mom, waiting for Rory to pick her up. As they drank iced tea and chatted about the leaf-peeper road trip her parents planned to take to Maine over the next few weeks, she wished she could say she'd spent the day relaxing. Instead, she'd been a ball of nerves, despite sleeping late, going for an easy run, and grilling sausages and corn with her dad for lunch. She couldn't stop wondering what Rory was doing, not to mention dreading the long drive home cooped up in his car together.

"Have you heard one word I've said in the last five minutes?"

"Huh?" She jerked her attention back to her mother. "Sure. You were talking about the campgrounds you made reservations at on your route through New England. I'm glad you and Dad are enjoying your RV so much."

"Then I told you I was going to cut your dad's hair in a mohawk and dye it pink, and you just nodded and smiled. What's on your mind? That missing painting, your evening at the Governor's Ball, or Rory?"

"Sorry I'm so distracted." Annalise pushed her toe against the floorboards to set the porch swing swaying. "I suppose all of the above."

"When you came in after the party, you said you had a new lead to follow." Her mother's brows pinched above her hazel eyes. "If you're determined to find the stolen painting yourself, that's a positive step, right?"

"Yes, but until last night, I hadn't realized just how many risks Rory is willing to take to recover it. I may not be able to forgive him for lying to me about damn near everything while we were together, but I certainly don't want him to get hurt—or arrested."

"Knowing Rory, he'll land on his feet." Her tone held an edge. "You're not the only one who has issues with the man. I can't forgive him for breaking your heart, and I definitely don't want you to go through that pain again."

"I'm trying my best to stay objective about working with him."

Her mom snorted. "How's that going?"

Her cheeks heated as she remembered the feel of his strong arms holding her close while they slow danced, the whisper of his breath across her ear setting her nerve endings tingling. "Not great, but he's literally the only one who can help me get that painting back, so I don't have a choice."

"This would be easier if you had a special man in your life to focus on."

"Well, I don't, although the new guy working in the museum gift shop asked me to lunch next week." She grinned. "I told him maybe."

"For heaven's sake, go out with the man. At this point, you need to be social rather than hanging out at home by yourself if you want to keep your mind off Rory."

Somehow, Annalise doubted Callen Ives would provide much of a distraction, but she nodded. "I suppose I can do that."

"Speaking of Rory, there he is."

His black Porsche turned into the driveway, and he parked next to her dad's Chevy Blazer. She pushed up off the swing as he got out and strolled toward them.

"Afternoon, Ellen." His gaze shifted to Annalise. "Ready to go?"

She nodded. "I need to tell Dad goodbye first. I think he's in the garden." When her mom stood, she reached over to hug her. "Love you, Mom. I'm sure I'll see you again soon."

"I hope so." She hugged back before stepping away. "Here's your dad now. He must have heard the car."

Annalise grabbed the suitcase she'd left beside the door and carried it down the steps as her father followed Buttercup around the side of the house. Reaching Rory first, he shook his hand. "Good to see you again, Rory."

"You, too, David. Don't worry about your daughter. I'll take good care of her."

"I can take care of myself, thank you very much." She slid her arm around her dad's waist and squeezed. "Bye, Dad. Have fun on your trip. Send pictures."

He dropped a kiss on the top of her head. "We will. Have a safe drive."

"Thanks."

Rory put her bag in the trunk while she bent to pet Buttercup. With a final hug for the dog, she got in the car, rolled down the window, and waved as Rory backed down the driveway. When her parents disappeared from view, she faced forward.

"I'm glad I got to hang out with them today. I probably don't come down to see them as often as I should."

"It's easy to get sucked into our routines and not take time for the important people in our lives."

"Yes, it is."

With his seat tilted back, he drove through town with a sure hand on the wheel and the radio playing softly, the picture of cool confidence. By contrast, she sat with her fists clenched in her lap. Deliberately, she relaxed them. When the silence began to bug her, she cleared her throat.

"I looked for the man Kat Lemmon was with last night on the William & Mary website. His name is Simon Kingsley, and he's a professor in the philosophy department. Maybe he was the one who was invited to the ball and brought her as his date."

"That's possible, although I checked into her, too. Business appears to be booming for Kat. She might have earned her own invitation since her interior design company, Concepts by Kat, now has offices in both D.C. and Richmond. Based on her social media posts, she also has an active social life and keeps company with several men, most of whom are older and wealthy."

"She's very pretty. I guess they don't care that half her family was indicted for grand larceny, racketeering, money laundering, attempted murder, and other assorted crimes."

"They're probably the type of guys who like arm candy and would never consider a woman like Kat is capable of casing their homes for potential art to steal."

"Unless one of them is the buyer." Annalise raised her knees and wrapped her arms around them. "How do we figure out who paid for the Pissarro?"

"We, or rather I, check them out, one by one. I spent an hour in Kat's Richmond office this morning, going through her files."

She turned to stare. "You broke into her office?"

"No one was working on a holiday, and their security really needs an upgrade. It took me less than two minutes to disable the alarm system and get inside."

Her breath caught. She'd asked him to help her, and that's exactly what he was doing. She needed to get over the fact that he was breaking and entering to get the job done.

"Did you learn anything useful?"

"First, I think we have to make a few assumptions. Since Archie showed up in Florida earlier this summer and has only been seen around the Richmond area for about a month, I would say the painting was stolen from your museum fairly recently."

Outside her window, the Virginia countryside whizzed by as they merged onto the interstate. After a moment, she nodded. "That makes sense. Also, I stop to admire *Sheep in the Meadow* fairly often. It's one of my favorite pieces, and I probably would have noticed sooner if the forgery had been hanging there for months."

"Good point. So, my working hypothesis is that we're looking for a person Kat has been in contact with, either through her business or socially, during the last month. The Richmond branch of her company worked with two clients within our timeframe. Interestingly, one of the jobs was for the Starmers. They used her company to decorate their vacation home on the beach in Chincoteague."

"Isn't that the island off the Virginia coast that has wild horses?"

"Yep. Cool place. I've sailed in the area before."

Annalise dropped her feet to the floor and sat up

straighter. "So, that's why Kat talked to the Starmers at the party. She knows them."

"Or they were inquiring about when their next piece of stolen art would be delivered." His tone hardened. "The Starmers definitely make our short list of suspects."

"Who was the second client?"

"An author who lives in Williamsburg. She just had one of her books made into a movie and apparently decided to remodel her old home with the profits." He smoothly passed a big rig and flipped on his lights as dusk settled. "I checked out her place after leaving Kat's office."

"Oh, my God, Rory. I'm surprised she wasn't there on a holiday weekend."

"She was, and she had family visiting. They were in the backyard, barbecuing and playing croquet. All the doors were unlocked. I took a tour of the house and got a distinctly modern vibe from her taste in décor. If she was into stealing art, she would have gone for something abstract, not your Pissarro."

She closed her eyes and took a few deep breaths. "Unbelievable."

"What? We can definitely cross Kesia Adams off the list. As for Kat's D.C. clients—"

"Wait. Wouldn't those job profiles be kept in her Washington office?"

"The hard copies, sure, but all her digital records are stored within the same online system."

"How did you—never mind."

"That's what I do for a living these days. Private businesses and government agencies hire me to break into their computers to show them where potential breaches are most likely to occur. I also personally demonstrate any weakness in their onsite security systems and then fix the problems."

"I knew that. I should have realized you can use your talents for both good and evil."

He laughed. "You make me sound like a cartoon villain. Anyway, Kat's D.C. office has been working on a huge project all summer for a high-profile federal judge. Abraham Blankenship completely renovated his home in Georgetown. The only other job she took this summer was last month for a VIP living in Chevy Chase, Maryland who wanted to give her master suite a quick facelift."

"Let me guess, another entitled politician?"

"Much better. Zenith Jones."

Annalise turned and gaped at him. "Superstar legend Zenith Jones? Are you kidding?"

"Nope." He flashed a wide grin. "I get to check out the home of the most iconic rock goddess of all time. How cool is that?"

Chapter Nine

Rory parked at the edge of Zenith Jones's upscale neighborhood and turned off the engine. Leaning one arm on the steering wheel, he faced Annalise. "I can still take you home and come back another time."

"We're here now. If you're worried about me, don't be. Since I'll be in the car, I'm not the one in danger of being arrested for trespassing."

"Make sure you stay put."

"I will. I'm not an idiot." She scowled. "Or a cat burglar. If I came with you, I'd just be a liability."

"If you're sure, I'll head out." He switched off the interior light before handing her the key fob and opening the door. "I should be back within a half hour. If you hear sirens, drive away. Wait twenty minutes at the gas station near the freeway where I changed into dark clothes. If I don't show up, go home."

"Just so you know, hearing that makes me feel sick to my stomach."

He reached over and patted her arm. "I don't expect any trouble, but it's always good to have a backup plan. Lock the doors after I get out."

"I will. Please be careful."

"Always." He stepped out onto the street and shut the door, wondering why she was so concerned. Was she worried that if he got caught, he wouldn't be able to get the Pissarro back? Or did she actually still care a little? The last thought was enough to warm his heart against the chilly, evening breeze.

When the locks clicked, he walked quickly away. No point in drawing attention to himself by running, although he wasn't really worried that anyone would notice since the homes in this neighborhood were set well back from the street, many behind tall fences. Wearing black athletic pants, a long-sleeved black T-shirt, and a navy ball cap pulled down low, he blended into the darkness and reached Zenith Jones's address four minutes later without having encountered a soul.

He'd driven by her home earlier, noting the high brick walls surrounding the property and the electric gates that could only be opened remotely. He doubted she had security guards patrolling her yard, but signs posted on the wall made it clear there was a canine presence inside. Good thing he always came prepared for dogs.

Taking the package of beef jerky he'd bought in the convenience store at the gas station from the fanny pack strapped around his waist, he broke the sticks into pieces. Walking along the side of the property, he tossed the chunks over the wall then gave a low whistle. A sharp bark broke the stillness of the night before what sounded like two large dogs thundered across the lawn. He quietly ran around the far end of the wall, found a toehold on a loose brick, and heaved himself up to the top. A glance in their direction assured him the two Dobermans were busy hunting for jerky.

Taking a moment, he surveyed the sprawling home while he snapped on latex gloves. Voices and soft music drifted from what he assumed was the living area. Upstairs, all the rooms on the back side of the house were dark. Likely, no one had locked up yet for the night, but he preferred to avoid a chance encounter on the main floor until he got his bearings. A large oak tree with branches stretching toward a second story balcony looked like his best option for entry.

After checking to make sure the dogs were still rooting through the grass, he dropped to the lawn below. Avoiding the security lights that illuminated most of the yard, he skirted the kidney-shaped pool and large patio area to climb nimbly up the old oak. Hoping the branch he chose would hold his weight, he crawled out a good six feet, then gripped the limb to swing back and forth. Getting some momentum, he let go and flew toward the balcony. Grabbing onto the wrought iron pickets, he dangled precariously before hoisting himself up and over the railing with a small thump.

When one of the dogs barked and galloped in his direction, he crossed the balcony to the set of French doors. The handle didn't turn. Working quickly, he pulled a set of picks from the fanny pack, inserted the sharp tool, and the lock clicked. Stepping into the room, he shut the door, which muted the barking, and used a small flashlight to scan the interior. A king-sized bed dominated the space, along with the usual bedroom furniture. The artwork on the walls consisted of framed photographs of flowers scattered in a random, eye-catching pattern. A two-minute search of the remaining upstairs rooms assured him the Pissarro wasn't hanging in plain sight.

Descending to the first floor would be a little trickier with people awake and potentially roaming about. Running lightly down the stairs, he walked through the kitchen, checked the large cupboards in the laundry room, then entered the attached garage. It took two more minutes to make sure there weren't any paintings stored in the shelving units.

A smile curled his lips as he noted the accumulation of junk. For a Rock & Roll Hall of Fame superstar, Zenith Jones's garage looked much like every other garage he'd ever been in. Heading back into the house, he hurried down the hallway to a set of stairs that led to a basement. The lower terrain seemed most likely to house stolen artwork, but the entire level was open to view. A home gym occupied one corner, while a theater area that included a giant movie screen filled the wall opposite the workout station. A recording studio took up the remainder of the below ground space. After making sure nothing was stashed in the soundproof booth, he ran back up the stairs.

Although he was pretty certain he was wasting his time, he checked the formal dining room, the library with its built-in shelves crammed full of books, and then edged toward the spacious living room that looked out onto the backyard and pool. Barking came faintly from outside, audible over the classical music playing in the background. An older black man with wavy gray hair and heavily tattooed arms stood by a large window. Rory recognized the drummer from Zenith's band.

"I don't know what the hell is bothering the dogs. They're standing by the oak, staring straight up. Maybe they treed a squirrel."

Zenith lounged on the couch facing Rory's direction, but her attention was focused on the drummer. She wore pink, silk pajamas and no make-up, looking much older than the stage version of herself. "Good for them. They're probably bored out of their minds being watch dogs for me. No excitement."

"At least the neighbors are too far away to hear and complain." He turned away from the window and walked back to the couch. Dropping onto the edge of the cushion, he pressed Zenith down into the nest of throw pillows. "How about we create a little excitement of our own?"

Cringing, Rory backed away. The last thing he wanted was to stick around and watch the old rocker couple getting it on. Since the living room walls were decorated with hanging tapestries that had a vaguely Middle Eastern feel, he was one hundred percent certain Zenith Jones wasn't their buyer. Her artistic taste definitely didn't lean toward nineteenth century Impressionism.

Now to get across the yard and over the wall without having a chunk bitten out of his ass by the Dobermans.

The front door seemed like his best option since it was the farthest exit from the dogs. Silently, he crossed the slate entry, noted the alarm had not been set, and pulled open the heavy front door. It squeaked slightly, but based on the sounds coming from the living room, no one was paying any attention.

Keeping his head down to avoid the security cameras, he sprinted across the lawn. The dogs stopped barking, and paws thundered against the ground as they apparently picked up his scent. Silent but deadly, they tore around the side of the house and gained on him as he neared the wall. Slowing only slightly, he jumped up onto the bricks, searching for finger and toeholds. As he scrambled upward, hot, damp breath fanned his ankle, and he jerked his foot away from a set of sharp teeth. Clinging to the top, he pulled himself clear and rolled over the edge, landing on his feet on the far side with a thud that jarred his clenched molars.

Deprived of their prey, the Dobermans howled like the hounds of hell.

Getting his breathing under control, Rory pulled off his latex gloves and shoved them into the fanny pack as he hustled up the sidewalk in the direction of the car. Mission accomplished. Another suspect eliminated, not that he'd really expected Zenith Jones to be the guilty party. Still, it paid to be certain.

As his Porsche came into view, he heard the locks pop. Clearly, Annalise was alert and waiting anxiously for his return. A few seconds later, he opened the driver's side door and slid behind the wheel.

"Thank God. I was a nervous wreck the entire time you were gone." She slumped against the seat. "I'm not cut out to be a criminal."

He grinned as he started the engine. "You didn't break any laws, and I didn't get caught, although one of Zenith's dogs nearly bit off my foot. And just so you know, our rockstar is in the clear."

"That's good, I guess." Her brows knit as they drove past a streetlight. "How was I not aware you had an insane fascination with danger?"

"Probably because I didn't need to live on the edge when I had you in my life. I was happier than I've ever been, either before or since."

She was quiet for several minutes as they got back on the freeway and headed north. Finally, she turned to face him. "It hurts that you didn't trust me with the truth, Rory, that you thought I wouldn't love you if I knew you weren't exactly perfect."

"Would you have?"

"Yes." She looked away and stared out the window. "I probably still love you, but I don't forgive you. Getting over you is still a work in progress, but I'm determined to succeed. I need to find a man I can trust with my heart. One who will trust me with his. One who won't lie to me."

His chest ached as her words pierced his soul. "Believe me, I'll live and die by the truth going forward. I learned my lesson."

"I hope so." She hesitated for the moment. "For the sake of the next woman you charm into your life."

He could declare he only wanted her. He could promise he'd never love anyone else. But he was pretty damn certain she didn't want to hear it. Not right now, anyway. Instead, he'd stick with his new plan to wear down her resistance, little by little, until she admitted she didn't need any other man but him. Sometime in the not-too-distant future, he was determined to put her engagement ring back on her finger where it belonged.

They rode in silence for several miles before she spoke again. "What's next? I have to work tomorrow, but—"

"You don't need to do anything except go about your normal routine while I search a few more of our suspects' homes. I'll head back to D.C. in the morning and investigate the judge's house. Also, two of the men

Kat has been dating live in the D.C. area, so I'll check them out at the same time."

"If that's your plan, maybe I should catch a train home so you can stay here tonight."

He glanced over and shook his head. "No way. I don't mind the drive. It's not much more than two hours if I avoid rush hour traffic."

"I guess that means you'll be spending the night in Philly again."

"I'll get a hotel room. At this point, we're in too deep to try to hide the fact that you've been in contact with me."

"I suppose so. If we don't find that painting, I think we're both pretty much screwed."

"Don't worry. We'll find it."

* * * *

Annalise woke the following morning with a bad case of déjà vu. After showering and dressing in black pants and a pink blouse, she headed for the kitchen, doing her best not to wake Rory, who was once again asleep on her guest mattress in the middle of the living room floor. At least she'd had the foresight to grind beans and fill the coffee pot with water the previous night. Right after she'd caved in and told him he could stay at her apartment. Not that he'd actually asked.

Guilt had overridden her urgent desire to send him packing once they'd arrived home. He'd been on his best behavior during the long, quiet drive, probably knowing she wouldn't have the heart to kick him out when he was only trying to help her. As a punishment for her altruism, she was treated to an unrestricted view of Rory's hard, bare chest and rigid abs, to go with her morning coffee. Thankfully, the sheet was pulled up to his waist.

Hoping the caffeine would clear away the mental cobwebs, she drained her first cup while she toasted a bagel then slathered it with cream cheese. Determined to sneak out before he woke up, she skipped making a lunch and took her breakfast to go, along with a travel mug filled to the brim with coffee. She left enough in the pot for Rory to have a cup and tiptoed around him on her way to the door.

"Morning."

Annalise stopped three feet short of her goal and closed her eyes. After a moment, she opened them again and turned. "Morning. I'm headed to work."

"So, I see." He sat up and swung his bare legs off the mattress, disturbing Maizie the Traitor in the process. The cat rose and stretched then sauntered toward the kitchen.

"Shoot. I didn't feed her."

"I'll do it." He pushed to his feet and followed the cat, wearing nothing but a pair of boxers. "Can I keep your spare key? I'll lock up when I leave." He tossed the comment over his shoulder as he got out kitty food and poured it into Maizie's bowl.

"I suppose so." *At this rate, he might as well move in.*

"Great. I'll call and let you know what I learn in D.C. I'm hoping to get in and out while both of Kat's gentlemen friends and the judge are at work. With any luck, I'll be back before you get home."

She kept her gaze above his waist when he walked around the counter and perched on a bar stool. "Don't you need to work today?"

"I work for myself, mostly remotely, so it's not like

I have to clock in. I should, however, put in a few hours on a couple of projects, but I can do that this evening."

Which made it sound like he intended to set up camp in her living room again. Annalise gritted her teeth. "Okay. Please be careful. I don't want to hear on the news that you've been arrested."

"That won't happen." He leaned his elbows on the bar counter behind him and smiled. "By the way, you look pretty in pink."

Ignoring his compliment, and the fact that he was lounging on her bar stool like a men's underwear model, she frowned. "You got busted before, if you'll recall, so clearly you're not invincible."

"Only because I didn't want the security guard to bleed out. Since no one is going to get shot today—"

"What are you talking about?" She glanced at the clock on the stove behind him. "Never mind. I don't want to be late for work. You can explain later."

"Have a good day, Annalise."

She opened the door. "Let's hope so. Bye." Shutting it behind her, she let out a breath.

Am I really desperate enough to deal with a mostly naked Rory every damn morning? A groan escaped. Unfortunately, she was, so she'd better suck it up and handle it. *No, not handle. Anything but handle.* She fled down the stairs. Right now, she simply needed to escape.

Annalise arrived at work a few minutes early, finished her bagel, and discovered Lydia waiting for her first tour of the day to arrive. She gave her an abbreviated version of her weekend that didn't include any mention of Rory.

"Sounds like you had a relaxing couple of days in

Virginia."

"I did." A total lie, and Annalise cringed just saying it. "Spending time with my parents was nice." At least that was the truth. "What did you and Sebastian do?"

"The usual. Caught up on housework, played tennis, went out to dinner, and . . ." A broad grin stretched across her face as she held up her hand. "He proposed."

"Oh, my God!" Annalise gripped her friend's hand and stared at the stunning, oval cut diamond ring on her finger before grabbing her in a tight hug. "That's awesome. I'm so happy for you both. Congratulations."

"Thanks. I'm happy for us, too, but there's so much to do to plan a wedding." She groaned. "We want to get married next spring, so I have less than a year. Am I crazy?"

"No, but I remember how much work was involved. Eloping is always an option."

Lydia's brown eyes clouded. "I don't want to throw my plans in your face if it'll bring back bad memo-ries—"

"Don't be ridiculous. I'm thrilled for you." Annalise hugged her again. "It's been two years since I cancelled my wedding, and I'm over Rory." Another big, fat lie, but she really was happy for her friend.

"I hope so. I want you to find someone as wonderful as Sebastian." Her gaze darted toward the entry where a couple dozen school children had just arrived and were making a beeline for the gift shop, followed by a harassed-looking teacher. "There's my tour. A bunch of fourth-graders." She grimaced. "Oh, shoot. I almost forgot. Marcus wants to see you right away. I told him I'd let you know."

"Just the way I dreamed of starting my morning." She rolled her eyes. "Have fun with the kids."

"I'll be ecstatic if they don't break anything. See you later, Annalise."

Straightening, Annalise dodged a few more children and headed down the hallway toward the curator's office. Just off the kitchen in what had once been an open breakfast nook when the museum was a private home, the room was now enclosed. She knocked softly."

"Enter."

Opening the door, she stepped inside. "Morning, Marcus. How was your weekend in Atlantic City?"

"Entertaining but expensive." Her boss glanced up from the paperwork on his desk. Behind him, a window looked out onto a garden where a couple of hardy hydrangeas still bloomed. "I hope you made progress on those pictures I picked up at auction."

"I still have quite a bit of work left to get them clean enough to display, but I was able to identify the artist. Thomas Moran."

"No shit?" His brows shot up. "That's quite a find since I paid fifty bucks apiece for them. When will they be ready?"

"Hopefully later today. Then, after we close, I want to examine the clothing in the Lenape tribe exhibit to make sure there's no dampness on any of the garments. Moisture got into that display, and I don't want to risk mold. Can you let Oscar know I'll need those cases unlocked?"

"I'll put in a requisition. With a building this old, leaks are always a problem, but maintenance assured me they made the necessary repairs." He set down his pen and crossed his arms over the navy blazer he wore with a white shirt and red tie. Not his usual, casual attire.

"Thanks." Annalise edged backward. "Is there anything else?"

His gray eyes were piercing beneath short, dark hair threaded with gray. "I have a report here that you asked security to remove *Sheep in the Meadow* on Friday." A frown etched grooves in his forehead. "Why was that?"

Her breath stalled in her throat, and her grip tightened on the travel mug clutched in her hand. It took every bit of composure she could muster not to freak out. "I noticed a hairline fracture in the frame. Rather than risk the crack getting worse, I repaired it." Her voice was calm, even if she was sweating bullets. "Since the painting was only down for a couple of hours, I didn't want to disturb your weekend to get permission."

He nodded. "I'll check it out the next time I'm up there."

"If you're able to see the repair, I'm not doing my job right."

"Good point." His hands came down on his desk with a slap as he pushed to his feet. "I have a breakfast meeting with some of our biggest donors. We could use an influx of cash, so I'd better not be late. Good work on those paintings."

"Thanks. I'll see you later, Marcus." Turning, she left the office, keeping her pace slow and dignified, even though she felt like running. Had he been unusually interested in the Pissarro? He didn't normally question her when she removed pieces to clean them, but this time she hadn't made a formal request first.

Her legs trembled slightly as she passed the security office, waved to Jim, the guard on duty, and then unlocked the door to her dungeon. She needed to get her act together, do her job, and behave like nothing was wrong. Like she wasn't a quaking jellyfish inside. Even if Marcus did take a look at the painting, he'd never be able to tell it was a fake. He didn't have the critical eye for nuances necessary to detect a master forgery.

Thank God.

Unless he was the inside man who'd helped the thief.

Goose bumps rose on her arms at the thought. More than likely, someone she worked with was part of the heist. Someone was undoubtedly keeping a very close eye on the painting. And if that person figured out she knew it was a forgery—

She nearly dropped her coffee mug as she tripped on the bottom stair, and a chill slithered through her. If they discovered she—or Rory—was nosing around in their business, what might they do to tie up loose ends?

A whimper slipped out as she regained her footing. She was damn sure she didn't want to find out.

Chapter Ten

Rory had almost forgotten the adrenaline rush involved in his previous career as a thief. Not that he intended to take up robbery again as a hobby. He wasn't tempted in the least—not much, anyway.

Even breaking into a secret FBI facility, one that wasn't supposed to exist, to prove that he could, didn't offer the same nail-biting stress because there was no risk he'd be tossed in jail if he was caught. Or shot. Unless the agency forgot to put out the word they were running a test . . .

He inserted the thumb drive into the server that would have infected the mainframe—if it hadn't been completely harmless—and immediately began his extraction. Twenty minutes later, he was back in the rental car, calling the man who'd hired him. To say Special Agent Ferris wasn't pleased he'd gotten in and out without detection was an understatement.

Grinning, Rory started the engine and headed down the dirt road that would eventually take him to the interstate and the SeaTac airport. Once he wrote up his recommendations for improving security, his bank account would be substantially fatter as a result of tonight's work. And since he didn't have any other urgent projects, he could take some time off to focus exclusively on Annalise's problem. More importantly, on Annalise, herself.

Glancing at the dashboard clock, he grimaced. Eleven o'clock West Coast time was way too late to call her. He'd reserved a red eye flight from Seattle to Philadelphia and wouldn't land until sometime the next morning. No point in waking her up just because he wanted to hear her voice. Instead, he'd finish his reports on the plane, catch a couple hours of sleep, and then surprise her when she got off work. If he didn't warn her he was coming, she couldn't tell him to stay away.

Which was why he found himself waiting in a café with a view of the museum a few minutes after six o'clock the following evening, wondering if she planned to work late. Just as he pulled out his phone to text her, Annalise walked through the doors. Wearing a black skirt that hit just above her knees, a pale-yellow top with a cream-colored sweater, and a bright smile, she was so pretty all he wanted to do was rush over and pull her into his arms. Except she wasn't alone. The weasel who'd asked her to lunch the previous week was walking by her side, laughing at something she'd said.

"I might have to kill him." Rory muttered the words beneath his breath as he left a five-dollar bill on the table to cover the coffee he'd ordered. As soon as the two passed the café, he strolled out to the sidewalk and followed, leaving a ten-yard gap between him and Annalise. Not that she would have noticed if he'd been right on her tail. She seemed completely unaware of her surroundings, which was just plain careless and potentially dangerous, engrossed in her conversation with the dweeby man at her side.

They reached the intersection, and the guy gave her arm a quick squeeze before turning left across the street when the traffic stopped. While Annalise waited for the light to turn green, Rory caught up to her.

"You look gorgeous. Hot date?"

She pressed a hand to her chest, and her eyes widened as she jerked around to face him. "My God, Rory. You scared the heck out of me. What are you doing here?"

"Waiting for you to get off work. I flew into town earlier today."

The walk sign flashed, and she set out at a fast clip. "Why didn't you go home instead?"

"I left my car at the airport here, and Philly is a lot closer to the Virginia coast than New York. You didn't answer my question."

She frowned. "What ques—oh, a date. No, I don't have a date. Did you *follow* me while I was walking with Callen?"

"Since I was waiting for you to exit the museum, and you came out with the dweeb, I didn't have much choice. I didn't want to interrupt what looked like an intense conversation."

"We were talking about the fall exhibit I convinced Marcus to pursue. Some incredible Egyptian artifacts are touring the country, and they had a cancellation at a museum in Ohio, which means we could potentially scoop up that timeslot. This will be huge for our museum if we get the show."

"No wonder you looked so animated. I couldn't

imagine—Cullen, was it—inspired such passion."

"Callen. You're a real jerk, Rory."

"Just looking out for your best interests, love. You're way out of that guy's league." He put a hand on her back as they turned down her street. "If you don't have a date tonight, I'll take you out to dinner since you look so pretty in that outfit."

Her lips moved, and he had a feeling she was counting to ten as she unlocked the door to her building. Maybe he'd better cool it a little, but he was so damn happy to see her after four days apart to take care of some pressing business that he couldn't pull off casual civility.

"Or, we can *not* go out. Did you forget we have a working arrangement only?"

"Your choice for the evening. I'm good with staying in. We can order pizza or Chinese, or even better, I'll rummage through your fridge and find something to turn into a fine dining experience."

She gritted her teeth as she marched up the stairs. "Are you going to tell me why you're here?"

"You're off Sunday and Monday, right?" When she nodded, he continued, "I thought we'd drive down to Chincoteague in the morning. Since my search through the homes of Kat's recent D.C. connections didn't turn up the painting, we're left with the Starmers and the professor she's been dating, Simon Kingsley." Rory followed her into her apartment and bent to scoop up Maizie when the cat ran to him. "Of course, you don't have to go with me if you don't want to."

"What makes you think the Starmers would keep the Pissarro at their vacation home and not at their main residence in Richmond?"

"I don't know that they would." He rubbed Maizie beneath her chin, and her eyes slitted in sheer bliss. "I'm trying to cover all our bases. Since I had to take a few days off to deal with an urgent request by an important client, I intend to get back on track with our search."

Annalise dropped her keys and purse on the counter and walked over to the refrigerator. Opening it, she stood staring into the interior. "How, exactly, can I help by going with you?"

"You could keep me company, and once I've investigated the Starmers' house, we can drive out to the refuge on Assateague to see the wild horses. The island is very cool."

She shut the door without taking anything out of the fridge and leaned against it. "So, basically, a fun weekend getaway?"

"If the Starmers are on the island, you can keep watch while they're in town and call to warn me if they head home."

She rolled her eyes. "You don't actually need my help. Hell, you searched Zenith Jones's house while she was in the living room. And didn't you mention Judge Blankenship came home while you were rooting around in his attic? You got out just fine without me acting as a lookout."

Setting down the cat, he approached slowly. "You seem a little stressed. I bet you could use a day at the beach to ease some of that tension."

"I was perfectly relaxed until you snuck up on me at the corner."

"Fine. I'll go alone. And if the painting isn't there, I'll head to their Richmond home after a quick stop in

Williamsburg to check out Kat's professor boyfriend's place. Hopefully I'll have the painting returned to you by the end of the weekend."

She closed her eyes and rubbed the back of her neck. "No, I'll go with you. This is my problem. I can't expect you to do everything alone."

Strolling across the kitchen, he stopped in front of her. "Do you have a headache?"

"I'm getting one. You're right about one thing, at least. I've been a stress case all week, wondering if the person who helped the thief would realize I figured out the painting was a fake."

"If you were aware it was a forgery, wouldn't they expect you to report it?"

"I guess. Unless they discovered you were breaking into homes to hunt for the original. That might tip them off that something was up."

"I don't leave a calling card on my way out, for heaven's sake. No one is going to learn about my recent activities. I promise." He turned her around and kneaded the stiff muscles along her rigid shoulders.

Surprisingly, she relaxed and hung her head forward on a moan. "That feels good."

"Why don't you go soak in the tub while I make dinner?" He'd rather move her massage into the bedroom but was pretty positive that wasn't an option. So instead of suggesting it, he rubbed her neck for another minute before pulling his hands away. "Go. You'll feel better."

"Okay." She stepped away from him. "There's chicken and veggies in the fridge."

"Great. Take your time in the bath. I'll have dinner ready in forty-five minutes."

With a nod, she disappeared into the bathroom and shut the door with a soft thump.

Rory glanced down at Maizie. "First, I'll feed you. At least someone missed me while I was gone."

After scooping kibble into the cat's bowl, he turned on the oven and took a package of chicken thighs from the refrigerator. Poking through the produce drawer, he came up with potatoes, an onion, a red bell pepper, and a bag of baby carrots. A few minutes later, he'd cleaned and chopped the veggies, added them to a pan with the chicken, drizzled olive oil and sprinkled seasonings over everything with a lavish hand, and stuck their meal into the oven to roast.

With time to kill, he needed something to think about other than Annalise, naked in the tub. Dropping onto the loveseat, he pulled out his phone and scrolled though texts, pausing when he found one from Theo he hadn't noticed earlier. It must have come in while he was breaking into the FBI facility.

Did you find Archie?

His fingers hovered before deciding a phone call was in order. Tapping Theo's number, he waited while the phone rang.

"This is getting to be a habit, Rory."

"You texted me. I'm responding. Archie is definitely working out of Richmond."

"Did you locate the painting you were after?"

"I'm still working on that. What's your end game, Theo?"

"What do you mean?" His tone was suspiciously innocent. "I was curious? That's it."

Rory pondered how to get information without tipping him off that he was onto Kat. "Is Felix running his old operation out of his prison cell? Is Archie working for him again?"

"How would I know? I'm not in contact with my uncle, nor was I ever involved in his business. I merely did you a favor by telling you what I'd heard about Archie."

Why? Theo had to have an ulterior motive. He wished he knew what it was.

"Do you have any other tips for me? Like who hired Archie to paint that forgery? We both know he isn't the one who organized the heist. He's an artist, not a criminal mastermind."

"I've no idea."

Rory didn't believe him for a minute. "I saw your cousin while I was in Richmond. She was at an outdoor café with an older dude. I thought she lived in D.C."

"She does, but Concepts by Kat has expanded to Richmond. Last I heard, she was dating some professor at William & Mary."

"He looked like the scholarly type. Good for her. Kat was always a go-getter."

"Did you talk to her?" Theo's question sounded just a little too casual.

"No. I was driving by, and her distinctive red hair caught my eye. Are you sure you don't know anything else about Archie? A bartender recognized him. Unfortunately, I couldn't track down where he's staying."

"Are you still in Richmond?"

"No. I had some pressing business to take care of. I may head back down that way to try again, but without a solid lead . . ." He let his voice trail off.

"You should reach out to Kat. She'd recognize Archie if she saw him, and maybe she noticed him around town. If you do talk to her, tell her I said hi."

"Good idea."

"Look, while this has been fun, I've got nothing more to say. Good luck finding Archie and that painting you're after. Sounds like you'll need it."

The connection went dead.

Rory tossed his cell onto the couch cushion and scowled. Before he had time to mull over the conversation, the bathroom door opened. Moist air, fragrant with the scent of lavender, preceded Annalise into the room. She wore a pair of tie-dyed yoga pants and a UPenn sweatshirt. Her pale blond hair was secured in a loose topknot with a few damp strands escaping, and she looked so sweet and pretty he itched to pull her down onto his lap.

"I heard you talking to someone." She bent to pick up Maizie, and the cat rubbed her head against Annalise's jaw and purred.

Rory wished he could do the same.

"Theo. He texted me to see if I had found Archie so I called him back. The jerk is up to something, but I can't figure out what."

"You think he knows Kat's involved?" She sat down on the chair opposite him with Maizie curled on her lap.

"Hell, yes. When I casually mentioned driving by his cousin in Richmond, just to feel him out without mentioning the Governor's Ball, he suggested I ask her if she's seen Archie."

"That's kind of wild. Why would he do that?"

"I don't know. I'd swear he's playing me somehow. I wish I knew what he has to gain."

Her brows lowered in thought. "Let's see if we can

figure it out."

"Okay, but we'll have to do it while we eat." He rose to his feet and headed into the kitchen. "Our dinner is probably done by now."

"Something smells good."

"Roast chicken and veggies." Using a potholder, he pulled the pan from the oven. "Yep, it's ready." Taking two plates from the cupboard, he dished the food onto them. "Come and eat."

Maizie growled when she shifted her onto the chair and stood. "Thanks for cooking."

He glanced across the counter at her and smiled. "It's the least I could do since I forced my company on you for the evening."

"I'm not trying to be difficult, Rory. This is just . . . hard."

"I know, and upsetting you isn't my goal." He carried the plates to the small table tucked against the wall. "Have a seat."

She took the chair facing him, and they dug into the food.

"This is excellent. Restaurant quality. Having to fend for myself in the kitchen was an adjustment."

Meeting her gaze, he bit into a piece of potato and swallowed. "Cooking for one isn't much fun."

"I don't want this to become a habit." Her fingers tightened around her fork. "No personal chatter. Let's talk about Theo. What's he hoping to accomplish?"

"He can be a sneaky bastard." Rory narrowed his eyes as he chewed. "First he told me where to find Archie, but wasn't specific enough so that I could actually walk up and kick down his damn door. Then, when I mentioned Kat, he tells me to give her a call."

"Does that mean he wants Kat to know you're looking for the painting? Why not simply warn her himself, and why would he have tipped you off to begin with?"

"I've no idea. Unless he wants Kat to feel threatened."

"Do you think he was working with her and she tried to cut him out of the deal? Wouldn't that be classic?" Annalise grinned. "You're delivering Theo's message loud and clear. Play nice, or he'll tell you where the painting is."

"If that's the case, I give him major credit for thinking on the fly. The text he sent me a couple of days ago must have been his way of fishing to see what I'd accomplished before he dropped the next tidbit of information." A frown drew his brows together. "Now that we're putting the pieces together, I suspect he's helping her launder the money."

"And you brought up Kat's name without him having to do it."

"Convenient for him." He ate another bite of chicken. "Theo knows who paid for the Pissarro. However, since I didn't tell him I'm onto Kat, he doesn't know I've been looking into her contacts."

"Okay, then. How does this change our plans?"

"I don't believe it does. If we find the painting, it's all good. If we don't, I can force Theo to talk."

"Sounds messy—and dangerous. He'd probably call the cops since you can't tell them the truth without revealing the Pissarro hanging on the wall of the museum is a forgery."

"I'd rather wait until we actually have the painting in our possession to initiate an official investigation.

Also, if either Theo or Kat tips off the buyer, you can bet we'll never locate the stolen art. They'll hide it somewhere untraceable, and Archie will disappear again. We'll be left looking guilty as hell with no evidence that anyone but us was actually involved in the theft."

"This conversation is *not* reassuring me."

"Me, either." His tone was glum. "I say we stick with the plan and head to Chincoteague in the morning to check out the Starmers' vacation house. Afterward, we'll determine our next step. I'd rather not approach Kat and spook her unless we have to."

"That makes sense, but honestly, whatever game Theo is playing scares me."

He snorted. "I can kick my old pal's ass into next week, if it comes to that, but I don't want the situation to get out of control." He reached over to squeeze her hand. "You don't need to worry about Theo. I won't let him—or anyone—hurt you."

"Okay." She was mostly quiet as they finished their meal. Rising from the table, she cleared their plates and took them to the sink. "Dinner was delicious. Thank you."

"You're welcome." He walked up behind her and resisted placing his hands on her shoulders the way he had earlier. All he wanted was to pull her backward against his chest and drop a lingering kiss on her lips when she looked up at him. Instead, he kept a couple feet of space between them. "I'll take off now. What time do you want me to pick you up in the morning? Unless you've changed your mind? It's fine if you'd rather stay here this weekend."

"I'll go with you." She squirted soap on the sponge

and quickly washed the plates and silverware, then filled the baking pan with water to soak. Finally, she turned. "It's simpler if you spend the night here." Her tone was resigned. "We can watch a movie or something."

"You sure?"

"Yeah. It's stupid to send you to a hotel, simply on principle."

He didn't argue further. "After I get my suitcase, we can pick out a movie."

"All right."

He hustled down the stairs and stepped out of the building into the cool evening air. Striding up the block to where he'd parked his Porsche, he removed his bag of freshly washed clothes from the trunk. Earlier in the day, he'd spent two hours at a laundromat since he was beginning to smell like a vagrant. A smile curled his lips as he locked the car. Hopefully Annalise would appreciate his sacrifice.

On his way back, he eyed a middle-aged man who stood on the sidewalk opposite her apartment, talking on his phone. The guy glanced up, made brief eye-contact, and then strolled away.

No point in getting paranoid.

An older woman walking her teacup poodle approached, pausing near where the man had stood while her dog sniffed a shrub. When her gaze drifted toward Annalise's window, he crossed the street and entered the building. This was a busy neighborhood, and suspecting every person loitering in the area of spying was pointless. Shutting the door behind him with a firm click, he ran up the stairs, pushed open her door, and locked it behind him. Heading straight to the window overlooking the street, he shut the blinds.

"Good idea. The glare from the streetlight reflects off the TV." She set a bowl of popcorn on the coffee table. "What sort of movie do you want to watch?"

He didn't mention that he'd shut the blinds because he didn't want anyone outside looking in. "You know me. I prefer action flicks, but we can watch a romcom if you'd rather."

"I wouldn't."

She didn't say it, but he knew exactly what she was thinking. No way in hell did she want to watch people falling in love or making out. They agreed on a vintage mystery, settled into their respective corners of the loveseat, and put the popcorn between them. An hour later, the bowl was empty, the movie half over, and Annalise was sound asleep.

When she slumped toward him, looking uncomfortable as hell with her neck bent at an odd angle, he moved the bowl, scooted over, and pulled her into his arms. Her lids flickered slightly but didn't open, and a soft sigh slipped out. With her cheek resting against his chest, he stroked her pale, silky hair and simply held her. Happier than he'd been in a very long time.

Chapter Eleven

Annalise woke slowly, feeling warm and secure and strangely at peace. Until she opened her eyes and realized exactly where she was. Tucked against Rory's chest with her nose buried in his neck and his arms cuddling her close, they were twisted together like a pretzel on the love seat. The TV screen was blank, but the light was still on. Clearly, she'd fallen asleep watching the movie, and he'd taken advantage of the situation.

Okay, maybe he hadn't done anything more than simply let her sleep while he held her. And if the early morning light creeping around the edge of the blinds was any indication, she'd slept more soundly, despite the contortionist position, than she had in months. This was what she'd been afraid of. Letting Rory into her life and falling hard for him all over again, despite the fact she didn't trust him. She knew in her head that she deserved more than a man who'd lied to her, but her heart still ached with memories of their good times together.

Lying there, all wrapped around him, certainly wasn't helping. She raised her head, her chin brushing against his bristly jaw, to take a peek. Thick, dark lashes brushed lean cheeks, and his mouth was open slightly. The man slept like the dead. Now to extricate herself without waking him. She eased the big, warm hand splayed across the bare skin of her waist beneath her sweatshirt to the couch cushion. Extracting her knee from between his thighs was a challenge, and when she bumped up against a distinct bulge, she froze.

His eyes opened. Slightly disoriented, he blinked, before the green depths took on a warm gleam. "Morning, love."

Before she could move, or even protest, he cupped the back of her head and pulled her face down to meet his lips. Covering her mouth with his own, he kissed her the way he always had, with enthusiasm, skill, and passion. Her whole body quivered at the assault of pure pleasure. Her nipples tightened as heat flowed like liquid lava to her core.

Kissing him back was about the stupidest thing she'd ever done, yet she couldn't seem to tear her lips away as his tongue pressed into her mouth. Her traitorous body strained against his. Intimately aligned the way they were, there was absolutely no denying exactly how turned on he was. She responded with a whimper.

The small sound of distress must have triggered something in his brain. Breathing hard, he pulled back a few inches and stared into her eyes. "Are you okay?"

"No."

He pressed his forehead against hers. "I didn't intend for this to happen last night. I only planned to hold you for a while and let you rest."

"But you fell asleep, too."

"I guess so. I was just lying here with my eyes closed, feeling so relaxed and happy . . ."

When she pushed against his chest, he let her go. Struggling to untangle herself, she sat up. When Maizie strolled into the room and jumped onto her lap, she stroked her back with shaking fingers.

"If we're driving to Virginia this morning, let's get moving."

He seemed to accept her change of subject. "I need to shower, and then I'll make breakfast."

"I'll cook eggs. I'm not completely incompetent in the kitchen."

"I know you're not. I just like doing nice things for you."

She ran a hand through her hair and let out a long, slow breath. "If you want to do something I'll appreciate, forget the last few minutes ever happened."

"Short of hitting me over the head with a sledgehammer, I definitely won't forget. But I won't push the issue." He touched her arm. "Quit squeezing Maizie so hard. She looks like she's about to bite you."

Annalise winced when the cat dug sharp claws into her leg. "Sorry, sweetie." Loosening her grip, she handed the irritated feline to Rory and stood. "I'll only be in the bathroom a minute."

Stepping around the coffee table, she fled from the room. After shutting the bathroom door, she leaned against it and stared at herself in the mirror. Her color was high, her eyes were wide and filled with something resembling panic, and her hair straggled around her face.

"Just shoot me now," she muttered as she squeezed

paste onto her toothbrush. After scrubbing her teeth and splashing cold water on her face, she ran a brush through her hair and pulled it back in a ponytail. Looking slightly less frazzled, even if her emotions were still a jumbled mess, she left the bathroom and paused beside her bedroom door. "It's all yours."

"Okay. I fed Maizie."

"Thanks." Without meeting Rory's gaze, she entered her bedroom and closed the door with a soft click. "You can do this, Annalise." She took a few deep breaths. "You've got this."

The pep talk didn't help. Probably because her tone lacked conviction.

It would be so easy to let him break down her barriers, to cave in to the attraction between them. But if she slept with Rory, she'd have to admit, at least to herself, that she'd never fallen out of love with him. And if she acknowledged that, she was setting herself up for a whole lot of pain. Rory might be thrilled to pick up where they'd left off before his arrest, before all his secrets had been exposed, but she couldn't simply forgive and forget. If that made her less than compassionate, uncharitable, or even cold, then so be it. She'd needed to be all those things to survive.

Or, as Brielle had pointed out, she was simply protecting her heart.

So, she'd suck it up and pretend like they hadn't kissed, hadn't come damn close to doing a whole lot more. She'd walk out of this room, put on a pleasant smile, and not let him see that she was nearing a breaking point. Maybe today would be the day they'd find the painting, and this nightmare would be over. And Rory would be out of her life, for good.

An hour later, she was dressed in capri pants and a short-sleeved top, had eaten breakfast, cleaned up the apartment, and packed for what might turn into another overnight stay. On their way out, she stopped to ask her neighbor to check on Maizie and feed her. Once outside, they hurried up the sidewalk to Rory's car. He opened the trunk and dropped their bags inside, glancing over as a man stepped out of the shelter of a doorway across the street and walked with his head down toward the end of the block.

A frown creased his brow.

"What's wrong?" Annalise slid onto the passenger seat while he got in and started the engine.

"I don't know. Just wondering if that guy was waiting for us to come out. Did you recognize him?"

She eyed the twenty-something man wearing saggy jeans, a beanie, and a jacket that looked far too warm for the sunny, fall morning as he disappeared around the corner. "If he's a neighbor, I've never seen him before."

"He's dressed for colder temps, like maybe he spent the night watching your apartment."

Goose bumps rose on her arms, and she rubbed them. "What would be the point?"

"I've no idea. Let's see if anyone follows us."

"What are we going to do about it if he does? Engage in a high-speed chase through the streets of Philadelphia?"

"I'm not going to risk lives, but I can try to lose him." Rory glanced in the rearview mirror as he made a lefthand turn. "An older Saab just pulled away from the curb. It's a few cars back so I can't see who's driving."

She turned in her seat. "Which one's the Saab? I

know zip about cars."

"The yellow one three back." He made a right at the next block.

"Yep, it followed us."

"Well, hell." He made a few more turns, as did their shadow, then ran a light just as it turned red.

"The Saab had to stop." Annalise fist-pumped the air. "Good job."

Rory turned into a parking structure, cruised through until they neared the exit, and idled in the shadows behind a large van. "Let's see what happens since he knows we came this way. Can you see the entrance?"

Annalise rolled down her window and leaned out. "Yep. An SUV just entered the garage. Wait. The Saab is right behind it."

"Perfect." He darted down the ramp, paid the fee, and waited for the arm to rise. Reaching the street, he headed back the way they'd come.

"Once he figures out we aren't in the garage, he won't know which way we went. That guy was a total amateur, probably hired off the street for cash to watch the building."

"Hired by whom?"

"The only one who knows I'm looking for the painting is Theo, and even though I didn't mention your name or tell him I was in Philly, he's smart enough to make an educated guess."

"You think he wants to stay up to date on your movements, just in case you don't contact Kat the way he suggested?"

As he approached the onramp to the freeway, he nodded. "It's the only thing that makes any sense, unless there's more to the situation than we know."

Annalise shifted to face forward. "The Saab is nowhere to be seen. You ditched him."

"Then we'll head to the Starmers' vacation home the way we planned. It shouldn't take much more than three hours if the traffic is light."

"Do you really expect to find the painting there?"

He glanced her way. "I've no idea, but it's worth taking the time to look."

"Then we will. What else can we do to be proactive?"

"I'm not sure. After my plane landed yesterday, I spent some time hacking into Kat's financial records while I was at a laundromat that had decent wi-fi."

"If you needed to wash a load of clothes, why didn't you just do it at my place? You still have my spare key."

"I didn't feel right about barging into your home without permission. I know you want to set some boundaries."

So, he draws the line at throwing his dirty clothes in my washer, but doesn't hesitate to kiss me senseless?

She clamped her lips together and refrained from commenting on his skewed priorities.

"Anyway, I discovered several large deposits into her business account had been funneled through a shell corporation. She also made a couple of transfers that looked suspicious, at least to a trained eye. Those eventually landed in a bank account in the Cayman Islands and were probably a payoff to Archie."

"Who deposited the money into her account?"

"I wish knew." He changed lanes to pass a slow-moving sedan. "However, I'm pretty certain the payments originated in Boston."

Annalise frowned. "Kat doesn't do business that far north. Why would any of our suspects have a bank account up there?"

"They wouldn't, but Theo lives in Boston. My guess is he laundered the client's money through his law firm and the shell corporation, probably taking a cut before funneling it to Kat. Unfortunately, I couldn't trace the payments. There are too many accounts associated with Theo's law firm, and he wouldn't have used the client's actual name."

"So the money trail is dead?"

"For now, anyway."

"That sucks."

"Yeah, it does." He drummed his fingers on the steering wheel. "Between the money coming out of Boston, and Theo's conversation with me, it's a given he's involved up to his eyeballs. Still, there's clearly trouble in paradise between him and Kat."

"Maybe Theo simply has trust issues. He suspects everyone of screwing him over, which is why he hired someone to watch my apartment."

"That could be the case. He always had a bit of a persecution complex."

She tucked a strand of hair that had escaped her ponytail behind her ear. "Out of curiosity, how much money did the buyer pay for the Pissarro?"

"One point five million was transferred to Kat, but I can't be sure it was all for that one painting. Maybe Kat has several deals in the works."

"What a bargain. *Sheep in the Meadow* would probably go for over twice that at auction."

"I guess you don't get top dollar on the black

market."

Annalise stared out toward Delaware Bay and frowned. "I wonder if the Starmers have that kind of cash lying around."

"Her family is loaded. She could get her hands on the funds if she wanted to."

"What about Kat's professor boyfriend?"

"I haven't looked into his background yet. There are only so many hours in the day."

"You're slacking, Rory." Her tone held a teasing note, and he grinned in response.

"I'll get on it just as soon as we check out the vacation house. Unless we find the painting there."

"Let's hope. Do you mind if I put on some music?"

"Not at all."

She plugged her phone into the dash, pulled up her favorite road trip playlist, and cranked the tunes. Singing along with the music was better than getting too chummy with Rory and letting the conversation turn personal.

It was nearing noon when they reached Chincoteague Island and drove toward the Starmers' home on Little Oyster Bay. Since they couldn't get near the house, which was right on the water, without driving down their private road, Rory passed the turnoff and kept going.

"Now what?"

"I checked out the area on Google Maps while you were getting ready to go. There's an inn just up ahead, and their website states they have kayaks available for their guests. While you head inside to see if there's a room available, I'll snag one of the kayaks and paddle down to the Starmers' property to do a little reconnaissance."

She turned to stare at him. "You want to stay here tonight?"

"No. They're fully booked, but it'll give us an excuse for parking in their lot."

"What if someone on the dock questions you?" She frowned as he pulled up near the entrance of the pretty, white inn. Fall flowers bloomed in profusion in pots along the front porch.

"I'll tell them I'm a guest and don't have my key with me. If you sound confident and look the part, people believe you. I'm not worried."

"If you say so." She unbuckled her seatbelt. "Do you want me to leave or make an excuse to stick around?"

"I'll call once I get to the Starmers' place." He handed her the key fob and reached into the backseat for his daypack. "If no one's around, I'll search the house. If they're home, it'll be risky to walk up from the dock in broad daylight."

She nodded and got out. Her gaze locked with his over the roof of the car. "Good luck."

"Thanks. See you in a bit."

Not waiting to watch him stroll away, Annalise headed up the walkway to the porch steps and entered the building. She took her time, glancing into the dining room where a server carried plates to one of the occupied tables, then wandered toward the front desk.

An older woman with silver hair twisted into a bun glanced up from her computer screen and smiled. "May I help you?"

"I was wondering if you had any rooms for tonight? We drove out here on a whim, so I'm afraid I don't have a reservation."

"Sweetie, I wish we did, but we're booked solid. First openings aren't until next month." Her accent was as smooth as honey.

Annalise lifted her shoulders in a resigned shrug. "I figured, but it didn't hurt to ask. This place is lovely."

"The lodge is a real gem, and the views are wonderful. Book ahead next time, and we'd love to accommodate you."

"I'll do that. Do you mind if I check out the grounds while I'm here?"

"Of course not. Take your time."

"Thank you. I'd stay for lunch since it smells wonderful, but my friend went for a run. I'm killing a little time before I pick him up."

"That's fine, hon. Enjoy yourself."

Annalise headed back outside and walked across the lawn to a spot with a view of the dock. Rory was nowhere in sight. Raising a hand to shade her eyes, she peered up the shoreline and spotted a kayak gliding through the water, powered by quick, sure strokes. Though she couldn't see his face, she recognized Rory's wind-ruffled, dark hair and strong back beneath a pale blue T-shirt.

Judging the distance, she figured he was almost to the Starmers' dock. Turning back toward the car, she'd just reached it when her phone rang.

She swiped to connect. "Everything okay?"

"Yeah. The place is empty right now, but it looks like someone's been here recently. There's a jug filled with cut flowers on a table on the deck, and a towel is draped over the railing. No cars parked near the house. I'll go look around inside."

Her breath caught. "What if they come back?"

"You can be my lookout. Pull over near the entrance to their private road and call if you see them coming. That'll give me time to get back to the dock."

"Okay. I'll leave the inn now."

She disconnected, hit the remote to unlock the door, and got into the car. Clutching the wheel in a fierce grip, she backed out of the parking spot and forced herself not to speed up the driveway. A couple minutes later, she pulled into a turnout about ten yards past the lane to the Starmers' vacation home and let the engine idle. When a minivan approached, she slouched down in the seat, but it continued down the road.

Tapping her phone, she called Rory.

"Are they back?" He didn't sound terribly worried.

"Not yet. I don't suppose you know what kind of car they drive?"

"She drove a Bentley to the plantation house last weekend, but they could be in a different car. I'm in the house now. It took two seconds to pick the lock, and they hadn't set the alarm."

"Well, hurry." She sat up straighter. "Oh, God, a really sweet convertible is barreling down the road toward me." She drew in a breath. "False alarm. Looks like teens on a joy ride, going way too fast."

"Hopefully they won't hit something—or someone." He was quiet for a few moments. "No sign of the painting in any of the main rooms, and there's no garage. I'm heading upstairs now."

"I don't know how you can act so calm."

"It's not an act, love. Panic will trip you up every time. Focus and logic keep you safe." A door squeaked. "What do we have here?"

"Did you find the painting?" Annalise's pulse sped up, and she gripped the armrest on the door.

"There's a stack of framed paintings leaning against the wall in the guest bedroom. Damn. No sign of the Pissarro. They're all beachscapes."

"If Kat redecorated the house recently, maybe those were the pictures she took down."

"That makes sense." Faint footsteps sounded through the speaker. "The master suite has photographs on the walls. No paintings."

"There's a car coming. I think it's a Mercedes, but I'm not positive." Annalise turned her face away as the car slowed when it passed her. "Oh, crap. It's turning down the road to the house. Get out of there, Rory."

"On my way. I'm checking the final bedroom's closet now. Nothing stashed in there."

"Jesus, Rory. They're going to catch you in the house."

"No, they won't. Gotta go. Pick me up near the inn."

The connection went dead. She dropped the phone on the passenger seat and rolled the window down. When she didn't hear any screams, or worse, gunshots, her pounding heart finally slowed. People were known to shoot trespassers on sight, and she had no idea if the Starmers were armed. Finally, she shifted into gear, pulled into the next driveway to turn around, and headed back toward the inn.

But she didn't relax until Rory strolled up from the dock, his gait easy and confident, acting like he didn't have a single concern. He flashed a smile when they made eye contact through the open window. She scowled in response. He might think breaking into homes was no big deal, but she'd nearly had a full-blown panic attack.

His smile faded as he reached the car. "You okay? You don't look so good."

"Maybe because I was afraid Howard Starmer would whip out a handgun and shoot you."

He opened the door, hunched down to eye-level, and took her cold hands in his. "They had no idea I was there. Do you know where I was the last few days?"

She frowned at his question. "You said you were dealing with an important client."

"That's right. Actually, I was breaking into an FBI facility to prove they had some security problems. The FBI, Annalise, and I got in and out without detection."

A chill shivered through her. "What if you hadn't?"

"The agent in charge who hired me put out the word he was running a test. Hopefully, they'd have apprehended me and asked questions rather than shooting an intruder."

"*Hopefully?*" Her voice squeaked on the end of the word. "That's crazy."

"My point is, I'm very good at what I do. You don't need to worry about me." He squeezed her hands a little tighter. "I can take care of myself and you, too. Want to go chill on the beach and check out the wild horses?"

Her mouth dropped open a little as she gaped at him. "That's the end of our discussion?"

"Sure. There's really nothing else to say."

"Fine." She pushed him away and stepped out of the car. "You can drive. By all means. Let's go see the wild horses."

Chapter Twelve

They sat on the beach, eating sandwiches they'd picked up at a deli and gazing in awe at the herd of mares running in the surf a short distance away. Manes and tails flying, they kicked up their heels and galloped away, spooked by something only a horse could understand. Possibly the crab skittering across the white sand or the seagull feather fluttering in the breeze.

"So beautiful." Annalise let out a sigh and turned to face him, her blue eyes sparkling in the sunlight beneath her Phillies ballcap. "I'm so glad you suggested this."

"You needed a dose of nature and relaxation." Rory crumpled the paper wrapper and stuffed it into the bag before taking a swallow from his water bottle. "I can practically see the tension draining out of you."

She wiggled her bare toes in the sand. "Maybe I overreacted earlier. I know you're a pro at breaking and entering, even though I cringe just saying that. Still, I can't help worrying."

He brushed a strand of hair off her cheek with a

gentle finger. "I'm glad you care enough to be concerned."

"Caring has never been the issue." Her tone was grim as she slapped his hand away.

Deciding it was time to change the subject, he leaned back on his elbows and stared across the breakers rolling into shore. Sunlight shimmered off the vast expanse of deep blue sea, and he wished they could spend the rest of the day exactly where they were. Unfortunately, getting back on the road was the smart move.

"Instead of stopping in Williamsburg to check out Simon Kingsley's residence, we should go straight to the Starmers' Richmond house since we know they won't be home yet. No risk involved in searching their place this afternoon."

"Kingsley was Kat's date, right? I'm trying to keep these people straight."

"Yeah, the philosophy professor at William & Mary. I want to look into his finances to see if he could even afford that painting."

"I'll drive while you do that." Annalise put their trash and the water bottles into his daypack. "Sounds like it's time to go."

"The horses have deserted the beach, anyway." He rose to his feet, gave her a hand up, and slung the pack over his shoulder.

She slid her feet into her sandals and followed him up the path leading to the parking area. "If you want to search Kingsley's house tonight, we can stay at my parents' instead of driving back to Philly. They left on their camping trip a few days ago so they won't be there, but I have a key."

"I'd definitely rather not drive back tonight. But if you'd like some time to yourself, I can bunk at your brother's place. He probably wouldn't mind."

"It's a big house. I'm sure we'll manage."

He glanced over his shoulder and grinned. "I promise to do my very best to resist you if you fall asleep on me again."

"Very funny."

"Just trying to lighten the mood. You need to smile more."

"I'll smile plenty once we have that painting back." When they reached the car, she took the key and got in behind the wheel. "Your Porsche drives like a dream, a whole lot nicer than my ancient Bug."

"You still have that thing?"

"Yeah, but I put it in storage after I moved downtown. I don't need a car to get to work, and there's not much parking."

Apparently, she wanted to avoid personal topics. He'd cooperate for now, but eventually he intended to plead his case for getting back together. Still, it wouldn't hurt to soften her up a little more first. Maybe he was wishful thinking, but she seemed to be slowly letting her walls down, even if it was only one brick at a time.

While Annalise confidently navigated her way off the island and through the afternoon traffic heading south, he opened his laptop and dug into Professor Kingsley's background. They'd almost reached the Chesapeake Bay Bridge when he closed his computer.

She glanced his way before refocusing on the road. "You've certainly been busy. What did you learn?"

"I have an E-ZPass so you can get over to the left."

As she changed lanes to merge onto the bridge, he leaned back in his seat to enjoy the view. "I uncovered some interesting facts about the guy Kat's dating. Simon isn't rich, but he's comfortably well-off. However, he likes to gamble and has scored some major wins and a couple of big losses over the last six months. I'd say the guy has a gaming addiction."

"Did he win enough to pay for that painting?"

"Not unless Kat gave it to him at cost. Archie certainly doesn't work for free. But the professor's cash flow problems could be why Theo has his panties in a wad. Maybe Kat cut him out of his share because her boyfriend lost the money he owes for the painting at the craps tables in Atlantic City. I searched his accounts but couldn't find any records of big transfers."

Annalise frowned. "He could have paid Kat in cash."

"I was thinking the same thing. Simon's online vibe doesn't shout Impressionist painting lover, but maybe he has a few secret fetishes he keeps to himself. The guy is definitely worth pursuing if we don't find the painting in Richmond."

Her grip on the wheel tightened as they descended into the tunnel. "What if we don't find it at either the Starmers' house or at the professor's home? Any one of the suspects we've already ruled out could have stuck the Pissarro in a storage unit as a precaution until he—or she—gets the all clear that no one at the museum discovered the forgery."

"If I learned one thing about collectors while I was stealing artwork, it's that they have a compulsion to see the masterpieces they've acquired. Usually, they have them on display somewhere easily accessible, not stashed in a closet, and definitely not in storage." He patted her knee. "Don't worry. My gut tells me I'll find that painting hanging on someone's wall where he can admire it whenever he chooses."

She blinked as they came out of the dark tunnel beneath the bay into the bright sunlight. "You believe the buyer's a man?"

"I used the masculine pronoun because I just researched the professor, but Georgette Starmer could be our woman. She was born a Wentworth, after all, with a proverbial silver spoon, and she's used to getting what she wants. If she fixated on that painting . . ." He shrugged.

"What Georgette wants, Georgette takes."

"Something like that. We'll know soon enough."

"I guess that's true. Did you see any indication she's into old French masters in her vacation house décor?"

"Not in the least, but that doesn't mean she won't have a room full of them at her main home." He was quiet for a while as they continued across the magnificent bridge. Finally, he turned in his seat to face her.

Back straight and both hands clamped around the steering wheel, she bit down on her bottom lip.

"Relax and stop thinking about that damn painting. Tell me what you've been doing for the last two years. I really want to know how you've been."

She eyed him for a fleeting moment before letting her tense shoulders droop. "Just work. After Josephine retired, the board of directors hired Marcus Poole. He's good at his job but isn't as relaxing to work for as Josephine was. I feel like I have to prove my worth all over again, and I have. I'm damn good at what I do."

"Hell, yes, you are. What about for fun? Have you been on any interesting vacations? We were planning to—" He broke off and winced. *Explore France on our honeymoon.* She probably wouldn't appreciate the reminder.

She gave him a brief, hard look. "I haven't left the country recently. Bri and I took a trip to California and toured Napa's vineyards last spring. We were both determined to do something that wasn't remotely related to art or history, and we had a great time."

"I'm surprised you dragged your sister out of her world of genealogy research to go wine tasting. Brielle isn't exactly a party animal."

"She did it because she knew I needed to cut loose for a change." Her lips curved slightly. "All the alcohol helped."

Just imagining Annalise and her very pretty sister, partying with a bunch of single guys while they drank their way through a dozen vineyards, made him slightly nauseous. "Maybe I don't want to hear the details of that trip."

She rolled her eyes before concentrating on the road. "I can do what I want, Rory."

"You're right. Doesn't mean the idea of you dating other men doesn't hurt. Just so you know, I haven't slept with anyone since we split up."

When she turned to stare, he grabbed the wheel. "Careful."

She focused on the traffic, which grew heavier as they left the bridge and drove through Norfolk. "Why not?" Her tone was curt. "It's been two years. Is chastity some sort of self-inflicted punishment?"

"No. I went out on a few dates, but I didn't care

about those women. I only wanted you, so I didn't think it would be fair to pretend otherwise."

"Dammit, Rory." She sounded like she was about to cry.

"I'm just telling you the truth."

"Well, don't. I don't want to know about your personal life."

"I guess I keep hoping you'll forgive me, even if I don't deserve it."

"No, you don't. You would have married me with a huge secret hanging over our heads. In my mind, that's worse than your criminal history."

"I know I made mistakes. How can I fix this?"

"I honestly don't think you can. It's easier to put the past behind us and move on."

"You're wrong." He stared straight ahead, feeling like he might choke on raw emotion. "I can't put you behind me. I tried, and it didn't work. I've just been going through the motions since you walked away."

"Okay, *easier* was the wrong word. Nothing about this is easy. How about *necessary*." Her tone was as sharp as broken glass. "Maybe we both need to try harder." She swiped a hand across her eyes and blinked a few times, clearly holding back tears. "You can go home to New York and forget about the damn painting if this is too difficult. I'll tell both my boss and the police I discovered the forgery and simply hope for the best."

"I'm not going to do that." His voice nearly cracked. "I fully intend to finish what we started."

"Then we need to stop letting these conversations destroy us." Her voice rose. "I can't keep doing this."

"Okay." He released a shaky breath. She sounded

close to falling apart, and that was the last thing he wanted. "I won't say anything more about how I feel. If you change your mind, you can let me know."

She swallowed hard and nodded. "Thank you."

They didn't talk for the rest of the drive, not until they reached Richmond and he gave her directions to the Starmers' house, an impressive colonial home set back on a large property with a surrounding fence.

"Keep going." He turned in his seat as they passed. "There's a park close by."

"Okay."

Following his directions, she drove a couple of blocks farther and turned into the lot next to a neighborhood park with a playground. Late on a Sunday afternoon, the place was filled with young families. Kids ran wild, screaming and laughing and having fun.

Rory got out, pulled the daypack off the back seat, and emptied the trash into a nearby can. After making sure he had what he needed to get into the house, he bent to give Annalise a sober smile. "This shouldn't take long."

"Please be careful."

"I will. They might have live-in help, but I know how to avoid trouble."

She shook her head. "Could have fooled me."

* * * *

Long shadows stretched across the driveway as Rory pulled up in front of her parents' house and turned off the engine. When Buttercup scrambled to her feet on the porch and barked before running down the steps to greet them, Annalise frowned.

"That's weird." Opening her door, she stepped out of the car. "I figured Lincoln would keep her at his house while Mom and Dad are gone." Bending, she rubbed the dog's ears. "What a good girl. Are you excited to see me?"

"Someone's home. There're lights on inside. Maybe your parents didn't leave yet." Rory got out and stroked Buttercup's head when she ran around to his side.

Before Annalise could answer, the front door opened and Nash walked out onto the porch. Deep blue eyes beneath longish brown hair darted from her to Rory and back. A scowl knit his brow, and his jaw tightened beneath a few days' worth of scruff. Her oldest brother was looking a little rough around the edges.

"Nash!" Hurrying up the walkway, she met him at the bottom of the stairs. Careful of the sling holding his bandaged left arm, she hugged him tight. "It's so good to see you. I didn't know you were planning to be in Wildwood."

"I'm watching the house and Buttercup for Mom and Dad. He released her and slowly stepped back, eyeing Rory. "I can't hold a camera until I take off this sling, so I figured I might as well do something useful. Besides, I'd rather hang out here than in my D.C. apartment."

She fisted her hands on her hips. "I thought you only had minor injuries. That arm doesn't look minor."

"If I'd told Mom I got hit by flying shrapnel during a bombing, she would have worried herself sick. A hunk of metal did some nerve damage, but the doctors say the surgery went well, and my arm will heal without complications. I'll have a few more scars, not that I care. I'm just pissed I can't work."

"Since you never take a break between assignments, you could probably use the rest."

"Maybe so." He faced Rory. "You're about the last person I expected to see with Annalise. Lucky for you, I'm not at my best, or I'd kick your ass."

Annalise put a hand on his good arm. "He's helping me so just chill. I don't need a protective big brother."

Nash snorted. "Dad mentioned you had a problem with a forgery at the museum. He didn't say a word about Rory."

Rory held up both hands, palms out. "You still have one good fist. Take a punch at me. I deserve it, so I won't hit back. Then, I hope we can at least be civil."

Nash's lips twitched in a hint of a smile. "I'll pass. For now. But thanks for the offer."

Annalise looked from one to the other. "If you two are through with your pissing contest, can we go inside? We planned to spend the night here, if you don't mind."

"I'm happy to have company. Come on in. You can tell me all about this problem Rory's helping you with. I'm bored. Maybe there's something I can do to help."

"I wish. We sure aren't making much headway." She followed Nash up the porch steps, while Rory and Buttercup brought up the rear.

"Let's head to the kitchen. I made chili and cornbread. I guess I won't have any leftovers, but I'll survive. You can toss a salad to go with it. Chopping veggies one-handed is a struggle."

Annalise smiled. "Wow, I wasn't expecting to be fed, but I won't turn down your chili."

"What can I do?" Rory stopped just inside the kitchen doorway.

Nash glanced over his shoulder. "Feed Buttercup. Her food's in the pantry. Then you can open a couple of beers." One brow rose. "Unless Annalise wants one? Or Mom might have wine stashed somewhere."

"I'll stick to water. It's been a long day, and if I have a drink, I'll have to fight to stay awake."

"What's wrong with crashing early?" Her brother pulled bowls and plates from the cupboard.

"Rory still has one more house to break into tonight, and I don't want to fall asleep in the car while I wait."

"I told you I can go alone." He scooped kibble into the dog's bowl. "I know you want to do something productive, but I can manage just fine on my own."

"What the hell are you two talking about?" Nash dropped the dishes on the table with a thud.

"Long story." Annalise strolled over to the refrigerator to pull lettuce, spinach, tomatoes, and carrots from the crisper drawer. Frowning at a moldy cucumber, she tossed it into the trash. "I'll let Rory tell you all about it while I make the salad."

He nudged her away from the refrigerator and took out two beers. Using the bottle opener Nash handed him, he opened them and pointed toward the kitchen table. "Sit down and relax. I haven't coerced Annalise into a life of crime, if that's what you're thinking."

"It was."

"Based on the fierce scowl, I figured. Believe me, you aren't half as angry as I am about the situation."

Annalise stirred the chili and sliced up veggies while Rory gave a brief rundown of their search for the Pissarro. When the salad was finished, she added a few pine nuts and craisins and dressed it with balsamic vinegar and oil. After cutting the cornbread into squares, she carried the food to the table.

"So, you just came from searching the Starmers' house in Richmond, but you didn't find the painting?" One-handed, Nash scooped chili from the pot into a bowl and sprinkled cheddar cheese over the top.

"No sign of it, and their taste in art doesn't jibe with a love of Impressionism."

"Unfortunately." Annalise dropped onto her chair. "I just want this to be over."

"Whose house do you intend to search tonight?"

"Simon Kingsley's home in Williamsburg. He's a professor at William & Mary and is currently dating Kat." Rory took a bite of chili. "This is good."

"Thanks." Nash frowned. "What if the painting isn't there?"

"I honestly don't know. Kingsley is our last viable suspect. We've searched the homes of all the people Kat's been in close contact with in the last couple of months. I suppose the buyer could be a random stranger, but I don't know how they would have known she took over her father's business. I've searched the dark web, and there isn't a single hint she's active."

"Maybe this professor has it, then." Nash bit into his cornbread and chewed. "I don't like the fact that you're taking my sister anywhere near these houses you're searching. What if you get caught?"

"Rory assures me that won't happen. He's too good at breaking and entering." Her tone had an edge. "Anyway, I'm always blocks away, waiting in the car."

"Just the same, I'll go with him tonight. You can hang out with Buttercup. My guess is Kingsley will be home on a Sunday night, so the threat of discovery is a whole lot higher."

From her spot near the table, the dog lifted her head and thumped her tail against the hardwood floor. Annalise stretched out her foot and rubbed Buttercup's belly.

"No one has to go with me." Rory stabbed a tomato in his salad. "I don't need backup."

"Too bad. You're getting it." Annalise glanced between them. "But Nash can go if he wants. As long as he promises not to ditch you if something goes wrong."

Her brother smiled. "Tempting, but since Rory seems like your best option to get that painting back, I'll rein in my grudge against him."

"Gee, thanks." Rory dropped his spoon in his bowl with a plop.

"Can we not do this?" Annalise drew in a deep breath and let it out slowly. "I don't need any more hostility. I don't need you to be mad at him on my behalf."

Her brother's eyes darkened. "I don't want you to get hurt again."

"I'm not going to hurt her." Rory brought his elbows down on the table. "She's made it clear she doesn't want me in her life after we find the original painting. I respect her wishes, so lay off, Nash."

"Look, I have nothing against you personally. I always liked you just fine, but protecting my little sisters is a hard habit to break."

"I'm glad she has your support." Rory met Nash's gaze head on. "However, I don't intend to take advantage of Annalise or the situation, so stop with the attitude."

"If that's the case, we're good. Both of you, finish

your dinner. I don't want to see my excellent chili go to waste."

Annalise eyed both men's clenched fists where they rested on the table. Despite their words, anger simmered in the air. "I'm a big girl, Nash, and Rory is doing everything he can to help me. Trust me, I've got this. Seeing you two at odds isn't helping."

Finally, he nodded and held out his hand. Rory took it in a firm clasp, and they shook.

"Sorry. I appreciate what you're doing for my sister."

"No problem. I'm damn glad you didn't get hurt worse. You'll have to tell me about your adventures in Ukraine."

The conversation turned general, and the two men went back to eating. Annalise slumped in her chair as some of the tension drained out of her. She could tell Nash's animosity hurt Rory, and her heart ached for him. Their emotions were in tune, whether she liked it or not, and she didn't want to think about the reason why she felt his pain so deeply.

His gaze met hers, and she closed her eyes, afraid of what he might read in their depths. Reaching over, he squeezed her hand and released it just as quickly. She had a feeling he already knew.

Chapter Thirteen

"So, you intend to stroll into this guy's home while he's sitting in his living room, watching TV?" Nash's tone made it clear he thought Rory was a reckless idiot.

"It's really not that difficult." He glanced over from the driver's seat of his Porsche. "Odds are, the back-door is unlocked, and if it's not, I'll pick it. People don't usually set their alarms until they go to bed."

"Then they should be more security conscious."

"No kidding. Anyway, when I checked Kingsley's social media earlier, I found pictures of an aquarium full of fish. Not a single photo with a dog, so I don't believe he has one. Always easier without a canine warning system."

"Buttercup would lick an intruder to death."

Rory grinned. "Probably, but she'd make plenty of noise doing it."

"That's true." Nash stared at him for a moment. "How long do you expect to be gone?"

"It won't take more than fifteen minutes to search the place from top to bottom. The house isn't very big."

Rory raised a brow. "Any more questions? You worry more than your sister."

"Doubtful. Annalise keeps her feelings bottled up until I'm afraid she'll explode. I just want to know the score before you go in."

"Since I'm good at adjusting on the fly, there's no reason for concern. Plan to stick around for a half hour. If something does happen and I'm not back, go home."

Nash snorted. "And tell my sister I deserted you? I don't think so." He held out his good hand. "Let me have the key fob. If the homeowner shoots you, I'll come pick up your body."

Rory tossed it to him then pulled on gloves before stepping out of the car. "You do that. See you shortly."

He shut the door and headed up the sidewalk, his black clothes blending with the shadows. Kingsley lived in an older neighborhood with well-kept homes on large lots with plenty of mature trees. No security fences, but the neighbors probably all had doorbell cams and wouldn't hesitate to call the cops if they saw suspicious activity. He kept his head down and Annalise's Phillies ballcap pulled low over his forehead as he walked. When he reached the professor's two-story brick home, he slowed his pace. A TV flickered in the main room where the blinds were still open, and a light glowed from the back of the house, probably in the kitchen. The front walkway was lit up with decorative lights.

Staying close to a row of blue and purple hydrangeas planted between Kingsley's yard and the neighbor to his west, he reached the back yard and ran across a small patch of grass to the detached, single car garage. The padlock took only a few seconds to open, and he pushed the door aside far enough to slip through. Taking a small flashlight from his fanny pack, he shined it around the interior.

An antique roadster squatted on the center of the cement pad. Various car parts were lined up on the bench behind the vehicle, and tools hung from the walls. A large mechanic's box sat in the far corner. Clearly, Simon Kingsley used this space to work on a car restoration project. There was no sign of the painting, and a quick look in the toolbox assured him he hadn't stashed it there.

Turning off his flashlight, he headed outside, shut the door, and relocked it. The backyard was dark as he approached the rear door, and the knob turned easily in his gloved hand. He opened the door a crack and listened intently before stepping inside. The combination laundry and storage room held a good-sized closet filled with cleaning supplies and a vacuum, along with golf clubs and ski gear. Apparently the professor was a man of many interests.

The light was on in the empty kitchen. Rory hurried across the tile floor and took a look into the dining room. The old home had not been remodeled with an open-concept floorplan, which made wandering through the lower floor a heck of a lot easier. Voices came from the living room at the front of the house, and it took him a moment to realize the female speaking wasn't on the TV. Kingsley had a guest. Avoiding that area, he searched a small office and then ran lightly up the stairs. A master suite and a guest bedroom and bath turned up no sign of the painting. Pull-down stairs at the end of the hallway led to an attic, and he cringed when they squeaked as he lowered the steps.

Heart beating a little faster than normal, he waited, letting out a sigh of relief when the occupants in the living room didn't come to check out the noise. After a moment, he climbed up to the third floor. The ceilings sloped downward, and the area was packed with old furniture and boxes. Shining his flashlight around the crowded space, he noted a trail of scuff marks on the dusty floor that led to a big trunk. Stepping carefully to avoid leaving additional prints, he stopped in front of the old, leather trunk and opened it.

The professor might have a secret obsession, but it wasn't Impressionist paintings. Sex toys, velvet lined hand cuffs, and several women's costumes had been neatly stored in the chest. The short plaid skirt and white blouse reminded him of a school girl uniform, and there was also a pink dress with ruffles. The dude was seriously disturbed, and Rory couldn't help wondering if Kat knew about the games he played. Hell, maybe she was a willing participant.

With a shudder, he lifted the outfits to make sure the painting wasn't hidden beneath them and then shut the lid. Since there were no other tracks disturbing the dust, Kingsley clearly hadn't stashed the Pissarro anywhere else in the attic. Following the trail back, he descended to the second floor and raised the stairs into place The creaking hinges grated on his nerves, but there was nothing he could do about it except hope the TV was loud enough to cover the sound. He still needed to take a quick look into the living room. For all he knew, the painting was hanging on the wall in plain sight.

Hurrying back to the main stairway, he listened for movement before running silently down to the entry.

The TV was blaring, but neither Simon nor his guest were talking. Rory risked a quick peak into the room. Someone had drawn the blinds, and the man he'd seen with Kat at the Governor's Ball was stretched out on the couch, facing the big screen, wearing nothing but a pair of boxer shorts. The program holding his attention looked like a documentary on ancient Egypt. An aquarium gurgled against one wall with a grouping of seascapes above it. There was no sign of the stolen painting.

Time to get the hell out of the house.

Kingsley lowered the TV volume with the remote and turned toward the doorway as Rory flattened himself against the entry wall near the coat tree by the front door.

"Hey, Kat," he yelled. "Bring the whole bottle."

"I had the same thought." She appeared from the direction of the kitchen, wearing a lace bra and panties, carrying two shot glasses in one hand and a bottle of tequila in the other. Stopping abruptly, her gaze locked on Rory.

He pressed a finger to his lips and shook his head.

Her brown eyes narrowed as recognition flared, but she simply stood there without saying a word.

Rory opened the door and slipped outside.

"Kat? Did you find the limes in the—"

He shut the door softly, cutting off the professor mid-sentence. Crossing the lawn to avoid the lighted walkway, he reached the sidewalk and forced himself not to run. Sprinting up the street would only draw attention if a neighbor looked out a window, and If Kat called 9-1-1, he'd still reach his car well ahead of any police response. What he couldn't do now was panic.

He was still two blocks from where he'd parked when his Porsche pulled around the corner and stopped next to him. He jerked open the passenger door and slid onto the seat.

"Take a left. Don't drive by Kingsley's house."

"You were late so I came looking for you." Nash glanced over at him as he turned at the corner. "What happened?"

"I got made just as I was leaving." He clenched his hands into fists. "Let's get the hell out of here."

"The professor saw you?"

"No, Kat Lemmon did. She's the one running the opera—"

"You told me who she is. So, this woman, Kat, was there with Kingsley?"

"Yes, but I don't think she'll report me. She probably won't say anything to good old Simon, the pervert, either. Now that I think about it, the last thing Kat will want is to draw attention to herself by talking to the cops. And since there was no sign of the painting anywhere in his house, Kingsley probably has no clue what his girlfriend is doing on the side."

"Why did you call him a pervert?" Nash merged onto the freeway and headed west, having no difficulty driving one-handed.

"The dude is into some seriously kinky sex games, but he isn't our buyer so I don't care about his personal habits. Right now, damage control is my top priority, or that painting will disappear for good."

"Sounds like you blew it." Nash's tone was hard.

"Without a doubt, but since we've run out of potential suspects and houses to search, I was going to have to approach Kat, anyway. Tonight's little mishap will shift the impetus to her."

"You think she'll call you?"

"Definitely. Right after she talks to my old pal, Theo, to see what he knows about my activities. That should be an interesting chat." Rory slumped against the seat as they left Williamsburg behind. "However, nothing is going to happen while she and the professor are getting drunk on tequila and playing dress-up. I probably have until tomorrow morning to plan my next move."

They didn't say much for the rest of the drive, and it was just after ten when Nash parked in front of his parents' home. The porch light was on, and the door opened as they walked up the steps.

Annalise wore a bathrobe and slippers, along with an anxious expression. She hugged her arms across her chest. "I was getting worried."

"We haven't even been gone two hours." Rory followed Nash into the house and offered what he hoped was a reassuring smile.

"Well? Did he have the painting?"

"I'm afraid not." Entering the living room, he bent to rub Buttercup's belly when she rolled over onto her back and thumped her tail against the rug. "Kat was there. She saw me."

"Rory!" Annalise's eyes widened, and her mouth dropped open. "Did she call the cops?"

"I'm pretty sure she didn't, or we would have heard sirens as we were leaving the neighborhood."

"Then what—"

"As fascinating as this conversation will surely be, I'm going to take a pass and catch the highlights in the morning." Nash gave his sister a quick, one-armed hug.

"Get some sleep. You look tired."

"Probably because I am. Good night, Nash."

Rory straightened from petting the dog. "'Night, Nash. Thanks for being my getaway driver this evening."

"Sure." He eyed Rory steadily. "Whatever you decide to do next, make sure it doesn't involve any danger to Annalise."

"No one's going to hurt her." He spoke between gritted teeth.

With a nod, her brother left the room, and his steps faded as he headed up the stairs.

Annalise turned to Rory, a frown creasing her brow. "What do we do now?"

"I imagine I'll hear from either Kat or Theo, or maybe both, tomorrow morning. The painting definitely wasn't in Kingsley's house, so I have no idea who has it. Maybe the buyer is just a random connection of Kat's . . . or possibly Theo's. Our best bet might be to tell them we intend to notify the police, who will initiate a major investigation into both their affairs."

"Is that what you want to do?"

"No, since we can't be sure they'll believe us, but we might not have any other option. I didn't think finding the painting would be this difficult."

"Won't Kat threaten to tell the cops you broke into her boyfriend's house last night?"

"I'm sure she will, but there isn't any proof. I made sure to keep my head down and avoid security cameras. Anyway, if she does that, she'll have to explain to Kingsley why I was searching his house. If he gets belligerent about going to the authorities, I can threaten to leak his perverted sexual habits to his coworkers at the university. I doubt he'd want anyone knowing about those. You should have seen—"

She held up her hand. "Eww. I definitely don't want to know."

"You're right. You don't."

"So your solution is to wait until you get a call from Kat?"

He nodded. "Then, depending on how she wants to play this, I'll make a counteroffer. Maybe I can convince her to give me back the Pissarro in exchange for not ratting her out to the FBI. It's possible Archie has painted several forgeries for her by now, and she won't want those sales jeopardized."

"Then I guess we go back to Philly in the morning and see what happens." She inhaled deeply before letting out a gusty breath. "Nerve-wracking, but everything about this situation has me on edge."

"The fact that Kat saw me isn't the worst thing that could have happened. It exposes our hand, but now she knows I'm a player. That should worry her."

Annalise nodded. "If there's nothing more to do tonight, I'm going to bed. I put your bag in Lincoln's old room. Since mom uses Nash's room for sewing, he took over their master bedroom."

"Sounds good. What time do you want to leave tomorrow?"

"I don't care."

"If you aren't in a rush, maybe I'll see if I can pry Archie's address out of Theo before Kat has a chance to contact him. I'd like to pay my forger pal a visit, just to see if he knows anything I can use against Kat. We can drive back after lunch."

"Sure. I don't have anything urgent to do at home

except laundry." She gave him a tight smile. "Good night, Rory."

"Sleep well, love—uh, Annalise."

After she disappeared upstairs and a door shut, he slumped onto the bottom step of the staircase. Seeming to sense his mood, Buttercup strolled over to lean against him, and he rubbed the dog's ears.

"Maybe I'm just wishful thinking, believing she'll let me back into her life." He pressed his fingers to his eyes, wondering how he could stand it if she didn't. Life without Annalise would be . . . empty. Lonely days and nights, one after the other without end.

"I'm doing my best, Buttercup." Rising to his feet when the dog walked over to the door, he let her out and waited on the porch while she strolled around the yard and peed. Then strolled around some more.

"Let's go, girl."

The dog finally returned. After locking the door, he headed upstairs to bed. If he wanted to win Annalise back, he needed to be patient. He wouldn't give up hope, though. Ever.

Rory woke early the next morning. Unusual for him, but with so much on his mind, sleep had been elusive. Since neither Annalise nor Nash was up yet, he made coffee and then called Theo. And kept calling him every couple of minutes until the man finally answered.

"What the hell is your problem? Jesus, Rory. It's six in the morning."

"I wanted to catch you before you went to work. I saw Kat yesterday, but she wasn't talking." He grinned. Not a lie, and Kat would undoubtedly tell her cousin the circumstances of the meeting soon enough.

"Oh, did she say anything at all?"

"Nope. Nothing. She just seemed surprised when I appeared out of the blue. Anyway, since I haven't been able to locate Archie, it looks like I'll have to go to the cops about the stolen painting. Of course, you might not care if they start digging into all Felix Lemmon's known associates again, but I thought I'd ask one more time if you'd learned where Archie's staying."

Theo was quiet for a moment. "Actually, I did hear a rumor he's living in a loft in the warehouse district. Lots of natural light for painting. I believe he's above a business that imports textiles. That's all I've got."

"Let's hope it's enough."

Rory disconnected and ran a quick search on his phone, using Richmond, textiles, and Lemmon as key words. A few seconds later, he had the address for an import business owned by Hugo Lemmon. Undoubtedly, one of Felix's relatives.

He glanced down when Buttercup wandered into the kitchen. "I guess I know where I'm going this morning."

"Where's that?"

He jerked his head up and smiled as Annalise walked in behind the dog. "Good morning."

She headed straight to the coffee maker and stared at it as the machine sputtered and drizzled. "It'll be better once I have a cup of coffee. My brain isn't functioning very well yet."

He took a mug from the cupboard, pulled out the pot, and poured her a cup. "Here you go."

"Thanks." Taking the milk from the refrigerator, she added a splash and sipped. "Excellent."

His lips twitched at the look of sheer bliss on her face. "To answer your question, I have an address for

Archie. I'm going to pay him a visit."

"I'll get dressed and come with you."

"Probably best if you don't. The fewer people who know you're involved, the better."

She frowned. "Theo must know I'm the one who contacted you since the painting was stolen from the museum where I work."

"Except I've never mentioned which painting I'm looking for. *Sheep in the Meadow* probably isn't the only piece Kat's been involved in stealing recently. Let's try to keep your name out of the mix."

"That guy in the Saab followed us, so he must have been watching my apartment. Maybe Kat or Archie saw us at the Governor's Ball."

He frowned. "That's true, and it worries me. The dude knows I've been staying with you since he saw us come out together. I'm just not sure how he's connected."

"If it'll make you feel better, I'll stay here. Do you want breakfast before you go?"

"I'll eat a banana or something while I drive. I want to make sure I catch Archie before he leaves his apartment."

Annalise's eyes darkened. "Do you think he'll be a threat if you corner him?"

Rory filled a travel mug with coffee and screwed on the top. "Not in the least. Archie avoids conflict whenever possible, which is why he got away when the rest of Felix's crew went to prison. You don't need to worry." He met her gaze and smiled. "Not that I don't appreciate it."

"I don't want you to get hurt because of me."

He squeezed her shoulder beneath the soft fleece

robe. "Archie's a wimp. I'll be fine." He opened the pantry door and held up a Ziploc bag. "Oh, wow. Homemade blueberry muffins. Can I?"

"Of course. Mom must have made them before she left."

"Hey, I baked those yesterday." Nash sounded slightly offended as he strolled into the room. "Go ahead and have a couple. Are you leaving?"

Rory nodded. "I'm off to have a conversation with an art forger. I'll be back in a couple of hours."

"Be careful, Rory." Annalise's brows drew together over concerned eyes. "I don't care how big of a wimp you think he is."

"I will." He resisted the urge to pull her close and drop a kiss onto her lips. Instead, he took his coffee and muffins and left.

He had plenty of time to think while he drove into Richmond and parked down the street from the warehouse. Catching Archie unprepared seemed like the best option to get some straight answers. Even if Theo had given him a heads-up, the man probably hadn't had time to pack up and leave.

At this hour, the neighborhood was still mostly deserted. Rory walked around the building, located a fire escape, and jumped to grab the lowest rung of the ladder. Swinging himself up, he quickly climbed to the third-floor window above the warehouse and slid it open. Stepping over the sill, he walked around an easel with a partially-finished canvas propped against it and stopped in the middle of the cavernous room. Snoring came from the bed in the far corner of the huge, open space.

"Get up, Archie."

"What?" The blanket jerked as the man in the bed rolled over and shot upright. "Who the hell . . ." He fumbled for the glasses on the bedside table and slid them onto his nose. "Shit! Cavanaugh? How did you—"

"Never mind how I found you. Drag your ass out of bed. I have a few questions."

"I'm not answering them." He grabbed a pair of sweatpants off the floor and pulled them on.

"Yes, you are. I have the FBI on speed dial, and I'd be happy to call them. In fact, that might be the simplest way to—"

"What did I ever do to you, huh? Nothing. It's not my fault that last job went south." He crossed his arms over his skinny, bare chest. "What do you want to know?"

"Who's Kat's buyer? One of the paintings you forged could get a friend of mine in trouble. I want the original back."

"Hell, I don't know. She doesn't talk to me about the business end of the deal. I've actually only seen her a couple of times since I got back into the country."

"You were both at the Governor's Ball."

His eyes widened. "Were you there?"

"Doesn't matter. I know more than you think, so don't lie to me, Archie."

"I'm not." His tone was defensive. "That night, she handed me a note with the name of a painting and a date for completion. That's how she works. No emails or phone calls that can be traced. She's punchy as hell about getting caught."

"Where do you take the painting once it's finished?"

"Nowhere. Someone comes here to pick it up on the due date. Afterward, money is transferred into my account."

"Who collects the paintings?"

"I don't know him. A youngish, blond dude. We weren't formally introduced."

Rory stared at him for a minute. "If you aren't any use to me, why the hell shouldn't I turn you in?"

"I told you I don't know shit!"

"How many forgeries have you done for Kat since you left South America?"

"Two. I'm working on a third. The quality I produce takes time." Archie rubbed his hands up and down his arms. "The first time the guy showed up, he whistled and said he couldn't tell my painting from the original. I told him that was the goal. He mumbled something about not getting them mixed up."

"You think he's the thief?"

Archie shrugged. "Could be. Makes sense to avoid middlemen if possible. I was standing at the window after the dude left and saw him drive by in a black SUV. That's all I can tell you, and I need to pee. Now get the hell out of here. I'm done talking."

"If Kat calls you—"

"She won't. I don't even have a phone."

The man didn't look him in the eye. Definitely a lie, but Rory simply nodded. "You take care, Archie. I'll see you around."

"Don't count on it."

Turning, he left the way he'd arrived, through the open window. It wasn't much, but he had a little more ammunition for his conversation with Kat. Now to wait for her call before he made his next move.

Chapter Fourteen

The museum was closed, and the sun had long since set when Annalise straightened from a stooped position over her work table and tried a few yoga moves to ease the pain in her back. Not that she could see daylight from her domain in the bowels of the building, even at high noon. Despite the fact her body ached from meticulously removing the top layer of paint from the canvas to get to the picture beneath, she'd worked steadily, well past quitting time. The excitement of what she might find under the mediocre portrait of a pompous looking gentleman in a tight suit drove her to keep going.

When the door to the basement creaked open, she glanced up in surprise as tall black boots and a maroon skirt appeared at the top of the steps. "Lydia?"

"Yes, it's me." Her friend continued down the stairs. "I couldn't believe it when Oscar told me you were still here. It's after seven."

"So why are you hanging around? I thought you had a hot dinner date with your fiancé."

"He's working late, too. It seems to be an epidemic. Anyway, he's meeting me at the restaurant. I forgot my iPad so I stopped by to get it on my way there." She put her hands on her hips and scowled. "What's your excuse?"

"Yesterday, my new buddy, Gladys, an octogenarian who's as sharp as a Maizie's claws, brought in a painting for me to look at." She nodded toward the portrait on the worktable. "Apparently, her uncle fancied himself an artist and painted over a few old pictures her family had owned for several generations. She found this one when she was getting her house ready to sell and hoped I could uncover the original painting under her uncle's self-portrait."

Lydia's brows shot up. "Can you?"

"I'm making progress, although it's a slow, tedious process. Gladys said she'd donate the piece to the museum if it's something we want. Curiosity is driving me crazy, even though the hidden painting might be nothing special."

"But it could be a lost masterpiece."

Annalise grinned. "Exactly."

"Either way, it'll still be here tomorrow. Go home. Didn't you mention a friend from out of town is visiting? At least that was your excuse for not going out for drinks last night."

"He left this morning."

"*He?*" Her brown eyes brightened. "You didn't tell me your mysterious guest was a *he*."

"Because I knew you'd get the wrong idea. I thought you were meeting Sebastian."

Lydia glanced at her watch. "Crap. Now I'm going to be late. Promise me you'll go home."

"Fine. I'm too tired to keep working, anyway. I'll clean up and take off."

"Good. See you tomorrow." With a little wave, her friend headed up the stairs.

Annalise's shoulders slumped. She hadn't lied about being exhausted. All the frantic energy that had kept her going the past couple of weeks seemed to have drained through her fingertips into her work, leaving her a little shaky. Still, it took another fifteen minutes to clean up her area and put away the chemicals she'd been using. After shrugging on her wool coat, she climbed the stairs, switched off the basement light, and locked the door. Turning, she nearly bumped into JR as he came out of the security office.

Letting out a gasp, she pressed a hand to her chest. "You startled me."

"Sorry." He smoothed back his wild red hair and resettled his cap. "You leaving now?"

"Yes. Definitely time to call it a night. Have a good evening, JR."

"You, too. I'll lock up after you." He turned away as quickly as he'd appeared.

With a shrug, she walked down the silent corridor to the main entrance and let herself out. The mild weather of the previous week was gone, and a chill wind blew, sending colored leaves skittering down the street. Pushing her hands deep into her coat pockets, she set out for home, then on a whim, detoured in the direction of Independence Hall. It wasn't much out of her way, the cold night air seemed to be reviving her, and she wasn't in the mood to hang out alone in her apartment. Because once she walked through the door, she'd have to admit she missed Rory.

He'd received an urgent call from a client the previous day, and she'd encouraged him to go take care of business. He certainly wasn't accomplishing anything waiting around her apartment for his phone to ring. After his visit to Archie on Monday morning, they'd driven back to Philadelphia, both anxiously waiting for Kat to contact him. She hadn't. Nor had she called the next day, or the one after that. Rory was losing patience, wondering what sort of game she was playing.

Annalise walked down the path leading to the venerable old building and stopped near the statue of Commodore Barry, one of the lesser-known heroes of the Revolution. For once, the usual crowd of tourists was missing, and the square was deserted. Maybe because it was late and the dark sky was threatening rain. Whatever the reason, she was happy to be alone with her thoughts as she stared up at the clocktower on Independence Hall.

Her troubles seemed trivial compared to those of the Founding Fathers who had created a new nation in this very building, but she felt like they would have applauded her desire to buck the system and solve her own problems. *If* she and Rory could actually find the damn painting and return it to the museum where it belonged. She was just as frustrated as he was, but she hid her emotions a whole lot better. She'd had plenty of practice keeping her feelings under wraps, especially when it came to him.

A foot scuffed against the paving stones somewhere behind her, and Annalise swung around to peer into the darkness. She didn't see anyone in the deep shadows cast by the trees, but the fine hair rose on her arms. Walking alone at night in a city rife with crime wasn't the smartest move she'd ever made. Clutching her purse tightly to her side, she pulled her keys out of her coat pocket and gripped them between her knuckles like a weapon, wishing she'd actually bought mace instead of just thinking about it. Heading across the lawn, she reached Walnut Street and let out a sigh of relief. The steady stream of traffic and other pedestrians was exactly what she needed right now.

Except as she walked farther down 5th Street toward her neighborhood, thunder rumbled in the distance, and raindrops spattered the pavement. The few remaining pedestrians seemed to vanish like rats, scurrying for cover. Shivering, Annalise glanced over her shoulder. Only one other man remained on the sidewalk, striding quickly with the hood of his sweatshirt pulled up against the drizzle. Picking up her pace, she practically ran the remaining distance to her street and across the intersection.

Only two more blocks to go.

Maybe she was acting like a fool, imagining a threat where none existed, but when she glanced back and saw hoodie man continue down 5th without even glancing in her direction, she pushed the damp hair out of her eyes and exhaled the breath she'd been holding. *Scared of my own shadow, for God's sake.* She was generally safety conscious, but not overly nervous by nature, and there was no reason at all for her to freak out. Still, if Rory hadn't left town, he would undoubtedly have met her at the museum to walk her home.

One more block to go.

A figure moved out of the shelter of a doorway as she passed, and before she could let out a squeak, the man wrapped his arm around her neck and held her clamped against his chest. She gasped for breath as the pressure of his forearm cut off her air supply. Kicking backward, she connected with his shin, but he didn't even flinch. Instead, he tightened his hold until her vision darkened and wavered.

"Stop looking for the painting, and keep your mouth shut." Hot breath hit her neck as his low voice growled in her ear. "You won't get another warning."

A shove sent her sprawling face-first onto the sidewalk. By the time she pushed to her knees and turned around, he'd disappeared around the corner. Shaking and wet, the heels of her hands burned where she'd scraped her skin. Biting her lip to hold back tears of fear and anger, she picked up the keys she'd dropped, scrambled to her feet, and ran the rest of the way to her building. Fingers trembling, she finally got the right key inserted in the lock and let herself into the building.

Pressing her back against the door, she took a few calming breaths to steady her shaking legs. "You've got this," she muttered.

After a moment, she crossed the polished oak floor, her footsteps echoing. Only the muted strains of classical music coming from the unit on her right disturbed the silence. By the time she climbed to the second floor, her hands were nearly steady as she unlocked the door and entered her apartment. Pushing home the deadbolt, she flipped on the light, staggered into the living area, and collapsed onto the loveseat. When Maizie strolled into the room and jumped up beside her, she stroked her soft fur and let out a long, shaky sigh.

"Well, that sucked." She glanced down, noting a

rip in the knee of her pants. At least she hadn't worn a dress to work today. Turning her hands over, she picked tiny bits of concrete and dirt out of her raw palms. "I need to go soak in the tub, Maizie."

The cat meowed, jumped down, and sauntered into the kitchen.

"Okay, after I feed you. Sorry I'm home so late."

She needed to eat something, as well, but the thought of food made her stomach churn. When Maizie meowed again, she got up and followed her into the kitchen, poured cat chow into her bowl, and then headed into the bathroom to fill the tub. When she sank into the warm water a few minutes later, some of her tension eased and she began to relax.

Short-lived as her ringing phone jarred her out of her lethargy. Leaning over the side of the tub, she pulled her cell from the pocket of her ruined pants. Rory. There were also two missed calls from Callen, but apparently he hadn't left a message. Taking a moment to compose herself, she swiped to connect.

"Hi."

"How was your day?"

She gripped the phone a little tighter. "My day was fine, but someone was waiting for me on my street when I got home."

"What happened?" His tone was sharp. "Are you okay?"

"Yeah, just scraped up a bit. He grabbed me around the neck and basically told me to stop looking for the painting, or else. When I was feeling faint from lack of oxygen, he shoved me down and took off."

She put her phone on speaker and set it on the edge of the tub while he swore.

"I just scraped my hands and knees, and I'll probably have a bruised neck. It's not like I'm dying, Rory."

"Doesn't matter. I'll get back there as fast as I can."

"Why? If I'm being watched, seems like your presence would only piss them off more. Have you heard from Kat?"

"No. Maybe I should call her instead of waiting."

"And say what?" She frowned. "Where are you, by the way?"

"Back in New York, staring out over Central Park, feeling the need to punch something."

"You should take a bath. That's what I'm doing, and I'm not nearly as uptight and freaked out as I was before." When he didn't respond, she sat up a little straighter. "Rory?"

"Sorry." His voice was low and rough. "Just picturing you naked in the tub."

Her cheeks heated, and she sank beneath the water. "Don't start."

"Can't help it."

"Yes, you can. Stay on topic. What do you intend to say to Kat?"

"I'm not sure. This attack on you changes things. Did you recognize the guy?"

"I didn't see his face since he grabbed me from behind. All I know is he was strong." She stared up at the ceiling. "Do you think we should follow orders and simply drop this?"

"I guess that's one option. Your safety is more important than anything else."

"Maybe Kat didn't call you because she sent her guy after me to make a point, instead."

"You could be right." He paused for a moment. "What can you tell me about the man?"

"I don't think he was super tall, but he held onto me with an iron grip. He wore a leather jacket, and his voice was kind of raspy."

"Any accent?"

"I don't think so, but he only said a few words, and my focus was on trying to breathe."

"I don't like you being home alone. Or walking to and from work by yourself."

"I left later than I should have, and it was raining. Usually there are plenty of people around. My apartment is locked up tight, and I'll be more careful in the future." She bit her lip. "Did you finish your emergency job?"

"Not quite. I worked late, which is why I didn't call until now. I was planning to wrap it up tomorrow, but—"

"No buts. I'll be fine going to work in broad daylight."

"I still think it's best if I head straight down there. If not tonight then—"

"Stop, Rory." She raised her voice to cut him off. "Instead of coming here, maybe you should go see Theo after you finish your project. I bet he knows a whole lot more than he's saying."

"That's actually a pretty good idea. Let me think about it." His tone softened. "Are you sure you're not hurt worse than you're telling me?"

"My neck is a little sore, and I need to put some antibiotic ointment on my hands and knees when I get out of the tub. That's it. Mostly, I'm just angry."

"I take it you didn't call 9-1-1?"

She rubbed her arms as the water cooled. "What would be the point? He was long gone, and I couldn't even give the police a description. I just came home."

"Will you check in with me tomorrow morning?"

"I'll text you when I get to work." A smile curved her lips. "I could always ask Callen to walk me home. He wants to take me out, but I've been putting him off since I've been a little preoccupied with looking for that damn painting."

Rory grunted. "The gift shop dweeb? Fine. You, do that. After an hour or two in his company, my guess is you'll miss me more than ever."

He was probably right. *Damn him.*

"My bath is getting cold so I'm going to hang up now. I'll talk to you tomorrow."

"Okay. Good night, Annalise."

"'Night, Rory."

She touched her phone screen to disconnect and then slumped into the water. Maybe she *should* agree to have dinner with Callen. She clearly needed something to distract her since she was spending way too much time thinking about Rory.

Standing, she drained the tub and showered off, then dried and put ointment on the abrasions. If she had trouble working tomorrow because her hands hurt, she was going to be royally pissed. Holding up her pants, she scowled. With one shredded knee, they were a total loss. She wadded them up and chucked them in the trash. She'd force herself to eat a light meal and then go to bed. As evenings went, she couldn't wait for this one to be over. Hopefully tomorrow would be a better day.

The next morning, Annalise arrived at work with a positive attitude, determined to reveal the identity of the artist whose work had been painted over. There'd been no sign of any strangers loitering near her apartment, and she'd reached the Chestnut Street Museum without being accosted. A big win in her book. By noon, she was feeling jubilant after uncovering a signature at the bottom of the painting.

Violet Oakley had been a local artist, known for her murals in the state Capitol building. But she'd also painted historic Americana pieces. If that's what was hidden under Gladys's uncle's crappy self-portrait, Marcus would be thrilled she'd taken on this project.

Though she was making slow but steady progress, she needed a break. Heading upstairs to see if Lydia was free, she took her bag lunch out of the refrigerator in the kitchen, waved at Jim, the daytime security guard manning the office, and continued down the hallway. Francine stepped out of the gift shop just as she reached it and beckoned her over.

"How's your day going, Francine? Is the museum unusually busy, or is it my imagination?"

"It is busy, and unfortunately, I don't have any help—not that I can't handle the shop alone." Her tone was curt. "Do you know why Callen didn't show up for work this morning?"

"I've no idea. He tried to call me yesterday evening, but we didn't connect."

"He's usually a very reliable young man, but this new generation doesn't have the work ethic of more mature employees."

Annalise resisted the urge to roll her eyes since she probably put in more hours than anyone, and she was on salary. What that said about her, she wasn't sure. Probably that she was an idiot and needed to get a life.

"I hope nothing's wrong. Did you call him?"

"Of course, but he didn't answer. Maybe if you try, he'll pick up. Callen has a bit of a crush on you."

"I can do that."

Francine glanced over her shoulder. "Shoot. I have customers ready to check out. Let me know if you speak to him."

"I definitely will."

Annalise crossed the entry to the main stairs and glanced upward when she heard voices above. Off the second-floor balcony, Lydia held court, surrounded by a group of Asian tourists. Apparently, her friend was in the middle of a tour so Annalise headed down the east wing where visiting exhibits were displayed. The space was currently set up with suits of armor dating back to the middle ages, along with weapons that looked capable of severing heads in a single swipe. Shuddering, she exited through the rear door into the enclosed garden space behind the museum and chose a bench beside a rosebush with a few late blooms to eat her sandwich. The sun was shining, warding off the chill in the air.

First, she'd check in with Callen. She should have returned his call the night before but hadn't been in the mood. Pulling her phone from the pocket of her skirt, she accessed her recent calls and tapped his name. After several rings, it went to voicemail, and she waited for the beep.

"Hey, Callen, it's Annalise. Francine was worried when you didn't show up for work this morning. Give one of us a call. I hope everything's okay."

A frown furrowed her brow. He was definitely the reliable sort, and missing work was completely out of character. Setting her phone aside, she'd finished her ham on rye and was crunching baby carrots when he returned her call. She swiped to connect.

"Hey, did you forget you were supposed to work today?"

"Annalise?" His voice sounded slightly slurred.

She sat up straighter. *Is he drunk or sick?* "Is something wrong?"

"I don't know. My head feels messed up, like I drank a fifth of vodka, except I didn't." He grew slightly more coherent. "Oh, hell. It's after noon. Francine's going to fire me."

"What the heck happened?"

"I'm not sure. Jesus, my head aches."

"Maybe you should see a doctor. If you fell or something . . ."

"Not that kind of hurt. I haven't felt this crappy the morning after since college." He let out a shuddering breath. "I was hoping to see you last night, and when you didn't answer your phone, I decided to stop by your apartment. You weren't home."

"That's because I worked late."

"Oh. I waited around then called again, and when it went to voice mail, I thought you might be blowing me off."

She sighed. "Not intentionally. I turn my ringer off when I'm trying to focus."

"Makes sense. I probably should have left then, but I'm the stubborn sort."

When he hesitated, she gritted her teeth. "Then what?"

"I got out of my car and went back to check your apartment. One of your neighbors was coming out and said she hadn't seen you. Anyway, I walked back to my car, determined to wait until you got home, and the next thing I remember is hearing my phone ring a few minutes ago."

"Are you still in your car?"

"Yeah, I am. Just down the block from your apartment. I know this sounds bad, but I swear to God I wasn't doing drugs or drinking anything stronger than a giant cup of soda while I waited. I only drove over to your place instead of walking because I hoped you'd agree to go out to dinner with me."

She fisted her free hand so tightly her nails cut into her scraped palm. Had Callen been passed out in his car while she was accosted on the street? She didn't even know what sort of vehicle he drove.

"Did you see anyone when you went to my apartment? Maybe someone walked by you?"

"Just your neighbor. You must think I'm some kind of freak." His voice was glum.

"No, I don't, but maybe you should get checked out by a doctor."

"Maybe I should. Man, this sucks. I need to call Francine."

"I'll tell her you have some sort of twenty-four-hour bug and just woke up feeling horrible."

"That would be great. I'm heading home now. I feel a little better, but if I'm not back to normal in a few hours, I'll go to a clinic. I haven't been getting enough sleep lately, so maybe I dozed off and hit my head on the steering wheel or something." His tone darkened. "Either that or I have a brain tumor."

"I'm sure it isn't anything that horrible. I'll see you at work tomorrow."

"Okay. Bye, Annalise."

She disconnected and sat there staring at the fading roses. Had the asshole who'd grabbed her drugged Callen because he didn't want a witness? Maybe he'd slipped a Mickey into the soda he was drinking while he was at her building, talking to her neighbor. If her attacker had recognized Callen, it must mean he'd been following her on previous occasions.

The whole situation made her queasy, and she swallowed hard. Whoever had grabbed her wasn't afraid to play hardball. If she and Rory kept searching for the Pissarro, he could escalate even further, and next time, he might not stop at a warning.

Chapter Fifteen

Rory left the terminal at Logan International in a drizzle of rain. It was nearing dark as he headed toward the line of taxis when a blue Miata pulled up next to him. The passenger window lowered, and the driver waved an arm.

"Get in."

Stooping, he made eye contact with Annalise's sister, Brielle. Deciding she probably wouldn't kill him in the middle of Boston's crowded airport, he waited for her to pop the trunk, dropped his carry-on bag into the small space, and then slid onto the passenger seat.

"You're about the last person I expected to see, let alone offer me a ride. How did you even know I was here?"

"I talked to Annalise earlier. She told me you were flying in to confront Theo. I decided we should have a little chat first." Her tone had an edge.

Maybe she does intend to murder me in cold blood, despite all the witnesses.

He offered a hesitant smile. "It's good to see you,

Brielle. You look great."

Two years younger than her sister, Brielle was a few inches taller and had a quiet, understated beauty, though she always seemed completely unaware of her appeal. Long, brown hair was pulled back in a no-nonsense braid, and her Quintrell blue eyes were direct and intelligent, always focused on her goal. Of all Annalise's siblings, Brielle was by far the scariest.

"Don't try to charm me, Rory. I'm here because I'm worried about my sister." She merged with traffic heading toward the tunnel, the wiper blades slapping away the rain. "She said some idiot grabbed her on the street yesterday."

"That's why I intend to have a conversation with Theo. I'm pretty sure he knows exactly what's going on, and if I have to beat the crap out of him to get answers, I will. I'm finished playing his game."

"Maybe you should have done that to begin with."

He slouched in his seat. "Apparently so. I thought it would be a piece of cake to find the stolen painting. Kat isn't operating a large-scale operation the way her father was. It seemed likely someone she knew tempted her into using her connections to liberate a couple of paintings, earning a handsome profit from the deal."

Brielle glanced over as they came out of the tunnel and, with heavy traffic, drove in fits and starts through Boston's North End in the direction of Little Italy. "Annalise said none of your suspects have the Pissarro."

"Unfortunately not, and now Kat knows I'm involved. I don't intend to let her target Annalise as a way of controlling me." He stared out the window at the falling rain and steady stream of brake lights. "On the other hand, it's possible Theo is the one who sicced the thug on her. Maybe he thought we were getting a little too close when his original plan had simply been to make Kat take notice and play nice. Either way, I want answers, and I won't leave here until I have them."

Brielle zipped into a spot in front of a fire hydrant near an Italian trattoria. "I ordered takeout while I was waiting for you at the airport. If you want to run in and get it, I'll circle the block and be right back. There's never anywhere to park around here."

"Okay." Opening the door, he stepped out of the car and dashed through the puddles on the sidewalk to enter the brightly lit restaurant. After giving the hostess Brielle's name, he inhaled deeply, the scent of marinara making his stomach growl. A few minutes later he was back on the street, clutching the bag of food as he waited for her Miata to appear.

When she pulled up in front of him, he jumped in. "Please tell me you ordered enough for two. This smells amazing."

"I did. You still have some explaining to do, but we can eat at my apartment while I grill you."

"I'm happy to tell you whatever you want to know."

"We'll see about that." She parked in a garage not too far from the restaurant, and they got out. "I've moved since you and Annalise broke up. This is a great neighborhood."

"Especially for food." He shut his door and gestured toward the trunk where he'd left his suitcase. "Am I taking a cab from your apartment, or do you intend to dispose of my body once you're finished torturing me?"

She grinned. "I always liked your sense of humor, Rory. Although, in this case, you might not be too far off the mark. Leave your bag. I'll drive you to Theo's after we eat."

"I appreciate that. He lives in Beacon Hill so it isn't too far."

"What hotel are you staying at?"

"I didn't make a reservation." Still carrying the food, he followed her out of the garage. "I'll decide what I'm doing once I hear what Theo has to say."

She nodded and flipped up the hood on her jacket. "The rain's letting up. I'm only a couple of blocks away so at least we won't get soaked."

Brielle lived in one of the old brick buildings ubiquitous to the area. Her apartment was on the fourth floor above a dress shop.

"Lots of stairs. It's a good workout." She glanced over her shoulder as she climbed up the stairwell past the third-floor landing without even breathing hard. "I like being on the top story. No one tromping around over my head so it's pretty quiet." She led the way down the hall to the end unit and fished her keys out of her coat pocket to open the door.

He followed her inside and went straight to the window. "This is super cool. You have a view of the Old North Church tower."

"That's why I took this apartment when I moved across the river from Cambridge. You can practically smell the history in this part of town."

He glanced around the high-ceilinged room, which was lined with bookshelves stuffed full of well-read books. Old radiators hissed and steamed, and homey furniture seemed to invite visitors to sit down and put up their feet.

"The place suits you." Setting the food bag on the small table near the miniscule kitchen that looked like it hadn't been updated since Eisenhower was president, he raised a brow. "Do those antique appliances still work?"

"They made things to last back in the good old days. Have a seat. I'll get some plates. I don't have any beer, but I might have a bottle of wine somewhere."

"Water's fine." His eyes narrowed as she carried dishes to the table and went back to fill glasses from the tap. "You're being much nicer to me than I expected or probably deserve. What's the catch?"

She sat opposite him and opened a container filled with spaghetti and meatballs and another of salad while he unwrapped garlic bread in foil. "I actually appreciate the fact that you dived in to help Annalise without hesitation, despite the risk of landing back in jail if you're caught. However, when I talked to my sister, she said your methods haven't been very effective."

"Not so far, although we've ruled out a few people." He dug into the spaghetti and closed his eyes as the rich flavors melded in his mouth. "This is unbelievably good."

She frowned at her fork as she stabbed a bite of lettuce. "Now there's the added threat that this creep might hurt her. After he drugged her co-worker—"

His eyes opened wide. "What?"

"Didn't Annalise tell you? That guy who's been asking her out, Callen, was waiting outside her apartment for her to get home last night. Someone must have slipped him a mickey because he woke up in his car at noon today, feeling totally wasted."

"Are you serious?"

"Yep. Annalise figured whoever attacked her recognized Callen as a friend and didn't want any witnesses when he grabbed her on the sidewalk."

"Which would mean he's seen her with the dweeb at the museum. Shit."

"The dweeb?" Her brows rose.

"The guy looks at her like a sad puppy waiting for a pat on the head. I'm not a big fan."

"Which brings us to the second reason I wanted to talk to you." She twirled spaghetti around the tines of her fork and narrowed her eyes as she stared at him. "If you break my sister's heart again, I'll definitely kill you and dump your body in the bay. No joke."

"All I want is for Annalise to be happy." The pasta settled in his stomach like a chunk of granite. "Do I wish she'd admit I'm the man who can bring joy back to her life? Hell, yes, but I won't force the issue. Right now, my only intention is to find the painting and support whatever decisions she makes."

"Why in the world didn't you trust her with the truth before you got engaged? Lying to her was the biggest mistake you could have made."

"I know that now. At the time, the risk of losing her seemed too great. The most important people in my life had let me down, and I couldn't stand the thought of Annalise walking away."

Some of the ice in her blue eyes thawed. "I don't know if she'll ever be able to forgive you."

"Maybe not."

"If you keep pushing her to give you another chance, and she isn't willing, you'll tie her up in knots. You weren't here to see how badly hurt she was, Rory.

I won't let you put her through that again."

"I'm doing my best not to overstep the boundaries she sets. Honestly. But it's hard when I love her so damn much."

"I can see that. Still, it's her decision. You know how I feel so I won't say anything more on the subject." She took a bite of bread, and the light in her eyes grew speculative. "So, what's your plan for Theo? Is there anything I can do to help?"

"I intend to make him tell me everything he knows. Then I'll book the first flight to Philadelphia. The fact that someone is keeping such a close eye on Annalise makes my stomach churn. I don't want her to be alone."

"Maybe it's time to take your story to the police."

"If we can't prove anything, they won't be able to do much more than question Kat. Since I spooked Archie, he's probably already fled the country. Likely, both Annalise and I would be considered persons of interest in an investigation, if not actual suspects."

"I'm sure you're right." Brielle frowned as she poked at her salad. "Her job at the museum means a lot to her. I know she doesn't want to jeopardize it."

"Exactly. Still, if I don't feel like I can protect her, I'll call the cops. But first, I want to see what Theo has to say. That might change everything." He popped a meatball into his mouth and chewed. "Would you be willing to stay with her for a few days if I get a lead on the painting and have to go somewhere?"

"Of course. Nash could play watchdog, as well, since he's on a break between jobs right now."

"If I have to leave Philly, I'll definitely call for backup."

Brielle smiled. "Even though my sister will say she

doesn't need a babysitter?"

"I don't care. I don't want her to be home alone."

They finished their meal and headed back to the garage. As Brielle navigated Boston's traffic-clogged streets, Rory mentally refined the details of his plan. The trick was to uncover Theo's biggest weakness and use it to make him sweat. If it came down to saving himself or his cousin, Rory was pretty sure it wouldn't be a contest.

"Do you want me to wait for you?"

"Huh?" He jerked out of his thoughts and glanced over at Brielle.

"I can check flights and drive you to the airport after you pressure Theo for answers."

"I'm sure you have better things to do with your evening."

"True, but I don't like the idea of Annalise being alone, either. If I can get you back to Philly a little faster, I don't mind playing chauffeur."

"In that case, I'd be happy to accept your offer. Theo's address is just around the corner. Why don't you drop me off here and find somewhere to park. I'll text you when I'm ready to be picked up."

She nodded and rolled to a stop. "Good luck."

"Thanks. Hopefully this won't take too long."

Rory got out and ran across the street behind her car. A couple of minutes later he'd reached the townhouse where Theo lived. The place looked the same as the last time he'd been there, and he just hoped his old pal didn't have either a live-in girlfriend or company for the evening. He'd have to take his chances.

Outdoor lights illuminated the short walkway leading to the front door. Inside, the first floor was dimly lit, and upstairs, a light shone behind drawn blinds. The good news was, Theo's townhouse was an end unit. He rounded the block and stared at the high brick wall stretching between the rear of his building and the one on the next block. Each townhouse undoubtedly had a small, fenced-in yard behind the unit.

Gripping the rough edges of the bricks, he quickly scaled the wall and dropped over the other side into a shrub. Extracting himself from the bush, he crossed a patch of grass to a stone patio. A sliding glass door opened into a combination kitchen and dining area where a light had been left on over the sink. Apparently Theo hadn't bothered to lock the back door when he'd gone upstairs to shower. Rory could hear the water running, which gave him a few minutes to settle in.

A single lamp burned next to the couch in the front room, and the TV was turned to a cable news channel, though the sound had been muted. He took a seat in a chair in the darkest corner and faced the staircase.

The water turned off, and a few minutes later footsteps sounded as Theo appeared on the stairs. Of medium height and slightly stocky, he was dressed to go out in slacks and a blazer. With dark, razor cut hair and a trim beard, he hadn't changed much since Rory had last seen him. He stopped by the front door, slid his wallet into his back pocket, and scooped up his keys. Turning, he walked over to the end table and grabbed the remote to turn off the TV.

"Have a seat, Theo. You aren't going anywhere."

He spun around and dropped the remote on the rug at his feet. His eyes widened as he stared at Rory. "What the hell are you doing in my house?"

"You left your back door unlocked, not that I couldn't have gotten in, anyway." His tone was hard. "Sit down. I have a few questions."

"Or, I can just call the cops."

"I don't think you want to do that. If the FBI got a tip you've been using your law practice to launder money—"

Theo dropped onto the edge of the couch cushion and scowled. "What do you want to know that I haven't already told you?"

"Let's start with why you brought up Archie's name in the first place and then told me to contact Kat. Seems counterproductive from your standpoint."

"Look, I've got nothing to do with Kat and whatever game she's involved in."

"You're a horrible liar, Theo." Rory resisted the urge to walk over and punch him in the face. "I know money was transferred from a Boston bank your firm uses to an offshore account. Since I'm not in the mood to dig through all your client records to figure out which one's fake, I'd appreciate a straight answer. The consequences for lying won't be pleasant."

His eyes narrowed. "What're you going to do, beat me up? Are we ten-year-olds on the playground?"

"I might, just because you're pissing me off. But don't forget I have the skills to plant all sorts of evidence on your computer and then hand you over to the FBI. I won't hesitate to burn your ass if you don't cooperate with me."

"Jesus, Rory. We were friends."

"Yeah, we were, but you and Kat picked the wrong target when you stole a painting from the museum where Annalise works. And then you compounded your error by sending some thug to threaten her. My loyalty lies with the woman I love, and I intend to fix this problem for her."

"Even though she dumped your ass when you got arrested?"

"That's right, so start talking."

"I didn't send anyone to threaten her. And I certainly didn't choose the painting Archie forged. Kat told me she knew someone who wanted a couple of original paintings and was willing to pay to get them. She asked me if I knew where Archie might be hanging out. He'd turned up in Miami not long before then, so I put her in touch with him. That's the sum total of my involvement."

"Not quite. You took a payment when you transferred the money through some shell accounts. Who bought those paintings?"

"I've no idea." He leaned forward, arms resting on his knees, the picture of honesty. "An extremely large retainer check from a guy named Joe Smith was sent to me in the mail. I created an account for him and then moved the money out after giving him a history and a crap ton of billable hours. Kat cut me out of the loop when the second painting was purchased. I'd just found out and was ticked off when you called me, so I dropped Archie's name. I should have kept my mouth shut."

Rory's lips curved in a grim smile. "Kat shouldn't have messed with you."

"Damn right. Anyway, I'm completely out of the loop now. Maybe she got someone else to launder her funds. Or it's possible she's simply stuffing her mattress full of cash."

"Not helpful. Let's get back to Joe Smith."

"Look, I'm meeting a woman for drinks, and she's going to think I stood her up. I don't know anything about the buyer, and I'm sure Joe Smith is an alias. If I knew, I'd tell you."

"What bank was the check drawn on?"

"I have no idea." He frowned. "Actually, I believe it was a bank in Philadelphia. I remember that much because the address for Joe Smith was a post office box in Philly. I was kind of surprised since Kat doesn't do business that far north."

"She never said anything else about the buyer?"

"Not a word, but it makes sense that he—or she—is from the same place as the painting. Maybe a regular visitor to the museum has some sort of weird passion for that particular piece of art and wanted it for themselves."

"The painting is by Pissarro."

Theo lifted his hands. "I didn't even know that much, let alone where it was stolen from."

"Who's the thief?"

"No clue. Kat didn't ask for a recommendation." He rose to his feet. "I need to go."

Rory stood and crossed the room, stopping inches from his old buddy. "If I find out you're lying about anything you've said this evening—"

"I'm not. If you want answers, talk to Kat."

"You damn well better not tip her off that I'm coming after her."

"I won't. I like my life exactly the way it is, and I know you have the computer skills to shit all over my world. Are we finished here?"

"For now." Rory followed him as he headed

toward the front door. "Hey, don't forget to lock that slider."

Theo swore but detoured in the direction of the kitchen. Smiling, Rory left through the front door and pulled out his phone to text Brielle as soon as he reached the sidewalk.

I'm waiting out front.

She responded with a thumbs-up emoji.

Exiting his townhouse, Theo made an elaborate show of locking the door before hurrying down the walkway to the street. "You know, I'm beginning to regret I ever hooked you up with my uncle. You've become a real pain in my ass."

"You and me both. Biggest mistake I ever made. It cost me everything I've ever wanted."

As he strolled away, Theo glanced over his shoulder. "Maybe she'll forgive you."

Rory sighed. "I keep hoping."

Chapter Sixteen

Annalise sat up in bed when the door to her apartment squeaked slightly as it opened. With a shrill meow, Maizie jumped down and shot out of the room.

"Rory?"

"Yeah, it's me." His voice sounded tired. "Sorry. I was trying not to wake you."

She slid out from under the covers, turned on the bedside lamp, and stuck her arms through the sleeves of her robe. Padding across the floor on bare feet, she walked into the living room where she'd left a light on for his arrival. "I wasn't asleep, just lying there wishing I was. It's after midnight. We'll both be exhausted in the morning."

"We're young. We'll recover. My flight got delayed, which is why I'm so late." He dropped his bag and scooped up the cat when she twined around his ankles.

"How was your trip?"

"Quick. Semi-productive. Your sister was nice to me."

Her brows shot up. "You saw Brielle?"

"She picked me up at the airport, fed me, and gave me a lecture. Then she drove me to Theo's place, waited while I talked to him, and chauffeured me back to the airport."

"Wow." She settled onto the couch and grinned. "Looks like you're still in one piece. I'm kind of surprised."

"Me, too. Maybe she's mellowing with age, like a fine bottle of scotch."

"Maybe." She yawned and tucked a strand of hair behind her ear. "So, what happened at Theo's?"

"Don't you want to go back to bed and talk in the morning?"

"If you give me some good news, I might actually be able to sleep."

Still holding Maizie, he took a seat on the chair opposite her. "Unfortunately, Theo didn't know as much as I'd hoped. Our mystery buyer contacted Kat and offered her a lot of money to procure a specific painting. She reached out to Theo since she didn't know where Archie was, and he hooked them up. He also laundered the money for the first painting through his law firm."

"He admitted that?"

Rory nodded. "I made it clear lying wasn't an option. Anyway, Kat cut him out of the deal for a second painting, which was why he gave up the info about Archie in the first place. He was ticked off at his cousin."

"We figured as much. He doesn't know who the buyer is?"

"No, but the check came from a Philadelphia bank.

The name on the account was an alias, Joe Smith, with a Philly post office box for an address. Theo suggested the buyer might be a regular at your museum. The guy developed a passion for *Sheep in the Meadow* and decided he wanted it for himself."

"Which means the second painting was likely stolen from a local museum, as well, either ours or the Philadelphia Museum of Art."

Rory nodded. "Archie was working on a third forgery, but after I confronted him, he probably cut his losses and left the country without finishing it. He's a cautious dude."

"So that leaves us with Kat, the thief, and whoever threatened me—unless they're one and the same."

"Theo didn't know who she used for the job." He frowned. "There's also the inside man at the museum. Someone had to have disarmed the alarm system and reset it afterward."

"My head hurts just thinking about all this. What do we do now?"

"It's time to confront Kat. I'll call her office in the morning to find out if she's in D.C. or Richmond. Right now, you should go back to bed."

"We both need to get some sleep." She rose to her feet. "I slid your mattress under my bed. You can come get it and the bedding."

"Okay." He shifted the cat off his lap and followed her into the bedroom. Stopping beside her, he touched her neck with gentle fingers. "You have bruises from that asshole grabbing you. Are you really okay?"

Her breath caught in her throat, and she swallowed. "I'm just a little sore. My knee scabbed over, so my legs won't win any beauty contests right now."

He stroked her cheek with the pad of his thumb and grinned. "You always know how to make me smile." After holding her gaze for a moment, he stepped back. "I'll take the mattress and get out of your way."

Walking over to the closet, she lifted a spare pillow and blanket off the shelf and followed him into the living room. "You've gone above and beyond to help me, Rory. I hope you know how much I appreciate it."

He dropped the mattress onto the rug in the middle of the floor and turned around. "It's the least I can do. I'm furious you were hurt, and I don't intend to leave you alone again. If I have to go somewhere, we'll ask Brielle or Nash to stay with you."

She rolled her eyes. "You might be afraid of my sister's wrath, but I doubt the thug who attacked me would be."

"Safety in numbers, love. Uh, I mean Annalise. I promised Brielle I wouldn't push you or add any more emotional scars. I won't try to take advantage of our enforced closeness."

His eyes held a wealth of caring and earnestness, tempting her far more than his lighthearted charm ever had. But now wasn't the time to cave in and do something stupid, not when she was too tired to think straight.

"Good to know." She handed him the bedding. "Good night, Rory."

"'Night, Annalise. Sleep tight."

She went back to her room and shut the door, leaving Maizie with Rory. The cat was thrilled he'd returned, and maybe she was, too. She simply wouldn't think about it.

After a fitful night's sleep, she woke feeling

sluggish. A shower revived her slightly, and she dressed for work in a pair of plaid tweed pants, a green sweater, and comfortable flats.

A grim smile curled her lips as she left her room. If she needed to run from the bad guys, at least she wouldn't be wearing heels.

As usual, Rory was sprawled out on the mattress, the blanket draped across his waist, with Maizie curled against his side. The cat blinked at her and purred, rubbing her head against his chest. Annalise rolled her eyes at the blatant display of favoritism as she walked into the kitchen. By the time she'd made coffee and scrambled eggs, he sat up and stretched, dislodging the cat. She avoided looking at his hard, muscled abs.

"Good morning. Do I smell breakfast?"

She nodded. "You do. Would you like a bagel or toast with your eggs?"

"A bagel, please." He blinked. "I must have crashed hard. What time is it?"

She dropped a bagel into the toaster. "A little after seven."

"Definitely time to get up and get moving." He threw off the blanket and rose to his feet, wearing nothing but a pair of boxers. Bending, he dug through his bag and straightened with a handful of clothing. As he headed into the bathroom, he called over his shoulder, "I'll get dressed and be right out."

Closing her eyes, Annalise swore softly. He might not be trying to torture her, but he was damn sure doing an excellent job. Ignoring the heat suffusing her body, she scooped eggs out of the pan onto two plates, added a bagel to his and a piece of rye toast to hers, and set the food on the table. She'd poured a cup of coffee with a splash of milk for him and topped off her own cup when he emerged from the bathroom.

"Wow, you didn't have to go to so much trouble." He took the cup she handed him, and his green eyes sparkled with humor as he met her gaze over the rim. "I might get used to it."

"Well, don't. Just sit down and eat. I want to get to work early, and I knew you'd insist on walking with me."

"Darn right. What's the rush?"

"I have a special project I'm trying to finish, and in the meantime, my other work is backing up. There aren't enough hours in the day."

He swallowed a bite of eggs. "You should get a raise."

"Without a doubt." She sipped her coffee. "You'll call me once you know where Kat is?"

"Yes. I don't suppose you want to call in sick so you can tag along with me when I drive down to confront her?"

"I really can't."

He frowned. "I guess I'll see if Nash is free to come up here and stay with you."

"Or, I can hang out with Lydia and Sebastian tonight and save my brother the trip if you insist I need a babysitter."

"They drugged your friend, for God's sake. That's a step up from a verbal warning and a shove. By the way, how did your attacker manage that?"

"Callen was waiting down the street from my apartment. I told you I worked late that night, and he wanted to take me to dinner. I guess he left his car to ask my neighbor if I was home. All I can figure is the jerk who grabbed me slipped a mickey into the cup of soda he'd been drinking while he was away from his car."

"Jesus. We're lucky he didn't do worse than push you, and we definitely aren't taking any more risks."

"Fine." Considering the circumstances, she wasn't crazy about spending time alone in her apartment. Every creak and groan in the old building made her flinch. "Maybe you can talk to Kat this afternoon and won't get back too horribly late."

"Let's hope. I'll keep you posted."

They finished their breakfast and left a short time later. The weather had improved as the rain moved out, and the day was sunny and cool. Autumn had settled in, turning the leaves to rich golds and crimsons that drifted from the trees onto the sidewalk.

"I love this time of year." She stuck her hands in her coat pockets. "I'd like to spend my weekend hiking in the Poconos to see the fall colors instead of in my apartment, worrying.

"That's not out of the question if I can convince Kat to talk."

"Why would she tell you anything?" Annalise stopped at the corner and glanced over at him. "You aren't the kind of guy who would beat answers out of a woman."

He grinned. "No, ma'am. I promise to use my words instead of brute force to convince Kat to be reasonable."

"Funny, Rory."

"I try. Anyway, my pitch will be that I'll swap out the fake painting currently in the museum for the original, without the buyer ever knowing a second switch was made. She doesn't lose any money, and her customer stays completely in the dark. That forgery is so damn good I doubt anyone but a trained professional would be able to tell the difference."

"True. I wasn't completely convinced until I ran tests on the pigment." When the light changed, she headed across the intersection. "You think she'll agree to that?"

"If she doesn't, I'll threaten to tell the FBI everything I know. Even if we can't prove she arranged the theft, she isn't going to want the feds digging into her business."

"Most people wouldn't. Especially those with something to hide."

"Exactly."

The pedestrian light blinked walk just as they reached the next corner, and Annalise stepped off the curb. When a black SUV came up from behind them and hung a hard right into the intersection, Rory grabbed her around the waist and jerked her back against his chest. The bumper of the vehicle caught the edge of her coat and ripped it as she staggered against him. Exhaust clouded the air as the driver gunned the engine and sped away.

"Oh, my God." Her heart pounded and her breath came in gasps. "That guy could have killed me."

"Are you hurt?" His hands shook as he loosened his tight hold and turned her to face him.

"Thanks to you, I'm not." She glanced down at the ragged hem of her wool coat. "My coat was the only casualty."

"Bastard." Rory stared up the street, but the SUV had turned the corner and disappeared.

She clung to his arm, afraid her wobbling legs wouldn't hold her upright. "Do you think the driver did that on purpose?"

"I wouldn't bet against it." He met her gaze. "Are you sure you're okay?"

"Just a little shaky. Thank you. If you hadn't—"

"Don't think about it. I'm pissed I couldn't see the person behind the wheel. Those damn smoked windows obscured my view completely, and I was too focused on you to get a plate number before he disappeared."

"Maybe the driver was a she. What kind of car does Kat own?"

"I've no idea, but I'll find out. Can you walk? The light is changing again."

"Yeah. I just needed a moment."

He slid an arm around her waist as they crossed the street, and a few minutes later, they reached the museum. His gaze was worried as he finally released her. "I can stick around while you work."

"I'll be fine. The place is full of visitors on Saturdays, and I'll tell security not to let anyone into the basement without checking with me first. I won't be alone."

"I'll walk in with you, just to be on the safe side."

"Here comes Lydia." She let out a long breath. "No one will accost me with her as a witness, not that I expect any trouble inside the museum."

"Except someone on the staff is undoubtedly working with the thief." His tone was hard.

"Well, it isn't my best friend. Give me a call as soon as you know anything."

"I will." He smiled at Lydia as she approached, her eyes widening at the sight of him, then turned to rest both hands on her shoulders. "Don't go anywhere alone. Promise me."

"I won't. Bye, Rory."

He walked away, and all her bravado went with him. When it came to Rory, her emotions were so tied up in knots, she didn't think she'd ever be able to untangle them.

Lydia stopped in front of her. "Was that your ex-fiancé, or do I need to have my vision checked?"

"It was Rory." She turned and trudged up the shallow steps to the big front doors. Pulling her keys from her coat pocket, she unlocked them. "We're both early this morning."

"That's all you have to say? After what he did to you, why are you talking to Rory?"

She opened her mouth . . . and then shut it. Explaining about the painting wasn't something she was prepared to do, even though she trusted Lydia completely. "He's in town for work and called me. We had breakfast."

"You aren't getting back together with him, are you?"

"No. I mean, I don't think so. No. No, I'm not." She stuttered to a stop while Lydia gave her a long, discerning look.

"Did you sleep with him?"

She shook her head. "No way." At least she could answer that one with conviction.

Her friend waited while she relocked the door, then walked beside her as they passed the gift shop where Francine was already busy restocking shelves. They headed down the west wing toward the kitchen. "Sounds like you wanted to."

"Maybe, but I didn't."

"I'm here to support you no matter what. Even if you make a boneheaded move."

Her lips curved in a smile. "I appreciate that, but I'm trying my best to be smart."

"I imagine it would be easier if he wasn't so good looking. The man is extremely hot."

Annalise sighed. "You're right about that." She stopped at the top of the stairs to her subterranean lair and touched the knob. It turned beneath her hand. "Why's the basement unlocked?"

Oscar strolled out of the security office and gave them a tired smiled. "'Morning, Annalise. 'Morning, Lydia. I opened it to get some supplies for Francine. I figured you'd be along shortly so I didn't relock it."

"Oh." Her brows lifted. "Shouldn't you be off duty by now? You look beat."

"My relief is running late, so I stayed. He had a flat."

"How's your wife doing, Oscar?" Lydia headed over to the refrigerator to put her lunch inside.

"Exhausted from the chemo, but her numbers are good. She's kicking cancer's butt."

"That's great news." Annalise gave him a high-five. "Well, I have work to do. I'll see you both later."

Lydia's eyes narrowed as she shut the refrigerator door. "Definitely. We'll talk."

With a nod, Annalise pushed open the door, flipped on the light, and headed down the stairs. She didn't need a lecture on how stupid she'd be to cave in and sleep with Rory. She knew better than anyone how devastating it would be to walk away from him again.

Unless you forgive him.

The little voice in her head was hard to ignore. Could she find a way to trust him moving forward? Could she get beyond his lies?

As much as she might wish otherwise, love alone wasn't enough to build a solid future, and she did love him. She'd never stopped. But acknowledging her feelings and doing something about them were two entirely different things, and right now wasn't the time to make any big decisions. Not when she was so stressed out about the missing Pissarro.

She was hard at work, carefully removing the top layer of paint from what was turning out to be a beautiful Oakley painting of the signing of the Declaration of Independence when Rory called. Pulling off her latex gloves, she swiped to connect. "What's the news?"

"Kat is at her D.C. office, working this weekend. Her assistant said she was busy and has a pretty full schedule. I claimed to be an old friend in town for the day, who was hoping to take her out for drinks. The assistant said Kat's attending a charity event this evening at seven so probably wouldn't have time since she has a client meeting at five."

"That means she'll go straight home to get ready."

"Yep. I'll make sure I'm waiting in her apartment when she gets there." He paused. "I can't imagine our talk will take long, so I expect I'll be back by nine or so this evening."

"In that case, I'll invite myself over to Lydia's for dinner. She wants to grill me about why I'm spending time with you, so she'll be thrilled."

"Do you plan to tell her about the painting?"

"I'd rather not. The fewer people who know the

one currently hanging in the gallery is a fake, the better."

"Good decision. She'd probably confide in her boyfriend—"

"Fiancé. She and Sebastian got engaged."

"That's great. He's a good dude, but a real straight arrow. What if he convinced her the right decision is reporting the theft to your boss?"

"She wouldn't blindside me, but I'd rather not put her in an awkward position. It's easier to let her think I couldn't resist seeing you again."

"I wish," he muttered. When she didn't comment, he continued, "Are you sure you don't want me to call Nash?"

"Positive. If you'll be late getting back, I'll sleep on Lydia's couch. After that SUV nearly ran me down this morning, I don't want to take any chances."

"I don't want you to, either. If that was another warning, they're not playing around." He sounded frustrated as he let out a harsh breath. "I'll leave food for Maizie before I take off."

"Okay. Good luck, Rory."

"I'll pick you up this evening. Talk to you later."

She disconnected and laid her phone on the table before pulling her gloves back on with hands that shook slightly. Maybe Kat would tell him who had the painting, and this would all be over soon. She sure hoped so.

At noon, she cleaned up most of her mess and left the basement. No one was in the security booth, which was odd, but maybe they'd had a situation somewhere else in the building. With a shrug, she went in search of Lydia. As she walked past the gift shop, Callen waved a hand and beckoned her over. She waited until he finished helping his customer to approach.

"How're you feeling?"

"Fine." He picked up his soda and walked out to meet her, swirling the ice in the cup. "Maybe whatever flattened me was some sort of twenty-four-hour bug, after all." He nodded toward his boss, who glanced in their direction as she rang up a purchase. "Francine was pretty understanding about my no-show. At least I didn't lose my job."

"It wasn't your fault. It's not like you went on an all-night bender."

"Sure felt like I did."

"I'm just glad you recovered quickly." She glanced toward the stairs as a family with three kids, all talking at the tops of their voices, descended. "Have you seen Lydia around?"

"Her most recent tour ended about twenty minutes ago. I heard her say something about eating lunch in the garden before her next one since she only had time for a short break."

"I think I'll join her. Thanks, Callen." Turning, she bumped into someone, and flinched when a hand gripped her arm.

"Steady, there. How's the restoration on the Oakley painting coming along?"

She glanced up as her boss released her and stepped back. "Better than I expected. Removing the top layer of paint is a slow process, but I think the finished product will be exceptional."

"That's good news." Marcus checked his watch. "I have an appointment, but I'll check in with you later."

As he strode away, Callen touched her shoulder.

"Maybe we can go out after work sometime soon." His tone was hesitant.

She should simply turn him down, but she didn't have the heart to do it. Instead, she waffled. "I've been working late most nights. I seem to have a lot on my plate right now."

"Let me know when you're free."

She offered a quick smile. "I'll do that. See you later, Callen."

Dodging tourists and displays of antique weapons, she headed through the east wing, wishing she'd packed a lunch, but she'd been in a hurry this morning. Her stomach growled as she pushed open the door into the walled garden.

"Lydia?" When her friend didn't respond, she walked along the path lined with shrubs. A bird chirped nearby then stopped abruptly, leaving nothing but silence.

"Well, damn." Apparently her friend had finished her lunch and gone back to work.

When a door shut softly, a chill shivered through her. "Lydia?" Turning, she headed back the way she'd come.

No one was in sight. As she reached for the door handle, a flicker of movement to her right caught her eye. Before she could turn or call out, pain exploded in her head, and her legs crumpled as fell forward into blackness . . .

Chapter Seventeen

Rory locked Annalise's apartment door and was heading down the stairs when his cell rang. Her name popped up on the screen, and he swiped to connect. "What's up, love, uh, I mean Annalise?"

"Rory? This is Lydia." Her voice trembled slightly. "Annalise asked me to call you."

He froze with one hand clutching the smooth, oak railing. "What's wrong? Is she okay?"

"She has a big lump on her head and is a little disoriented. They're taking her to the ER at Jefferson University Hospital on 11th Street to get checked out. The EMTs said she probably has a concussion." She sounded close to tears. "I wanted to go with her, but I have a huge tour group scheduled in a few minutes."

"I'll meet her at the hospital and take care of her. Thanks for calling me."

"I'm giving Annalise her phone back. The ambulance is leaving with her now. Bye, Rory."

He disconnected and ran the rest of the way down the stairs, through the lobby, and out to the street.

Sprinting the two blocks to where he'd parked his car, he jumped in and pulled out in front of the driver of an old Chevy who slammed on the brakes and blasted his horn. He didn't care in the least. His only goal was to reach Annalise.

Traffic was brutal, and it took fifteen minutes to get to the parking garage near the hospital and another few minutes to reach the admitting desk at the ER. Waiting in line behind a guy who was dripping blood all over the floor from a serious gash in his arm, he was pretty sure he was going to lose it.

"Can I help you, sir?" An older woman waved a hand as a young mother with a toddler went back to the waiting area. Bloody guy approached her, and Rory stepped to the front of the line.

Finally, a pretty brunette finished with the elderly couple she was helping and beckoned to him. "What can I do for you, sir?"

Rory planted his hands on the counter and leaned forward. "My fiancé was brought in by ambulance with a concussion a short time ago. Her name is Annalise Quintrell. Can I go back to see her?"

"Let me check her status."

She tapped her computer keyboard and frowned. "It looks like she's still being examined. Are you her ride home once the doctor releases her?"

"Yes, but I want to go see her now. Please." He offered his most charming smile. "Have a heart. She got hit over the head. I'm freaking out here."

"Yeah, there's a note the police want to talk to her." Her eyes softened when he steepled his hands beneath his chin. "Fine. She's in cubicle eight. I'll buzz you back, but don't get in the way."

"I won't. Thank you."

He headed to his right and pushed the door open as soon as the buzzer sounded. Dodging a nurse and an orderly, he approached cubicle eight and tweaked the curtain to peek inside. Annalise sat propped up on the bed while a woman in a white coat shined a light in her eyes.

"Can I come in?"

She blinked, and some of the stiffness in the set of her shoulders relaxed. "Rory." Her voice cracked.

He pushed aside the curtain, shut it behind him, and hurried to the side of the bed opposite the doctor. Taking her hand, he brought it to his lips and kissed it. "How're you doing?"

"My head hurts. Someone hit me."

The doctor lowered the light. "She sustained a concussion, and there's a cut on the back of her head. We dressed it and gave her meds for the pain." Assessing eyes narrowed behind her glasses. "I noticed fading bruises on her neck, as well."

"I got mugged a few days ago." Annalise's lips trembled. "The universe is out to get me."

"At least the man didn't stab you." The doctor refocused on Rory. "Keep an eye on her for the next couple of days to make sure she doesn't have any unusual dizziness or nausea. If she loses consciousness, bring her in immediately, but I don't really expect any problems other than a tender head until that laceration heals."

"A concussion is bad enough." He tightened his hold on her hand. "I nearly had a heart attack when Lydia called me."

"It happened so fast, I didn't even have time to be

afraid." Annalise winced as she shifted against the pillow. "When can I leave, Doctor Gupta?"

The ER doc pushed her glasses up her nose with her index finger and rose to her feet. "As soon as the CT scan results come back, I'll release you. You were lucky I was able to get you in there as fast as I did. Provided we don't find any unexpected complications. It shouldn't be much longer."

"Thank you."

"You're welcome." She glanced up to meet Rory's gaze. "Take good care of her."

"I definitely will."

After the doctor left, he turned to face her and gripped both her hands. "What the hell happened?"

"There's a little walled garden behind the museum. Callen told me Lydia was eating lunch outside, so I went to find her and invite myself to dinner. Except no one was around. When I heard the door into the museum open, I walked back down the path. Someone came out of the shrubs and hit me."

"Did you see the person?"

She shook her head then winced. "Ouch, that doesn't feel great. I hope those pain meds kick in soon."

"Why don't you just close your eyes and relax."

"I'm fine. I want to go through what happened step by step so I can give the police a coherent account. I was kind of out of it earlier and didn't talk to them."

"The woman at the desk mentioned they're waiting to see you once you're released."

"So I gathered. Anyway, the creep came at me from behind, and I didn't have time to turn around. I must have been out cold for a minute or two because Lydia discovered me passed out and called 9-1-1."

"So, she was in the garden, after all?"

"No, she'd gone inside, and I must have missed seeing her since there were a lot of people milling around the medieval exhibit. When Callen told her I was looking for her, she returned to the garden, and that's when she found me."

"Was the person who hit you still there?"

"I'm not sure. The police arrived while the EMTs were loading me onto the stretcher. Lydia told the officer she saw movement near the back wall, but she was on her knees, focused on me, and didn't see anyone clearly."

He tightened his hold on her hands. "The guy who hit you probably heard her coming, bolted, and climbed over the wall."

"That's what one of the cops said."

"They'll want to know if you were targeted for a reason."

"I intend to tell them I have no idea why I was attacked."

"Are there security cameras in the garden?"

"I think so." She closed her eyes for a moment, looking completely wiped out. "I'm sure the police checked them."

"We can ask when they talk to you." He glanced up as a nurse in blue scrubs pushed back the curtain.

She smiled as Annalise opened her eyes. "The CT scan was normal so you're all set to go as soon as you sign these forms. I highlighted the spots." She gave Rory a quick glance as she handed Annalise a clipboard. "You're her ride?"

"Yes."

"Great." Taking the paperwork from her when she

finished, she stepped back as an orderly arrived with a wheelchair. "There's an officer in the lobby waiting to take your statement. I hope your head feels better soon."

"Thank you. So do I."

Rory helped her down from the bed, and she sank onto the seat of the wheelchair with a grimace. "I've got your phone." He picked it up off the bedside tray and slid it into his pocket. "Can I push her out?"

"Sure." The nurse pointed. Head straight down that hallway. The door at the end opens into the main lobby." She nodded toward the big man who'd brought the wheelchair. "Jerome will wait with Ms. Quintrell while you bring your car around."

"Okay, thanks." He grabbed the chair handles and turned it around in the tight space. "Lead the way, Jerome."

In the lobby, an officer approached them as they moved toward the doors. "Ms. Quintrell, I'd like to take your statement now, if you're feeling up to it."

"Of course, although I didn't see the person who hit me."

Rory leaned down. "Shall I wait with you or go get the car?"

She glanced up, her gaze much more direct. "I can handle this."

With a nod, he left her with the orderly and the cop. At least she'd be safe until he returned. By the time he'd retrieved his Porsche, paid the exorbitant fee to exit the garage, and double parked on the street, Jerome had pushed her across the sidewalk to the passenger side of the car. After settling onto the seat, she thanked the man, and Rory eased back into the stream of traffic.

"How'd it go with the officer?"

"I told him what happened, assured him I didn't know why, and asked if there was security footage. He said the angle of the cameras only caught a rear view of a man in saggy jeans and a hoodie sweatshirt with no identifiable features. He also admitted the chances of finding the guy were minimal without a description. Can we go back to the museum before we go home? I left my purse in my workroom. Thankfully, I was able to access my insurance info from my phone."

"Sure. Why don't you call Lydia and ask her to bring your purse outside?" He reached in his pocket and pulled out her phone.

She took it and tapped the screen. "Geez, I have a bunch of texts. Marcus told me to take the rest of the day off and let him know if I wouldn't be back to work on Tuesday."

"Good of him." His tone was filled with sarcasm.

"God forbid I take a long weekend." She tapped the screen again and waited. "It's going to voicemail. Lydia must still be on her tour. I'll—oh, I thought I missed you. Yeah, I'll survive. My head still hurts, but the pain meds are helping." She listened for a few moments. "I promise to take it easy. Hey, can you ask security to bring me my purse and coat. We'll be out front in a couple of minutes, and there won't be anywhere to park." Another pause. "Thanks. I'll let you know how I'm doing. Bye, Lydia."

Rory stopped at a light and glanced over. "You sound a lot better."

"They gave me good drugs." She gently touched the white bandage, mostly covered by her hair. "I begged them not to shave off any hair."

He smiled. "Did they listen?"

"Yep. Everyone was very nice." Cautiously, she turning her head. "Lydia's still in the middle of a tour, but she said she'd send someone for my things."

"Good. I just want to get you home."

"What about talking to Kat?"

"To hell with that. Right now, you're all that matters." He pulled up in a no parking zone in front of the museum, and a few seconds later a guy in a security uniform came out."

Annalise rolled down her window and took the purse and coat he handed her. "Thanks, JR. I didn't realize you were working the day shift."

"Getting some overtime while one of the guys is out sick." His eyes narrowed on Rory before he stepped back from the car. "You okay?"

"Still a little shaky, but I'll recover. Oh, I left the basement open. Can you—"

"I already locked up." He nodded abruptly. "I gotta get back to work. See you, Annalise."

"Sure. Thank you."

He didn't respond, just turned and headed into the museum.

"That dude seems to have a stick up his ass." Rory flipped on his blinker and pulled away from the curb.

"After you and I broke up, JR asked me out. I turned him down. It's been a little awkward ever since."

Rory rolled his eyes. "Do you work with any single guys who don't want to date you?"

"Marcus is single. He doesn't seem interested."

"Maybe he's gay."

Annalise laughed and then held her head. "Oh,

wow, don't do that."

He turned when he reached the corner and then stopped at another red light. "I'm wondering what the guy who hit you hoped to accomplish. Let's assume it was the same asshole who grabbed you on the street. He already gave you one warning."

"Maybe he would have stuck a knife between my ribs to finish the job if Lydia hadn't come outside again." She shuddered. "I don't feel like this guy is going to give up until we stop him. I can rest in the car. Let's drive to D.C. the way you'd planned. You need to confront Kat."

He glanced over as the light changed. "Are you sure you're up to it?"

"It's not like I'll be doing anything but sitting. If I'm totally beat, we can spend the night at Nash's apartment. He can ask the manager to let us in."

"Fine, but I don't need the manager to get in."

"Of course you don't." Her tone held more than a touch of irony. "Whatever was I thinking?"

His lips quirked upward in a smile. "Did you forget how clever I am?"

"Apparently."

"All right, we'll go to D.C., but first, we'll stop by your place to get what we need for the night. Did the doctor order a prescription to pick up before we leave town?"

"No. She told me over the counter pain meds should be enough."

"Right, then let's do this."

A half hour later, they'd quickly packed overnight bags and his laptop, left a disgruntled Maizie, and were on the interstate headed toward the nation's capital. It was pushing three o'clock, and Rory was praying traffic wouldn't keep him from reaching Kat's home before she got off work. Next to him, Annalise was quiet. His grip tightened on the steering wheel. He wanted to kill the guy who'd hurt her.

"I don't like the idea of you sitting in the car alone while I deal with Kat."

"Why not? She lives in a safe neighborhood. I'll be fine." She turned slightly to face him. "What are you going to say to her?"

"Honestly, I'm not sure, but this second attack on you changes everything. If my conversation with her doesn't go well, I intend to call my FBI contact and tell him the whole story. Let Special Agent Ferris pass along the information. Maybe the cops won't believe a word I have to say and will drag me in for questioning, but it'll take the heat off you."

"If there's even a shadow of a doubt in people's minds that I had something to do with the painting being stolen, I'll never work in my field again." Her tone was flat.

He met her gaze. "I'm aware, but it's better than you winding up dead."

"Then you need to do whatever it takes to get answers from Kat." She clenched her hands into fists. "Or let me come with you. I won't hesitate to hit the bitch."

"If I thought it would help, I'd get physical, too. But finesse will probably be more effective. I've got this, love."

"I hope so."

They reached Kat's Logan Circle neighborhood a little after five, and Rory parked on the street a block from her home. Turning, he touched Annalise's arm. "How're you feeling?"

"Fine. No dizziness or nausea. Just a bit of a headache. I'll call Nash while you're inside and ask if we can stay at his apartment tonight." She grimaced. "We could get hotel rooms, but since I might not have a job if this doesn't go well, why spend the money?"

"That's not going to happen. I promise." He opened the door and got out. "I'd better get moving, just in case Kat leaves work early. If you have any problems, call me."

"Sure. Go kick some butt, Rory."

He smiled. "You bet."

Shutting the car door, he jogged across the street and hurried up the sidewalk, keeping his head down and the ballcap he wore pulled low. Reaching her address, he climbed the steps, shielding his face from the doorbell camera with his hand. After covering the camera lens with a round piece of adhesive, he pulled his picks and a small container of graphite powder from his jacket pocket, jimmied the lock, and was inside in under a minute. As the security alarm began to beep, he dusted the keypad on the control panel for prints. The one, two, three, and four buttons showed prints. Rolling his eyes, he touched them in order. The beeping continued. Apparently Kat wasn't a total idiot. He quickly reversed the order, and the sound stopped.

Something thumped behind him, and he whirled around, relaxing when an arthritic bulldog hobbled toward him. The old dog sniffed his ankles, and he bent to scratch his ears.

"Hey, I know you. How're you doing, buddy?"

Waldo had been Felix's dog. Apparently Kat had

inherited him after her father went to prison.

"Do you want to go outside?" He relocked the front door, then walked through the townhouse to the French doors off the dining room and opened them. Holding one door wide, he waited while Waldo wheezed and snorted as he maneuvered down the steps to the small, fenced yard in the back. "Take your time. I'll leave the door open for you."

While the dog did his thing, Rory took a quick tour of the house, checking the upstairs bedrooms and all the closets, just to make sure Kat didn't have the painting stashed somewhere in her home.

"That would have been too easy," he muttered as he returned to the main room just as a key turned in the lock. Stepping out of sight, he waited as Kat breezed into the house, paused, and then frowned at the control panel.

"Did I forget to set the damn thing again?" With a shrug, she slipped off her coat, hung it on the tree beside the door, and then kicked her heels into the corner. "Waldo? Where are you, boy?"

The dog's toenails clicked as he crossed the dining room floor.

"There you are." Squatting in her slim skirt, she patted the dog.

"Hello, Kat."

With a squeal, she toppled onto her butt as she tried to spin around. Reaching down, he grabbed her hand and pulled her to her feet.

Brown eyes narrowed beneath the wispy red bangs of her short, stylish hair as she stared at him. "What the hell are you doing here, Rory?"

"We need to talk." He pointed toward the couch.

"Have a seat."

"I don't have time. I have a fundraiser to go to. Get out now, or I'll call the police."

"You'd no more call the cops than Waldo, here, would bite me. If you don't want to be late for your event, make this easy on both of us and tell me who has the Pissarro."

"Honestly, I have no idea." She let out an irritated huff. "A payment was made from an account held by Joe Smith. I don't know if that's the client's real name, but I doubt it. We've never met."

"What about the payment for the second painting, the deal you cut Theo out of?"

Her eyes widened. "My cousin's been talking."

"He's pretty irritated with you, in case you didn't know."

"Oh, I'm aware." She dropped onto the couch. "I was compensated for that one with a very nice diamond and ruby necklace that I sold to a local jeweler. The necklace was delivered by mail to my office. I didn't need Theo's services, and I gave Archie his cut in cash."

"How'd you hook up with the buyer?" He stared down at her, hands fisted on his hips. "Neither of us is leaving here until I have some answers."

She rubbed Waldo's bristly back with her foot when he thumped down beside her legs and groaned. "Why are you involved in this, Rory? Annalise dumped you. I don't see why you care."

"You shouldn't have stolen a painting from her museum."

"Not my choice. I swear to God, I don't know any more about who has the paintings than you do. All I did was ask Theo where I could find Archie and then collect the payments."

"Someone with skills stole the damn paintings. You hired the thief."

"No, I didn't. Dad took care of that end."

Rory stood very still, anger heating his blood to the boiling point. "Felix is running this show from his prison cell?"

"I guess. When I visited him last summer, he told me to find Archie and set him up in the apartment over my uncle's business. He only needed me to do that much because Theo wouldn't have anything to do with him."

"Why would you get involved? You have a legit business, for Christ's sake. Why would you risk that?"

"Dad said there wasn't any risk since I wasn't doing anything illegal." She shrugged. "And I got a nice bonus to compensate me for my time. All I did was give Archie a couple of messages with the names of the paintings. Someone else picked up the finished pieces."

"Who?"

"I don't know. I never saw him. Look, I really need to get dressed for my event."

"Some asshole attacked Annalise. Twice. What do you know about that?"

Her eyes widened. "Nothing. I swear. You shouldn't have butted into my dad's business, Rory. I told him you were sneaking around Simon's house, and he was plenty angry."

"What's in this for Felix? He's not going to see a penny of the money for those paintings while he's in prison, and chances are he'll die in there before his sentence is up."

A frown creased her forehead. "I asked him that. He said he was doing a favor for an old friend."

"Tell your father to leave Annalise the hell alone. If you don't, this isn't going to go well for you."

She laughed. "Like he listens to anything I say. My dad does what he wants, and you aren't exactly his favorite person."

Rory gritted his teeth. "I can take everything I know to the cops."

"What good will that do? I'll deny we ever had this conversation. Theo isn't going to risk his career by admitting his part. My uncle told me Archie took off, and my dad certainly doesn't have anything to lose. You'll only make him more irate. Just walk away from this before you or Annalise really get hurt—or worse." She rose to her feet. "I'm finished with this conversation. You can let yourself out."

Rory stared after her as she ran up the stairs without a backward glance, and fear slithered down his spine. They were totally screwed.

Chapter Eighteen

Nash lived in an older apartment complex in Foggy Bottom, not too far from the Capitol. After walking through the small, central courtyard and up two flights of exterior stairs to his third-floor unit, Annalise's head was throbbing. She leaned against the wall while Rory picked the lock, swung open the door, and gave her an anxious look.

"You okay?"

"Tired, and I have a headache. I'll take some Tylenol in a minute." She flipped the light switch and preceded him into the large studio. "I don't know why my brother lives in this dump. He can afford something a lot better."

"Maybe because he's rarely home. This is a convenient place to land between jobs before he flies to some other war-torn corner of the world." He pushed the door shut with his foot and glanced around. "It's not bad if you don't need a lot of space. Not much personality."

"At least it's clean. Nash is my tidy brother." She headed straight to the worn, leather couch in the middle of the room, facing a large-screen TV, and flopped down. The furniture was solid and functional. No frills. A bike hung from ceiling hooks in one corner.

Rory set down their bags and walked over to the single picture hanging on an otherwise naked wall, a family portrait taken after Brielle had graduated from Harvard. "With all the amazing photos Nash has taken over the years, you'd think he'd put up a few more."

"Most have such a haunting quality, they'd be hard to look at and relax." She patted the cushion beside her. "Sit down and tell me what happened with Kat. You've been very grim since leaving her house."

He dropped onto the scarred leather and ran one hand through his hair. "She doesn't know any more than Theo did. Her father is the one who orchestrated the operation from his freaking prison cell."

"How is that even possible?"

"I guess the buyer is a friend of his, possibly someone he owed a favor. Felix recruited the thief. Or maybe the guy who stole the paintings is an associate of the buyer. Kat had nothing to do with him and didn't know."

"So Felix brought the buyer, the thief, and the forger together with a little help from Kat and Theo. They switched out two specific paintings, and intended to steal a third, when you confronted Archie."

"That's the short version. Archie skipped town. Probably left the country. Felix is fuming because I got involved. Terrorizing you is his way of telling me to back off. Kat swore she knew nothing about any of the attacks."

Annalise frowned. "That old criminal must be in direct contact with someone other than his daughter.

Either the buyer or the thief or the guy who hit me."

"That's true. Look, if you want, we can report the theft of the Pissarro to the police and tell them everything we know, but since we can't identify the other players involved, they'll probably believe I stole the painting. Kat and Theo will deny any involvement, and Archie's gone, so they won't be able to question him."

"Even if we go to the authorities, why would Felix drop his vendetta? He'd probably be even more determined to see that you pay for screwing up his plans."

"You're right." He rose to his feet and paced to the window overlooking the side street and back again, his lips pressed in a tight line. "Which means you can't go home. Not until we identify the guy who attacked you and make sure he's locked up. You're not safe."

"What do you suggest? I hide out indefinitely?" She straightened and frowned. "What about my job? I have to go to work on Tuesday."

"By then, hopefully we'll know more."

"I don't see how since we're out of suspects to question. Are you going to request an interview with Felix and ask him nicely to call off his thug?" She knew she sounded pissy but couldn't help it. The whole situation was spiraling out of control, and she wanted her damn life back.

"Maybe I'll sic you on him. Right now, you look mad enough to spit nails."

"Preferably straight into his skull."

They both smiled at the ridiculous image, and Annalise relaxed slightly.

"I was thinking more along the lines of hacking

into the prison's computer system and accessing their visitor and phone logs to see who Felix has spoken to in the last few months."

Her brows shot up. "You can do that?"

"If I can hack into an FBI database, I'm pretty sure a state penitentiary won't be much of a challenge."

"In that case, go for it. Seems like a better option than calling the police."

He nodded. "We can stay here while we're trying to determine who Felix has been in touch with. I assume no one you work with knows where your brother lives?"

"No. Well, Lydia knows he lives in D.C., but not his address. I don't think I've mentioned even that much to anyone else."

"What about personnel forms? Emergency contact, that sort of thing?"

"After we split up and I moved, I updated my file and used my parents as a contact."

"Then you should be safe here."

She hugged her arms across her chest. "Do you think someone who works at the museum hit me while I was in the garden?"

"Either that or a coworker saw you head out there and tipped off the asshole. He could have been waiting in the vicinity, intending to follow you when you left the building."

A shiver slid through her. "I was standing in the lobby near the gift shop when I told Callen I was going outside to find Lydia. Anyone nearby could have heard me."

"Security also has live camera footage of the entire museum. It would be difficult to pinpoint who made the call. Let's hope we can find a connection between an employee and the person Felix has been in contact with. Once we put all the pieces together, we can go to the police."

She let out a long breath. "I should eat something since I need to take a couple of Tylenol. You must be hungry, too."

"Starving. I'll order takeout. There are plenty of restaurants in the area to choose from. What're you in the mood for?"

"Maybe some soup. Nothing spicy. The headache is making my stomach a little queasy."

He walked behind the couch and squeezed her shoulder. "Then let's get some food into you. Do you want a glass of water to wash down the pills?"

"Please."

He headed into the kitchenette, filled a glass with water, and brought it back. "Here you go."

"Thanks." She took the water, shook a couple of tablets from the bottle she kept in her purse, and swallowed them. "I'm going to sit here and not move instead of going with you, if you don't mind."

"Not at all." He squatted beside her and stroked the side of her cheek. "I hate that you're hurting."

"The Tylenol will take the edge off, but I probably won't be great company this evening. I just want to go to sleep."

"Not until you eat something." He took the glass from her to set on the coffee table. "I'll be back shortly. Does Nash have a spare key?"

"Check the junk drawer in the kitchen. That's where we always keep them."

She closed her eyes while he pulled open a couple

of drawers. "Got it. I'll lock up and be back shortly."

"Okay." She opened her eyes. "Thanks for taking care of me. You've been great."

"I'll always be here for you, Annalise. Always."

He shut the door behind him and turned the key in the lock, making sure she was safe.

A few tears trickled out. The man was doing everything in his power to show her how much he cared, to show her she could trust him. Maybe he'd changed. Maybe she really could trust him to tell her the truth going forward. More than anything, she wanted to believe in him.

She must have fallen asleep because the sound of the door opening startled her awake. Pushing her hair out of her face, she eased upright from her slumped position as Rory walked into the apartment carrying two big bags.

"How're you doing?"

"Better. I slept for a little bit. My head doesn't hurt as much."

He set the bags on the counter. "I went grocery shopping while I waited for our order. Now we have food for breakfast."

"Smart." She rose to her feet. "What did you get?"

"Chicken and dumplings for you. The ultimate comfort food, and a little more filling than soup. I got a club sandwich and fries and a salad for me."

"It smells amazing. My stomach is growling."

"Have a seat. I'll put away the groceries, and we can eat."

A few minutes later, they were settled side-by-side on the bar stools at the counter. Annalise savored the delicate flavors of the chicken stew. "This is perfect.

Both my stomach and my head feel much better."

"Good. When you're done with that, you can take a shower and get some sleep while I do a little computer hacking."

She touched the back of her head. "My hair feels sticky."

"There's some blood in it. Hopefully Nash has first aid supplies. We'll need to replace the bandage on that wound."

"I'm sure he does." She rested her spoon in her bowl. "You must be tired, too. We've had a long day. Can't you look into Felix's activities tomorrow?"

"I'll put in a couple of hours and then crash on the couch. The sooner we have answers, the better."

"I feel bad. All I've done since the beginning is tag along while you do everything."

"Yet, you're the one Felix's righthand man is targeting. Which is why I want to nail this creep as soon as possible." He popped a fry into his mouth. "We're a team. We'll figure this out together."

"I hope so. By the way, where is Felix locked up?" She forced herself to keep eating, even though she'd lost her appetite.

"In Baltimore. His business was technically run out of Maryland, so that's where he was charged for most of his crimes."

"Easy driving distance for anyone in Philly to go see him."

"Definitely." He covered her hand where it lay on the counter. "Finish your meal so you can get some rest."

She ate most of her chicken and dumplings and then took a shower. The lump on her head didn't seem quite as prominent, and it felt good to wash her hair. After putting on pajama pants, a T-shirt, and her robe, she left the bathroom carrying a gauze pad, antibiotic ointment, and tape.

Rory glanced up from where he was stretched out on the couch, swung his feet to the floor, and set his laptop on the coffee table. "You look better."

"The shower felt great, but I need some help with the bandage."

"Come sit down."

She settled on the cushion next to him and turned her back. He lifted her hair and gently touched the wound.

"The cut is scabbing over already but let's cover it for tonight. They shaved a small area around the laceration, but your hair is plenty thick to cover the spot."

"So, I don't look like a total freak?" As he finished applying the bandage, she turned to face him.

"You look beautiful." He hooked a strand of hair behind her ear. "You'll always be beautiful to me, even when we're both old and wrinkled and gray."

"Rory." Her voice broke and she swallowed back a hard knot of burning tears.

"What's wrong, love?" He pulled her into his arms and cradled her against his chest. "Is your head still hurting a lot?"

"No. It's you. Us." She drew in a ragged breath. "I want what we had before I found out about all the lies. I want to be able to trust you with my heart, and I don't know if I can."

"I swear to God, I'll never tell you anything but the truth, even if it's something you don't want to hear. If we have a problem, we'll talk it out." He pulled back and looked straight into her eyes. "But right now you're way to vulnerable to be making important decisions. Get some sleep, and we can talk about this tomorrow." He hesitated for a moment. "If you want."

She stroked his rough cheek with her thumb and pressed a quick kiss to his lips. Before she could pull away, he deepened the contact, and she moaned low in her throat.

After a moment, he released her. "Sorry."

"Don't be. That was my fault." She forced herself to put some distance between them. "You're right, though. I'm not thinking very clearly right now. I'm going to bed."

"Good idea." His tone was deep and a little rough. "Sleep well."

She rose to her feet. "Don't stay up too late."

"I won't."

Annalise walked over to the alcove, dropped her robe, and slid beneath the covers, hoping Nash wouldn't mind that she was borrowing his bed. Rory had turned on a lamp near the couch and switched off the overhead light. She watched him for a while as he went back to work on his laptop, but she couldn't keep her eyes open . . .

A thump in the night woke her. She bolted upright in bed, heart pounding, and it took a moment to remember where she was. "Rory?"

"Yeah. Sorry. I smacked the coffee table returning from the bathroom."

The room was completely dark with only the faintest trace of light showing around the edges of the drawn blinds from the streetlights beyond the window.

"What time is it?"

"Late. Nearly two in the morning."

She felt more than saw him move as he approached the bed and stopped a couple of feet away.

"How does your head feel? It's been several hours since you took those pills."

"Actually, it doesn't hurt much at all." She frowned in the dark. "Have you been working all this time?"

"Yeah. I searched through online prison visitor logs until I couldn't see straight."

"That's crazy. You need to get some sleep."

"I will. Uh, can I use one of the pillows. The little ones on the couch feel like they're filled with cement."

"Of course." Reaching for the second pillow, she paused. "The couch isn't comfortable, either. The leather is cold and slippery." She took a breath and let it out slowly. "You can sleep in the bed, as long as you know it isn't an open invitation. I just want to go back to sleep."

"Deal." He slid under the covers before she could even scoot over, and pulled her close against his chest, spoon fashion.

"Rory." Her voice held a warning.

"We'll just cuddle. Nothing else." His face rested against her hair, and his voice rumbled in her ear. "Promise."

"I'm too tired to argue." Not that she really wanted to. The heat from his warm, bare chest encompassed her. Wrapped in his arms, she felt like she'd finally come home. "'Night, Rory," she whispered.

"'Night, Annalise." He pressed a kiss against the side of her neck. "I love you."

She didn't respond. Couldn't let herself say she

loved him, too. Not until she forgave him completely. And she still wasn't sure she could. His arms tightened, but he didn't say anything more, and finally she drifted back to sleep.

The room was gray with morning light when she slowly opened her eyes. She was curled against Rory's side with her cheek pillowed on his chest, much the way they'd always slept together. Tilting her head, she studied his face. Dark lashes fanned against his cheeks, and tension was etched in the lines that bracketed his firm lips, despite the fact he was still deeply asleep. He'd been through a lot in the last couple of years. Stress, self-reproach, and regret had left their marks.

She'd probably contributed more than a few of those lines. She saw them in her own face when she looked in the mirror. Heartbreak and bitterness carved deep. Maybe it was time to let go of the anger and disappointment, to absolve the hurt he'd caused. He'd owned up to his mistakes and never once downplayed her feelings. That alone said a lot about his character. That and the fact he'd turned his life upside down to help and protect her when she needed him the most. Didn't he deserve her trust? Hadn't he earned it?

"Those must be some pretty serious thoughts. Are you okay?" His voice was a little gruff as he raised a hand to stroke the side of her face.

She blinked and focused on his beautiful green eyes that reflected concern, caring, and a little bit of fear. "Sorry, I didn't realize you were awake. I was trying to get a few things straight in my mind."

"And did you?"

"Maybe. Let's compare my life to a treasured bowl, shattered into pieces around me. All my hopes and dreams lost in the chaos."

"The last thing I wanted was to break you." Tears glistened in his eyes, but he didn't bother to brush them away.

Her heart ached with the desire to comfort him, but she needed to express her feelings first. "I know that. Honestly, I do. What I also realized is that resenting the damage didn't fix the bowl or make me feel any better. If I want to be happy, I have to either glue together the pieces or find a new container for my dreams."

"Should I sweep up the mess I made and then send you shopping?" His tone was hollow.

"No, but you can buy me a bottle of super-strength adhesive. My passion is for taking beautiful things that have been damaged and putting in the hard work to make them shine again. A few cracks may remain, but I feel like we should try to fix what was once so special."

He cupped her chin in his hand. "Do you mean it, or will I wake up and realize I've been having one hell of an awesome fantasy?"

She couldn't help smiling. "I don't know? Does your fantasy end in morning sex?"

"Absolutely."

He pulled her up until she was stretched out on top of him and then gently threaded his fingers into her hair, being careful of her wound. His lips covered hers as he kissed her the way she'd been wanting him to, with an intensity that spoke of all they'd missed for the last two years.

"I love you, Annalise. I never stopped."

She touched his bristly cheek. "I love you, too, but this isn't a get-out-of-jail free card. This is a *let's see if we can build back trust and move forward* card."

"Totally fair. I'm simply ecstatic you're giving me a second chance."

"Then kiss me because I've really missed your kisses."

"Among other things, I hope."

He covered her lips with his, stroking his tongue into her mouth, making her want so much more. When he ran his hands up under her T-shirt, brushing the sides of her breasts with his thumbs, tingles shot straight to her core.

Finally, he pulled back enough to nuzzle her neck. "You're wearing way too many clothes."

"I definitely am."

He helped her shimmy out of her pajama pants and carefully pulled the shirt over her head. After rolling her onto her back, he jerked off his boxer shorts. "How's your head? I don't want to hurt you."

"It's fine." She wiggled beneath him as he stretched out over her. "I haven't felt this good in two long years."

"I guess that means I was a tough act to follow." He pressed his face between her breasts, his rough stubble scraping lightly.

"No one followed you, Rory. I didn't let any other man get close because I wasn't over you no matter how much I wanted to be."

"I won't pretend I'm not glad." He lifted his head and met her gaze. "I guess we both struggled to let go."

Then he was kissing her and touching her and giving her all the feels, all the butterflies. She returned the favor until they were both crazy with need.

"Please tell me you're still protected." His voice was a faint rasp beside her ear as he held perfectly still, his weight balanced above her.

"Yes." She dug her fingers into his back. "No more waiting."

"Thank God." He pressed home, his breath leaving him in a whoosh. "I'm in heaven."

She smiled against his neck as they moved together. Loving each other completely as she let go of the past and focused on the present. Never wanting this moment to end.

Chapter Nineteen

Rory glanced up from his computer and gave a little fist-pump. "Got you, asshole."

Annalise turned away from the sink, holding a sponge. "You found the person who visited Felix Lemmon?"

"He's had several visitors and received quite a few phone calls in the last three months. Kat and his ex-wife both visited, along with a few of his old friends. There were also some names I didn't recognize. No one visited more than once. I've been trying to connect phone calls to visitors. Again, no unusual activity to any one number."

"Felix is a careful man."

"He's a cagey bastard. I finally tracked two calls to burner phones that were purchased at the same store in Philly. The first was paid for in cash, but the second was bought with a credit card. Big mistake. The name on the card matches a visitor from last July. Brady Murphy."

Annalise dropped the sponge in the sink and

walked over to the couch, settling onto the cushion beside him. "You think Brady Murphy bought both burners?"

"I'd bet on it. Maybe he was in a hurry and didn't have cash on him the second time. He probably felt confident no one would ever check."

"I imagine a cautious guy like Felix would be furious at such carelessness."

Rory grinned. "Without a doubt. Anyway, Murphy made the first call shortly after you discovered the Pissarro was a fake and I showed up at your apartment. The second call happened the day you were attacked on the street." He started typing rapidly on his keyboard. "My guess is this bastard lives somewhere near the store where those burners were purchased. Let's see if I can find him on social media."

"Brady Murphy." Annalise frowned. "I feel like I've heard that name before."

"Yeah?" Rory met her gaze. "You've met this punk?"

"I'm not sure. Maybe someone just mentioned him, but I can't remember who."

"A person you work with?"

She hunched one shoulder. "Possibly. Or maybe it was someone I went to college with if the connection is in Philadelphia. Or I could be completely mistaken."

"The memory might come to you if you don't try to force it." He scrolled through social media accounts using Murphy's name and Philadelphia as key words. A few minutes later, he paused. "Does this guy look familiar?"

Annalise scooted over to stare at the screen as Rory enlarged the photo. A blond, twenty-something guy with a scruffy beard leaned against the door of a yellow car parked on a city street. The distinctive tower of Christ Church was just visible in the background.

"I can't see the whole car, but the guy who tried to follow us the morning we went to Chincoteague drove a yellow car."

"Yeah, a Saab. He could be that dude, although I didn't get a good look at his face when we were on the street. This profile picture is for a private account. There's more than one Brady Murphy in Philly, but none of the others seem to be likely candidates. I'd bet he's our thug."

"Excellent work. Now what do we do?"

"I'll dig some more to see if I can come up with any additional info on this guy. Like where he lives or works."

"In that case, I'll finish the breakfast dishes and throw the sheets into the washer while you do your thing." She rose to her feet. "Unless you want to spend another night here?"

"I think we should go back to Philly since that's where Murphy is bound to be. I want to get my hands on that guy pretty damn badly, but I won't risk taking you to your apartment. We can check into a hotel room."

"Do you really think that's necessary?"

"Absolutely." His fingers hovered over the keyboard. "Except if we register under either of our names, there's a chance Felix's associates could track us. I don't want this asshole anywhere near you."

"What if we book a vacation rental under a different name? No one is going to ask for ID when we arrive since those places usually have lockboxes with a key."

"You're right. I'll look for a house somewhere nice and safe out in the burbs while you're doing laundry." He glanced around the tiny apartment. "Except I don't think Nash has a washer and dryer."

"There's a laundry room on the first floor of the complex and a bag of quarters in his junk drawer. I'm all set."

He ran a finger down her arm and smiled when she shivered. "I guess it would be rude to leave those sheets on his bed after what we did . . . three times."

Her cheeks colored. "Very rude. It'll only take me a minute to toss them in the washer."

While she stripped the bed and carried the sheets downstairs, Rory found a vacation rental for a cottage near the college campus in Bryn Mawr, a short drive west of the city. Using a fake name to register, he cringed as he paid with his credit card, even though he didn't enter his name on the form. Chances were good Felix didn't have the ability to track his card, but Brady Murphy had probably thought the same thing.

When Annalise entered the apartment, he glanced up and smiled. "I rented what is described as a quaint cottage in Bryn Mawr for two nights. Let's hope that's enough time to nail this bastard."

"It better be because I have to be at work on Tuesday. Can we pick up Maizie before checking in?" I don't want to leave her alone for two more days.

"How about if I drop you off at the rental and then retrieve the cat. Actually, if Murphy is waiting for you to show up at your apartment, it'll save me the trouble of tracking him down. Going there might be a smart move."

Her forehead crinkled in a frown as she sat on the

arm of the couch. "What if he's armed? You aren't bulletproof any more than I am."

"I'll scout out the area before I go in, but I can handle that little shit if he tries to attack me the way he did you."

She stared at him for a moment, lips pressed in a tight line, but she didn't argue. "Do you think Murphy knows who the buyer is?"

"It makes sense. Someone hooked him up with Felix."

"And if the man isn't lying in wait outside my apartment? Then what?"

"I'll do some more digging online and try to track him down. We'll find this guy."

"I hope so." She rubbed her hands up and down the arms of the pink flannel shirt she wore over jeans. "I need to work. I'm already behind with my projects from taking half of yesterday off. My head doesn't hurt at all anymore so I could actually go in today."

"No way. Someone in the museum is working with this idiot. We're not taking any risks until we figure out who else is involved."

"Since I have enough new scrapes, bumps, and bruises, I'm on board with being cautious." She rose from the couch arm. "I'll let you get back to your online sleuthing while I call Nash to tell him we'll be leaving sometime today." Her lips tilted in a quick grin. "But I don't plan to mention why I washed his sheets."

"You're not going to tell your family we're back together?"

"No, because we aren't. We're working on it."

"We will be." His voice rang with conviction. "I won't blow it again."

"I hope not."

He decided not to press the issue, and instead, returned to his online research. As he dug deeper into Murphy's social media profiles, all of which were private, he was vaguely aware of Annalise talking on her phone, assuring her brother she wasn't in any kind of danger and didn't need him to come stay with her. A short time later, she ran downstairs and had just walked through the doorway when he finally hit paydirt.

"Check out this video."

Annalise sat beside him as he replayed the clip. A younger looking Murphy could be seen scaling the side of a building with ease, launching to a tree limb, and doing a flip to land lightly on his feet. Cheers sounded, and the guy recording the action spoke, "You're like a damn cat, Brady. We should call you Nine Lives." In the background, a second male laughed. "More like a cat burglar."

Annalise's brows shot up. "Did Murphy post that video on one of his pages?"

"No. His accounts are private. A guy named Charlie Lee tagged Murphy in the video, which was posted a few years ago. Our boy Brady has some serious ninja skills. My guess is he's not only the asshole who followed us and hit you, but also the thief who switched the paintings."

"Can you learn anything more about him through his buddy's account?"

"I'll see what I can discover. Are the sheets finished?"

"I put them in the dryer. Do you want to eat before we go?"

"We might as well since I bought lunchmeat. Or

we can make sandwiches and take them with us."

"Sounds good since I'm not hungry yet. You keep working, and I'll take care of packing lunch."

Before she could push up off the couch, he tugged her into his arms and kissed her, taking his time. Finally, he drew back and caressed her cheek with his thumb. "We always made a great team, and that hasn't changed. Together, we'll find the guy who hurt you, as well as the missing painting, and I'll damn sure make him pay."

She leaned into him, resting her cheek against his chest. "I know you will. You're stubbornly determined when you want something. I've always appreciated your perseverance."

"Which is why I would have showed up on your doorstep, even if you hadn't called me." He ran a finger down the side of her neck and smiled when she quivered. "I told myself I had to give you time to let go of your anger . . . and to miss me. I fully intended to have you back in my life whenever you were ready."

"I didn't think that day would ever come." She tilted her chin and met his gaze, a wealth of emotion laid bare in her beautiful eyes. "I'm glad I was wrong. I hope we can start a fresh chapter going forward." A frown puckered her brow. "Once we've put this current mess behind us."

"We will as soon as I get my hands on Brady Murphy."

She pressed a quick kiss to his lips before pulling away. "Then get back to tracking him down."

By the time Annalise had assembled sandwiches, packed up the other food he'd bought, and remade the bed, Rory had uncovered a few more clues. While he hadn't found a current address, Murphy was friends with a group of people who'd apparently grown up in the same affluent Philadelphia suburb. Possibly, the bastard still had connections there.

He shut his laptop. "Ready to hit the road?"

Annalise dropped her small suitcase next to the door beside the bag of food. "I'm all set."

"Let's get out of here." He stuffed his computer into his overnight bag and smiled at her. "Thanks for doing everything."

"I certainly didn't mind since you were busy and I was bored." She opened the door. "When you fetch Maizie, can you bring me my laptop? And a couple of books? And a few more clothes?" She grinned. "I'll make a list."

"I can handle that." Scooping up the bag of food, he flipped off the light and shut the door behind them, trying the knob to make sure it was secured. "After we get settled in the rental, maybe we can go for a run. Seems like forever since I've had any exercise."

She led the way down the stairs. "Excellent idea. I need to get back into some normal habits. The way we've been living has done nothing but raise my stress level and probably my blood pressure."

After unlocking his car, he popped the trunk and dropped their bags inside. "We'll keep the food up front and eat while we drive." As she opened the passenger door, he met her gaze over the roof of the car. "We're closing in on him. It won't be long now."

She gave him a smile that rocked his world. God, he loved this woman.

Once on the road, they deliberately avoided the topic of Brady Murphy and the forged painting, and instead, talked about everyday things. Her latest project at work and the book she was reading. Lydia's engagement, and how much she was looking forward to her friend's wedding in April. His business's increasingly prestigious portfolio of clients and his new addiction to Thai food. How he was ready to step away from the frenetic pace of Manhattan and live somewhere a little more laidback. He also wanted to take a relaxing, cross-country road trip to see a few of the National Parks.

"Who are you, my parents?" Annalise laughed out loud. "They've planned similar trips for their retirement. What about sailing? That was always your thing."

"After we split up, I didn't get out on the water as often as I used too." He met her gaze for a brief moment. "Too much time alone to think, to regret, to wish I'd made different choices. Instead, I filled my days with work so I wouldn't go crazy."

"Same. The museum was the only place where I felt in control. I missed you so much." She let out a sigh. "Anger isn't great company, and Maizie seemed to blame me for your absence. All I had to go home to was a pissed-off cat."

"Maizie knows what she wants." He reached over to squeeze her hand where it rested on her thigh. "So do I."

Two hours later, they'd just crossed the Pennsylvania state line when Annalise turned to face him. "It's ridiculous to leave me at the rental house, drive to my apartment, and then back to Bryn Mawr. We can cruise through my neighborhood to make sure Murphy isn't somewhere nearby. Once we're relatively sure it's safe,

I'll drop you off and go park. You can call when you're ready to be picked up."

He met her determined gaze before focusing on the traffic, which had slowed to a crawl. Apparently, there was an accident up ahead. "What if that asshole is waiting there? I don't want you anywhere near—"

"What do you think he's going to do, launch himself at my car door or take a potshot at me from the sidewalk? I won't go inside since you seem to think he might be lying in wait. Of course, if he is, you could probably use the backup."

"Not happening." He drummed his fingers on the steering wheel as they crept past a fender-bender blocking the slow lane and finally picked up speed. "Fine. I guess if you drop me off a few blocks from your apartment and then drive around for a while, you'll be safe enough. *If* there's no sign of his Saab."

"I still don't like the idea of you going one on one with that guy, especially if he's hunkered down, waiting for an opportunity to take us out."

"I don't plan to walk through the front door into an ambush. I intend to go through your bedroom window. It'll be easy money to access it from the passageway between your building and the one next to it."

"I always keep that window locked and the shade drawn since the only view is of a brick wall. Plus, you'd have to scale the exterior wall to get to the second floor."

"I'll manage."

She was quiet as the traffic thinned. "Do you really expect him to be waiting in my apartment? If he hurt Maizie—"

"I'd bet on the cat if that freak tried to mess with

her." He offered a reassuring smile. "My guess is he's been checking your place off and on, but I don't imagine he set up camp there." When she opened her mouth, he continued, "However, I intend to be cautious, just in case."

"I suppose I'll have to live with that."

They didn't talk much during the rest of the drive, and when they exited the freeway and neared her neighborhood, Rory could feel Annalise tensing in the seat beside him.

"Hey, if this is upsetting you, I can come back—"

"I'm not worried about me. I'm worried about you."

"You don't need to be. I can handle myself." He circled the block a couple of times but didn't see any sign of the yellow Saab or Murphy lurking in a doorway. When he was convinced no one would follow her, he double parked, got out, and waited for her to walk around the car. "This shouldn't take too long. I've got your list." He patted his pocket.

"The cat carrier is in my bedroom closet."

He cupped the back of her head, being careful of her injury, and kissed her. "I'll be fine."

"You'd better be. Don't try to be a hero and do something stupid if that freak shows up."

"I won't. If you park somewhere, make sure there're plenty of people around."

"No back alleys." She rolled her eyes. "I'm not an idiot."

He grinned. "You definitely aren't. I'll see you shortly."

With a nod, she slid onto the driver's seat, shut the door, and drove away. Turning, he headed in the opposite direction, quickly walking the two blocks back to her street. When he reached the corner, he paused to take a long look around. No one sat in a nearby car, and the only pedestrians where a pair of women pushing strollers, an older man leaving a building with his dog, and a young woman texting on her phone who nearly walked into a lamppost.

Confident he wasn't being watched, he hurried down the sidewalk to the narrow passage next to Annalise's building and flipped up the latch to open the gate. Avoiding several garbage cans, he stopped beneath her bedroom window and stared upward. There were plenty of rough edges on the brick wall for finger and toeholds, and he should be able to grip the edge of the sill while he jimmied the old lock open with the thin blade on his pocket knife.

With quick movements, he scaled the wall, pulled his knife from his pocket, and had the window open a few seconds later. Hanging from the sill, he inched the window upward and paused to listen. When he didn't hear any movement inside, he slid it up far enough to crawl through the opening and cringed when it screeched.

"Dammit!"

Knowing anyone that wasn't completely deaf would have been alerted, he yanked on the shade to send it flying upward and levered himself over the sill. Landing in a slightly crouched position with the knife clutched in his hand, his gaze darted toward the open doorway.

When something shot out from under the bed and brushed against his ankles, he nearly had a heart attack. Maizie meowed and twined between his legs.

"Jesus." He let out a long breath. "I guess no one's here. I could have used the door."

Stepping around the cat, he crossed the room and froze in the doorway. Framed pictures had been pulled off the living room wall and dropped on the floor below. Glass littered the hardwood, glittering in the afternoon light streaming through the front window. A chill shivered down his spine. On the bare surface, red paint ran like trails of blood from big, block letters.

YOU CAN'T HIDE.

Chapter Twenty

Annalise checked her phone for the fifth time, wondering why Rory hadn't called her yet. It had been twenty minutes since she'd driven away. How long did it take to grab a few clothes and put Maizie in a carrier? Vivid images of him lying in a pool of blood, unable to reach his phone, while Brady Murphy stood over him, knife in hand, were freaking her out. After another minute passed, she couldn't stand it any longer. Tapping his number, she held her breath.

He answered on the second ring. "Hey, love. Sorry, it's taking me longer than I expected."

"Is Maizie resisting the carrier? She probably thinks you're taking her to the vet."

"I haven't got that far yet. Murphy was here. At least I assume it was him. He left a message."

The fine hair rose on her arms, and she shivered. "What did that freak do? Did he tear up my apartment?" She pressed a hand to her chest. "Please tell me he didn't hurt Maizie."

"She's fine. She hid under the bed like a smart cat

and didn't come out until I got here."

"Oh, thank God."

"There's not much damage. He broke the glass in the picture frames hanging in the living room, but that can be replaced. I swept up the pieces and am scrubbing the paint off the wall. It didn't have a chance to dry, so it's coming off pretty easily with soap and water." His tone more than his words revealed just how angry he was. "There may be a faint pink tinge left, but we can paint over it with the original cream color after the wall dries."

Tears threatened, and she blinked hard to keep them from falling. "What did he write?"

"You can't hide, which is bullshit. He's the one who won't be able to hide. I can't wait to punch this son of a bitch in the face before I hand him over to the police. After I find out who has the Pissarro."

It could have been worse. She pressed her fingers against her eyes and struggled to get her voice under control. "I'll help clean up. It'll only take a few minutes to get there."

"No, you won't because I've no idea when he'll come back, and I don't want you to run into him out on the sidewalk. Anyway, I'm almost finished. Give me fifteen more minutes, and I'll be ready and waiting for you to pick me up out front."

"Okay." She spoke quietly, holding back her rage, feeling violated because someone had defiled her home. "Thank you, Rory. Knowing he was in my personal space is bad enough, but at least I won't have the memory of his evilness etched on my mind."

"I didn't want that, either. I'll see you in a few minutes."

She disconnected, set her phone on the seat beside her, and then covered her face with her hands, letting the sobs come. If it wasn't for Rory . . .

Everything he did showed her just how much he loved her. She'd been a fool for not giving him a second chance sooner. Clearly, he wasn't the only one who'd made mistakes. She'd been so busy feeling betrayed, she hadn't realized she was hurting herself with her bitterness.

The minutes ticked by slowly, and she was close to screaming before it was finally time to turn on the engine and go pick up Rory. She was stopped at a light a few blocks from her street when the yellow Saab that had followed them before drove through the intersection. The man at the wheel turned to stare, and their gazes locked for a brief moment before he continued down the street.

Her hand shook as she fumbled for her phone and tapped the screen to call Rory. When the light turned, she made a left, three cars back from the Saab.

"I'm on my way downstairs. Where are you?"

"A couple of minutes away. Brady Murphy just drove by, headed toward my apartment. He saw me. I'm following him."

"Damn. I wonder what his plan is. I'm going to put Maizie back in the apartment and then go outside to wait in the passageway. If I can surprise that asshole and grab him, I will."

"I bet he'll take a detour to give me time to park and get into the apartment before he shows up. He won't know I recognized him."

"You're right." A door opened and shut again in the background. "Since I wasn't in the car with you, I wonder if that'll make him cocky or careful."

Her fingers tensed on the steering wheel as the Saab reached the next intersection and drove through. "He kept going straight instead of turning just now. If I follow him, he'll wonder why."

"I don't want you to tail him."

"What if he gets suspicious and doesn't return to my apartment? If I hang back far enough, maybe he won't notice and—"

"No." His tone was sharp. "Just come get me."

"Fine." She gritted her teeth as she reached the stop sign and flipped on her blinker. "Do you want me to park while we wait to see if he shows up?"

"What I really want is for you to be somewhere safe, but he'll know you aren't home if he doesn't see my Porsche . . ." His voice trailed off. "Yeah, go ahead and park, and we'll figure this out."

Before he'd finished speaking, she whipped into a spot the second a red compact pulled away from the curb. "I got lucky. I'm half a block away."

Rory stepped out onto the sidewalk in front of her building and waved. "I see you."

"I'll be right there." She disconnected and slid the phone into her pocket. After locking the car, she hurried toward him. "Now what?"

Encircling her waist, he dropped a kiss on her upturned lips. "Can you go hang out with your neighbor?"

"If someone's home, I'm sure they wouldn't mind." She followed him into the lobby and paused at the bottom of the stairs.

"The girl who feeds Maizie when you're gone is there. She was going in when I was coming out. What are you going to tell her?"

"I'll make something up. Are you planning to wait for Murphy outside or in my apartment?"

"Inside is probably best since I'm not sure how he intends to gain access. He might use the window. I suspect that's how he got in earlier. Other than squeaking, it slid up easier than I expected, which probably means it was pushed up recently."

She glanced over her shoulder as she hurried up the stairs. "Not by me. I haven't opened it since I burned a batch of cookies at least six months ago and was trying to air out the place. It was pretty stiff, if I recall."

"Murphy will be in for a surprise if he does show up." Rory practically growled the words.

Pulling her keys from her pocket, she unlocked the door and pushed it open. When Maizie yowled from her carrier, she picked it up and stared at the living room wall. Faint pink streaks marred the cream paint.

"What does he hope to accomplish by harassing me?" Her voice quavered slightly. "I don't get it."

"Clearly, their warnings haven't worked. We aren't giving up. Kat probably told her dad about our little chat. My guess is he wants to get to me through you. If they shut us both up, everyone involved walks away in the clear. Right now, we're the only threat to their success."

She poked her fingers through the carrier door to stroke Maizie's soft head. "When you put it like that, we seem like idiots to keep what we know to ourselves."

"Maybe, but I bet we're a whole lot smarter than Brady Murphy, and we still don't know who has the Pissarro. I don't want to go to the cops without it." He pressed a hand to the small of her back. "Head next door. That bastard should be here shortly, and I want to be ready for him."

"Be careful, Rory."

"I will." He cupped her chin in his palm and kissed her. "Go."

Carrying Maizie, she crossed the hallway and knocked on her neighbor's door. Serenity, the fourteen-year-old who took care of her cat, opened it, her deep brown eyes widening in surprise before she smiled.

"Hi, Annalise. My mom is at the store if you're looking for her." Her gaze dropped to the carrier. "Or do you need me to watch Maizie?"

"Actually, I'm planning to take her with me, but this weird guy keeps bugging me to go out with him. I told him no, but he's persistent. Can I wait in your apartment until I'm sure he's gone, just to be on the safe side?"

"Of course." She stepped back and waved her in. "You're not talking about the guy I've seen with you a few times. He was here earlier."

Annalise set down the carrier and ignored Maizie's plaintive howl. "No, that's Rory. This is a different guy."

"Wow, you have a stalker? That's kind of freaky."

"It definitely is." She walked to the front windows and stepped to the side to look down at the street. A chill shivered through her as the yellow Saab appeared at the corner and slowed before continuing on. She pulled out her phone and texted Rory. *Did you see him?*

Her phone beeped. *Yes. He's probably parking out of sight.*

Serenity walked over to stand beside her. "Why

don't you call the police if someone's bothering you?"

"Right now, I'd rather just avoid him. I plan to be away for a couple of days. Hopefully, he'll have given up by the time I get back."

"You can't be too careful. My friends and I try not to walk anywhere alone. It's safer that way."

"Smart girls. Your mom trained you well." She stepped farther back from the window as a man rounded the corner and walked with his head down and ballcap pulled low. Despite not being able to see his face, she was pretty sure it was Murphy.

"Is that the guy?" Serenity eyed the approaching man. "You stiffened."

"Your people-reading skills are excellent. Yes, it is. I didn't want to be alone in my apartment in case he gets pushy. Not that I expect trouble, but—"

"Better safe than sorry. That's what my mom always says."

"Exactly." When Murphy disappeared into the walkthrough between the buildings, she left the window. Unease curled through her as she imagined the creep confronting Rory. He knew how to handle himself, and Murphy was a thief, not a killer.

What if he's both?

She rubbed her hands up and down her arms as the thought preyed on her mind.

Rory was smart, competent, and determined. He'd be just fine. She couldn't let herself believe anything else.

* * * *

Rory turned up the music a little louder as Murphy entered the narrow passageway between the buildings. Since the window seemed to be his intended mode of entry, let the asshole think Annalise wouldn't hear the squeak as he raised it. Get his confidence soaring. That's when mistakes were made.

Standing flat against the wall next to the window, he waited as the man scrambled up the exterior and jimmied the window lock, all in under a minute. The guy was good, but then, Felix always hired the best. His skills were no real surprise.

As he slipped through the opening, quiet as a cat, Rory grabbed his wrist, jerked him off balance, and jammed his arm up behind his back at an angle guaranteed to cause pain. Murphy let out a yelp but didn't struggle when Rory wrenched harder.

"Let's talk, asshole."

"Shit, dude. You're gonna dislocate my arm."

"I will if you don't answer my questions. Who has the Pissarro you stole?"

"That would be telling, and Felix isn't the only one who'd be ticked off. You can break my arm, but I still won't talk."

Rory pulled his knife out of his pocket with his free hand, flipped open the blade, and held it against the guy's neck. "How about if I slit your throat, instead?"

He swallowed, and the blade nicked his skin. "You won't do it. You got arrested rather than let that security guard die. You don't have the balls."

"The guard didn't deserve to bleed out. You do. You messed with the woman I love." He pressed harder, and a rivulet of blood streamed down his neck.

"I could have killed her, but I didn't. Walk away from this, Cavanaugh. No one will ever realize that Pissarro is a forgery."

"Annalise figured it out. Archie might have incredible technical skill, but you can't fake emotion. There's a reason the original artist is so revered." He cut a little deeper. "Tell me who has the damn painting."

His breathing was harsh as he swallowed again. "I can't do that."

"Let's start with an easier question, then. Which employee helped you steal it? Someone turned the alarms off and switched them back on again. You didn't have enough time between security rounds to do everything yourself without inside cooperation."

"Damn, Cavanaugh. I can't tell you that, either. Kill me or let me go."

"The problem is, dead men don't talk. Torture seems like a better solution." He jerked on Murphy's arm until he yelped. "Let's see what your tolerance for pain is. Move it. I don't want to get blood on the bedroom floor."

Lowering the knife, Rory marched him out of the room. When his phone vibrated in his pocket, he loosened his grip for a split second. Murphy lunged against his hold and broke free with a howl of pain. Before Rory could grab him, the man sprinted to the door, threw it open, and raced toward the stairs. Running after him, Rory hit the staircase at full speed and was halfway down when his foot slipped. Throwing out his arms, he grabbed the railing and barely managed to keep from faceplanting against the treads, but the damage was done. Murphy reached the floor below and disappeared out the door onto the sidewalk.

"Shit." Dragging himself upright, he picked up the knife he'd dropped and headed back upstairs.

Annalise opened her neighbor's door a crack and

peered out. When she saw him, she stepped into the hall. "I heard a commotion. What happened?"

"The bastard got away."

"Are you okay?"

"The only thing hurt is my pride." He ran a hand through his hair. "Dammit. I was so close to getting answers."

"I'll grab Maizie and be right over."

He nodded. "Okay." Leaving the door open, he heard the murmur of voices in the other apartment before Annalise reappeared with the cat carrier. "I'll lock your bedroom window, and then we can go."

She followed him inside. "Do we still need to stay somewhere else tonight? What're the chances Murphy will come back after confronting you?"

"My guess is he'll bring reinforcements next time. We should probably stick to the original plan." Walking into the bedroom, he took a stack of sweatshirts off a shelf in the closet, removed the board, and jammed it in the window frame. "Now it won't open from the outside. Of course he could still come through the door since the lock isn't exactly state of the art."

"If he paints more nasty messages on my wall, we'll clean them off." She set the carrier on the bed, wrapped her arms around him from behind, and rested her cheek against his back. "What happened?"

Turning to take her in his arms, he tucked her head beneath his chin and simply held her for a moment. "I grabbed him when he came through the window, asked him who had the painting, and threatened to slit his throat. He wasn't talking. I figured if I cut off one of his fingers, he might be more cooperative."

"Rory!"

"I wasn't going to let him simply walk away." He heaved out a frustrated breath. "Anyway, once I put his hand on the chopping block, I figured he'd cave. I was marching him toward the kitchen when my phone buzzed. I lost my focus like a complete idiot, and he yanked out of my grip. The only positive is I think he did some major damage to his shoulder."

"He won't be scaling any walls if he dislocated his shoulder."

"Maybe not, but I didn't get the answers I wanted. Interestingly enough, Felix didn't seem to be his main concern. I got the feeling the buyer was the person motivating him to keep quiet. Either he's afraid of the person or extremely loyal."

"Well, I'm glad you weren't forced to play amateur butcher in my kitchen."

"I wasn't looking forward to it, but I would have done whatever was necessary." He released her. "Let's take off."

She picked up the cat carrier and a tote bag he'd packed earlier, while he grabbed the cat supplies and litter box. After locking up, they headed down the stairs and out onto the sidewalk.

"Who called you?"

"What?" He took the key fob from her and hit the remote when they reached the Porsche.

"You said someone called, which is what distracted you."

He squeezed everything into the trunk while she put Maizie's carrier on the passenger side floor. "I forgot all about that." Retrieving his phone from his pocket, he slid onto his seat. "I have a missed call from Theo."

Annalise frowned. "I wonder what he wants."

"Let's find out." He started the engine, pulled away from the curb, and then tapped the dash screen to return Theo's call.

His so-called friend picked up immediately. "I hear you're causing all sorts of trouble, Rory. I got a message from Felix."

"Oh? What did your uncle have to say?"

"That you'd better heed the warnings you've been given and go back to New York. He said you'll regret it if you don't."

"I thought you weren't talking to the old bastard."

"Someone left me a voicemail, but she didn't identify herself. She just said Felix is concerned and wanted me to pass along his message to you. She said it would be in everyone's best interests if I could get you to see reason. That was it."

"You don't know who the woman was?"

"I didn't recognize her voice, if that's what you mean. It definitely wasn't Kat, and she didn't sound like my aunt, Felix's ex-wife." He hesitated for a moment. "He had a couple of lady friends before the FBI busted him. Maybe one of them is still in touch with him. All I can say is you're pushing your luck, bro."

"Maybe I am, but you can tell Felix I'm not afraid of him or his minions." His voice rose. "I'll get that damn painting back if it's the last thing I do."

"Message received. Damn, Rory, you used to be so laid back. What happened?"

"I grew up." He disconnected and gripped the steering wheel so hard his knuckles turned white. "If they think they can intimidate me, they're wrong."

Annalise reached over and squeezed his thigh. "Don't let them get to you. I think they're worried we're close to finding the painting."

"That's because we are. Let's go check into the vacation rental and get Maizie out of her carrier. She doesn't seem too happy."

Grinning, Annalise wiggled her fingers through the grate to stroke her cat. "What gave it away, her growls or the fact that she's in there scratching the crap out of the walls?"

"She never was a big fan of the carrier. After we get settled, I want to check out the Penn Wynne neighborhood where Murphy grew up. Hopefully, we can find someone who'll tell us where he's living now." He scowled as traffic stalled and taillights flashed. "When I get my hands on that shithead, I'll do more than cut off a finger. I'll hack off his damn balls to get answers."

"Seems to me, Felix and company should be afraid of you instead of the other way around." Her tone was dry.

He finally smiled. "Okay, that may have been a bit dramatic. No way am I touching that dude's junk, but I *will* make him talk."

The sun was setting when they reached the rental house in Bryn Mawr, unloaded the car, and released Maizie from her prison. The cottage was small but quaint, with a well-kept, fenced yard and comfortable furnishings.

Annalise dropped her suitcase in the bedroom and stood with her hands on her hips, looking around. "Do you really want to question Murphy's old neighbors in the evening when they're probably busy making dinner? Wouldn't it be better to casually show up and talk to them outside in their yards during the day instead of knocking on doors?"

"You're right. Stupid plan." He shoved his fingers through his hair. "No one wants to open their door to strangers after dark. I'm just so damn anxious to get this situation resolved, I wasn't thinking straight."

"Tomorrow is soon enough." She walked over and slid her arms around his waist. "I can think of better things to do right now."

His whole body heated as he gazed into her eyes. "Yeah?"

She smiled back. "Absolutely."

He took her face in his hands and kissed her. "Excellent idea."

Chapter Twenty-One

"This is Indian Creek Drive, so we must be in the right neighborhood." Rory slowed the car to a crawl. "One of the recent photos in Charlie Lee's account was labeled the old Indian Creek gang."

Annalise eyed the large homes set deep on spacious lots, all with plush, green lawns and mature shrubs and trees. Clearly, the people who lived in this section of Penn Wynne were comfortably well-off, if not actually wealthy.

"He's the childhood friend who posted the video?"

"That's right."

"Do any of the homes look familiar?"

"That stone house over there with dormer windows and a big oak tree was in one of the throwback pictures. The tree is bigger now, and there aren't any bikes lying on the lawn."

"One of the boys in the group must have lived there." She pointed. "Since there's a car parked in the driveway, someone is probably home."

"Let's get out and walk around." He pulled to the

curb and turned off the engine. "I'd rather take your suggestion and find a person in their yard to talk to instead of knocking on doors."

"I'm sure we'll see someone. It's a beautiful fall day, even if the breeze is a little brisk."

They left the car and strolled side-by-side up the street. She nudged Rory with her elbow when she noticed a middle-aged woman on her hands and knees, digging in a circular flower bed around the base of a tree. A sack of bulbs sat next to her. Pulling one out, she placed it in the ground and covered it with dirt.

Glancing up, the woman caught sight of them and smiled. "Morning."

"Good morning." Annalise spoke in a cheerful tone. "Isn't it a lovely day? Your yard is beautiful with all the leaves turning colors."

"Thanks." She grimaced. "This time of year, the trees are gorgeous, but I miss having my sons at home to rake. Are you visiting someone in the neighborhood?"

Rory shook his head. "Actually, we're thinking about moving out of the city and have been checking out different suburbs. A guy I used to know grew up around here. He always said it was a great place for families, so we thought we'd check it out."

"It really is. My boys ran with a whole pack of kids back in the day. Do you have children?"

"Not yet." He looped an arm around her waist. "We're hoping to soon, though."

Annalise froze. Unable to speak, she swallowed against a hard knot of emotion. Is that what she wanted, to marry Rory, have kids, and buy a house outside Philly? Two years ago, she'd forced herself to stop thinking about what her future with him would look like. And even though he was spinning a story for the sake of getting answers, his voice was filled with sincerity.

"I'm sure you'd love it here, although I don't know if there are any homes for sale close by." The talkative lady pushed to her feet and bent side to side to stretch her back. "Who recommended our neighborhood? I might know him since I've lived here for what seems like forever."

"Brady Murphy." Rory's tone was the epitome of casual.

She took off one glove, pushed her glasses up her nose, and smiled broadly. "I do know Brady. He was friends with my boys. I think my oldest still sees him once in a while."

"Small world. I lost touch with him a few years ago. I tried to call when we moved to Philly, but his number had changed. Do his parents still live around here? Maybe they can give me current contact information for him."

"His father was never in the picture. Just his mother, a really hard-working woman, and an aunt who helped the family out. His mom cleaned houses in the area but didn't actually live here. However, she brought Brady to work with her during the summer, and he rode the bus after school with his friends and was part of the Indian Creek gang. That's what they used to call themselves."

"I guess he felt like this neighborhood was his home. It's too bad we won't be able to hook up. I couldn't find him on social media. That's usually how I track people down."

Tugging off her other glove and letting them both

drop to the ground, she slid her phone from the pocket of her dirt-stained pants. "Let me text my son. He probably has his address." She started tapping away on her cell. "It'd be a shame if you couldn't reconnect. I always liked Brady, even if he was a daredevil. I used to tell my boys they couldn't jump off someone's roof just because Brady did."

Rory laughed. "That sounds like the guy I knew. Thanks for checking."

"Sure."

Annalise stood silently by his side, feeling like an observer rather than a participant in this charade. It amazed her how easily Rory created a scenario that sounded completely believable. Uneasiness curled through her. Was he simply telling her what he knew she wanted to hear when he promised never to lie again? She gave herself a mental shake. He loved her. He wouldn't hurt her.

Their new friend glanced up from her phone. "My son says Brady lives on Johnston Street near Marconi Plaza in South Philly. I have a phone number for you."

Rory pulled out his cell. "That's great. Go ahead." He typed in the number as she read it off. "Thanks so much. It'll be great to catch up. I'll definitely give him a call."

"I'm glad I could help."

"We should probably let this nice woman get back to her gardening." Annalise finally spoke. "You've been wonderful, taking time out of your day for us."

"It was a pleasure. Enjoy your tour of the neighborhood. I hope you find the perfect house to buy."

"We'll definitely consider this area." He took Annalise's hand. "Have a great day."

"You, too."

As she knelt beside her flower bed, they strolled down the street, waiting until they were out of earshot to say anything.

Rory squeezed her fingers and grinned. "Well, that couldn't have gone much better. Thank God for trusting people."

"We only know the street, not Murphy's exact address. We can't exactly call him to ask."

"No, but I can easily hang out, wait for his Saab to show up, and then follow him."

Her brows rose. "I? Don't you mean we?"

They looped around the block and reached the Porsche a few minutes later. After popping the locks, he regarded her over the roof. "I don't want you with me when I confront that asshole, especially since I don't know what it'll take to make him talk."

"You're not really going to cut off his fingers." Her tone was flat. "That's not the sort of person you are."

They got into the car, and he leaned back against the seat to rub his eyes. "I don't know what else to do."

"If we locate his house or apartment or wherever it is he's living, why can't you bug the place or hack his computer or just grab his phone and run?" She frowned. "Surely he must be in contact with whoever has the painting."

"You're right. There has to be some sort of communication trail. I'd need access to his computer long enough to break any password protection and search through emails. Same goes for texts on his phone, if I can get my hands on it. Considering he's a thief by trade, he probably has a high-tech security system in place for his residence."

"Maybe not. The neighborhood he lives in isn't the best. Clearly, he isn't raking in the big bucks."

"Good point." He started the engine and made a U-turn to head toward the expressway. "Either his life of crime is just an occasional side gig, or he blows all his money. Maybe he has a gambling problem."

When Rory rolled up to a stop sign, she turned to face him. "Are we going back to the rental house or to look for Murphy?"

He gripped the wheel with both hands. "Every part of me wants to take you someplace safe."

"I don't need you to envelop me in bubble wrap. I'm not fragile. While I don't intend to court danger, a few minor risks won't kill me."

"What if they do?" When the car behind him honked, he stepped on the gas and turned left.

"This whole big, strong man protecting the feeble, little lady routine is beginning to bug me. I can take care of myself."

"I know you're a competent, intelligent woman. The problem is, I love you so damn much, I don't want you to get hurt again. This guy already gave you one concussion."

"Have you stopped to think I feel the same way about you? Yet, I don't complain when you put yourself in jeopardy. I know you'll make smart choices."

"I will, and you're right." He met her gaze. "Sorry for acting like a caveman. We'll go look for Murphy now. The sooner the better, before our chatty informant's son tips him off that someone was asking about him."

"Good point." She stared out the window as he

merged onto the expressway. "All I want is to find that man and learn who he's working for so you can steal back the Pissarro."

"Poetic justice. I can't wait."

It took twenty minutes to reach the South Philly neighborhood where Murphy lived. Neither of them said much after they exited the expressway and found Johnston Street.

"Murphy will recognize your Porsche if he sees it."

"You're right. We'll do a little reconnaissance to look for his car, but we definitely can't hang out in plain sight on his street."

They searched an eight-block section up from Marconi Plaza, a neighborhood of brick rowhouses, many with small, covered front porches. There was no sign of the Saab.

Annalise craned her neck, hoping for a flash of yellow, but didn't see anything. "He must not be home."

"Doesn't look like it." Rory drove back toward the main artery and parked on a cross street. "If he's coming off the expressway, we should spot him from here. I can run back to Johnston Street, stay out of sight while he parks, and see which unit he enters."

"I guess waiting is all we can do at this point." She settled in, sipping from the water bottle she'd brough with her. "Do you intend to break in while he's at home?"

"I'd love to get my hands on his phone, but those houses are small. I'd need eyes on the asshole to try such a risky move, and I can't watch him through a window unless I have cover. I'll probably have to wait until he goes out again and hope he leaves his computer at home."

"Sounds like we'll be here for a while. I hope Maizie doesn't get into trouble in our rental cottage."

"She isn't going to claw up the furniture, and maybe this won't take too long."

"Can I do something other than hanging out in the car? Act as lookout?" She hugged her arms across her chest, feeling chilled. "If he leaves and you go inside, you'll need to know if he returns."

"Let's see what happens." His tone was noncommittal. After a few minutes, he straightened and pointed. "Well, look at that. There's the bastard now. We couldn't have timed this any better."

A yellow car had exited the expressway and turned onto the main thoroughfare. As it drew closer, she identified Murphy's Saab.

"I want to see which street he turns on." Rory got out and stood in the shadows cast by the building as the Saab cruised by, then hurried up to the corner. A few seconds later, he gave her a thumbs up and sprinted down the street.

Annalise watched him in the rearview mirror as he reached Johnston and loitered near the building on the corner. After a minute, he crossed the street and disappeared from sight.

All she could do now was cross her fingers, hope for the best, and trust Rory. Worrying wouldn't help, but she'd do it anyway. Waiting was the hardest part.

* * * *

Murphy got out of the Saab and bounded up the steps to the door on the left side of the rowhouse duplex. Its neighbor to the right had an awning that sagged slightly over a porch where two plastic chairs sat on either side of a small, glass-topped table. Murphy's half had only a dark blue painted door with a window to the left of the stoop, nearly covered by an overgrown shrub planted in the dirt below. The blind was drawn down halfway.

Once he disappeared inside, Rory hurried down the block, keeping an eye out for anyone in the neighboring homes who might be watching the street. No one was outside, although there were a few cars parked next to the curb. He slowed his pace as a van drove by and then darted behind the prickly bush below Murphy's window. Wearing jeans and a dark gray jacket, he blended well enough with the foliage that a casual passerby wouldn't notice him pressed up against the side of the building where his face was on level with the bottom of the sill.

At least he hoped no one would notice him and call the cops to report a peeping Tom.

A light flashed on in the front room. Standing to the side of the glass pane, he was able to see Murphy moving around the living area. A laptop lay on the coffee table in front of the couch. Beside it was a black burner phone. Returning from the kitchen with a beer and a bag of chips, he dropped onto the cushion, picked up the remote, and pointed it at the TV.

Faintly through the wall, Rory heard what sounded like sports commentators talking. Maybe the Phillies had a day game today. If Murphy had settled in for the duration, he'd have no chance of grabbing either his phone or his laptop while the game was on.

The man pulled a second phone from his pocket and was texting rapidly while munching chips. Something on the TV made him glance up sharply as he reached for his drink. The can slipped from his hand, hit the table, and beer sprayed all over him. A stream of profanity followed as he leaped to his feet, stuffed his phone in his pocket, and pushed his computer and the burner out of the path of the foaming liquid. Still swearing, he ran to the kitchen and grabbed a wad of paper towels to mop up the mess.

Brushing ineffectually at the wet stains soaking his sweatshirt and jeans, he left the room and headed up the stairs. A few seconds later, the shower turned on and pipes creaked as the water heated. Rory couldn't believe his luck. He shot around the bush and ran up the steps. The door wasn't even locked.

Avoiding the wet spot, he dropped onto the couch, picked up the burner phone, and went to work. Greasy prints marred the surface, but four of the numbers were smeared more than the rest. It took him eight combos to open the phone. Recent calls included a number he recognized from the penitentiary where Felix was incarcerated. A second, local number that he'd called more than once was unfamiliar. Taking out his cell, he snapped a picture of the screen.

When the water turned off upstairs, he set down the burner and opened the laptop. "Come on. Come on," he muttered as it fired up. Using the same four-digit access code, he held his breath. If it didn't work—the lock screen opened. He pulled up Murphy's emails to scan the contents.

One titled *artist out of town indefinitely* caught his eye, and he clicked on it. After taking a photo of the message, he closed the email, exited the account, and shut the computer. Footsteps sounded overhead as he crossed the room. Cringing when the front door squeaked, he shut it softly behind him and was down the stairs and out on the sidewalk within seconds. Reaching the corner, he glanced back, but the door to Murphy's unit remained closed. A relieved breath slipped out as he headed toward the Porsche.

Annalise turned in her seat and regarded him with wide eyes as he slid behind the wheel. "That was pretty quick. What happened?"

"First, let's get out of here." Starting the engine, he pulled forward and turned onto the main street.

"You were able to get into his house?"

"Lucky for me he spilled beer all over himself and went upstairs to take a quick shower. I got a number off a burner phone that might be useful, along with an interesting email from his computer. I didn't have time to read it, but I took a picture." He handed her his cell. "The code to unlock the phone is your birthday. Check out the content of that email."

She gave him a long look before tapping in the numbers. "Murphy didn't see you?"

He shook his head. "If this doesn't give us the info we need about the buyer, I can always go back. As it is, he'll have no reason to warn the guy."

"And you didn't have to amputate any fingers during the process." She tapped the picture icon and read aloud as he merged into traffic on the expressway. "*Artist out of town indefinitely. I regret to inform you that the painting you requested has been placed on hold. When it's possible to fulfill your order, I'll be in touch.*"

"Sounds like our buddy Murphy was letting the buyer know Archie fled the country. Since he used his own email account, he worded it so he wouldn't incriminate himself if he got hacked."

"Why didn't he just call the buyer on the burner phone?"

"Maybe he couldn't reach him right away and followed up later. There was a recent call to Felix, plus several to another number with a Philly area code."

"The number on the second picture you took?"

"That's right. Who's the email addressed to?"

"Aesthete1962. No name."

Rory glanced over. "Isn't aesthete just a fancy way of saying art lover?"

"It is. The 1962 could be a birth year, but how is this going to help us?" Her tone sounded frustrated.

"When we get back to our rental house, I'll do a little digging. Maybe Aesthete1962 called Felix from the same number as the call made to Murphy. I can get into the prison logs again easily enough. I can also search through social media to see if anyone is using that handle." He reached over and patted her thigh. "Actually, I'm encouraged. We'll know who this guy is before the day is over."

"When you put it like that . . ." She covered his hand with her own and squeezed. "I feel a lot better."

"You said you need to be at work tomorrow. I'm trying to make sure that happens."

"Have I told you how much I appreciate everything you're doing for me?"

"Yes, but thanking me isn't necessary. Wouldn't you come to my aid if I was in trouble?"

"Of course. Even when I was so furious I couldn't look at you without feeling like my head would explode, I still would have jumped in with both feet to help you." She turned his hand over and threaded her fingers through his. "Because as much as I longed to hate you, I didn't. A lot of my anger was because I couldn't stop loving you, no matter how much I wanted to."

"Selfishly, I'm glad. It would have killed me if you'd found some other guy, one who was far more worthy of you than I can ever hope to be."

"Everyone makes mistakes. As long as we both learn from our errors, we'll be stronger going forward."

"I know I can trust you with the truth, no matter what." He spoke softly, wishing he could pull over and kiss her right now. But they'd be—if not home—back in their own private cottage soon enough.

"And I realized that being judgmental and holding a grudge only hurts me in the long run. I should have let you explain after the robbery. I should have been more understanding."

"After what I did, you put up protective walls. I don't blame you for that. I blame myself. All I want to do now is look to the future. The past is behind us."

"The last two years haven't been much fun. We have nowhere to go but up."

He gripped the steering wheel a little tighter. "What did you do with your engagement ring?"

She met his gaze briefly before staring out the windshield. "I was home in Wildwood a week after you were arrested, standing on the bank of the James. I was going to throw it into the river, but Lincoln stopped me."

He took his attention off the road to stare at her. "You would have done that?"

"I was ready to fling it in the water when Lincoln grabbed my hand. He told me that rock was worth a big chunk of change, and being hurt and angry wasn't a good enough reason to toss it in the river."

His stomach clenched. "Wow."

"So, I handed the ring to my brother and told him to hawk it and donate the proceeds to charity." She clasped her hands together in her lap. "That's the last time I saw it."

He'd been hoping the big diamond was tucked away in her jewelry box because she couldn't bear to part with it. Apparently, the pain he'd inflicted had cut deeper than he'd ever imagined. The wound might be scarred over, but he doubted it would ever fully heal. Which meant he had his work cut out for him.

Chapter Twenty-Two

Annalise had made and eaten lunch, cleaned the litterbox, and thrown a load of laundry into the washer, which was conveniently tucked into a closet off the kitchen of their rental cottage. All while Rory worked on his computer and nibbled at his sandwich, muttering to himself every now and then. Maizie was curled up beside him on the couch, and the baseball game was on with the volume turned down low. At least the Phillies were winning.

She was in the process of transferring the clothes to the dryer when he let out a whoop that disturbed Maizie. The cat jumped down, tail swishing, and strolled over to her food bowl to see if anything new had magically appeared.

After shutting the dryer door and pushing the button to start it, she crossed the open room and leaned over the back of the couch. "Did you find something?"

"I did indeed. I have a name and an address. Got you, you bastard." He stretched an arm over his head to pull her down for an awkward kiss. "I knew it was only a matter of time."

"You're amazing. Who has the painting?"

"A guy named Walter Bates. He lives on Rittenhouse Square."

"That's one of the most expensive neighborhoods in Philly. I wonder how Brady Murphy and Felix Lemmon are connected to him."

"I don't know, but he's been in contact with them both. I dug up his home address through his company, which doesn't have the best cyber security." Rory grinned. "He should hire me to beef up his firewalls. Anyway, Bates owns several jewelry stores along the East Coast—here in Philly, and also in D.C., Baltimore, Richmond, Manhattan, and Boston."

"So the buyer and Felix could know each other from just about anywhere. I guess how they're associated doesn't really matter."

"No. The important thing is getting the painting back. I'll make a call to his local store and ask to speak to Mr. Bates about a special purchase."

Annalise walked around the couch to sit beside him. "They'll just send you to the manager."

"True, but I can leave a fake name and contact number and ask if Mr. Bates is currently in Philly or at one of his other stores. The manager will give me that much information."

"I guess learning if he's home or out of town will be key to breaking into his house."

"Exactly. We could take what we know to the cops, but it probably isn't enough for a search warrant, and if Bates finds out he's a suspect, that painting will disappear for good."

"You intend to steal it back tonight?"

"Damn right. I'd rather return the original painting to the museum, even if I screw up the chain of evidence and this bastard walks. If the police can make a few arrests afterward, based on some anonymous tips, that'll be a bonus."

She nodded. "In that case, call the jewelry store. The sooner we can get this over with, the better."

He pulled out his phone, tapped in the number to the store, which was still up on his computer screen, and smiled broadly. "Yes, hello. I'd like to speak to the owner, please. That's right, Mr. Bates."

Annalise slapped a hand over her mouth to keep from laughing at his very realistic British accent."

"He's not? Maybe a manager can help me." He waited a few moments, his green eyes bright with humor. "Hello, there. Yes, I'm trying to reach Mr. Bates about a very special necklace he was having custom made for me." His accent grew slightly thicker. "No, I'd rather speak to him directly. Do you know if he's currently in Philadelphia?"

The tinny sound of a voice came through the receiver, and Annalise wished he'd put the call on speaker so she could hear the manager's response.

"I understand you can't release personal information, but perhaps you could give him a message that, uh, Harry Prinz is following up on our previous conversation . . ."

Her eyes widened, and her jaw sagged. "Oh, my God!" The whispered words burst out. "Rory, no!"

He grinned in response. "If Mr. Bates is by chance at his Manhattan store, I could possibly arrange a meeting—" He listened for a moment. "Oh, I see. No, I won't be in Richmond. Just ask Walter to contact me at his earliest convenience. I believe he has my number. Thank you."

The second he disconnected, Annalise flopped backward into the corner of the couch, tears of amusement flowing. "Isn't impersonating royalty illegal?" she choked out between giggles.

"I didn't say I was a prince, and it isn't my fault if the guy made assumptions. When Bates tells him he's never spoken to Harry in his life, the manager will look like a fool who fell for a practical joke, but that can't be helped."

"Your accent was perfect. I didn't know you could mimic British nobility."

He followed her down onto the cushion and kissed her before running his lips along the side of her throat and nipping the lobe of her ear. "I guess I have a few talents you don't know about. Want to explore them?"

She tingled all over as she threaded her fingers through his hair and kissed him back, taking her time. Finally, they came up for air.

"I thought you wanted to steal a painting?" She gasped when he pressed against her, rubbing in exactly the right spot.

"I intend to, but not until this evening. The manager informed me that Mr. and Mrs. Bates are in Virginia for the rest of the week."

"How convenient."

He nuzzled his nose between her breasts. "Which gives us plenty of time to have a little fun before I go on a reconnaissance mission. Recovering the painting will be faster and easier if I know what to expect when I enter their home."

"What about going for a run to get some exercise,"

she teased, stroking the pad of her thumb along his rough jaw.

"We can do that afterward." Sliding his hands beneath her shirt, he pulled it up over her head and covered one breast with his warm palm. "Anyway, my heartrate is already up . . . among other things."

She laughed helplessly. "In that case, we should probably move to someplace less exposed. Anyone could walk right up to the window, and there are kids in this neighborhood."

"You're right." Rory rolled off the couch and scooped her into his arms. "We'll get naked behind closed blinds."

As he carried her into the bedroom, she pushed the door shut, leaving Maizie in the living area to fend for herself. He lowered her to the bed, tugged her shoes from her feet, and stripped off her pants before she could blink. Lying on the comforter in her bra and panties, she relaxed against the pillows while he dropped his clothes on the floor.

A smile curved her lips as he approached, completely naked and fully aroused. "You seem to be in a bit of a hurry."

"All that wasted time to make up for." Sitting at her side, he leaned in and kissed her, slowly, thoroughly, stroking with his tongue while he managed to unhook her bra at the same time. Tossing the scrap of silky material aside, he raised his head as his gaze drifted down to her bare breasts. "However, since I have you exactly where I want you, we don't need to rush."

"Except now you've got me all worked up." She closed her eyes, and her muscles clenched as he kissed his way across her stomach to the edge of her panties. Drawing them down her legs, his lips followed, and she couldn't breathe, couldn't think. "Rory." His name came out on a gasp.

"For two years, all I could think about was you. This. Wanting you back more than life itself." He inched his way up again until their bodies were perfectly aligned. Cupping her face in his hands, he met her gaze, his eyes reflecting sincerity, pain, and a deep well of love.

She ran her finger over his lips. "I was miserable without you. Lonely. Unfulfilled. Missing my other half."

"Never again." He sank into her and held perfectly still. "Now we're both complete."

They made love with the ease of familiarity, but with a new sense of urgency. Recapturing what they'd lost and feared they'd never find again. Touching, tasting, moving in sync until they both reached release and clung to each other. Holding on in the aftermath because neither of them wanted to let go.

"Is this real?" Annalise spoke quietly as she rested her cheek against his chest, breathing in the scent of his damp skin. "Or am I just wishful thinking?"

His arms tightened. "I hope this is our future. I don't want you to have any regrets. Ever."

"I don't either."

"Because I'll do whatever you need to make this work."

"Our relationship can't be about you changing into what you think I want." She propped herself on one elbow to meet his gaze. "That's what I meant by real." She spread her fingers against the warm flesh directly over his heart. "I know you won't lie to me, but you also can't lie to yourself."

"I'm not. When I met you, I thought I'd put my past behind me. The guy you fell in love with was the real me. That's who you're looking at now."

"Good." She bent and kissed him. "That's all I need to know."

He kissed her back and groaned when he finally pulled away. "As much as I'd like to go for round two, we have work to do. But first, I really do want to take a run and get some fresh air. There's a jogging path not far away."

She sat up. "Let's do it. Then you can scout out the Bates' house, and we'll pick up dinner on our way back."

"Excellent plan. I'll probably wait until late tonight to actually break into their place."

They got dressed, took a quick, three-mile run, showered, and headed into the city. It was early evening when they reached the upscale Rittenhouse neighborhood where the Bates' home was located. The elegant brick mansion with beautiful bay windows stood on the corner facing the square.

"Impressive." Annalise turned to stare as they drove by. "Now what?"

"I'll park a few blocks away and walk back. I want to assess their security system. I can wander around in the park and not look like I'm casing the place before I take a peek inside."

"Let me guess. I get to stay in the car." Her tone held a trace of sarcasm. "I feel so useful."

He squeezed her arm. "You can pick me up when I call, but there's no reason for you to be caught near that house on door cam video."

She turned to face him as he pulled to the curb and parked. "You're not worried about being seen?"

He tugged the Phillies cap he was wearing low over his forehead. "I know how to avoid being caught on cameras. At any rate, I doubt Walter Bates will call the police to report a thief lifted his stolen painting. My main concern is not tripping silent alarms that will notify a security company, or getting spotted by a neighbor breaking and entering. This trip is about figuring out the best ways to avoid that."

"I get it. You're a professional and know what you're doing."

"I'll call if I need anything." He leaned over to kiss her. "Promise."

"You do that. Stay safe, Rory."

"I will." He handed her the key fob and got out of the car. "See you shortly."

Uneasiness crawled through her as he walked away, despite the fact he didn't believe there was anything to worry about. Lately, unexpected complications seemed to be a given.

Rory had been gone fifteen minutes when a flash of yellow up the street caught her attention. The familiar Saab cruised toward her, stopping at the intersection before continuing in her direction. She ducked down low in the seat as Brady Murphy drove by. Pulling out her cell, she called Rory.

He picked up on the first ring. "What's up?"

"Murphy is headed your way. He just drove past me. I kept out of sight, but he may have recognized your car."

"There are plenty of Porsches in this neighborhood,

and he won't be expecting us." He was quiet for a moment. "I wonder what he's doing here. Surely he knows Walter Bates is out of town."

"If he sees you—"

"He won't. I'm standing beside a big oak and can stay out of view. He just snagged a parking spot half a block away."

"Then obviously it's not a coincidence he's in the neighborhood." She turned around in her seat but couldn't see past a minivan sticking out from the curb. "I wonder if he's housesitting while the Bateses are out of town."

"If he was, why wouldn't he have watched the game in much nicer surroundings than his own place?"

"You're right. What's he doing now?"

"He ran across the street to the front steps. Now he's waiting at the door." Silence stretched for several long seconds. "Someone just let him in. Looked like an older woman."

"Mr. and Mrs. Bates might have live-in help."

"That's a definite possibility. I wish I knew what the hell Murphy's game is."

"Does this change our plans?"

"Maybe. I'll hang out for a while and try to get a look inside. If he leaves soon, great. If not, I want to see what he's up to in there."

"I think I'll take a walk around the neighborhood." She shifted on her seat. "Sitting in the car for an hour or two sounds horrible. How do cops handle stakeouts? I'd lose my mind."

"You could go get take-out while you wait. If we're stuck here for any length of time, we can eat dinner in the park and keep an eye on the house."

"I'll do that if he doesn't leave right away."

"Great. I'll call you in ten minutes if the status doesn't change."

She disconnected and slumped in her seat. A stiff breeze rattled the leaves in the trees along the street, sending down a shower of gold and red, but it was still warm inside the car. Her mind wandered, reliving the last few hours with Rory, and a smile curved her lips. She hadn't been this happy since before she'd learned of his arrest, and her whole world had blown up in her face. Forgiving him felt good—knowing they had a future together, even better.

A silver Lexus that looked vaguely familiar drove by, waited while the van that had blocked her view pulled out onto the street, and then parallel parked in the spot with ease. As she watched in her rearview mirror, the driver's door opened and her boss stepped out. Marcus Poole pulled keys from his pocket, crossed the street to unlock the door of another stately townhouse, and disappeared inside.

"Well, that was unexpected," she muttered as she tapped her phone to call Rory.

"Hey, love. Murphy's still inside. You might as well—"

"My boss lives just down the street from Walter Bates. At least I assume it's his house. He showed up, opened the door with a key, and walked inside."

"You didn't know he lived on Rittenhouse Square?"

"Not a clue. Marcus has never invited the staff to his home."

"If they're neighbors, it's possible he and Bates know each other. Keep in mind, someone working at the museum was helping that punk, Murphy."

"I can't believe Marcus would risk his job to steal a painting. What does he get out of it, money?"

"Cash is what motivates most people. After I get the Pissarro back, I can look into your boss's finances. If he's guilty, we'll see that he gets busted."

"This is crazy." Her voice rose. "How many other pieces in the museum are fakes? I feel like marching up to his door and confronting him."

"Except you won't because you're too smart to make a dumb and dangerous move like that."

"You're right, but I'm livid." She took a few, calming breaths and relaxed her clenched fists. "Do you want me to wait for you or go get food?"

"You can—" He broke off abruptly and lowered his voice. "Murphy just walked out carrying a basket. Good God, did he come here to pick up his laundry?"

"The Bates' maid washed his clothes for him? That's kind of weird."

"No kidding. Murphy's heading straight to his car. Give me a few minutes to find the best point of entry and figure out what I have to contend with inside. It won't take long."

"Okay. See you shortly." She disconnected and stared at Marcus Poole's house. "Bastard." She forced the word through gritted teeth.

While she waited, she checked her email and texts. One from Lydia asked how she was feeling. So much had happened since Murphy had knocked her unconscious in the museum's garden, she'd almost forgotten about her concussion. After responding that she was fully recovered, she kept scrolling and stopped at a text from her sister.

What's up with Rory? Are you sleeping with him yet?

She grinned. Typical Brielle, to the point and no boundaries. She typed rapidly. *We're trying to work things out.*

Her phone dinged a few seconds later. *Which means yes. I figured you'd cave. He loves you.*

She stared at the words for a moment before responding. *I love him, too. I never stopped.*

I know, but if he hurts you again, I'll kill him.

Annalise smiled. *He won't. Thanks for caring.*

Her sister liked her comment with a heart emoji. She'd just set her phone on the center console when it rang. Her boss's name appeared on the screen. Drawing a quick breath, her gaze darted to his house. Had he seen her lurking on the street?

Cautiously, she swiped to connect and turned on the speaker. "Hello, Marcus."

"Hi, Annalise. I thought I should check on you. How're you feeling?"

"I'm fine. My head doesn't hurt anymore unless I touch the spot where I was hit."

"That's good to hear. I had a couple of messages from the museum's board of directors. I think they're worried you'll file a lawsuit or something because you were attacked on the property while you were working."

"I wouldn't do that." She glanced up when Rory opened the car door and pressed a finger to her lips.

His brows shot up, but he slid silently onto the driver's seat.

"So, you'll be at work tomorrow morning?"

"I plan to be. Is there a problem?"

"No, not at all. I picked up some eighteenth-century, carved wooden panels at an estate sale. They need a lot of restoration work, and I know you have a few other projects to finish, as well."

She rolled her eyes. "My work won't get done if I'm not there to do it."

"I don't mean to sound unsympathetic, but I'm leaving tonight for a two-day conference in Boston. I wanted to confirm everything will run smoothly while I'm gone."

"I'm sure we'll survive. Enjoy your trip, Marcus."

"Thanks. I'll see you on Thursday."

He disconnected, and she stared at Rory. "That was odd."

"Your boss called you?"

"Yes, and what he said wasn't out of character. It's just the timing. The fact that we're sitting practically outside his house."

"He doesn't know you're out here. If the call, itself, wasn't suspicious—"

"It wasn't. He just wanted to make sure I'd be at work since projects are piling up. Apparently he'll be gone for the first part of the week."

"I'll feel better about you going into work if he isn't there." He started the engine and pulled out onto the street. "Provided we're able to return the Pissarro to the museum and take down the forgery, I'm not sure how quickly the cops will round up everyone involved. They won't be happy about our involvement."

"Probably not. Did you check out the Bates' house?"

"Yep. I should be able to get in through one of the side windows upstairs. Those don't appear to be wired for security. As long as I wait until after the housekeeper or whoever she is goes to bed, I won't have any trouble." He grimaced. "Except for the Chihuahua."

"They have a dog?"

"Unfortunately, yes. Yappy little dogs are far worse than big ones for sounding the alarm."

Annalise smiled. "Bring a bowl of smelly, wet cat food with you. That dog will be your friend for life. Buttercup always tries to eat Maizie's food when I take her with me to my parents' house."

"Not a bad idea. I'm afraid to use tranquilizers on an animal that small. Hopefully, the damn dog sleeps in the bedroom with the woman and won't even know I'm there."

"Dogs love me. I could come with you and keep it occupied if it's wandering around."

He glanced her way and shook his head. "No way. I'll handle the mutt." Facing forward, he continued, "What do you want for dinner?"

Her eyes narrowed as she stared at him. "How about Thai?"

"One of my favorites. Excellent choice."

"This discussion isn't over, Rory. Not by a long shot."

Chapter Twenty-Three

Rory removed the screen, inserted a flat blade to flip the latch, slid open the window, and stepped across the sill. Turning on a small flashlight, he kept the beam low as he shined it around what was clearly the master bedroom. A small, brown head lifted from a nest of pillows on the otherwise empty bed, and bulging eyes met his gaze. Lips curled back from sharp, white teeth as the dog snarled. Lobbing, pieces of hotdog toward the Chihuahua, he hoped the little menace didn't expect steak.

The dog stood up and snatched the nearest bite, nearly choking in his eagerness to gulp it down. Apparently, the dog wasn't too highbrow to eat hot-dogs. Turning, Rory gave Annalise a hand as she stepped into the room, then pulled up the rope ladder, detached it from the sill, and shut the window. He'd completely lost his mind, agreeing to let her come with him, but she'd refused to back down.

She headed straight to the bed and sat beside the dog. The little guy stopped eating long enough to close his eyes in sheer bliss as she scratched him behind the ears and cooed to him in a low voice. Obviously, they'd do just fine together.

Giving her a thumbs-up, he crossed to the open door and surveyed the hallway beyond. Antique sconces spaced along the wall offered enough light to see by. A door at the end of the hall was shut. Chances were good it was the room where the woman he'd seen earlier slept, although he had no intention of checking.

Moving stealthily toward the stairs, he glanced through each open doorway and used his light to scan the walls. Guest bedrooms and baths, with no sign of the painting. Running lightly down the stairs, he entered the living room. The only piece of art on the wall was a still life of a bowl of fruit beside a vase filled with sunflowers that hung over the fireplace mantle. Backtracking, he checked the dining room where a huge seascape covered most of one wall. His nerves were tingling as he took a quick look into an office lined with shelves, then walked through the kitchen. If, after all this, the painting wasn't here, he would be beyond pissed.

Climbing the main staircase again, he walked silently down the hall to the far end. Narrow stairs opposite the closed door led to the third floor. When the home was built, the top level would have housed servant quarters and possibly the nursery. Cringing as a stair squeaked, he stayed near the wall and hurried up. Entering a huge, open space, his breath caught. He shined his light around the vast room with discrete groupings of furniture and walls hung with paintings. The Pissarro was on the back wall.

Sliding his phone from his pocket, he took photos

of the entire room, including close up shots of each painting. He had no idea how many of the others were stolen, but the Pissarro was one of two forgeries Archie had completed. He'd take what he'd come for and let the authorities sort out the rest.

Moving through the room, Rory stopped in front of *Sheep in the Meadow* and shined his light around the edge of the frame. It was wired, but not to the main security system. He guessed disturbing the painting would activate an alarm on a cell phone. Bates definitely wouldn't want the cops showing up. He probably had a thug on standby if the alarm was triggered.

The mechanism wasn't terribly sophisticated. All he needed to do was put in a breaker to bypass the trigger. Taking what he needed from his backpack, he went to work and was able to lift the painting from the wall a few minutes later. Turning it over, he pried loose the backing, holding the canvas in place.

His phone vibrated in his pocket, and he pulled it out to check the screen. Annalise had simply typed a string of question marks. He tapped a response. *Found it. Almost done.*

Shoving his phone into his pack, he removed a poster of a Monet masterpiece they'd picked up earlier at a home décor store. He taped it to the mounting board and inserted it in the frame, hung the picture on the wall, and reset the alarm. Walter Bates wouldn't be notified the Pissarro was missing until someone climbed up to the third floor and took a good look around. Their impromptu replacement might pass a casual glance into the room but certainly not close scrutiny.

Still, if all hell broke loose tomorrow, it wouldn't be his problem. By morning, he intended to have the original painting back in the museum where it belonged. Carefully rolling the canvas, he slid it into his pack and headed down the stairs.

Annalise glanced up when he entered the bedroom. "You have it?" she whispered.

"Yep."

She let out a long breath. "Thank, God. Can we leave?"

"Will your little friend let you?" He eyed the dog curled on her lap.

"Let's hope." She lifted the Chihuahua onto the bed, and it grumbled and let out a yip.

They both froze, but there was no sound from down the hall. After a moment, he crossed the room, slid open the window, and secured the ladder. "Okay. You go first."

Annalise left the bed and turned her back to the window to step over the sill onto the hanging ladder. He could have dismantled the home alarm system to exit out the front door, but this way was faster. Since he'd unscrewed the bulb in the nearest streetlight, no one would notice them climbing down the wall in the dark of the night.

Once Annalise reached the bottom, Rory stepped out onto the rope rung and shut the window. The dog burst out barking, shrill yaps loud enough to wake the dead.

"Shit." Taking the few seconds necessary to replace the screen, he scrambled down, gave the ladder a flip to detach it from the sill, bundled it under his arm, and hurried to where Annalise waited at the corner. "Your damn, furry friend raised the alarm."

He glanced over his shoulder as a light flashed on

in the master bedroom. Crossing the street, they fled through the park. If the woman in the house looked out and saw anything, it would only be shadows. She'd have no reason to suspect a thief or head up the stairs to the picture gallery at this hour. More than likely, she'd tell the dog to be quiet and go back to bed.

They reached the car, and Annalise leaned against it. "I don't know why people get off on a rush of fear and adrenaline. But then, I don't like rollercoasters."

Rory squeezed her shoulder as he unlocked the car. "Thrill junkies are a unique breed, but I can find the same rush sailing in tricky winds or standing at the top of a cliff, checking out an amazing view." He opened her door and bent to kiss her upturned face. "Or making love to you."

"Very smooth." She smiled as she slipped onto the seat. "Did you practice that line?"

"Nope. You inspire me." He shut her door and walked around to get in behind the wheel. "However, the night isn't over yet."

She leaned back in the seat and rubbed her arms as he pulled away from the curb. "Maybe we should take the original painting to the police instead of returning it to the museum."

"What do you think they'd say if they caught me red-handed with stolen artwork? Even with the photos I took to back up our story, I won't risk it. The cops would throw me in a cell first and ask questions later. Not happening, love."

"Then we head to the museum, I distract whoever's working security, and you replace the painting." She sounded like she was trying to convince herself it would be as easy as one, two, three.

He glanced over as they cruised through the dark streets of Philly, fairly empty in the wee hours of the morning. "I can take you back to the vacation rental and manage on my own. That was my original plan."

"No. I want to do this. I dragged you into this mess, so the least I can do is help finish it."

"I don't expect any complications. Use your key to get inside. Once you're in the lobby, give a shout out to whichever guard is roaming the premises, and then maneuver both guards down into your work area while you turn off the alarm on the painting. Remember, you have a good reason for being there."

"Thanks to that email you sent me." She turned to face him. "I still don't understand how you made it look like it came from the museum."

"I copied the IP address from a message your boss sent you. Anyone with advanced computer skills could clone the address. My only concern is getting in and out of the building before the guards start searching for an intruder. Once they realize your cover story is a lie, they'll be looking for trouble."

"I'll do what I can to keep them downstairs as long as possible."

"Make sure your phone is on speaker in your pocket so I can hear what's going on." He pulled up to the curb not far from Independence Hall. "We'll walk from here. After you unlock the door, drop your keys outside because the guard will undoubtedly relock it."

"Okay."

They left the car and headed down the block, skirting around a guy with a bottle sleeping in a doorway. Only one car passed before they reached the museum. Standing in the shadows just beyond the reach of a streetlight, she called his phone, put hers on speaker, and stuck it in the pocket of her jacket.

"You've got this, love." He dropped a quick kiss on her lips.

"I hope so. Here goes nothing."

While she ran up the steps and unlocked the big front door, he pulled on thin, latex gloves and watched her every move. Holding the door open, she tossed the keys in his direction before disappearing inside.

Rory inserted his earbuds and turned up the volume. Footsteps echoed across the parquet floor, and someone called from a distance.

"It's me, JR. I got a message about water damage in my work area." Annalise's voice came through loud and clear.

"I didn't hear anything about a problem. Did you lock the door after you came in?" Apparently, the security guard had joined her.

"No, I didn't. Sorry. I'm freaking out, wondering how much of a mess there is."

"Just a second while I lock— Okay, let's go check out the basement. Who called you?"

Rory ran up the steps, grabbed the keys she'd thrown, and inserted the proper one in the lock as Annalise and JR headed down the corridor out of sight. Taking a moment, he studied the angles of the security cameras in the lobby while he listened to their conversation.

"No one. I got an email. I figured either you or Oscar sent it. Luckily, I was having trouble sleeping and was playing on my phone. If anything is ruined down there, Marcus is going to go ballistic."

"I certainly didn't send an email. Hey, Oscar, did

you contact Annalise about water damage in the basement?"

"No. I haven't had any reason to look down there this evening." The second male voice grew louder as the man approached Annalise.

Confident he could avoid the cameras, Rory carefully made his way up the stairs to the third floor.

"That's weird, but we should probably check to make sure there isn't a problem." Annalise spoke again.

"I don't like this." The deeper voice belonged to the second guard. "Stay here, Annalise, while we check it out."

"Okay."

Using the wainscotting, Rory climbed the wall and shifted the angle of the security camera mounted below the ceiling away from the Pissarro. He landed lightly on the floor and approached the painting as the green light went out.

"All clear," Annalise whispered.

"There's no water damage in here." The voice came faintly from a distance.

"I'm coming down." Stairs creaked as Annalise descended into the basement. "The floor's completely dry. Why would someone alert me if there wasn't a problem?"

"Let's see that email." JR's voice was abrupt.

Annalise must have taken her phone from her pocket and pulled up her mail because when she spoke, she nearly blasted out his eardrum. Rory adjusted the volume.

"See. It came from the museum. If neither of you sent the message, who else was in the building? I got the email over a half hour ago. It took me a few minutes to dress and run down here."

"It's easy enough to tell which computer the message was sent from." The younger security guard spoke again.

Rory had the picture down and the backing loosened. Detaching the forgery took longer than he liked.

"The IP address is for the computer in Marcus's office," JR said sharply.

"I'll go take a look." The older security guard sounded worried. "You're sure nothing's been disturbed down here, Annalise?"

"I don't think so. I hadn't put away all my supplies before I went to lunch and got clobbered over the head, but everything seems to be where I left it. Maybe someone was simply playing a joke."

"Well, it isn't funny." JR's tone was grim. "Why would someone drag you out of bed to come down here for no reason?"

"Could be the same person who hit me was hoping to catch me unaware outside my apartment." Her voice rose. "Maybe, since I was already awake, I left before he expected me to. He could have been on his way to grab me."

"You stay with Annalise, JR, while I go check the curator's office."

Carefully stretching the original canvas over the mounting board, Rory fastened it down using the technique Annalise had drilled into his head earlier in the evening. Her greatest fear was that he'd damage the painting.

"There's no reason for us to stay in the basement." The younger security guard spoke again.

"Since I'm down here, let me put away the supplies I had out on Saturday. It'll only take me a couple of minutes."

"I guess so." He sounded annoyed. "I don't like anything about this situation. Why would someone deliberately try to hurt you?"

"I've no idea. I thought getting hit out in the garden was completely random. Wrong place at the wrong time. But if someone was trying to draw me out of my apartment in the middle of the night—"

"What about that dude you used to date? I noticed you were with him when you came back from the ER to get your purse. Did he try something and you shut him down?" His voice was flat. "Unless you didn't."

"Rory has no reason to hurt me."

"If you say so. Are you done messing with that stuff?"

Rory attached the backing and lifted the heavy frame onto the wall. Sticking the rolled-up forgery into his pack, he headed for the stairs.

A radio squawked. "It doesn't look like anyone has been in Marcus's office. Nothing's out of place, and his computer is turned off. I don't know what to make of this stunt."

"We're coming up from the basement now," JR responded. "I want to do a quick walkthrough of the entire museum. This whole situation reeks of distraction."

Racing down the stairs, Rory sprinted across the lobby and out through the front door. Pausing, he used Annalise's key to relock it and then ran down the steps to wait in the shadows.

"Let's go, Annalise." JR's tone indicated he'd lost

patience.

"Sure. I'm right behind you." A moment later, she whispered, "Rory?"

"I'm out." He spoke in a low voice. "Rearm the painting if you have a chance."

Footsteps sounded, and the two male voices murmured in the background.

"Shall I stay here while you two do your rounds? Or maybe I should just go home?" Annalise spoke up. "Obviously, there isn't an emergency, and I'd like to get some sleep before I have to go to work in a few hours."

"I hate to send you out alone at this time of night." Concern colored the older guard's voice. "It isn't safe."

"I ran here because I was in a panic and didn't want to wait for an Uber, but you're right. Walking home wouldn't be a smart move. I'll call for a ride."

"Good choice. Hang out in the office while you wait." The older guard took charge. "You can start on the third floor, JR, and I'll search down here. We'll meet on the second floor." Footsteps and voices faded.

"I turned the alarm back on." Annalise's voice was soft in his ear. "Why don't you get the car and come pick me up. I'll tell Oscar my ride's here."

"Okay. I'll text when I'm outside. You can hang up now."

"See you shortly."

Rory took the buds out of his ears and stuck his phone in his pocket. Leaving the shadows, he crossed the street to walk close to the building fronts where he wouldn't be visible if someone glanced out one of the museum's upstairs windows. He reached the car a few minutes later.

Hitting the remote to unlock the door, he set his pack behind the seat and got in. Gripping the steering wheel, he let the tension drain out of him. The Pissarro was back where it belonged. Tomorrow, he'd call Special Agent Ferris, his contact at the FBI, but for now, he'd take Annalise back to the vacation rental. Murphy could have left any number of surprises at her apartment, and she sure as hell didn't need to face something ugly tonight. He'd check out her place after he dropped her off at work in the morning.

Starting the engine, he cruised toward the museum and pulled up to the curb half a block from the front steps. Sliding his phone from his pocket, he texted Annalise. *I'm outside.*

She responded with a thumbs up, and a couple minutes later, the door opened. She ran down the steps and glanced both ways. Spotting the Porsche, she hurried toward him. Leaning over, he pushed open the door.

"I can't believe we did that." Annalise dropped onto the seat. "Well, I can't believe *I* did it. You're used to playing those kind of games. I felt like was going to have a panic attack the entire time I was in there."

"You were very professional. I was impressed." He zipped past the museum and hung a right at the next street.

She leaned against the window and closed her eyes. "I'm exhausted."

"It's the adrenaline crash. We'll head straight back to the rental house so you can get a few hours of sleep."

"Is this nightmare really over?" She sounded completely spent.

"It is for you and me. I'll have a conversation with

my FBI contact. They can take it from here. I'm sure they'll want to investigate Walter Bates' home gallery once they see the photos I took, but the Pissarro is back on the museum wall where it belongs. I'll give him Murphy's name, and the feds can figure out how they're all connected."

"They won't arrest us for tampering with evidence?"

"Hell, no. I'll make it clear I was covering both your ass and mine. Ferris will be angry, but we didn't commit any crimes."

She reached over and rested her hand on his thigh. "Then we can put this behind us and focus on our future."

"Do you know how good that sounds?" He met her gaze as they passed beneath a streetlight. "A life with you beside me is my idea of heaven."

Chapter Twenty-Four

Six hours later, Annalise sat in the car, double-parked in front of the museum, feeling like she'd left six minutes ago. Her eyes were gritty from lack of sleep, and she was too tired to argue with Rory, who was having second thoughts about her going inside.

"It's not up for debate. I have a ton of restoration work to do, and I'll be perfectly safe since Marcus is in Boston. I won't leave the museum or take any walks alone in the garden. I packed my lunch, and I'll hang out with Lydia if I'm not down in my dungeon. I promise."

"If I'd been able to reach Ferris, it would be different, but he's off the grid until tomorrow. Which means Murphy is still on the loose."

Turning in her seat, she gripped his clenched fist in both her hands and squeezed. "I know you're worried, but that creep won't be able to get near me."

"Not if I stay with you, he won't."

"And leave Maizie in the car? Or in her carrier all day?" She glanced down at her feet where the cat pressed her nose against the grill and meowed. "She'd howl the entire time. Go check out my apartment like you'd planned. You can have lunch with me if you want, but I need to focus on my work, and I won't be able to do that with you sitting in the corner, staring at me."

He ran the hand she wasn't holding through his hair. "Fine. I'll be back at noon."

Leaning forward, she kissed him. "I'll look forward to it."

Annalise got out of the car, walked around a tour group waiting on the sidewalk for the museum to open in ten minutes, and entered the building. She smiled at Dana, the young woman manning the information desk, and was heading straight toward her basement kingdom when Callen left the gift shop to intercept her.

"I hear there was some excitement last night." He was dressed neatly in khakis and a polo shirt with the Chestnut Street Museum logo on the front. His blue eyes scanned her from head to foot. "You look pretty darn good for a woman who got hit in the head on Saturday."

"I had a headache for a day, but that was it." She grimaced. "Obviously news of my nocturnal adventure has spread."

He nodded. "Why would someone play a joke like that on you? Rumor has it Marcus was going to skip his conference after Oscar told him what happened, but since security couldn't find any breach, he's staying in Boston, after all."

"I'm glad that stupid prank didn't disrupt his plans. As for why I was a target, I have no idea." She eyed the empty gift shop. "Where's Francine? Are you all alone today?"

"She called to say she's running a little late. We're not usually that busy on Tuesdays, so I'll be fine."

Annalise grinned. "There's a huge tour group waiting outside. Prepare to be swamped." She turned as Lydia approached from the direction of the kitchen.

"Morning." Her friend's greeting was cheerful. "I'm glad to see you've fully recovered. I guess Rory took good care of you." Her eyes filled with speculation. "We need to talk."

Amused, Annalise nodded. "I'd eat lunch with you, but Rory's meeting me here. Come down to visit if you have a break between tours."

"I'll do that, but right now, I'd better go meet my first group. Catch you later."

Callen's scowl cleared as she faced him. "I need to get busy, as well. I'll see you later, Callen."

"Sure. Have a good day."

Annalise headed down the corridor and stopped to say hello to the guard on duty in the security office.

The retired police officer, who now worked day shift at the museum, frowned. "We're still trying to figure out who used the IP address for Mr. Poole's com-puter to send you that message, but honestly, I doubt we'll learn how it was done. These damn hackers are too smart to leave a trail." His voice brightened. "The good news is, we don't believe anyone breached museum security. We checked camera footage for the time the message was sent, and there was no unusual activity."

"I'm glad to hear that. Thanks, Jim."

"The only thing that caught my eye was a flash of movement on the third floor during the time you, Oscar, and JR were down in the basement."

Annalise froze. "You saw a person?"

"Not exactly. We pulled one blurry image, but that was it. Might have been a glitch in the system. Occasionally, a slight earth tremor or sonic boom will shake the cameras. If someone was up there, we would have found more evidence."

"Maybe it was one of the ghosts Lydia is always hoping to see."

Jim smiled broadly. "Wouldn't that be something?"

When his radio squawked and he reached for it, Annalise gave a little wave and headed over to the basement door. Her hands shook as she unlocked and opened it. Gripping the railing, she made her way down the stairs, dropped her bag on the floor, and collapsed onto a chair.

Apparently Rory had gotten in and out without detection last night. Barely.

After getting her nerves under control, she went to work. Two hours later, she was making solid progress. The relief of knowing the Pissarro was back where it belonged was immense, and with the weight of anxiety lifted, she felt ready to tackle the world. Or at least her corner of it. Lack of sleep would undoubtedly catch up with her later, but for now, she was riding the high of being back in her normal routine. Who knew having a completely ordinary day could be so liberating?

When the door at the top of the stairs opened, she glanced up as Francine descended. The older woman wore a skirt and heels and looked shaky coming down.

"Careful, Francine. What can I do for you?"

She reached the bottom step and produced a harried smile. "I spent the morning steaming labels for the Philadelphia Museum of Art off the packaging on the prints we sell and replacing them with our labels. What a pain."

Annalise frowned. "Why didn't you just send them back if they screwed up the order?"

"We would have run short of stock, but believe me, I gave the supplier a piece of my mind. Anyway, I have one more box to relabel. I was going to ask Jim to carry it out to my car, but there's some sort of situation with a rowdy visitor on the second floor that he's monitoring."

"I'll carry the box for you." She wiped her hands on a towel and followed the woman to the supply closet.

"Thank you, Annalise. I guess I should have sent Callen, but I wasn't sure he'd get the right container." She pointed. "It's that one. I could probably lift it—"

"Don't be silly. I'm happy to help." She hoisted the heavy box and waited while Francine led the way up the stairs. "Where are you parked?"

"I was lucky to get a spot just down the block since the loading zone out front was clogged with a tour bus. I suppose I could wait until we close, but I wanted to take care of this now."

"It's not a problem." They passed the security booth where Jim was studying the monitors with his back to them.

"Let's use the side door out of the kitchen instead of carrying the box down the front steps. It'll be closer to my car." She hurried past the refrigerator, slid the bolts on the door, then held it open.

Annalise took the shallow steps down to the alley running the width of the building. "Can you flip the latch on the gate for me?"

"Yes, of course." Francine wobbled as her heels clicked against the cobblestones. She opened the gate and waved a hand. "It's the black SUV two cars down. I'll open the rear hatch for you. I really appreciate this."

"Of course."

She hit the remote to unlock the big vehicle, raised the back door, and then stepped out of the way. As Annalise leaned in to set down the box, something slammed her in the back. Pain shot down her spine as her whole body jerked and twitched. Toppling forward, the breath left her as she landed on the box. Before she could draw air to scream, someone thrust her legs into the compartment, and the door slammed shut.

As she gathered her wits, and the pain radiating through her body eased, the car pulled onto the street and drove past the museum. She pounded against the smoked windows and yelled, but no one outside appeared to hear her.

"Shut up and sit down. You're not going anywhere." The driver met her gaze in the rearview mirror.

A metal grate was screwed in place between the cargo area where she'd been pushed and the rear seat of the vehicle. Though she could only see his eyes and the back of his head covered by a ballcap, she recognized Brady Murphy.

Panic wouldn't help. Forcing herself to think, she felt for her phone in the pocket of her pants, only to realize it wasn't there. She's left her cell in her jacket, which was hanging over the back of the chair in her workroom. Fear slid down her spine, chilling her to the bone. She'd have to talk her way out of this.

"Rory called his FBI connection early this morning. He's probably getting a warrant to search Walter

Bates' home right now, and you'll be arrested right along with him. Adding kidnapping to the charges against you is going to double your time in prison. Make the smart choice and let me go."

"Not going to happen. Even if you're telling the truth, every painting in that gallery is legit. My mom discovered the Pissarro was missing when she followed my aunt's stupid little dog up to the third floor. For once, that mutt proved useful. She called me immediately, and I removed the Grant Wood painting. The others were all purchased legally."

Annalise turned to stare at the square shape covered by a flowered sheet leaning against the side of the vehicle. Moving the box of prints out of her way, she pulled the sheet off the frame and gasped. *Rooster at Dawn* was one of Wood's smaller, lesser-known works, but Josephine, the previous curator, had been thrilled to acquire it before she retired from the museum. The depiction of a rooster strutting across a coop as the sun came up behind distant haycocks was one of Annalise's favorites. She couldn't believe she hadn't realized the painting currently hanging in the museum was a forgery.

"Archie is damn good. I know I've looked at his replica more than once in the last few weeks and never suspected it was a fake."

She rubbed her hands up and down her arms as goose bumps pebbled her skin beneath her silk blouse. *Think, Annalise.* She was smarter than this asshole. She needed to come up with a plan.

"I don't know how the hell you figured out the Pissarro wasn't the original." He merged onto the expressway. "Impressive work, Annalise."

"Rory took photos of Walter Bates' upstairs gallery last night. When he shows them to his FBI buddy, he'll see that the Grant Wood painting is missing. You won't get away with this."

"Oh, but I will. Your lover boy thief spent the entire morning at your apartment, cleaning up the new messages I left on your walls. I kept an eye on him before heading to my aunt and uncle's place when my mom called. He hasn't had time to hand over any evidence to the FBI. Hell, who's to say they'll even believe his story?"

"You underestimate Rory's influence with the feds. He's their go-to guy when they have security concerns they can't handle in-house."

"Doesn't matter. I left him a message that he'd better not do anything stupid if he wants to see you alive again. By the way, my mom has your phone so you won't be calling anyone for help."

His mom? Finally the pieces clicked in her brain. "Francine is your mother?" Vaguely, she remembered Francine mentioning her son a couple of times. Had she ever referred to him by name? Maybe that's why the name Brady had rung a faint bell.

"That's right. Her sister loves that Pissarro with the sheep and came to admire it often. Since Aunt Victoria always helped us out as much as she could, my mom wanted to give her something she knew she'd cherish."

"So, she decided to steal a painting?" Her voice rose. "Are you kidding me?"

Murphy met her gaze in the rearview mirror. "Don't say one negative word about my mother, or I'll make sure it hurts when I kill you."

The look in his eyes made her skin crawl. "Where

are you taking me?"

"Somewhere I won't have to worry about you yelling or Cavanaugh alerting neighbors when he shows up to rescue you. I've made it clear if he contacts the authorities, I'll slit your throat and take off. I'm almost as good as Archie at disappearing."

They were heading south at freeway speed. Even if she could somehow get the door open, and she was pretty sure it was locked since Murphy wasn't completely stupid, jumping out of the car would kill her. At this point, all she could do was wait until they reached their destination and try to create some sort of distraction. What she didn't want was Rory walking into a trap since she was one hundred percent certain he'd be coming to find her.

When Murphy's phone rang, he answered it on the dash. "I wondered when you'd get around to calling."

"What did you do to Annalise? I'll kill you, you bastard." Rory's voice came through the speaker, loud and clear.

"Tell him you're fine, and then we can get down to business."

"Don't listen to him, Rory. He'll kill both of us," she shouted.

Murphy took the phone off speaker and held it to his ear. "I'll definitely slice up your girlfriend if you don't follow my instructions. If you cooperate, maybe I'll let her live." His voice was sharp. "Where are you now?"

Annalise clenched her hands into fists as rage filled her. Grabbing the grate, she shook it, but the metal didn't budge.

Murphy gave her an irritated glance in the rearview

mirror. "Tell whoever you're talking to at the museum that Annalise just texted she isn't feeling well, that she has a migraine or something, and went home. Make them believe there isn't a problem." He was silent for a few seconds while Rory talked. "If you call the cops, or museum security gets suspicious and contacts them, she's dead. I have an inside source, so don't think you can slip one by me."

Stomach churning, she gripped the grate even harder, wondering what Murphy hoped to accomplish by kidnapping her.

"I want you to get in your car and head south on I95. Make sure you bring Archie's replica of the Pissarro with you. I'll give you further instructions in a half hour or so." He disconnected. "Good old Rory is no doubt planning an epic rescue. Except there'll be no saving either one of you this time."

"Why didn't you just shoot me in front of the museum and dump my body in the car?"

"My mom used a Taser." He reached for the weapon and held it up. "Very effective. She's stronger than she looks from all those years of cleaning houses. She heaved you into the back with no problem."

"I can't believe Francine—" She broke off and clamped her lips together. No point in riling him up by badmouthing his mother.

"Rory would spill his guts to the cops in a heartbeat if he thought I'd hurt you or worse, so I need you alive until he arrives. I thought about trying to grab him at your apartment but felt it was too risky. He was probably expecting me to show up and planned accordingly."

"Coward. You know you couldn't beat him in a

fair fight."

He laughed, seemingly not in the least offended. "Who ever said life's fair? My mom had two deadbeat husbands. She slaved her entire life to see that I had opportunities."

"So you squandered everything she worked to provide by becoming a criminal?"

"Hey, I have a legit job. This is just a side hustle. When it comes down to it, I'm really no different than Cavanaugh. Felix told me Rory got into the business to save his mother. Well, so did I. The extra cash I bring in allows her to live a good life. She works at the museum because she enjoys it, and she'll have a substantial nest egg when she decides to retire."

Annalise narrowed her eyes. "You're nothing like Rory. Maybe he made mistakes in his past, but he's never threatened to kill an innocent person."

"The two of you aren't so innocent. If you'd kept your mouth shut and left the forgery where it was, we wouldn't be in this situation. You created the problem, and now I have to fix it." He glanced at her in the mirror. "Glaring at me like I'm some sort of monster isn't going to have any effect. I'm done talking. We have almost two more hours to drive so you might as well get comfortable."

Annalise sat down and leaned against the side of the car. For now, she had nothing better to do than look at Grant Wood's cocky rooster strutting his stuff in the farmyard. They'd crossed the state line into Delaware and were nearly to Wilmington. Based on Murphy's schedule, their destination must be somewhere in Maryland, not too far from D.C. Clearly he didn't intend to give Rory the exact address until the last minute. While they were on the expressway, there wasn't a damn thing she could do to help herself. But if they got off . . .

She cleared her throat. "I have to pee."

"Too bad." He didn't even glance in her direction. "Hold it or piss yourself. I'm not stopping."

She braced her feet as he swerved into the fast lane to pass a slow-moving truck. Maybe the bastard would get pulled over for speeding. She could dream.

Exhausted, the rumble of the road beneath the tires lulled her into a stupor. When Murphy's phone rang again, she jerked awake. He didn't put the call on speaker.

"Where are you? That's it? Step on it, dude. I don't want to wait around all day for you to show up. Keep heading south into Maryland. Once you cross the border, call for more directions." He was quiet for a moment. "No, you can't talk to her. I guess you'll have to take my word for it that she's okay."

He must have hung up on Rory because a few moments later, he spoke in a completely different tone. "Did Cavanaugh leave the museum without anyone calling the police? Good. I didn't think he'd risk it. I'll be fine, Mom. I know this was supposed to go smoother than it has, but Aunt Victoria will get her paintings back, and no one will be the wiser. I've got this under control. I'll talk to you soon."

Annalise's lips tightened. Apparently, Francine was perfectly willing to sacrifice both her and Rory for her son's agenda.

"Where are we going?" She spoke abruptly.

"Why does it matter?"

"Curiosity. I want to know where I'll be spending my final hours."

His eyes narrowed as he stared at her in the mirror. "I guess there's no harm in telling you. It's not like you're going to be talking to anyone." He turned his attention back to the road. "Felix owns a home out in the sticks about twenty miles north of D.C. It's on the Patuxent River. Very scenic. I went there once with my aunt and uncle when I was a kid. Walter and Felix go way back, which is why he was willing to organize this job from his prison cell. The property is tied up in his estate, currently sitting empty."

"Sounds like a perfect place to bury bodies."

Murphy burst out laughing. "That's what I was thinking."

Annalise's chest burned with fear and anger as she clenched her hands into fists. "Too bad the only body getting buried will be yours."

Chapter Twenty-Five

"I'm about fifteen minutes out, but that bastard thinks I'm forty-five." Rory gripped the steering wheel so hard his fingers ached, while worry gnawed a giant hole in his gut. He had to stay focused. "I figured we'd need the extra time. Where are you now?"

"On the Beltway going north around D.C. Linc has been driving like a bat out of hell, and luckily, we haven't gotten stopped by a cop." Nash updated him on their progress.

"Excellent. You're about a half hour away. Get off on State Route 29 and head north."

"Wait for us to get there, Rory. You won't help Annalise by charging in solo and getting yourself killed."

"I don't intend to do anything stupid. I finally got ahold of Special Agent Ferris, my contact at the FBI. He's sending backup, but I told him any sort of police presence would jeopardize Annalise's safety. Murphy made it clear he'll kill her if he even thinks there's a cop in the vicinity."

"That's why you called us, to create a distraction. Just two good ol' boys, out drinking beer and shooting squirrels. We brought dad's shotgun and a sixpack of Bud."

For the first time since he'd learned Murphy had grabbed Annalise, Rory smiled. "Don't overplay your hand. I'll text you when I'm in position."

"Do you have the exact address?"

"I do, but no thanks to Murphy. All he told me was that I'd be getting off at State Route 198. I pulled over and spent ten minutes on my computer, running property titles in the southeastern portion of Montgomery County to see what popped. Turns out, Felix Lemmon owns a place on the Patuxent River. Very rural. Seems like a nice, quiet location if you're planning a murder and don't want to be disturbed."

"Bastard." Nash's tone was hard. "Send us the coordinates."

"I will when I ditch my car. I plan to walk in, circle the property, and approach the house from the direction of the river while you two head down the driveway and draw him out."

"Keep your cool, Rory." Lincoln spoke for the first time. "I know you, and I fear the second you see Annalise—"

"I'll stick to the plan. Gotta go. Murphy's calling." He hung up on Annalise's brothers and swiped to connect with her abductor. "Do you have an address for me? I'll reach 198 in about twenty minutes."

"Jesus. Could you drive any slower?"

"A big rig blew a tire, and some idiot tried to dodge it and smashed into the guardrail. Traffic was backed up, but I cleared the mess about five minutes ago. Just give me the damn address."

"In good time. Take State Route 198 to 650 north. Call me once you reach Ashton Road." He disconnected.

Rory smiled. The man was beyond cautious. He'd passed Ashton Road a few minutes ago. If he intended to direct the cops to the meeting location, they'd be looking in the wrong place. He tapped his phone to dial Murphy back.

"What the hell do you want? I'm not giving you an address yet."

"I'm not meeting you until I talk to Annalise."

"Fine." Footsteps sounded before he spoke again. "Rory wants to say hello."

When only silence followed, his stomach knotted.

Something ripped, and a cry erupted. "Ouch. Dammit!"

"See, she's alive." The call went dead.

Letting out a breath, he released his death grip on the steering wheel. The asshole must have put tape over Annalise's mouth, which meant she was probably tied up, as well. Reaching the access road to one of the area farms, he drove slowly along the narrow, rutted surface. After passing a big barn, he turned onto a dirt track and parked far enough into the trees that anyone heading to the farmhouse wouldn't notice his car. Other than the wind blowing through the overhead branches, all was quiet.

Getting out of the Porsche, he took a lockpick kit from his backpack and slipped it into his jacket pocket, then studied his surroundings. According to the online map, the road continued past the last of the fields and wound toward the river for another half mile before it dead-ended, presumably at Felix's property. He intended to avoid the road and stay under cover. After texting his location to both Nash and Special Agent Ferris, he walked at a steady pace through the trees. A few minutes later, he reached a house located in a clearing on the south side of the Patuxent River.

A black Chevy Tahoe was parked in front of the sprawling, single-story wood and stone structure. Definitely not your typical hunting cabin, or whatever the hell Felix used the place for. Staying deep in the thick woods where pines mixed with colorful oaks and maples, he did his best to avoid thorn bushes as he made his way down to the river. Watching his footing as he traversed the moss-covered rocks near the water, he angled up the slope at the rear of the house and ducked behind a rock wall bordering an overgrown lawn.

Glass doors opened off a low deck into what appeared to be a dining room. He could just make out the end of a table and a ladder-back chair. A bay window to the left of the doors contained a row of small pots filled with the dried remains of what had probably once been herbs or flowers. A light inside reflected off the stainless-steel surface of a refrigerator. He couldn't risk approaching the house until he knew Murphy wasn't in the kitchen, foraging for a forgotten box of crackers to snack on while he waited for Rory's call.

Sitting on the ground behind the wall, he texted Nash. *I'm in position.*

His phone vibrated a moment later. *We're five minutes out.*

After responding with a thumbs up, he inhaled a few deep breaths to calm his unexpected nerves. He'd never worried when he'd worked a job for Felix. He'd always been cool and purposeful, confident in his abilities. This time was different. Annalise's life was at stake. Any mistake on his part . . .

He swallowed hard. He couldn't think about what Murphy might do to her.

When his phone vibrated again, he read the message, this time from Ferris. *I'll have agents out of D.C. on-site in ten minutes. Stand down. I repeat, stand down. Let the professionals handle this.*

Turning off his phone, Rory shoved it into his pocket. He couldn't risk waiting. If Murphy somehow had eyes on the road and saw a couple of unmarked FBI vehicles approaching, he might simply kill Annalise and bolt.

The sound of an engine caught his attention, and he saw a flash of silver through the trees. Lincoln's pickup. Annalise's brothers drove straight up to the house, and car doors opened.

"Dude. It looks like someone's here." Lincoln's voice carried on the breeze.

"Well, damn. Our favorite beer-drinking spot has been invaded. I thought Lemmon was still in prison."

A screen door squeaked, and footsteps sounded on the front porch. "Hey, this is private property. Get the hell out of here."

Rory vaulted over the wall and sprinted across the yard. Reaching the glass doors, he tried the knob, found it locked, and pulled out his picks. He had the door open a few seconds later. No one was in the dining room, which opened into a large front room with big, leather couches. Murphy's back was visible through the front window. He'd descended to the yard and was still arguing with Nash and Lincoln.

Hurrying down the hallway, he glanced into each room. Annalise was cuffed to a bedpost in the last bedroom at the back of the house, her mouth covered with duct tape. Her eyes widened as he ran across the room.

Trying not to hurt her, he pulled off the tape. Noting the pink, raw-looking skin beneath, his vision blurred with fury.

"He has a gun, Rory," she whispered. "A revolver in a holster under his jacket. Hurry. I heard him talking to someone outside."

"Your brothers." Taking a smaller pick from his kit, he popped the cuffs and released her wrists. "Let's go."

Voices in the yard raised, an engine raced, and a door slammed. Moments later footsteps sounded on the hardwood floor in the living room."

A little whimper escaped as Annalise slapped a hand over her mouth.

Pulling her toward the window, he raised the shade and flipped the lock. The wood frame screeched when he shoved up the sash."

"What the hell?"

At the sound of running footsteps, Rory punched out the screen and lifted her up to help her through the opening.

"Don't make a move," Murphy shouted.

Rory turned and met the man's gaze over the barrel of a small, black handgun. "Run, Annalise. I've got this."

"Rory, no." Her voice broke.

"Go."

"Take one step, and he's dead. Get your ass back in here. Now!"

"I can't climb up without a boost. Don't shoot him."

Rory locked gazes with Murphy. The man was sweating. "Take off, Annalise. I'm not afraid of this punk."

"I'll run around the house and come in through the front door." A sob escaped. "Please don't hurt him."

"Make it fast." Murphy grabbed him and pressed the gun barrel to his temple. "Walk, asshole."

Where the hell are Lincoln and Nash?

Rory took his time as Murphy prodded him toward the main room. Surely Annalise's brothers hadn't gone far. Better to wait until his odds of success were higher before he tried to overpower Murphy.

The man released his grip on his arm to open the front door but held the revolver firmly against his temple as they moved out onto the porch. "Get over here, Annalise."

She walked around the side of the Tahoe, her hands held behind her, and approached the steps. "Don't do this, Brady. Think about your mom. You'll spend the rest of your life in prison if you kill us."

"I'll spend the rest of my life there if I don't. Without you two blabbing to the cops, I have a decent shot of getting away with this."

"The FBI is on their way here right now." Rory scanned the woods for any sign of movement. "You might be able to cut a deal if you let Annalise walk away."

"I don't believe you."

"Drop the gun, or I'll blow your head off." Lincoln

stepped around the side of the house, an old shotgun aimed straight at his target."

Murphy spun, his grip tight on Rory, the steel barrel bruising his skull. "Try it. With that relic, you'll kill Cavanaugh, too."

Footsteps pounded up the steps behind them, followed by a pop and a sizzle. Murphy jerked, and the revolver fell to the porch. Giving him a shove, Rory scooped up the gun as the man thrashed for a few seconds.

"Jesus." He glanced over at Annalise's colorless face. "What—"

"Stun gun. Francine used it on me. Murphy left it in the SUV."

"You're amazing." Bending, he gripped Murphy's arm and hauled him to his feet as Nash and Lincoln approached.

Lincoln lowered the shotgun. "Hell, you didn't even need us. Our little sis is the real hero."

She set down the Taser, grabbed the railing, and held on as a shaky laugh escaped. "I think I might pass out."

"Take this freak." Rory pushed the still limp man toward Lincoln. "There are cuffs in the back bedroom. Those should hold him until the feds arrive."

"They're here now." Nash nodded as several agents in tactical gear burst out of the trees, sidearms drawn.

"Drop your weapons. Hands where we can see them."

Rory lowered the revolver to the porch and gave it a gentle kick. Lincoln did the same with the shotgun.

"You're all under arrest." A big guy grabbed Rory

and spun him against the rail while he clamped cuffs onto his wrists.

"Hey, easy with those. I'm Rory Cavanaugh. Special Agent Ferris will verify I'm the one who called him. Annalise Quintrell and her brothers, Nash and Lincoln, are with me. The little shit in the hoodie is the man you're after, Brady Murphy."

"Special Agent English can vouch for me." Nash grunted as a very pretty brunette twisted his good arm behind his back.

She rolled her eyes. "Using me as a character reference might not be your smartest move. What kind of trouble have you gotten yourself into, Nash?"

"None at all, Tempest. Watch the injured arm."

"Right now, I don't care who any of you are. We'll sort this out once you're contained and I make a few calls." The agent who seemed to be in charge didn't sound terribly concerned about their comfort.

Apparently, Nash knew the female agent, although the woman didn't look too thrilled to see him. Rory jerked his attention back to Annalise and scowled at the man who was cuffing her.

"Dammit, buddy. You don't need to be so rough."

"It's okay, Rory." Annalise spoke softly. "I'm fine, and no one got hurt. Let the agents do their job."

The guy holding her loosened his grip a little. "Would you like to sit down, miss?"

"Thank you. I'm not sure my legs will hold me much longer. It's been quite a day." She dropped onto the porch step and smiled at Rory. "But it's over now. The good guys won."

He grinned back at her. "You're right. Murphy and everyone else involved will be locked up for years. As for you and me, we have our whole future ahead of us."

Her eyes were bright as she met his gaze. "I can't wait."

* * * *

Annalise sat on the porch swing next to Brielle while her brothers, her dad, and Rory played horseshoes in the yard.

Her mom sank onto the chair across from them and smiled. "Look at those boys. So darn competitive."

Brielle laughed. "Nothing much has changed since we were kids."

Watching Rory throw a ringer and high-five Lincoln, Annalise's heart swelled with emotion.

For her at least, everything had changed. Rory had put his Manhattan apartment up for sale and moved in with her while they looked for a bigger place. She knew without a doubt that letting him back into her life was the right decision. Her only regret was the two years together they'd lost.

"You're quiet." Her mom reached over and squeezed her knee. "Is everything okay?"

She nodded. "Everything is great. I'm finally happy again."

"Rory sure seems to be doing his best to prove you can trust him." Her sister pushed her toe against the porch floor to set the swing in motion. "I might actually forgive him."

"I hope you will. I have. I probably would have forgiven him a whole lot sooner if someone had told me he only got arrested because he stayed behind to make sure the security guard didn't bleed out."

"You didn't know?" Brielle frowned. "I remember Lincoln talking about it during the trial."

"Back then, I refused to listen. Linc told me yesterday, and it just reinforces what sort of man Rory is. Anyway, he shows me every day how much he loves me."

"Your love for him shines in your eyes whenever you look his way. You practically glow with joy." Her mom turned her attention to the yard where the men were playing. "That's the best gift you could give me for my birthday. All I want now is to see the rest of my kids find the right partners."

"Ha." Brielle gave her mom a poke. "Don't lie. You want grandchildren."

She winked. "Okay, that, too."

"Well, don't look at me. I'm the youngest. Bug your sons." Brielle rose to her feet and stepped over Buttercup, who groaned in her sleep. "I'm going to check on the ham in the oven. Do either of you want anything when I come back?"

Annalise's gaze drifted to Rory. "Nope. I have everything I want."

Hours later, they'd finished dinner and eaten the birthday cake when Rory walked in through the kitchen door and nudged her. "Let's take a walk."

"Okay." She dried her hands on the dish towel. "We're done cleaning up in here, anyway."

Dark had fallen as he took her hand and strolled beside her to the river. A full moon shed a silvery light across the flowing water, and the trees rustled in the breeze, the last of their colorful leaves drifting to the ground. Buttercup trailed behind them and flopped by their feet when they sank into the camp chairs left on the bank.

"What a beautiful evening." Annalise released a

contented sigh as Rory rested their clasped hands on his thigh. "I'm glad you drove down with me for the weekend."

"I wouldn't have missed your mom's birthday celebration, and I'm very grateful your parents welcomed me back into the fold. Even Brielle seems to be thawing."

"She said as much. They've all accepted that we're together again."

"I'm glad because I know your family matters to you. They matter to me, too."

"I love you for that . . . among other things." Tilting her head back, she stared up at the stars. "I hope you're having a good time. You looked a little grim when you came into the kitchen just now."

"Theo called, and I went outside to talk to him. I guess the DA doesn't intend to bring charges against either him or Kat. Not enough evidence since the money trail for those paintings has conveniently disappeared. No one can locate Archie."

She glanced at his profile, straight nose, firm lips, and strong chin. "Are you angry they won't pay for their part in the heists?"

"I guess not. They both made money off the forgeries, but they had no part in stealing the originals—or in Murphy's vendetta against us. I told Theo that if Archie ever reappears and goes back into business, they'd better stay the hell away from the artwork in your museum."

"I'm just glad both *Sheep in the Meadow* and *Rooster at Dawn* are back where they belong. It's a little ironic that Marcus hired you to beef up the museum's security system."

"My services will cost the board a pretty penny, but I'll make damn sure no one will steal anything from the Chestnut Street Museum again, with or without inside help."

"I hope Brady Murphy rots in prison." Her tone was hard. "I'm glad my boss wasn't involved, and I'd almost feel bad for Francine if she hadn't tased me."

"I don't. It was her idea to steal the Pissarro in the first place. As it is, she and her worthless son, along with Walter and Victoria Bates, will all do some serious time. Maybe Walter and Felix can renew their boyhood friendship while they're in prison."

Annalise grinned. "They deserve each other, but enough about those losers. The night is too gorgeous to waste time thinking about what's over and done with."

"I agree. I'd rather talk about the present . . . and the future."

"Do you want to do some more house hunting when we get back to Philly?"

"Sure, but that's not what I meant." He reached into his pocket with his free hand and pulled out a closed fist. "I have something for you. Well, it's yours already. I'm just returning it."

She turned to face him. "Did you find the earring I dropped? Was it under the bed? I didn't want to crawl under there to look."

His lips curved. "I'll brave the dust bunnies when we get back, but what I have now is a whole lot better than a lost earring."

Something in his tone made her mouth go dry, and she tightened her grip on their laced fingers. "What did you find?"

Opening his fist, moonlight glinted off the big

diamond solitaire. "Your engagement ring."

She drew in a breath, and tears threatened. "My ring?" Her voice cracked.

"Turns out Lincoln never pawned it like you asked him to. He kept it instead. Said he had a feeling you might want it back one day." His gaze met hers in the glow off the water. "Do you?"

"Yes."

He slid the ring onto her finger and kissed the back of her hand. "Will you marry me, Annalise? I don't think I can survive without you."

She nodded. "I'll marry you. I don't want to spend another day without you ever again."

Standing, he stepped over the dog and pulled her to her feet and into his arms. Holding her tight, he bent to kiss her. "I love you more than you'll ever know."

She smiled up at him. "I love you, too. What do you think about a small, Christmas wedding?"

"I think two months is too long to wait. How about Thanksgiving? Or better yet, we can elope tonight."

She laughed out loud. "Brielle wouldn't forgive me if she didn't get to be my maid of honor." Standing on her toes, she looped her arms around his neck and kissed him. "Soon, though. We've waited long enough."

He lifted her up and swung her around. "I'd wait for you forever. Forever and a day."

"You don't have to. You have my heart—now and always."

Coming Soon

Final Witness
Book Two in the Truth and Lies Series

The face of a killer could be the last picture he takes…

As a photojournalist, Nash Quintrell travels the world, capturing striking images of ordinary people in extraordinary situations. He certainly never expected to snap a photo of the assassin who shot the first woman president on her Inauguration Day. Discovering his pictures hold important clues to identifying the men behind the attacks on several high-profile figures is a shock. But they also provide the key to rekindling a relationship with the woman he once pushed away.

When FBI Special Agent Tempest English sees Nash in the inauguration crowd, camera in hand, she has no choice but to approach him. Her mission is to catch a killer, and she'll take whatever help she can get, even if the last thing she wants is to work with the man who dumped her years before. Nash may have broken her heart, but fate throws them together again, and his photos are the best lead she has.

In an effort to unmask the powerful players behind the conspiracy, Nash and Tempest must track a ruthless band of homegrown terrorists. Infiltrating their circle risks not only their lives, but the future together neither imagined was possible. . .

About the Author

Write what you know. Jannine Gallant has taken this advice to heart, creating characters from small towns and plots that unfold in the great outdoors. A recent empty-nester, she grew up in a tiny Northern California town and currently lives in gorgeous Lake Tahoe with her husband. An avid outdoor enthusiast, Jannine enjoys hiking and snowshoeing in the woods around her home with her dog, Ginger. You'll discover the beauty of nature woven into all her fast-paced romantic suspense novels. To find out more about this author and her books, visit her website or sign up for her newsletter.

Made in the USA
Columbia, SC
24 January 2025